Paradise

Books by Patrick Dennis

Auntie Mame
Around the World with Auntie Mame
Genius
The Joyous Season
Tony
How Firm a Foundation
Guestward Ho! (with Barbara Hooton)
The Pink Hotel (with Dorothy Erskine)
Little Me (with Belle Poitrine)
First Lady (with Martha Dinwiddie Butterfield)

 # Paradise

PATRICK DENNIS

Harcourt Brace Jovanovich, Inc.

New York

This book is a work of fiction. Certain renowned
individuals, not active participants in the events that
take place herein, are referred to by their true names.
No one of the characters who actively participate
in these events is fashioned after an actual person,
living or dead, and any resemblance between these
characters and actual persons is wholly coincidental.
The events described in this novel are equally
fictitious and should not be construed in any way
as depicting events that in fact have taken place.

For *J. P. M.*

CONTENTS

I

STRANGERS IN
PARADISE

Mi Casa Es Su Casa

"There!" Liz said to no one at all. "Done!"

She set her paintbrush carefully across the muffin pan filled with colors, lit a cigarette, and stepped back to admire the lily she had just painted on the door. This room—the least desirable—was called Alcatraz. To any American unfamiliar with the Spanish language and able to recall the forbidding federal prison sitting on a shark-encircled island outside San Francisco, this particular room might have depressing connotations. But a calla lily was easier to paint than, say, one perfect daffodil and, anyhow, Liz didn't know the Spanish for daffodil.

Liz had planned Su Casa very carefully. The rooms and bungalows were not to be numbered. That was cold, impersonal, hotelish; and, besides, there were so few of them. Instead, each accommodation would be named for flowers—*rosas, violetas, claveles, hortensias, gladiolas*—and, insofar as was possible, decorated to match. Liz was clever at decorating, at finding junk and spraying it white or pink or yellow, at running up things on her sewing machine, at making an expenditure of a hundred dollars look like a thousand. "Charming! Such taste!" That was what people had always said about everything Liz touched—her clothes, her rooms, her flower arrangements, her meals. For nearly twenty years now Liz had held jobs where charm and taste were the basic requirements. Non-jobs, really. Oh, they had been hard work. Drudgery, some of them—decorating; party planning; a disastrous venture into catering; that mad, mod little gift shop that Liz's loyal friends had described as "years ahead of its time and too good for the public"; a personal shopping service.

3

Since the day she had been graduated from Bennington, Liz had worked, exuding her charm and her taste. Liz had had to. "The men in my life, I suppose," Liz had always explained.

She strode to the balcony at the end of the corridor and looked out. There it was, Su Casa. Hers! Hers and Salvador's, just as it said in the discreet and expensive advertisements she had placed in *Holiday*, *Venture*, and the Mexico City *News*:

In Fabulous Acapulco
S U   C A S A
An Intimate Guesthouse on the Sea
Elizabeth and Salvador Martínez, Your Hosts
Reservations Essential

Yes, there it was on its own tiny point of land jutting out into the Pacific—the main house and its cluster of bungalows. Well, they weren't bungalows really. At least they hadn't been. They had been servants' quarters, a gardener's cottage, a tool shed, and a boathouse. But they were bungalows now, each fitted out with new Spanish colonial antiques, secondhand plumbing, and a flower name: Margaritas, Poincianas, Amapolas, and Nubes. Liz had been of two minds about *nubes*—babies'-breath. She had never had a baby and the breath of the few she had ever known had reeked of sour milk. But the flowers had been awfully quick and easy to paint.

"Charming!" Even Liz had to say so. And such taste!

Liz had been married to Salvador barely a week when they found this enchanting spot. In fact they had been on their honeymoon right here in Acapulco when they drove out in a hired, candy-striped Jeep to picnic in peace and privacy on some deserted beach and there, stretching out from beneath Acapulco's most precipitous cliff, this long, narrow finger of land with its rambling Spanish colonial house had beckoned—abandoned, tumble-down, *and for sale!*

Liz had known—positively *known*—right then and there that this was their future. Liz's own money wouldn't hold out forever and Salvador was such an unrealistic baby, the darling, momentarily expecting another revolution in Cuba so that the Martínez money that was tied up there (sugar or rum or tobacco or possibly all

4

three—Liz had never been quite certain as to the source of her husband's wealth) would all be straightened out and Salvador would be solvent once again.

"But, darling," Liz had said, "don't you see? If—I say *if*—we could afford to buy it, or even lease it, we'd have a perfect spot to live and we could take guests."

"Guests? Elizabeth! Run an *alberguería*? I mean, take lodgers?" Really, Salvador could be so quaint, so old-fashioned, so endearingly Hispanic. Rich or poor, he never forgot that he was descended in one way or another—Liz had lost track—from Cortés and a dozen or so viceroys of Mexico.

"Darling, not some grubby little pension. I mean a really chic guesthouse. Much nicer than a big, commercial hotel. I'd adore it. Honestly I would. I can't just sit and turn into a vegetable. I've got to be occupied. I always have been. I love people. And it would be good for you, too."

"Good for me, Elizabeth? How, darling? How?"

"Well, it would give you something to do until your own affairs get straightened out. If we didn't like it, we could always sell it. The land in Acapulco is going no place but up and . . . darling, let's scramble down this cliff and at least just *look* at it."

Like naughty children they had loped over the deserted property. A rusted iron grille protecting one of the huge windows had literally disintegrated in the grasp of her bridegroom's strong, brown hands. They had snooped through the cavernous house, peered through the cloudy windows of the outbuildings. They had swum naked from the sparkling beach, made love on the white sand, eaten their lunch, and made love once more.

"Salvador, I want it."

"Again? Elizabeth, you are insatiable."

"No, silly. I want *this*. This place. There is a telephone number on that sign. Let's see how much they're asking."

"But, darling, the Lopez-Mendozas have asked us for cocktails at . . ."

"Oh, bother the Lopez-Mendozas! We can have cocktails for the rest of our lives. An opportunity like this comes . . . By the way, did you count the bedrooms in the main house?"

5

"Twelve, I think."

"How many baths?"

"One."

"Oh, well! They can be installed easily. And a swimming pool and some sort of dock for boats and . . ."

"Elizabeth, you talk as though money were something you find in the streets. I've told you that my family's holdings are . . ."

"But *I* still have a little. And, besides, we'd be *making* money here. We could turn these sheds and things into bungalows and . . ."

And so the peninsula had been acquired. Goaded by Liz, Salvador and a cousin of his, a lawyer, had bought it from the Mexican politician's widow who was its owner. Liz hadn't been interested in who had owned it before as long as she owned it now. Nor was her Spanish quite up to reading the pages and pages and pages of the contract of sale. The only thing that had fascinated her was the incredibly low price of the place, and with ocean-front property in Acapulco fetching thousands of pesos the square meter! The fools! They were positively *giving* it away.

That had been a little over a year ago. Liz had counted on three months to chic the place up. The contractor had said six. It had taken twelve. Their estimates as to cost had been exactly proportionate. But no matter. Now it was ready. There it lay. Su Casa. "Your house." And that was just what it would be, a charming, tasteful home away from home for some twenty appreciative guests willing to pay quite a lot for extra comforts, little niceties that no big hotel could ever offer—the percale sheets smuggled in from the United States; the handwoven tablecloths and place mats; the blown Mexican glass; the plates and cups and saucers and even the ashtrays specially painted with a design of Liz's own creation; the careful color schemes in every room; Liz's fabulous flower arrangements; the menus written in Liz's large, stylish hand; and the food!

All along Liz had wished that Salvador would show a little more interest in their project—her project, really—and the millions of details to be seen to, such as writing to travel agencies, printing a brochure, establishing Su Casa with the credit-card firms, haggling in Spanish with plumbers and carpenters and restaurant supply people and petty government officials. But then Salvador was a

6

Latin and Latin men were different. And without Salvador and his Mexican citizenship, this land on the sea, the hard-fought-for liquor license, the dozens of tiresome little documents, would never have been possible.

But now Su Casa was ready. There was Aurelia in the kitchen to cook. There were Pablo and Florentino to act as bellboys and waiters. There was the gardener who came in every day to look after the grounds and clean the swimming pool. Surely they would be enough for a start. Liz had designed their liveries herself—aquamarine drill trousers with striped manta jackets for day; white sharkskin trousers, Mexican-pink cummerbunds and white lace bridal shirts for evenings. Cool, casual, infinitely smart and not a bit like those dreary hotel uniforms one sees in bigger places. Liz's brother, Laddy, was even now in Mexico City collecting them. At least Liz hoped that Laddy was collecting them—and the writing paper from the engraver's and the adding machine and the water carafes and the individual soufflé ramekins and the other last-minute things Liz had thought of. Laddy had promised to be back with the station wagon no later than last night. He still was not back. It worried Liz. The Acapulco road was dangerous and Laddy drove so fast. . . .

"Señora?"

Liz turned. It was Pablo, her favorite among the servants. He was tall, good-looking, meticulously clean. How old? Twenty-five, Liz supposed. "You can never tell with these lazy Indians," Salvador had said. (Salvador was pure Spanish; or at least he claimed to be.) Lazy? Liz had never in her life seen anyone work as hard as Pablo. From seven in the morning, when he tapped on her bedroom door with her breakfast tray, until after midnight, when he put out the lights in the sala, Pablo was working. And everything was done with an air. Even now the little stack of letters addressed to Liz was piled upon a silver waiter, a wedding present salvaged from Liz's first marriage.

Bills. Liz knew without even opening the envelopes. There would be "Please!" written on the bottom of the bill from the people who had built Su Casa's swimming pool; something rather rude in Spanish—Liz had once worked the message out and was sorry that

7

she had—from the maestro who had made the furniture for the,
sala; a dunning letter from the Swede in Mexico City who had
installed all of that beautiful stainless-steel kitchen equipment. Liz
was going to pay them all. Really she was. She hated to be in debt.
It was simply that the place had cost so much more than . . .

Ah, but here was something that looked interesting—a letter
written from a hotel in the capital. Liz tore the envelope open and
read:

> Liz dear,
>
> Remember me? Arthur Craine. I read in some dreary
> gossip column in Mexico's excuse for an English-language
> newspaper that Elizabeth Parkhurst de Martínez was open-
> ing a caravanserai in Acapulco. Of course it can be only you.
>
> Can you take me and my sister and brother-in-law, Mr.
> and Mrs. William Williams, for ten days or so commencing
> on Friday? A bungalow, if you have one, out of the line of
> fire and away from all touristy ladies and giggling honey-
> moon couples.
>
> Can't wait to see you again. Until Friday.
>
> Arthur Craine

"Arthur Craine!" Liz said aloud, remembering the amusing, the
debonair, the acidulous, the indestructibly elegant Dr. Craine. "A
celebrity in our midst! And three more guests! Why, the place will
be nearly full the first day it's open!" Liz leaned over the balcony
and looked down at her husband, Salvador. There he lay on the
diving board, wearing his indecent little bathing trunks, his beautiful black eyes closed against the hot Acapulco sun. Could it be
possible that he had not moved in more than two hours?

"Salvador!" Liz called. "Chavo!"

Salvador raised a long, slim hand to shield his eyes. He gazed up
at Liz and flashed a dazzling white smile that nearly made Liz's
knees buckle.

"Salvador! Great news. More guests. An old friend of mine. He's
quite famous really. His name is Arthur Craine."

The smile vanished. "Oh?"

Oh, dear! Liz had phrased it badly. Now would there be a scene?
Would Salvador go into one of his jealous rages, accuse her of

8

having had a long, sordid affair with an old gelding like Arthur Craine? Would he demand explanations, dates, places? Or, even worse, would he sulk, be huffily aloof, speak only when spoken to and then in sullen monosyllables? Liz raced on, hoping to cover her mistake. "He's a friend of Laddy's really. He was Laddy's English master at Princeton—years ago. Much older. He's a famous author now. He's coming with his sister and her husband. Laddy will be so pleased." There! It had worked. Her husband's gorgeous smile reappeared at half-staff. Liz drove her point home. "Arthur's awfully finicky. A real old maid. I think I'll put them in Margaritas and move that Mrs. Bullock and her girls into . . ."

"Elizabeth, have you a cigarette?"

"A cigarette? Yes, darling. Yes, of course. I'll bring some right down." Liz clattered down the tiled corridor, pausing for a second to check her face and hair at the massive carved Spanish mirror at the head of the stairs. The reflection depressed her. Really, she ought to spend a little more time on herself, use some of that marvelous new moisturizing cream, drive into town for the works at a really good hairdresser's. She wasn't getting any younger. It was simply that she'd been so busy fixing the place for the season . . .

"Elizabeth! The cigarettes!"

"Coming, darling!" Tired as she was, Liz smiled and hurried down the stairs, eager to serve the man in her life.

There had been quite a number of men in Liz's life. Liz always needed a man to need her. In an earlier age Liz might have been the genteel spinster daughter who stayed at home to look after a widowed father and a wastrel brother. But in the twentieth century a girl as energetic as Liz had been able to see to Daddy and Laddy, to go out and work, and to marry as well. Daddy, old Mr. Parkhurst, hadn't really been much trouble. Dotty to be sure, but sweet and housebroken. As a poor man of the fifties, he had wanted only to go on living as a rich man of the twenties—dressing for dinner; refusing to use the dials on telephones; talking of Florenz Ziegfeld, the Central Park Casino and his Willys-St. Clair roadster as though they still existed; reading and rereading and rerereading old copies of *Vanity Fair* and the *Literary Digest* and occasionally writing indignant letters to the circulation departments to find out why they were no longer fulfilling his subscriptions. Young Mr. Parkhurst—darling Laddy—had been even easier, and out of the house more often than he was in it. His only requirements had been love, sympathy, understanding, influence with useful people (of which Liz always had plenty), and money (which was a different matter entirely).

And Liz's first husband had been almost as childish as Daddy and Laddy put together. An actor. At least that was what he thought. But then Norman had finally made it.

Norman had made it all right. Beginning with Liz, he had made it by kowtowing and toadying and sucking up to anyone who he thought had money, background, breeding, power, or connections. Liz had met him at someone's cocktail party the year she got out of Bennington. One look at Norman's frayed collar and cuffs, his slightly soiled necktie, his untrimmed hair, and Liz felt that Norman needed her. One look at Liz's good little black (only thirty-nine ninety-five, but marked down from much more), a glance at Liz's late mother's pearls, a hasty inventory of the Revere silver, the Duncan Phyfe furniture, and the family portraits in Liz's father's townhouse, and Norman knew that he needed Liz.

Norman proposed that very night and Liz accepted. Effusive rather than efficient, Norman should have waited until he looked into the exact state of the Parkhurst fortune. True, there had once been one, but it had long since gone. The townhouse was mortgaged to the roof; the furniture, silver, and portraits willed to the American Wing of the Metropolitan Museum. Even the pearls turned out to be cultured.

And so they were married—for six, going on seven, years. Liz thought of the marriage as her flush-door-foam-rubber-and-lightpole period. "Charming! Such taste!" people had said of the series of cold-water flats she and Norman had occupied in the various mews and alleys of Greenwich Village. During that time Liz had held jobs in the Bridal Department of Henri Bendel's, the Then and Now Shop at Lord & Taylor, a moribund decorating establishment on Madison Avenue, a defunct magazine aimed at young marrieds, a travel agency, and a flower shop that wittily called itself Garden Variety. Norman had held even more jobs. He did one season in summer stock, played roles of varying importance in six off-Broadway shows (one of which lasted all of nine performances), got a part in a musical that folded in Philadelphia, recited poetry in a coffeehouse on Horatio Street, and eventually landed a bit part on a television show.

It had been the undoing of their marriage, that television show. Not that things hadn't been rocky enough since the day Daddy's will, including, as it did, denunciations of the Hay Diet, Calvin Coolidge, and the Eighteenth Amendment, was read aloud to Liz and Laddy and Norman. There was enough money left to bury old Mr. Parkhurst and that was about all. Seething with anger and disappointment, Norman stuck loyally to Liz. Not only was she his lawful wedded wife, she was also supporting him. But, ah, that brief appearance on television! It opened new vistas to Norman. The sponsor's daughter, restless, raunchy, and recently divorced, spotted exactly what she thought she wanted in Liz's husband. Norman, ever considerate of those who could be useful, was only too anxious to oblige. While Liz was doing clever things with eucalyptus leaves in Garden Variety, swollen with pride over her husband's success, Norman was lunching with the sponsor's daughter. While Liz was on her way back to the Village in the subway, Norman was on his way to fame, fortune, and another marriage in the sponsor's daughter's bed. A week later Norman signed the contract that would make him a famous television star. A month after that Norman divorced Liz on grounds of mental cruelty.

Thirty, attractive, and, she hoped, wiser, Liz played the field while she was getting over Norman, going from one man who needed her to another. At thirty-five Liz told herself that she was sick of looking after men and set out to find one who could look after her. Her mission was accomplished in the person of Mr. Hobson (he was so much older than Liz that even now she felt it disrespectful to speak of him by anything so intimate as his first name). Mr. Hobson was a big, jolly, florid man, widowed, childless, and rich. He enjoyed hunting, fishing, traveling, and entertaining. As Liz did all these things well, their marriage—it was more of a merger than a marriage —seemed made in heaven. Liz moved into his hideous yellow brick house in Duluth, did over its ugly rooms, licked the late Mrs.

11

Hobson's maids into shape, filled the house with flowers, and sent out invitations to Mr. Hobson's hunting and fishing cronies and their wives to come and look it over. But the housewarming never took place. On his way downstairs to greet his first guest, Mr. Hobson suffered a massive stroke. And so Liz had another man who needed her.

For the next five years Liz sat by the side of Mr. Hobson's bed, plumping pillows, giving tender pats and brave smiles of encouragement, and trying to make sense of, and sensible answers to, the incoherent gurglings of the helpless blob who was her husband. Mr. Hobson's death was called a "blessed release" by all Duluth and at his funeral everyone told Liz what a brick she had been. Liz rather agreed. There was some money, but not as much as people thought after the crippling expenses of Mr. Hobson's lingering decline. Liz sold the yellow brick house, bade her adieus to Mr. Hobson's hunting and fishing friends and their wives—strangers really—and drifted southward, where the word "snow" was virtually unknown. Mexico. Acapulco.

Forty, attractive, and solvent, Liz hoped to find something like romance at last. It was not immediately evident that winter in Acapulco. Liz felt old and alone, and for the first time in her life, afraid. In a fit of panic she wired the plane fare to her brother, Laddy, and begged him to join her. At least he would be a man to escort her in the evenings, even if she had to pick up every tab herself. And then . . . and then she saw Salvador emerging like a glossy seal from the hotel swimming pool. Yes. There was Salvador, young, charming and polished, broad of shoulder, narrow of hip, radiant of smile. Salvador smiled at Liz and she was as good as gone. Laddy arrived in Acapulco just in time to give his sister away in marriage.

Laddy could be awfully sensible about other people's problems. He disapproved of Salvador and the marriage. Salvador, Laddy pointed out, was some years younger than Liz, had no visible means of support, and was after Liz's money. (This was exactly what Salvador always said about Laddy.) Well, that was just too silly to dignify with comment, Liz railed, commenting plenty. With two mature, intelligent people, what difference did a few years—less than ten—

actually make? And would Laddy please remember his own sordid involvement with that awful Mrs. Pangborn—old enough to be his mother—who all but kept him under house arrest in her vulgar villa in Palm Beach until Liz flew down to intercede. As for Salvador's being interested in Liz's money, that was the sheerest nonsense. Liz didn't have any money; at least not that kind of money. If Salvador *really* cared about marrying money there were hundreds—thousands—of predatory women right here in Acapulco who could buy and sell Liz a dozen times over. Look at that Mrs. What's-her-name occupying three suites and two swimming pools at Villa Vera; or that trampy old movie star living it up at the Pierre Marqués; or the Princess-up-the-Hill. As for money, Salvador had plenty of his own, or he would have once his family's affairs were straightened out. And speaking of money, Liz just wished that she had a dollar for every hundred Laddy had sunk into harebrained, get-rich-quick schemes. Here was Laddy almost forty and he hadn't amounted to a damn yet.

The wedding had been a silent, thin-lipped affair, attended by Laddy and by Salvador's cousin Ignacio, who also disapproved. The ceremony was followed by a grim wedding breakfast at Voisin, after which Laddy borrowed ten thousand dollars from Liz to pay for a sloop. The boat was essential to Laddy's plans to bring to the surface a fabulous sunken treasure lying on the floor of the Pacific just off Manzanillo, according to the map Laddy had bought from such a helluva nice guy he'd met at the bar at Armando's. That had been the last of Laddy for a while. But six weeks ago, Laddy and the boat had turned up again. Laddy had a beautiful suntan but no sunken treasure. In fact, no money at all. The sloop bobbed gently at the end of Liz's new dock, totally unseaworthy but picturesque. And Liz now had two men to take care of—Salvador and Laddy.

"Elizabeth! Are you coming with the cigarettes?"

"Yes, darling. Coming."

The Money Literally Grows on Trees

Laddy Parkhurst gunned the Su Casa station wagon along the Costera. He was going much too fast for the traffic of Acapulco, but then he was a little late in getting back home—just twenty-four hours. He was also lacking a few of the essential items that he had been sent to the capital to collect for Liz. But Mr. Ackerman and his niece had run up quite a check at El Paseo last night and, naturally, Laddy had picked it up, paid it, and tipped lavishly. Who could do less for charming people like the Ackermans, who were offering an annual income of millions and millions of pesos just for the asking?

Laddy—he had actually been christened John Benedict Nicholas Parkhurst, although everyone had forgotten—was beyond doubt the cutest American boy of forty in existence anywhere. Tall, blond, snub-nosed, and slim (when he was watching his weight), Laddy loved life and life loved Laddy. He was good at tennis and swimming and sailing and golf. He spoke enough French to get by and even more Spanish. Men liked Laddy and women adored him. There really wasn't anything positive enough about Laddy to dislike.

"The money literally grows on trees," Laddy said aloud, quoting Mr. Ackerman's reticent sales pitch at El Paseo last night and again at the University Club today. Avocado trees. Acres and acres and acres of them. Once planted, they practically took care of themselves and all the owner had to do was pick and ship the fruit to the eager markets of the world. From an initial investment, so small that it was embarrassing to mention, would spring a return in the millions, and not just once, but season after season after season, just for sitting around and watching the trees bear.

How wonderful to have a little ready money once again; to pay Diane the back alimony she was always screaming about (not that she needed it—she was only being vengeful); to settle trust funds on his children by Barbara; to repay Liz the money she had lent him over the years—twenty or thirty thousand dollars. Laddy had for-

14

gotten the exact sum, but it was a piddling amount really. "Solvent. Really rich. New suits. A car of my own. Another boat. A little place in town and, of course, a big house on the avocado ranch."

It wouldn't be easy, at first, to get Liz to advance him the money. This kooky idea of opening a hotel had taken quite a lot of the capital poor old Hobson had left her, and then Salvador, with his imported cigarettes, his custom-made bathing suits, his forays in Mexico City, was a terrible drain—just as Laddy had warned Liz! And Liz, although she never came right out and said so, was probably a little miffed about that sunken-treasure fiasco of last year. Was it Laddy's fault that the man who had sold him that map was a crook and a known con man? Besides, didn't Liz have the boat to dress up Su Casa? Even if the miserable old tub did lap up water, it might be nice for beach picnics or little trips around the bay. Anyhow, Pablo could probably patch it up in his spare time. Mexican servants could do anything

For the moment, Laddy didn't mind being on hand to help his sister out. Su Casa was comfortable and the Acapulco climate the greatest. Anyhow, it did no harm to have someone on the spot to see that Salvador didn't bleed poor old Liz white. Liz was a pushover for any man who needed mothering!

And she was so gullible. Imagine, a woman in her forties actually believing that cock-and-bull story about the Martínez family having —or ever having had—money! Laddy had found out, quite by accident, that Salvador's mother, far from being dead and buried in the family mausoleum in Madrid, kept a second-rate girls' school in Guadalajara. And, equally by accident, Laddy had discovered that Salvador himself was keeping a second-rate girl in Acapulco—on Liz's money! Of course Laddy wouldn't tell Liz any of this in a million years. She'd find out for herself in time. When her money was gone and Salvador with it. Meanwhile, Laddy would stick around and take care of his sister. She certainly needed it.

Laddy didn't really mind looking after Liz and her insane notion of Su Casa for the moment. As Laddy understood it, he was to be a sort of auxiliary host. He was to meet planes with the Su Casa station wagon; arrange courtesy cards at the clubs; play golf, bridge, or tennis with anyone who lacked a partner; mix drinks in the *sala* at cocktail time; and make himself generally accommodating. Laddy

15

was good with people and, you could never tell, he might even meet someone halfway amusing. Of course Liz's whole notion of keeping a guesthouse was pure idiocy. It was a nickel-and-dime business and to think of someone with Laddy Parkhurst's background—Lawrenceville and Princeton—wasting his time as a hotel servant . . . Well! He'd have to get Liz aside, far from her interfering young husband, and tell her about Mr. Ackerman and the avocado ranch. Ackerman wanted only twenty-five thousand dollars and . . .

There it was below him, Su Casa, stretching out into the Pacific. As Laddy eased the station wagon down the driveway he had to admit that Liz had done a good job—a great job—on this white elephant of a house. Whether you liked Spanish colonial architecture or not (and Laddy didn't), you had to admire the layout, the thought and imagination, and the plain hard work that Liz had put into the place. There it lay, the big, glistening white main house with its grilles and balconies and its sprawling paved terrace, with the turquoise swimming pool, the vibrant flowers, the gay parasol-shaded tables. There were the cottages—silly, some of them, but charming. There was the new dock and there was the *Sea Urchin,* Laddy's boat. When Laddy's avocado ranch really got going, he'd buy up the whole place from the bank that held the mortgage and simply hand it to his sister as a present. Salvador would be gone by then and . . .

"Oh, oh!" With a wet thud one of the wheels of the station wagon sank into the gravel of the causeway. Laddy gunned the motor. The wheel spun helplessly in its soggy pit. Laddy sprang out of the car to look. There it was, the rear right wheel embedded in a foot-deep hole filled with brackish sea water. "Poor Liz," Laddy said. "She never could do anything right." Well, Pablo and Florentino and the gardener could get the station wagon out and then fill in the hole with gravel. Laddy had done more than his share of work that day. It would be only a matter of months—even weeks, perhaps—before Laddy could stop being handy man, errand boy, and general factotum in a glorified boardinghouse. The avocado business. Where the money literally grows on trees!

Whistling a happy tune, Laddy walked along the narrow causeway to tell Liz that he was back.

Just a Bottle of Vodka and Some Ice, Honey

"Liz, I'm telling you, I went there three times. The stationery wasn't ready. Do you think I'd lie to you?"

"I hope you wouldn't, Laddy. But *I'm* telling you that Mr. Gómez telephoned long distance yesterday, the day before yesterday, and this morning to say that the paper was ready and you hadn't been near the place."

"Oh, Liz, you know what the Mexicans are like."

"I also know what Mr. Gómez is like. He's never been five minutes late with any order in his life. This is an especially big order and he's anxious to be paid for it. And *I'm* anxious to have menus and writing paper and billheads and all the other things that have been sitting there waiting for you for the last three days. Just where have you been, anyhow?"

Well, this was no time to tell Liz about the avocado business. She was tired and she was angry and she looked it. It was no time to tell her *that*, either.

"Liz, about that hole in the driveway . . ."

"Don't worry about that, Laddy. Pablo filled it in while you were having a swim. Now, if you didn't bring the paper back, could I at least have the money I gave you to pay for it? Mr. Gómez is sending it out on the five o'clock plane and I . . ."

Oh, no. This was definitely no time to tell Liz about the avocado ranch, about Mr. Ackerman and his attractive niece, about the bill at El Paseo last night, about the shirts and jackets and shoes he had ordered, about . . .

The blast of a horn in the driveway saved Laddy. "What's that?"

"Don't change the subject, please, Laddy. What's what?"

"That tooting in the driveway. I didn't know you were expecting anyone until tomorrow."

"I'm not. Now about the money I gave you. . ."

"Señora . . ." It was Pablo, looking splendid, though ill-at-ease,

17

in his new uniform. "*La Señora Mayor está en la sala.*"

"Señora que?"

"Señora Mayor, creo."

"Mayor?" Now what could that mean? Greater, larger, older? Mexican servants were hopeless with names—even with Spanish names. "I don't know any Señora Mayor, do you, Laddy?"

"*Tiene una reservación, señora.*"

"Oh, my God! Meyers! Mrs. Meyers." Now it came back to Liz. It had been their very first reservation. It had been written in a rather painstaking hand on letter paper from Beau Rivage and signed "Mrs. Florence Meyers." Liz recalled being favorably impressed only by the address. "But she's early; a whole day early. Her room isn't made up. There's nothing, really, to give her for dinner. I . . ."

"Just a bottle of vodka and some ice, honey."

Liz and Laddy spun around and there, swaying unsteadily in the archway, stood Mrs. Meyers.

There is a certain kind of person who can be spotted at a hundred paces as Quality. American, Mexican, English, French, Italian, the look is international. Singly, in pairs, in family groups, you see their prototypes in expensive advertisements in expensive magazines, sniffing expensive brandies, sleeping between expensive sheets, driving expensive cars, wearing expensive clothes, well-bred, well-groomed, well-heeled to the end. In real life you see them more rarely, but they are unmistakable. There is something about them—can it be the cut and quality of their clothes, the way they carry themselves, or simply the aura of discreet wealth?—that announces in carrying, but well-modulated, tones, "Class!" There was nothing about Mrs. Florence Meyers that even whispered such a message.

Mrs. Meyers was certainly forty, possibly sixty, probably somewhere in between. It was impossible to tell. A fugitive, girlish prettiness hid itself somewhere in the bloated lard of her face, emerging coyly and fleetingly only when she smiled. She did not smile often. She had perhaps once been what was known as "pleasingly plump." Now she was a shapeless mass, an irregular cube confined within a girdle that had long ago surrendered to the inevitable. Swelling bulges revealed its uppermost and its lowermost reaches. Ah, yes! Her feet! Her feet must once have been beautiful, small and plump. They still were, but the task of supporting Mrs. Meyers had been too much. Her insteps swelled over the vamps of scuffed black suède wedgies. Her hands? Yes, they, too, must once have been lovely; dainty and boneless. "Boneless as suet," Liz thought as she contemplated with distaste the pudgy paws. There were rings, four of them, large and lackluster as the bottoms of bottles, pressing into the sausages of her fingers. Could they be real? Liz hoped not. What a waste of diamonds! And the nails! Each bore a chipped coat of a color Liz dimly recalled as being fashionable in the thirties. "Mahogany," Liz almost said aloud. "Where in the world can you buy that shade nowadays? Or perhaps she simply hasn't removed it since— since about nineteen-forty?"

Quite without knowing it, Liz had pounced on the exact year when time began to stand still for Florence Meyers. The hair, once perhaps a glowing chestnut, hung in a lank, ginger "glamour-girl" bob over a thickened neck. The face was ineptly powdered —or at least it had been some hours or days ago—a calcimine white. And the mouth! Could it have been put on with one of those old stencils which some demented cosmetics manufacturer introduced to the market just before the war? From the slightly frayed, black straw, cartwheel hat down to the wedge-soled sling pumps, Mrs. Meyers was pure nineteen-forty—the black crepe dress with its jutting shoulder pads, its "sweetheart" neckline clamped to the straps of a soiled brassiere by two dim star-sapphire clips, its coquettishly swinging skirt. Spotted and split at the seams as it was, it must have been a very good dress at one time just to have lasted for so long.

The coat really did it. *That coat!* Draped limply over one mottled bare arm was a mountain of bedraggled white fur from which shot trembling fronds of black. What had it been called? Liz forced herself back to the year when she had been a gangling adolescent wishing for the first time for something more glamorous than the navy-blue uniform of The Brearley School. And what had she wanted most? A full-length coat of Paradise fox.

Yes! That was what it had been called. Paradise fox! A man-made wonder—white fox with tendrils of black monkey fur grafted onto it. It had been available in pink, as well. Understandably, it had never achieved popularity.

In the dim *sala*, behind this apparition, Liz could see Pablo stacking heaps of luggage, very good old luggage, plastered with stickers proclaiming first-class ocean crossings and visits to far grander establishments than Su Casa could ever hope to become. Was this, this creature, really planning to move into Liz's lovely guesthouse? And if so, for how long? Then Liz remembered. Mrs. Meyers's letter had said "for the season"—however long that might be—and the enclosed check had covered three months' rent at daily rates. What was worse, Liz had cashed the check and spent the money. She had had to.

There wasn't a snobbish bone in Liz's body. She kept telling herself that. The years at Bennington, where one of her best friends had been colored, had disabused her of all of Daddy's nonsense concerning who was and who was not fit to know. And if Bennington hadn't been enough, marriage to Norman, with his beatnik, unemployed actor friends, had certainly turned the trick. It was simply that Liz had visualized a, well, slightly different kind of clientele for Su Casa.

"I'm awfully sorry," Liz stammered. "It's just that we weren't expecting anyone until tomorrow. We don't open, officially, until then, uh, Mrs. Meyers."

"Just call me Flossie," Mrs. Meyers said, and swayed on her wedgies across the tiles of the patio. "Nice place you got here. Cute. I think I'm gonna like it."

"It's awfully quiet, I'm afraid," Liz said.

"Swell. That suits me fine. I bin in Acapulco a lotta times before."

Indeed she had. In the past few seasons, Mrs. Meyers had been asked to leave Hotels Hilton, Presidente, Caleta, Mirador, Boca Chica, Las Brisas, and Villa Vera in that order. The mere mention of her name was enough to give hotel managers ulcers. Being new to the business, Liz knew nothing of this, but she was able to sense that Mrs. Meyers—Flossie—just wouldn't fit in. The word "common" floated to the surface of Liz's consciousness. Determinedly she drowned it beneath the waves of her liberalism. Smiling, she held out her hand. "I don't think I've managed the formalities just yet. You see, I'm quite new at this sort of thing. I'm Liz Martínez and this is my brother, Laddy Parkhurst."

"Please' to meetcha." Mrs. Meyers took a step forward, lurched, and clutched at the back of a wrought-iron chair for support. The word "common" was replaced by "alcoholic." It made Liz feel a little better about herself. After all, alcoholism was a sickness.

"Now, let me see," Liz said, "where we're going to put you." Liz knew quite well where she had *originally* planned to put Mrs. Meyers—in Rosas, a pretty room right in the midst of everything. Now, desperately, Liz chose one of the bungalows—Nubes, the farthest-flung of all. "Yes," she continued inanely, "I thought you'd like a little cottage all to yourself. It's called Nubes."

"Nudists?" Again Mrs. Meyers swayed menacingly.

"Nu-bes. You see, all of our accommodations are named for flowers. Nubes means babies'-breath."

"Babies'-breath," Mrs. Meyers whispered in wonder. "Babies'-breath."

"Pablo," Liz called. She'd get this tottering old lush planted as far away from the center of things as quickly as possible and worry about what to do with her later. "*Ponga el equipaje de la señora en la Casa Nubes, por favor.* About dinner. Mrs. Meyers . . ."

"Don't worry about me, honey. Just a bottle of vodka and some ice, like I said. But maybe a bowl of milk for Queenie."

"Queenie?"

"Yeah. Queenie. She's half spitz."

At the mention of her name, a mangy hank of hair waddled out to the patio on three legs.

"You—you didn't mention a dog in your letter, Mrs. Meyers," Liz said, eying Queenie disdainfully.

"She goes everywhere with me. She'll be sixteen in March."

"Just fancy," Liz said, with a shudder. Liz was fond of animals. So was Laddy. But there was something so, well, *repulsive* about this . . . this . . . Bracing herself, Liz looked down again. Queenie did have bright little eyes. Yes, Liz would give her full marks for that. Her eyes were bright, intent, even intelligent. But the rest of her! It was an obese ball of fur, bald down the back where half a dozen flies had settled to sup on the poor creature's raw skin. Her right forepaw was held rigidly out in a sort of Nazi salute.

"Has—has she hurt her paw?" Laddy asked.

"That was Cans."

"Cans?" Liz asked.

"Yeah. At the Carlton Hotel. The elevator boy closed the gate on her foot. Had to have about half of her leg amputated. I swear that frog done it on purpose."

"Oh, Cannes," Liz said, and hated herself for it.

Laddy, looking away distastefully as Queenie settled under an iron chair to scrape her back rhythmically against one of its rungs, felt that, had he been running the elevator, he would have settled for nothing short of decapitation, thus putting the poor beast out of its misery.

"I wonder if we have some bones in the kitchen," Liz said wanly.

"Don't worry about that, honey. Queenie hasn't had a tooth in her head for three years. Going on four. Just milk. And don't worry about her bothering anybody. She never leaves my room."

"Never?" Liz thought of the rugs in Nubes, white, thick, expensive, unpaid-for.

"Paper-trained, honey. Queenie doesn't hardly ever have an accident."

"Laddy, would you ask Pablo or Florentino for some copies of the News, Excelsior, El Heraldo—whatever we happen to have?"

"Now if you'll show me where this place is—this babies'-breath. I had kin' of a hard trip. Queenie, too."

"All the way from Lausanne?"

"No. From Nassau. Last six, seven weeks I stayed there."

"That must have been nice," Liz said dutifully.

"It stinks. Here," Mrs. Meyers said, foraging through her black suède bag, "give this to the bellhop." Along with some grubby gray bits of paper and crumpled Kleenex, she extracted a five-pound note, a ten-dollar bill, and twenty French francs.

"D-don't you think that's rather a lot?" Liz said. "If you need some Mexican pesos . . ."

"Just do like I say, honey. And don't forget to tell room service —a bottle of vodka and some ice."

In the apricot light of the setting sun, Salvador appeared from the pool the color of copper. From beneath her pleated eyelids, Mrs. Meyers looked him up and down. "Hi there, handsome," she said, and lurched after Laddy toward the cottage called Nubes.

Liz was aware of Salvador's look of horror and shock. She braced herself for what she knew was coming.

"Elizabeth," Salvador said, "I would like a word with you. Now."

I Want That . . . That One

The sun was still shining when the Princess-up-the-Hill awakened. That was bad. Insomnia again. That Swiss quack would have to go. Couldn't he do anything right? All of his fancy talk about rejuvenating shots with the placenta of a cow and he couldn't even prescribe a proper sleeping pill. He was a bore, anyhow. It wasn't that the Princess-up-the-Hill didn't *like* daylight. She adored it. It was exhilarating. Different. It was simply that she didn't want sunshine to get to be a bore.

She stirred on her silver-tissue sheets and looked at the place in her bed that was now empty. Good! She would have been *really* annoyed to have found Lars—yes, it had been Lars, the white one—still there. Lars had delicacy. But she would have to speak to him—well, not speak to him; send him a note—about his sunbathing. Lars was supposed to be white, not pink, not lobster red, not tan. He had been engaged for his whiteness. Now was he going to ruin his season *and* hers by lying out in the sun?

The Princess pressed the silver bell on the silver table beside the silver bed. The silver door opened and her maid, wearing a silver sari, entered with a silver salver bearing six silver pillboxes

and a silver goblet of water. The Princess nodded to the maid
—and very civilly. She had heard that her Mexican servants were
embarrassed by the costumes she had chosen for them. Not even
the salaries she paid (triple the going rate) were inducement
enough for some of them to stay on. To run this house properly
the Princess needed at least twenty servants. At the moment the
Princess had been given to understand that she was pigging it on
ten, plus, of course, the permanent staff that traveled with her
from one house to another.

Clockwise, the Princess helped herself from the array of pills
and capsules—the pink ones, the reds, the fuchsias, the speckled
green-and-whites, the turquoises, and the violets. She washed them
down with the Vichy water from the silver goblet. The water was
heated to exactly 150 degrees Fahrenheit so that the pills and capsules would dissolve sooner, get to work more rapidly. She nodded
to the maid. The maid nodded back and scurried out of the room
on bare, silent feet.

Except for a few isolated occasions when a four-letter word had
escaped her silvered lips, the Princess-up-the-Hill had not spoken
for nearly three months. It was part of the course her new guru
had given her. The other parts had been discarded, along with the
guru himself. Standing on her head made the Princess dizzy
and quite cross; running a silk thread up one nostril and down
the other gave her a nosebleed; squatting in a tub of water with
a straw to give herself an enema by means of muscular control
was unthinkable. Really! But the part about utter silence leading
to utter serenity—the Princess liked that. It was restful. Most of
the people she knew had very little of any importance to say. The
Princess herself had even less. In a house of silence, such failings
need not be evident.

In Acapulco, Her Serene Highness was known only as the
Princess-up-the-Hill; in Tangier, as the Princess-in-the-Kasbah; in
London, as the Princess-in-the-Park (Regent's); in Paris, as the
Princess-in-the-Ritz. This was largely because her current last name
was made up entirely of consonants and was totally unpronounceable. Then, too, the Princess acquired and shed last names with
such speed that, even in an age of instant communications, it was
impossible to keep up with them. The only thing consistent about

her was that in each of her marriages she was always a princess—Georgian, Papal, Transylvanian, Albanian; no brand of royalty like English or Dutch which you could really sink your teeth into, but a princess withal. No one knew for sure, but she was said to treat her husbands quite civilly and to leave them well-fixed for life.

The pills and capsules were beginning to work. Early as it was —nearly five in the afternoon—the Princess got out of bed and strode to the silver pier glass. Critically she examined the reflection of her naked body, studying every detail from her silvered toenails up to her silver hair. Not bad for forty-nine (actually fifty-four). Even the Princess, who was not easy to please, had to concede that. And, in truth, it shouldn't have been bad. The Princess had undertaken almost every kind of cosmetic assistance known to science, including a few bouts in surgery. When it was fashionable to be buxom, the breasts of the Princess were cantilevered forth like flagpoles; when the look was lean, the Princess was as flat as an adolescent boy. Similarly, her hips came and went with the changing vogue. She gazed at the metallic sheen of her silver hair and tried to recall what color it would actually be. Possibly even silver by now.

Grudgingly satisfied with herself, the Princess rang again for her maid. It was time to be bathed, massaged, oiled, coifed, scented, painted, varnished. But today the Princess wasn't going to bother with idle vanity, at least not until after dark. It was so rare that she was up with the birds that she thought she might just as well enjoy the last hour of sunshine, then tie a can to that rotten Swiss sawbones and find a doctor who could prescribe a halfway decent sleeping pill. Since she was going to make a long day of it, it might even be fun to pile the boys into the big silver Rolls and run over to Le Club at midnight just to watch the fun. Surely they could put a screen around her table so that she would not be discomfited by the rude stares of the public. Really, people could be such beasts! Hadn't they ever seen a silver woman surrounded by four boys dressed in silver before? She would wear . . . she would wear . . . well, time enough to worry about that later.

25

The silver-leafed doors of her dressing room slid open at the maid's touch. Vaguely the Princess gestured toward a silver lamé burnoose, loose, unconfining, and perfect for slopping about the house. Clothed, the Princess slid her bare feet into woven silver sandals. They hurt, rather. The Princess was beginning to weary of her silver period, but then she had nearly run out of colors. She had gone through her white, her black, her red, her blue, her green, her copper, and her gold phases. A new color! That might be something amusing to think about for the rest of the day.

The Princess nodded in the direction of the three silver Moresque arches that linked her bedroom to the terrace. Electronically the glass door slid back at the maid's touch and the Princess slithered out into the fresh air. Hot! She wondered if she couldn't have the garden air-conditioned to match the even temperature of the Moorish palace. Probably not. These Mexicans just didn't *want* to solve simple problems.

As it had amused the Princess to have a pure Tudor house in Morocco, so it amused her—or least had once amused her—to have a Moorish house in Mexico. Built of silver glass tiles vaguely along the lines of the Taj Mahal, although somewhat larger, it stood high on a hill commanding a view of the sea, the bay, and the town itself. The Princess liked to be up high, above other things, other people, so that she could look down on them.

She gazed down at the pool terrace (not to be confused with the morning terrace, the luncheon terrace, the cocktail terrace, or the dinner terrace) and at her boys, wearing their silver fig leaves, lolling on chaise longues and gossiping. Integration was the coming thing. The Princess felt that strongly. Thus, her *personal* staff this season consisted of a pure Caucasian (Lars), a Chinese, a Sioux Indian, and the blackest Negro her agents had been able to find. It made the Princess feel wonderfully democratic and *with* it. But didn't those boys understand the meaning of the word "obedience"? There was pure white Lars, basted in Skol, trying to get brown while that stupid, black buck lay in the shade fending off the sun's beneficial rays. The Princess would speak to them immediately. No. She wouldn't speak. That would shatter the serenity. Instead she pressed the bell marked Eunuch four times.

Her major-domo appeared, wearing a silver bolero, silver tissue pantaloons, and nothing else. He was not a eunuch, as anyone could see through the pantaloons. In fact, he was the father of five. But it amused the Princess to be as authentic as possible (within the bounds of human clemency) in such matters. He carried with him a silver inkstand and a fat packet of silver-bordered paper. Since the Princess had given up speaking, she had arranged a coded series of bell ringings. Four rings indicated that she wished to write something.

While the eunuch waited, the Princess took up her pen and wrote:

> Get that stupid Swede out of the sun and that
> black bastard back into it!
> And tell them to *stop talking!!!*

The major-domo took the note, salaamed, and disappeared. The Princess heard a squawk from above. Squinting up her tallest minaret, the Princess-up-the-Hill saw it again. That vulture! He, or she, or *it* had been following her all season. She could swear it. Of course one vulture looked quite like another, but it gave the Princess an uneasy feeling. Vultures were supposed to be interested only in *dead* things, weren't they? When the house was new, the Princess had hired a Moslem mouedhin to bleat out the call to *mezeuns* from the minaret every evening at sundown. He made an unearthly racket, but at least he let the household know that cocktails were being served.

In addition, he was picturesque and authentic. That is, the Princess had *thought* he was authentic until he was unmasked as not a Moslem at all, but a slick little mockie from the Bronx who kept shrieking the most outrageous things about the Princess in Yiddish. Even so, he and his caterwauling were preferable to the vulture. The Princess flapped her burnoose in the general direction of the minaret. The vulture flapped its wings and took off, indolently, arrogantly circling the vast central dome of the house three times. Then it flew away.

27

The Princess felt better. Should she send for one of the boys? She'd love to dig her long, silver nails into Lars's pink, sunburned back. Teach him a lesson. Or should she . . . Suddenly her attention was caught by something below; something far below. Ah, yes, those people who had done over that jiggery-pokery old house down on the peninsula. The workmen had finally gone and now there seemed to be a little action.

The Princess moved to her telescope and adjusted it expertly. It was a glass worthy of the Mount Wilson Observatory. Sometimes it amused the Princess to gaze through it and see whether anyone she knew—or might wish to know—was coming into port on a yacht.

The glass was so powerful that the Princess could read the lettering on the bath towel tossed on a chair beside the swimming pool. Su Casa. How quaint! Bath towels, quaint or otherwise, held no interest for the Princess. But now she saw something that interested her intensely. It was Salvador emerging from the pool. Mm-hmm. Like a scientist observing bacteria beneath a microscope, the Princess gave the focusing mechanism a slight touch. There. That was even better. And there, filling the lens, was Salvador. She could see everything now, each detail—the slim, brown legs, the diaper bathing trunks, the thin line of blue-black hair that ran up to his navel and then fanned out over his chest. Finally she studied his face, watched him as he lit a cigarette, exhaled a cloud of blue smoke, and then gazed, almost longingly, upward, upward, upward at the silver Moroccan palace. He practically seemed to *know* . . .

Without removing her eye from the telescope, the Princess reached out and pressed the Eunuch button once. In a moment the major-domo was at her side.

Still gazing into the glass, the Princess spoke for the first time in days. "I want that," she said. "*That* one."

"*Comment, madame, lequel voulez-vous: le Chinois, le sauvage, le* . . ."

The Princess, who detested being an American, generally spoke to her staff in French. They were very patient about it. Just now she had no time for Gallicisms. "No, you fool. None of *them*. Look! *That* one. That one down there in that grubby little hotel."

28

Just Think, Champagne All the Way!

The telephone rang a third time. And then a fourth. Bernice was frantic. Would the sales figures never come right? Or wouldn't Madam Kaye, just this once, interrupt the daily battle she was holding with her sister on the other telephone and take this call?

"Get the phone, wudja, Bernice," Madam Kaye said. "An' jus' one other thingue, Yetta, the next time your gonif son, Melvin, comes kvetchingue around here . . ."

Bernice picked up the other telephone. "Haute Monde Society Resale, good morning." Hectically busy as she was, Bernice had answered the call in the approved manner. Like the gilt, auction-room chairs in the showroom (the *salon*), like the Olde Englyshe type on the memo slips and billheads, like the worn-out Kern, Berlin, and Porter tunes issuing eternally from Madam Kaye's secondhand hi-fi, everything connected with the Haute Monde Society Resale Shoppe had to be what Madam Kaye called "high class."

"Yes, Miss La Grande," Bernice said patiently. "I know your dresses have been here since Labor Day. And we show them to every size twelve who comes in. But there just isn't much call for beaded things here. That's why Madam Kaye was only willing to take them on consignment. As soon as we can sell one . . . Hello?" Miss La Grande, as was her custom, had slammed her receiver down in mid-tirade.

The high-class notices Madam Kaye placed daily in the classified advertising sections of the Chicago newspapers specified that the Haute Monde Society Resale Shoppe trafficked in "slightly used one-of-a-kind creations worn by society leaders and others." Miss La Grande, who operated from a very small apartment just off the Drive, was decidedly one of the others. Even a girl as naïve as Bernice Potocki had been able to sense that immediately.

Madam Kaye crashed down her own receiver, terminating the day's war games while she was still ahead. "Who wuzzat?"

"Miss La Grande again, Madam Kaye."

"Nafka! Got the books balanced yet?"

"Almost, Madam Kaye."

"An' put on some more records, Bernice. Like 'Smoke Gets in Yer Eyes.' "

"Just a minute, Madam Kaye." Five and two to carry; seven, eleven, sixteen, twenty-three, thirty. There! At last! "The books are finished, Madam Kaye."

"Good."

Bernice hurried out to the gold-and-pink showroom—the salon!—darted behind the faded rayon-brocade screen and snatched out half-a-dozen record albums; gems from *Roberta*, *Jubilee*, *Jumbo*, *Show Boat*, *Annie Get Your Gun*, and, just for good measure, an old Xavier Cugat collection of Latin-American music to remind her that she was going to Mexico today—if she could ever get away from her job.

For all of her twenty years, Bernice Potocki had wanted to be someone else, somewhere else. She had thought that escaping from the dismal, gritty coal town in southern Illinois to Chicago three years ago would be the answer. It hadn't been. She had simply exchanged the dismal, gritty house of her Polish parents for her married sister's even more dismal and gritty apartment next to the elevated tracks out west in Polack Land. Sis—Mrs. Ignatz Wisniewski—with her loudmouthed, loutish husband, her runny-nosed kids, her overly bleached hair, and her still worse taste. That lamp in the living room! For more than a thousand nights, as Bernice bedded down on the studio couch, the last thing she had seen was that lamp, and for more than a thousand mornings it had been the first thing to greet her—followed rapidly by the rumble of the elevated train, the shrieks and screams of little Sandra Ann, little Iggy, Junior, and baby Debra-Jo, the barking of Blackie, the bellowing of Ignatz, and the shrill, perpetual whine of Sis.

Of course Bernice had had to work, to earn a salary and to hand over most of it to Sis and Ignatz for room and board. It was that ad in the Chicago *Tribune* that had brought her to Madam Kaye:

WANTED—Attractive model-secretary-bookkeeper
to work in high-class fashion salon

How impressed, how completely awestruck Bernice had been by this parlor floor in a Rush Street brownstone with its dusty pressed-glass chandelier, its machine-made Aubusson rug, its spermatic background music, and by Madam Kaye herself, imposing in a pearl-gray satin dress redolent of Shalimar and sweat. "It's a Ben Zuckerman original," Madam Kaye had explained archly. The interview had been interrupted once by a woman whose beautiful mink coat—"But I've practically never worn it"—was bought outright for five hundred dollars cash, and once by a dashing, blonde Lake Forest housewife with two suits and three evening dresses to unload. "Dja get a load of huh, dearie? She just happens tuh be in the Sussil Registah. I get only the best people here," Madam Kaye had said. "Now whudja say yuh name was?"

"Potocki," Bernice said softly, embarrassed by its very Polishness. Madam Kaye's eyebrows shot up. "Po-tot-ski?" She was the first person in Chicago Bernice had ever heard pronounce the name correctly. "A Polska?"

"Polish descent," Bernice murmured. Really, she might just as well pick up her bag and gloves and go. She'd never be hired in this grand, this truly exclusive shop. This salon. A poor little Pole from nowhere. "Potocki, eh?" Madam Kaye had rolled her opaque eyes and whistled softly. Years earlier, Madam Kaye, her sister, and her parents had lived in a miserable village on the lands of the Potocki family within the shadow of the vast magenta palace of the Potockis at Lancut. At least by hearsay, if not from personal acquaintance, Madam Kaye was well aware of the glory of the Potockis, their art treasures, their seven state dining rooms, their carriages driven six-in-hand, their constant stream of visiting royalty. Talk about high class! Through the smoke of her cigarette, through her stubby, beaded lashes, she gazed shrewdly at Bernice. A perfect size ten, dark, pretty, anxious to work. Good legs. She looked like a lady and not like some of the *kurvehs* who *called* themselves models. Her suit was terrible. Not one penny more than twenty dollars retail. But conservative. High class. With a shicksa like this working out front—

a shicksa named Potocki, maybe even *Countess* Potocki . . . "You want I should dictate a couple letters, doll? Test out your typingue and shorthand?"

"I—I took the commercial course in high school, Mrs. Kaye."

"*Madam* Kaye."

Miraculously the glamour job became Bernice's. She was dumb with amazement. She shouldn't have been. Not many girls were qualified or even willing to serve as model, secretary, and bookkeeper. There were other duties not mentioned in Madam Kaye's modest advertisement. Dusting and vacuuming the *salon*, filling in as saleswoman ("venduce," as Madam Kaye called it), dashing out to Walgreen's for Madam's lunch, collecting Madam's bills, and fending off Madam's creditors. All of these things Bernice did for minimum pay.

There were Potockis and Potockis. Bernice was not one of the noble ones. But after a few weeks at Haute Monde Society Resale she could have passed for one. It was hardly the aristocratic proximity of Madam Kaye that brought about the changes in Bernice. Madam Kaye was an ignorant, greedy, vicious bully; a cheat and a liar; a toady to the rich, a tyrant to the poor. Insecure and immature, Bernice made a perfect slavey at Madam's secondhand rag emporium. But as spineless as Bernice may have been, she was intelligent, she was observant, and she was ambitious. Day after day, she watched and listened to the women who came in to dispose of dresses seen too often. The way they walked, the way they talked, the way they wore their clothes. Nothing was lost on Bernice. With her first week's salary she bought a used Chanel copy, perfect but for a small cigarette burn, got some almost-alligator pumps, and stopped teasing her hair. Sis thought she looked terrible. "So plain!" Instead of "din't, wun't, shun't," Bernice was saying "didn't, wouldn't, shouldn't," just like the women who sold their old clothes to Madam Kaye. It was not long before Bernice noticed that customers preferred to deal with her instead of the Madam. Unfortunately, Madam noticed it, too. As a reward, pressing and minor repairs were added to Bernice's duties.

Nor had it taken a girl as bright as Bernice very long to see

Madam Kaye and her dreadful, threadbare surroundings for what they really were. Shlock. Bad imitations of the real thing. By the time she had completed her first year of servitude, Bernice had seen enough of the real thing to know.

On inclement days, willing Bernice, in her smart little second-hand suits and dresses, her gay little raincoat, had been sent out on buying trips to the nearby homes of really important Chicago women who had large quantities of unwanted finery to dispose of. Head held high, Bernice, the little West Side Polack from a downstate coal-mining town, had breezed past respectful door-men and gone right up in the passenger elevators to dicker with women who treated her almost as a guest. Thus she had visited the Astor Street penthouse of young Mrs. William W. Williams, the Ambassador-East suite of a famous star who was packing them in at the Shubert, an apartment on Lake Shore Drive that housed a collection of French Impressionists rivaling the one at the Art Institute. These little journeys through homes of the great had had a depressing effect. Where once Bernice had been satisfied to look and sound like her betters, she now wanted to live like them, to be one of them. For a time she even attempted a few night-school courses—conversational French, art apprecia-tion, decorating—as much to get out of her sister's clamorous apartment as anything else, until one night she caught a glimpse of herself reflected in a gum machine on the windy elevated sta-tion platform. "But this is crazy," Bernice had said aloud. "What do I think I'm doing? Me. A little Polish nobody who works in a secondhand store coming home to a West Side slum talking about Directoire furniture and wearing a Mainbocher coat that some man bought for some other woman. This is hopeless." The tears streaming down her cheeks, she had fought her way through the biting wind to the squalid bedlam called home, where Sis in her rollers and Ignatz in his undershirt would be fighting with each other while the television blared out the wrestling matches. Hopeless!

But not entirely hopeless. As easily imposed upon and bullied as Bernice could be, she had will and she had wile. She began to think more deeply about the women she envied, studied them

33

for more than superficial features, analyzed them. She was younger, better-looking and, now, better dressed than almost any of them. How had they got their furs, their jewels, their paintings, their perfect apartments? Marriage. Marriage was the only answer. And not a marriage such as Sis's to a dumb Polack truck driver like Ignatz. Who then? Someone like that foul-breathed old goat who had offered her a drink and then tried to date her while his wife was burrowing through a closet full of Givenchy dresses? No! Not that. Bernice was too nice a girl, too fastidious to be interested in another woman's husband. This had to be one of her own. But where to find him? At Madam Kaye's shop? Never. No real, no eligible male ever set foot there. At her instant-culture classes in art and decoration? Hardly. The few boys who attended were poorer than Bernice, given to tight pants and loose sweaters and to loud effusions over the smartness of her clothes. Bernice wanted a man. A man to supply beautiful things, not to coo over them. At Ignatz's weekly beer busts? Certainly not. The man for Bernice would have to be found elsewhere. Away. Far away from Sis and Ignatz and the easy-payments horror of their existence.

Of course there was Ralph. What a name! He was sweet, he was kind, he loved her. Bernice was certain of that. But why encourage him? It would be dishonest, indecent. Bernice might be just what Ralph wanted, but Ralph would never be what Bernice wanted. A garage mechanic from Cicero? Bernice knew where she was going, or at least where she *hoped* she was going, and it wasn't a garage in Cicero with a man who said "he seen" and "I done." A man whose nails were forever black with grease? A man whose best suit—whose *only* suit—was a peacock-blue horror from Goldblatt's? No, never. Not Bernice. She had seen twenty years' worth of poverty and ugliness in Mom's dust-colored frame house, in Sis's dark, crowded flat. It was time for a change.

Bernice began quietly but surely. She started by quitting her job. There wasn't a shop on Michigan Avenue that wouldn't welcome little Miss Potocki. Bernice knew that. So did Madam Kaye. Madam had thrown a fit of hysterics, feigned a heart attack, and offered Bernice a ten-dollar raise. Bernice stayed on. Twice in the last two years, in her quiet, unobtrusive way, Bernice had quit again, bringing on further hysterics, the curse of Jehovah, two more badly staged heart attacks, two more raises, a commission agreement, and a vague hint as to a small interest in the business in the indefinite future. Still Bernice stayed on.

There was money in the bank now—not much—but enough to take her away. There were clothes enough to take her anywhere; good ones, smart ones, lasting ones. Her two new suitcases were parked beside her desk. This was it. Bernice's quiet, ladylike man-hunt was on. Mexico next stop. If Madam Kaye would ever let her go.

But go she must and go she would. There was nothing, absolutely nothing, that Madam Kaye could think of to hold her back. Bernice had come in at seven o'clock this morning, removed her trim little traveling suit, and scrubbed the tile floor of the bathroom, swilled out the toilet with a Johnny Mop, poured Drāno down the sink. She had brought the inventory up to date as of closing time last night. She had written checks for the rent, the light, the advertising, and for all the bills Madam Kaye did not intend to pay as well as those she did. She had stocked enough cartons of Pall Malls and enough jars of Nescafé to choke the old bitch, which Bernice ardently hoped might happen.

She looked at her watch. She was due at the airport in just one hour and she intended to be early, not late. Madam Kaye was hovering, regarding Bernice with hostile, baleful eyes, her beefy arms slightly extended like those terrible wrestlers Ignatz was always watching on television.

"Well, everything's done," Bernice said with a hollow gaiety. "Now to call a cab."

"Haven't I astcha not to use the phone for personal calls? The bill this month is . . ."

"I'll give you a dime. By the way, the checks for the telephone and all the other bills are on your desk. The envelopes are addressed."

"So yer really goingue?"

"Yes, I've got my tickets, reservations, tourist card. I've left my address on your desk, too, in case anything unusual comes up. It's Su Casa, Acapulco, Guerrero."

35

"Seems to me you like can see all the spicks you want right here in Chicago."

"Not the same kind."

"Prob'ly get sick. I hear everybody does down there."

"It's a risk I'll be happy to take."

"You really planningue on two whole weeks?"

"At least. By rights I should stay away for six. I've never had a vacation—or even a day off—since I've worked here."

"I don't know what kinda gratitude you call it, leavingue me flat right in the busiest season."

"It isn't the busiest season, it's the quietest. Besides, you'll have your niece Sylvia to help out. You're always telling me how wonderful she is. Maybe she'll be so good I won't have to come back at all."

Madam Kaye considered another heart attack and decided against it. That shicksa bitch had no feelings at all. The last time Madam Kaye had staged a heart attack Bernice had poured a glass of water all over her and her Norman Norell original. Her defeat was total but, just for the record, she thought she'd get in one last dig.

"Well, missy, just don't be too sure that this job will still be waitingue."

"Oh? Would you like to sign a check for my severance pay right now?"

It was too much for Madam Kaye. Even worse than losing two weeks of the efficient Miss Potocki's services was the thought of losing two weeks of her salary from the bank account. Madam was worried, frightened even, to be without her paragon. Stretching her reddened lips into the shark's smile she employed on really big sales, Madam Kaye chortled hollowly. "Ah, Bernice, honey, cantcha take a little joke? Go! Enjoy! You're entitle'. An', look, doll, justa show there's no hard feelingues, I want you should take this . . ." Madam waddled off to the stockroom and came back with a sable jacket. "Here, honey. You can borrow this. Natural Russian sable and it hasn't hardly been worn at all." There! That would bring Bernice back. The coat was insured anyhow.

Waspish and surly, Madam Kaye was hard enough to take. Magnanimous, she was insupportable. But now even Bernice was stunned. That sable jacket was the star item in the used-fur collection. "W-why, Madam Kaye! It's—it's . . ."

"Go ahead, doll. Take it. Wear it in good health. We're only youngue once. Oh, by the way. There's a fella waitingue in the *salon*. I thought I tolja not to have friends comingue around your place of business."

"Someone to see *me*?" Bernice got up and went to the showroom. There, in his horrible peacock-blue suit, was Ralph.

Sitting on a hard, little serape-covered bench in the waiting room, Bernice began hating herself. The airline—a totally unheard-of one, offering the cheapest possible excursion rates to Mexico—had thoughtfully provided a vase of large, dusty, Mexican paper flowers and some scratchy, canned marimba music to establish a mood of frenetic Latin gaiety for its Economy La Fiesta Champagne Flight. It was all about as jolly as an interment. The other passengers were unprepossessing, to say the least; a couple of tarty-looking girls with outlandish pompadours and matted false eyelashes, some incredibly frumpish old couples wearing badges that read "Senior Citizens Sunshine Jamboree," and quite a lot of shabby Mexican families with incredible quantities of children. Bernice just knew that she was going to end up next to a sick Mexican baby. With her perfect little suit, her trim pumps and matching bag, *and* with the sable jacket, it occurred to Bernice that she, and not the rabble of fellow passengers, looked decidedly out of key. No matter. Her smart traveling outfit had been effectively ruined by Ralph. Not only had he taken the morning off to drive her out to the airport in his old car, he had bought her an orchid corsage. And what an orchid! In just the wrong shade and elderly to begin with, it had been further enhanced by the addition of a lavender tulle bow, by silver glitter sprinkled over it and, as the final touch, a rhinestone dewdrop. It fairly screamed Polish wedding—or funeral.

Ralph! Such a sweet, dumb, big ox. The peacock-blue suit, the white socks, the big garnet high-school graduation ring, that

37

wild necktie. He was so kind, so good, and Bernice was actually embarrassed to be seen with him. How she despised herself!

"Gosh," Ralph said glumly, "I wish you wasn't going."

"Why, Ralph! I've never had a vacation. You should be glad."

"I guess what I mean is that I wish I was going with you."

Bernice wished no such thing. "Ralph, it's not as though I were taking a trip to the moon. It's only for two weeks. I'll be back before you know it. And I'll write and send postcards."

"What I wish we was doing is going on a honeymoon."

"Now, Ralph, dear." Oh, no. Not this again!

"Bern, I'm makin' good money. Gus wantsta retire. Sell out the business. We could . . ."

Just in time, just in the nick of time, Bernice was saved by the astounding appearance of a middle-aged blonde hopefully got up in a great sombrero, a limp peasant skirt aglimmer with some tarnished sequin flowers, and a lot of eye make-up. "*Hola!*" she cried. "*Saludos amigos!* Announcing the departure of the Economy La Fiesta Champagne Flight for old Méjico. In addition to orthentic native Mexican music, complimentary champagne will be served all dooing the trip. Passengers will please board immedjitly. *Olé!*"

Bernice got to her feet. So did Ralph. "Well," she said, "I guess this is it."

Ralph colored, stammered, and began groping through the pockets of his suit. "Bernice, just one thing else." Finally he located whatever it was he had been searching for. He pulled out a small box covered in purple plush.

"Oh, Ralph," Bernice said. She felt tears smarting beneath her eyelids. Inside the box rested one of the ugliest little chip-diamond rings she had ever seen, like Sis's, only smaller. "Ralph, I . . ."

"Don't say nothing, honey. And you have a swell time. Boy! Champagne all the way!"

In a small, strangulated voice Bernice said, "Y-yes. Just think, champagne all the way." Blinded by her tears, she planted a quick kiss somewhere between the corner of his mouth and his ear lobe. Then she ran to the plane.

Whatever You Say, Arthur

Yes, there is a certain kind of person who can be spotted at a hundred paces as Quality. Even the most myopic could spot Mr. and Mrs. William W. Williams and their traveling companion, Dr. Arthur Craine, at a *thousand* paces as Class.

From a glossy black Cadillac limousine that was exactly Carolyn Williams' age, the three of them emerged at Gate One of the Mexico City Airport. The hired limousine had been Arthur's idea. Almost everything was Arthur's idea. But it had been easier than trying to whistle up those elusive Mexican taxicabs.

"*Muchas gra-thias, The-thilio,*" Arthur said in his pretty good Spanish, handing the driver a tip—large but not ostentatious. Even in Mexico, Arthur Craine persisted in using the Castilian accent. The Mexicans found it a scream, especially Cecilio, the driver.

"All ready, loves?" Arthur said.

"Not quite, Arthur," Bill Williams said, counting the luggage as it was unloaded from the trunk. "We've got the bags to think about."

"*Zut alors!* How too true," Arthur said. "*Oiga! Portero! El equipaje para Acapulco, por favor.*"

The porter, recognizing a better-than-average American tipper when he saw one, darted forward, loaded the Williams-Craine bags on to his hand truck and reverently rolled them twenty feet to the Aeronaves counter. Bill Williams, having nothing smaller, rewarded him with fifty pesos.

"*Zut alors!* We're hours early," Arthur said, glancing at the slim, elegant watch on his slim, elegant wrist. "Bill, dear boy, you check the baggage through and then join Carolyn and me up in the bar."

"Arthur, dear," Carolyn said. "I don't really think I want a drink."

39

"Of course you do, darling. We all do. Come, love."

Everyone in the airport stared as the tall, elegant, English-looking man and the fluffy, chic little blonde clicked their way along the marble floor. "*Preciosa! Que linda! Y guapo el caballero!*" It was the reaction created by the Williams-Craine entourage everywhere—in Moscow, Paris, London, New Delhi, Tokyo, Nassau—you name it. They were great travelers. Arthur saw to that. It kept them on their toes.

Carolyn supposed she was having a good time. It was always such fun to travel with her brother, Arthur. At least that's what everyone said. Arthur had been everywhere, knew everyone. Going places with Arthur never involved sightseeing buses, guided tours through museums, or wondering how to kill a long evening in a strange city. To travel with Arthur meant hotel suites or apartments or even whole houses; dinner in at least one embassy—and usually two or three—per capital; private parties in private mansions lovingly laid on for the lion, Arthur Craine. It was the way you really got to know a place. At least that's what Arthur always said.

Their week in Mexico City had been very gay, Carolyn guessed. The three of them had lived amicably in a duplex hotel suite at the Maximiliano. ("The only possible non-hotelly place to stay since the Villa Napoles closed," Arthur had explained.) They had dined at the American Residence, been entertained at the Jockey Club, at four splendid apartments, and eight opulent houses. They had met Dolores del Río, María Félix, Rufino Tamayo, Mayor Corona del Rosal, several people named López Negrete and López Figueroa and a lot of rich foreign residents. Carolyn would have liked to have seen the Ballet Folklorico, the Museum of Anthropology, a bullfight, eaten at least one meal in a good Mexican restaurant. But Arthur had said that those things were just too touristy for words. And besides, there hadn't been time. Yes, Mexico had been very gay. All except for last night.

Last night Arthur had to deliver a lecture at the Mexican-American Cultural Institute, then dine, then say some deliciously outrageous, but eminently quotable, things to the English-language press. Left alone together, Carolyn and Bill hadn't had much of an evening. After discussing for the better part of an hour where they might have dinner—"Where do you want to go?" "I don't care. Where do you want to go?"—they had dined joylessly, wordlessly in the near-empty hotel dining room. It had been early when Bill signed the check. "What would you like to do now?" "I don't care. What would you like to do?" They had returned to the large living room of their suite, where Carolyn pretended to read Patrick McHenry's *A Short History of Mexico* while Bill wrote a letter back to the office. "It's late. I think I'll turn in," Bill had said. Then he had crawled into his twin bed with the new issue of *Time*. After gazing moodily at Chapultepec Park from the terrace, Carolyn had gone to bed, too. Bill was asleep. No. Not a terribly stimulating evening. Maybe skiing at Aspen, which is what Bill had wanted to do, would have been better. But Arthur had stipulated Mexico. And Mexico was gay. Really it was.

"I think we'll sit here," Arthur said, after he had surveyed the airport bar. "Not too sunny for you, is it? That antelope suit is marvelous on you, my dear. I knew I was right when I made you buy it."

"Yes, Arthur. But it's awfully hot. Maybe back in Chicago in a high wind . . ."

"Ah, here comes Bill now. Sit down, William. What will it be?"

Arthur Craine gazed upon his handsome young brother-in-law, his beautiful baby sister, with proprietary pride. Americans of absolutely the best type, both of them. Really a stunning couple. Carolyn was twenty-seven now, but Arthur still thought of her as a baby sister. And with good reason. Arthur had just cast his first vote, was in his senior year in college, when, to the horror and surprise of everyone concerned, his middle-aged parents had presented him with a bouncing baby sister. The shock and embarrassment had been considerable to young Arthur Craine, but then he had bigger things to think about than formulas, teething, and diaper rash. Arthur had his career. Arthur would stay right on at Princeton and teach. Thanks to a trust fund left by his grandmother, Arthur could afford to. How wonderful to enter a selfless vocation like teaching and still be able to live like a gentleman!

As a young English instructor, Arthur was an unqualified success—elegant, witty, acerb, and popular. He might have gone on in his snug, smug, book-filled bachelor apartment for years had not Arthur found himself, at thirty-five, the sole guardian of his fourteen-year-old sister Carolyn. They were orphans.

Except to send the child little mementos at Christmas and on her birthdays, Arthur barely had known his sister. Having a shy, gawky, repressed teen-age girl move in on him struck Arthur as something of a mixed blessing. But there was a lost, helpless, utterly dependent quality about Carolyn that appealed to her older brother. After years of laying down the law to tweedy Princeton boys, Arthur was ready for new horizons. It might just be that Carolyn could provide them. Carolyn could and Carolyn did.

Oh, it hadn't been easy for Arthur being brother, mother, and father to a colorless little girl. But Arthur had coped and Arthur had triumphed. Under Arthur's constant supervision, Carolyn had turned first into a beauty, then into a hostess, and then into almost something of an intellect. Arthur had chosen her clothes, her schools, her friends. Docile Carolyn had developed fast. By the time she was fifteen, Carolyn, in the good little pastel wools Arthur had prescribed, was perfectly capable of passing canapés at Arthur's delightful cocktail parties. At sixteen, in decorous evening dress, she presided most creditably at Arthur's exquisite little dinners. At seventeen, Carolyn had become something of a legend on the Princeton campus. Miss Popularity! No hanky-panky, no funny business. Arthur always knew where Carolyn was going and, more important, with whom. Only the very nicest boys from the very best backgrounds took Dr. Craine's little sister to club dances.

Carolyn could have gone to any college she chose. Arthur had other plans. "She can learn more in my library and going abroad with me in the summers than she could in a lifetime at Vassar," Arthur said. Carolyn remained beneath her brother's roof and his wing.

At twenty, Carolyn married. It had come as no surprise to

Arthur. He had chosen the bridegroom himself from his own English composition class. One look at young William W. Williams and Arthur had known that he was the perfect brother-in-law. Young, nice looking, bright enough, well dressed and even better mannered. Bill was the only child of an imposingly rich Chicago steel magnate who was in notoriously poor health. It was the perfect setup to provide Carolyn with the perfect setup.

Obediently, Carolyn fell in love with Bill, accepted his proposal and Arthur's advice as to how their Chicago apartment would be furnished. Because old Mr. Williams had been too decrepit to venture far from what was soon to be his deathbed, Arthur staged —yes, that was the only word—Carolyn's wedding in Chicago the week after Bill graduated. Chicago was entranced. Carolyn was In.

But Carolyn's being In left Arthur slightly Out. His familial duty done, Arthur had to look for something else to occupy his time, his energies. He stumbled across his outlet and, incidentally, fame and fortune, by dashing off a little duty piece for the Princeton *Alumni Weekly*. Wittily, acidly, charmingly, it had dealt with how to and, more important, how *not* to write the English language. Within days a letter had arrived from a New York publishing house. Would Arthur care to expand his delightful little piece into a book-length work? The rest is now history. Arthur's book became one of those fluke best sellers. It had said nothing that a grade-school teacher could not have said quicker but, ah, how beautifully Arthur had put it! The yearly sales of the textbook edition alone were enough for Arthur to employ the weekly services of a good tax accountant.

Arthur wore his celebrity as elegantly as his suits. He resigned from Princeton regretfully. (He couldn't really afford to accept the salary in his present tax bracket.) Being ever so selective, he condescended to appear on a few of the better television panel shows. The things Arthur said on the air! But the higher IQ's in the audience were delighted. Lecture agents circled. Yes, Dr. Craine would deign to speak occasionally, but not oftener than twice a month, and not to fewer than a thousand people at a time or for less than a thousand dollars plus expenses. Any class magazine worthy of its name would give far more than the going rate for a short article by Arthur. (His essay on people who said "Good-bye, now" was a classic.) In the nicer houses, Arthur Craine was a household word.

Time to move on. Why hang around Princeton as a Wit Emeritus? Besides, the summers were too hot, the winters too cold. New York? Arthur had had New York. London was nice, but Arthur preferred being mistaken for English in America to being recognized as American in England. California? Nice for a visit, but . . . And so Arthur had moved to the place he had always known he was going to anyhow. Chicago. Just a block from Carolyn's apartment on Astor Street. Big brother and little sister were reunited, the trinity established.

". . . and so," Arthur was winding up one of the witty *petite histoires* that invariably accompanied his simplest statement of fact, "instead of having to stay in some Miami-style hotel with the jet set of the middle class, we'll be billeted at Liz Parkhurst's little pension. Liz is a pet and anything she has anything to do with is bound to be charming. Such taste!"

"Whatever you say, Arthur," Bill said.

Carolyn, who had heard the story before, allowed her attention to wander. A terribly pretty girl had just come into the bar. With a practiced eye, Carolyn took in her suit, her shoes, her bag. The best of everything and all of it topped by a sable jacket that made Carolyn's mouth water. "Stunning," Carolyn said aloud.

"What's that, dear?" Arthur asked.

"That girl. The one sitting two tables away. Isn't she lovely?"

"Hmmm," Bill said.

"Very attractive," Arthur conceded. "The tattiness of people who travel nowadays is exceeded only by . . ."

"I could swear I've seen her someplace before," Carolyn said. "Odd."

"Shall I try to pick her up, my dear?"

"Oh, Arthur. You couldn't! Never in a million years."

"She doesn't seem the type," Bill said.

"She's darling looking. And that sable!"

As with all conversations in which Arthur did not serve as

moderator or subject matter, his attention soon drifted. Blandly, he waited for a brief break and then leapt into the center of things again. "Now let me tell you a bit about our hostess, Liz Parkhurst—Señora Martínez she is now."

No elocution teacher had ever taken Arthur in hand. None had needed to. His voice, though not unduly loud, was a carrying one that delivered Arthur's most trivial message, his most subtle nuance, to the farthest drafty corner of the classroom, to the uppermost reaches of the auditorium. Hearing about Su Casa, the place where she was planning to stay, Bernice Potocki gazed guardedly through her big sunglasses at the table of the most handsome, smartly-turned-out people in the bar. And then her heart skipped a beat. The woman was Mrs. William W. Williams, the exquisite Carolyn Williams of Astor Street, whom Bernice had once visited in the interests of beefing up the stock of Haute Monde Society Resale. Bernice had not actually planned to falsify herself on this trip, to tell lies, to pretend to be something she was not. Rather, Bernice had hoped to get along on her looks, her wardrobe, and by saying as little about herself as possible. Now the dream was shattered. Carolyn would surely recognize her and unmask her as the little slavey who did the dirty work for Madam Kaye's secondhand clothing establishment in Chicago. In desperation, Bernice rose to her feet and, in doing so, sent the tiny bar table over with a noisy thud.

Arthur Craine and Bill Williams, gentlemen of the old school, were at her side in a flash, brandishing Irish linen handkerchiefs, swooping downward to snatch up her fur jacket, her alligator purse, from where they had fallen.

"Oh, thank you. Thank you very much," was all Bernice could say. Yet she was glad that Ralph's terrible orchid had been jettisoned on the plane to Mexico City.

"Zut alors, but you must let me replace the drink you have just lost," Arthur said. He winked at Carolyn. He'd shown his sister that Arthur Craine could pick up an attractive girl in considerably less than a million years.

"Oh, no. Thank you. Really. But I have to catch a plane in . . . in . . ."

45

"So have we. There's just time enough to have one more. *Mesero!*"
Safe. Safe as a church! Even safer. Of course Carolyn Williams
hadn't recognized her any more than she would recognize a little
salesgirl at Marshall Field's who had sold her a blouse two years ago
or the Mexican waiter who was even now bringing a round of
drinks.

Potocki. Arthur's chilly blue eyes had flickered just once when
he had heard the name. "Potocki," he had said, almost tasting the
name. "Ah, yes. Lancut. Near Kraków. I remember visiting the
Potocki house there." (He had. Several years after it had been
turned into a public museum.)

"Then you've done better than I have," Bernice said.

Slightly dismayed, Arthur said, "But you are one of the Polish
Potockis?" Indeed, there was no other kind.

"Oh, yes, I am Polish and a Potocki. But you see, Poland has
been behind the Iron Curtain since before I was born."

First in Spanish and then in English, the flight to Acapulco was
announced. "You must forgive me," Bernice said, "but that's my
flight."

"Well, isn't that a coincidence," Bill said. "It's ours, too."

I'm Sure You'll Be Very Comfortable

"I'm sure you'll be very comfortable here, Mr. Goodman."

"Goodwin," Lee said.

"I'm sorry. Mr. Goodwin. Alcatraz is the last room available. The
others are all taken. Or, at least, they're reserved."

Liz couldn't believe it; Su Casa just barely open and already sold
out. There were a lot of other things she couldn't believe, either.
She couldn't believe that Aurelia, assisted by Pablo and Florentino,
would actually get lunch out onto the buffet table. And yet they
had and the lunch had been good. The only drawback was that she
and Salvador and Laddy had been the only ones on hand to eat it.
There hadn't been a peep out of the incredible Mrs. Meyers—

46

Flossie—in spite of the terrible things Salvador had predicted. Mrs. Meyers neither ordered breakfast this morning nor appeared for lunch. Liz knew that she wasn't dead because she had heard her from Nubes talking to that woebegone dog.

Nor could Liz believe the bathing outfits on those two extraordinary men at the pool. She was glad Salvador hadn't seen them. They had looked only silly when they came out of Rosas in matching terry-cloth ponchos, but when they had peeled them off at the edge of the pool they had been left in nothing but matching bandanna jockstraps and quite a lot of gold St. Christopher medals, wristwatches, identification bracelets, signet rings, also matching. Liz had gasped aloud. Not that they were deformed or anything like that. They both had good figures—especially the younger one. They just looked so white, so terribly naked; like cold-storage turkeys. "I'd cover up the first day," Liz had said as they anointed one another with Bain de Soleil. "The sun here is terribly strong." That had been two hours ago. They were still lying motionless at the pool's edge, stirring only to sip the enormous planter's punches they had ordered. Perhaps a good second-degree sunburn would get them back under wraps. Failing that, they would at least look a little more, well, clad in coats of tan. Liz tried to tell herself that they were just pals, two men traveling together. She couldn't believe that either, and she knew that Salvador wouldn't. Liz had seen enough of such couples during her years in fashion, in decorating, and with Norman, to know better. Not that Liz cared; she rather enjoyed the company of les boys, but Salvador would be a different matter entirely.

And something else Liz wouldn't believe was that the couple who had arrived just after lunch were married. Rex Roman and April May. Tarzan and his Mate! Of course when she saw Rex, thirty pounds heavier than he had been thirty years ago, it all came back to her. Tarzan himself! Like Johnny Weismuller and Buster Crabbe, he had been a big star, lithe and lean, with the noble face of a tailor's dummy. He had swum like a porpoise and flown from branch to branch in the constant company of an ape that was far the better actor. Fat and florid, Rex Roman had seemed stupefied, rather than gratified, that Liz had remembered him, and

47

told him—quite untruthfully—how much she had enjoyed his jungle films. Well, Rex was all right. He might even add a certain dim luster to Su Casa's roster of guests.

But the bit of fluff with him, Miss April May! With her cotton-candy hair, her thrusting breasts, her tinny little-girl voice, she was a caricature of every trampy movie starlet ever mentioned in a publicity release. And what was Salvador going to say about her, about *them?* Plenty. Salvador, with his old-fashioned, almost quaint, set of morals. Salvador, however, had been gone since luncheon. Laddy was gone, too. But at least Liz knew where Laddy was—at the airport meeting Arthur and his sister and her husband and a Miss Potocki from Chicago. Dear old Arthur! If Arthur was still as determinedly grand as he had been as a lowly English instructor, he would go a long way toward making up for that common (no other word for her) Mrs. Meyers, for that obvious pair of men by the pool, for Rex Roman and his doxy, and, also, for this cold-eyed, faintly unpleasant young man—this Mr. Lee Goodwin—who had just appeared from the blue.

"Uh, yes, Mr. Goodwin. If there's anything you want, just ring. We run the bar on the honor system—self-service and simply sign for whatever you drink. Dinner is served on the terrace from eight o'clock on."

"Thanks," he said flatly.

"Well, I'll be running along now."

"Do that."

The door closed behind Liz, and Lee cast a scathing look at it. Christ, but these society-type dames gave him a pain in the ass! And no use turning on the old charm for this one. Forty if she was a minute, and probably didn't have two pesos to rub together. The place was decent enough; clean, brand new, but obviously being run on a shoestring. Lee could spot a smalltime operation immediately. He'd seen too many bigtime ones not to know the difference.

"Hell, I wonder if I should of come here after all?" It was a purely academic question. If Lee wanted to stay in Acapulco long enough to accomplish anything, he'd have to stay here or in some other little dump run by some other dizzy broad with no brains and less experience.

48

Earlier today, as Leonard Goodrich, he'd made it out of the Acapulco Hilton pretty well. Damned well. He'd nearly knocked the management cold with the V.I.P.-ness of his departure, the detailed list of forwarding addresses for his mail: "Until the fifth, Hotel Victoria, Taxco; from the fifth through the tenth, Posada de las Quintas, Cuernavaca; from the tenth on, Hotel Presidente, Mexico City." That was the way. Kill 'em with kindness, a month's worth of forwarding addresses—all to expensive places—then keep them busy figuring pesos into pounds sterling. Next a check drawn on Coutts's Bank, 440 Strand, London, W.C.2. (Established 1692. What could be more respectable? It would take about three months to discover that no Leonard Goodrich had an account with Coutts & Co.) Then a whole lot of big-shotism about a car for the air-port and away we go. For another buck another airport car could bring him back into town to another hotel where he could live under another name. Lee Goodwin, that had always been a lucky handle.

The Acapulco Hilton had been a washout. One whole, lousy, goddamned month wasted there. And the prices! Not that they really mattered. Just because some joker had told him that all the fat cats were stopping at the Hilton. There were fat cats there, all right, but none of them had much time for Lee Goodwin (or Leonard Goodrich), except for a daffy old dentist from Detroit who'd slapped back about a thousand pesos' worth of Lee's cham-pagne, showing the greatest interest in Lee's Texokla Petroleum Enterprises, and then left on the midnight plane without a single penny changing hands. Smart ass! Was Lee losing his touch?

And now he was stuck in this ditsy dump unless he wanted to leave Acapulco entirely. He had to be. No dice in going to the Hilton or the Caleta or any of the big places. Hotelmen were as thick as thieves, gossiping with each other like washerwomen. The minute it got around that Lee Goodwin/Leonard Goodrich/Lewis Goode/Lenox Goodhue was still in town after leaving all those fancy forwarding addresses . . . Lee had been caught that way once when he was younger, dumber. Little chance of being picked up in a dead-ass place like this. Anyhow, Leonard Goodrich had gone into the men's room at the airport wearing spectacles and a mus-

49

tache. Lee Goodwin had come out bare-eyed and clean-shaven.

He put his attaché case on the bed and twiddled with the combination lock. The lid sprang open. Inside were the many official effects of the many Lee Goodwins. There were the brochures and stock certificates for Texokla Petroleum Enterprises, the Happy Ending Retirement Fund, Sunset Estates Realty, Royal Canadian Mining and Smelting, Ltd. There, too, were the imprinted checkbooks, the credit cards, the papers of identification. Lee tucked Leonard away for safekeeping and took out the documents essential to Lee Goodwin.

It was so simple. You just stuck a few thousand dollars into a very good bank and, while you waited for a fat book of checks with your new name and address printed on each, you established credit with the Diners Club, American Express, Carte Blanche. Then you just withdrew the money and walked away with a nice new checkbook and new credit cards. Fly now, pay later! This checkbook from the First National City Bank proclaimed him as Lee Goodwin, 670 Park Avenue, New York 10021. There was no such address on Park Avenue, but it sounded good.

Yes. It was all so easy. You only needed a nice little piece of capital. Ten thousand, even less. That was the problem. The capital was going fast. You couldn't charge *everything* and Lee hadn't had a really big strike since he had taken fifty thousand off that horny old doll in Fort Lauderdale for the Happy Ending Retirement Fund. Acapulco certainly *ought* to be the place. Wasn't it full of people with more money than sense?

Lee went to the window and stared out. Dead. At least it looked dead. Only two guys practically bare-assed at the pool. Fags. Lee could sniff them out in a hurricane. Probably a pair of hairburners on two weeks with . . . oh, no. Two gold cigarette cases glinted in the sun, flashed up into Lee's eyes. Then two gold lighters. Lee looked more closely at the mated medalions, the watches, the bracelets. He hated dealing with queens, but these two might have some money. No. Not these *two*; one of them; the older one going artistically gray at the temples.

Another blinding flash caught Lee in the eyes. It came from the windshield of the biggest Buick made. Brand new. Pennsylvania plates. Stepping back, Lee looked down. A man and a woman. Forties. Well preserved. Man wearing tropical suit, necktie, coconut-palm hat. Conservative. Woman, good figure, charm bracelet, carried jewel case and mink jacket. Solid! Quiet, classy, solid, and loaded. Lee could smell it.

Maybe it wouldn't be a bad idea to be a little nicer to the dame who ran this place. Get the names and addresses of the other guests, do some quick checking. A cozy little joint like this one, where people got on first-name terms right away, might turn out to be better pickings than the whole Hilton chain.

"Screw the Acapulco Hilton," Lee said. "*Su casa es mi casa.*"

But This Is Going to Be Fun, Hon

"Hon?" Essie called from the dressing room.

"Yes, hon?" Walt answered.

"I just wish you'd come and see how cute this is. The suite's called Violetas and there are violets just every place—on the tiles; on the shelf paper; purple towels; even lavender Kleenex and toilet paper. I wish Madge were here to see it. Charming! Such taste!"

"Nice," Walt said. "I wonder if the bar's open."

"Now, Walter, remember how sick you were in Taxco."

"Never felt better."

"Well, just go easy at first. Now, I'm putting your things here on the left and in these three drawers and my things . . . "

As neatly and efficiently as they did everything, Estelle and Walter Dewlap, leading citizens of Anthrax, Pennsylvania, U.S.A., settled into Su Casa, Acapulco, Guerrero, Mex.

If the United States could be said to have a backbone at all, the Dewlaps were two of its sturdiest vertebrae. In Anthrax, Pennsylvania, a city of nearly fifty thousand souls some two hours' drive from Pittsburgh, Walt and Essie were *somebody*. Walt owned the Buick agency and also Dewlap Pipe & Valve, the business founded by his grandfather in 1880. He had gone to the Hill

51

School and the University of Pennsylvania. He had emerged as a captain from World War II. Estelle had graduated *summa cum laude* from Anthrax Country Day and done two years at Bryn Mawr before abandoning intellectual pursuits to become Mrs. Walter Dewlap. Their house on Duquesne Drive was locally famous for food, flowers, furniture and, as of a year ago, its swimming pool. Essie's every stitch came from the French Room at Weisenheimer's or Peck & Peck. Walter bought at Brooks Brothers, Pittsburgh. Essie was still a perfect size five. Yes, *five!* Walter, who stood six-feet-one in his socks, had most of his hair, all of his teeth, and had gained only three inches around the waist since V-J Day.

They were members of the Anthrax Country Club, the University Club, the Diners Club, the Book-of-the-Month Club, the Theatre Guild, the Fortnightly Discussion Group, *Le Cercle Français*, the Anthrax Assembly, and (Essie) the Clara Kissinger Muggeridge Crèche, which was Anthrax's equivalent of the Junior League. No worthy cause—the community chest drive, the school integration program, the new hospital wing, the Anthrax Beautiful campaign—was ever launched without the wholehearted support of Estelle and Walter Dewlap. Essie gave one day a week as a nurse's aide and another caring for the children of working mothers at the Crèche. Walt was active in the teen-age physical-fitness program and shot golf in the high seventies.

The Dewlaps subscribed to—and read—*Time, Life, Harper's, The New Yorker, The Saturday Review* (it was a rare Double-Crostic that Walt couldn't lick in less than an hour), *Vogue, Gourmet, House & Garden, Connaissance des Arts* (in French), the New York *Times*, and *Mad*. They had been to Europe twice, once with the children. Annually, they spent two weeks at the Plaza in New York, shopping, catching up on the theater, the opera, the galleries.

Their only failing, their irreparable sin, was that they had not been born and bred on the Eastern banks of the Hudson River. "White-shoe trade," said the wittier New York bellboys, ignoring Walter's bench-made cordovans. "Eeks frahm de steeks," said Puerto Rican chambermaids, splashing themselves with Essie's French perfume. "A coupla tourists," said the hat-check girl whose own travels had been strictly confined to the New Lots Avenue express. "Yokels."

Uncomfortably conscious of their hopeless provincialism, Walt and Essie were determined to do something about it before it was too late. "After all, hon," Walt said, "we've gotta realize that Anthrax isn't the world. With LeRoy in Culver and Elspeth in Wheaton, we ought to get away a little more. Live a little. Maybe a trip around the world."

In the dead of winter that had seemed just too ambitious. Essie was anxious to do Russia, the Scandinavian peninsula, but not at temperatures below zero. "Walter, I can freeze to death right here in Anthrax. If you want to go away, let's at least go to someplace warm."

"You mean like Florida, hon?"

"No, Walter Dewlap, I do not mean like Florida. And I don't mean some cruise with a social director and Funny Hat Night, either. I mean someplace warm and different. Like South America."

"But, hon, that's even farther than Europe. I oughtn't to be away for more than two weeks. Three at the most."

In a big, air-conditioned Buick, fresh from the floor of Walt's showroom, they had compromised on Mexico. As always, the Dewlaps had done everything Right. In the right clothes, they had gone to all the right places. They had stopped at Hotel María Isabel in the capital, dined at the Rivoli, Delmonico's and Jena; lunched at Restaurant del Lago, La Cava and Ambassadeurs. Essie had bought a suède coat at Aries and some cute little cotton things at Tomacelli. They had poked around the thieves' market and found a pair of old dueling pistols for Walt's study. They had spent a day in Cuernavaca, lunching among the tropical birds at Las Mañanitas and, over cocktails with Essie's second cousin, Clyde, who kept an antique shop and an Indian boy there, being told that they had done everything wrong. They had toiled up the perpendicular cobblestone streets of Taxco and bought a silver pitcher. Acapulco last stop! Their cultural lag caught up with, Acapulco was going to be nothing but sun, fun, and relaxation. No cathedrals, no museums. Just swimming, golf, tennis, deep-sea fishing, and nights spent in the company of the jet set.

"All unpacked, hon?" Walt said.

"Yes, hon. Now why don't you take a little snooze while I dash off notes to LeRoy and Elspeth and Madge? Nice paper. Engraved."

"Madge!" Essie's fashionable divorcée friend, Madge, was practically the only thing Walt and Essie had ever disagreed on in twenty years of happy marriage.

"Now, Walt, Madge is my best friend. Besides, she's lonely."

"With a tongue like hers, I don't wonder. Well, give my love to the kids. Maybe I'll just look the place over. See if the bar's open. You think this outfit is too informal?"

"Your shorts and that lovely silk shirt? I do *not!* Besides, if you could see those two men at the pool, you'd think you were dressed for the Assembly. I'm glad you don't wear bathing suits like that."

"Hm!" Walt said, glancing out of the window. "Well, I still could. I may have a bulge but it isn't in the stomach." He let the curtains fall and put both arms around his wife. "Come on, hon, let's live a little—before we're too old."

"Walter Dewlap! *Stop* that! We just got here."

"Did you want to do it in the car? *I* did. Come on, Essie."

"Oh, all right, Walter. But wait a minute."

"I can't."

"Well, you'll just have to. You turn down the bed while I'm getting ready. Is it a double?"

"Yes, thank God."

Walt skinned out of his clothes, draped them neatly over a chair. Through the dimness he glanced at his sideways reflection, pulled in his belly, stuck out his chest. Then he crawled between the sheets and lit a cigarette.

A minute later Essie appeared from the dressing room. Look at her! Forty years old, two grown children, and she was still like a little doll.

"But this is going to be fun, hon," Essie said.

"You bet your bottom dollar it is."

"Oh, stop it, silly. I mean this *place*. Now don't mess up my hair!"

My Girls Are Used to the Best

"Mrs. T. B. Bullock, Melrose Hotel (permanent guest), Dallas, Texas, U.S.A." Mrs. Bullock signed the register with a force that nearly made the legs on the Spanish colonial desk buckle. "There," Mrs. Bullock said. "Now, girls, you-all sign. First you, Julie, then Susan, then Lou Ann. Now I believe we said a bungalow at a daily rate of . . . "

"Yes, Mrs. Bullock," Liz said. "I have the correspondence right here. Quite a lot of it, in fact. You and your party will be in Amapolas—poppies. Sitting room, two double bedrooms, two baths."

Every hotel at which Mrs. Bullock and her cultural tours stopped had a lot of correspondence from her, each niggling letter pointing out the probability of some unforeseen contingency, requesting impossible privileges such as free limousine and chauffeur service for the duration of Mrs. Bullock's stay, and each letter trying to reduce the day rates. In all likelihood, Mrs. Bullock spent more on airmail postage than she saved on hotel bills, but she enjoyed trying for every advantage. "I hope it's nice," Mrs. Bullock said, displaying her cast-iron dimples, her too perfect teeth. "My girls are used to the best."

"Old fart!" Lou Ann McIver mumbled under her breath. Susan gasped. It was such fun shocking dull old Susan that Lou Ann went on. "Pretty pool and would you just dig the baskets on those two studs layin' there." She drew great satisfaction from the widening of Susan's china-blue eyes, from the rush of blood to her face. "That's what you need, Sue, honey—something long and hard and often. Me, too."

"Lou Ann!" Mrs. Bullock said sharply. "Would you please just sign, like I told you. I am ve-ry weary. And all this heat. You didn't *tell* me Alcapulca was so *warm.*"

"You didn't ask," Liz said. It was about all that Mrs. Bullock hadn't asked.

Lou Ann signed the register with a flourish and gave her famous glad eye to Pablo and Florentino, who hurried forward for the bags. Pablo blushed. Florentino smiled, twinkled, smiled again. Lou Ann had heard about Latin lovers. She intended to find out from firsthand experience. What's the point of being seventeen and out of Hockaday School if a girl couldn't have a little fun?

That blond Parkhurst guy who'd met them at the airport. Cute. But an antique. Thirty if he was a day. Still, he was an encouraging sign. At least old Miz Bullock wasn't bringing them to another old ladies' home. And would you get the one who was coming in now: Woweee!

Liz, interpreting correctly Lou Ann McIver's sudden brightening at Salvador's appearance, smiled and said smoothly, "Salvador, querido. You're just in time to meet Mrs. Bullock and the girls she's chaperoning through Mexico. Mrs. Bullock, Miss Juliet Noyes, Miss Susan Holt and Miss Lucy Ann—uh—I don't think I got your name, dear."

"Lou Ann. Lou Ann McIver."

"Oh, yes. Forgive me. Miss McIver. This is my husband"—pause —"Señor Martínez." Husband, eh? Lou Ann abandoned that project while it was still on the drawing board. Liz had known that she would. "Now, if you'll just come with me, Mrs. Bullock, girls, I'll show you Amapolas."

Liz was good with people, everyone said so; outgoing, kind, and understanding. Still, Liz wasn't a doormat. She had dealt with a lot of mean women before—hair-splitters, price-cutters, and rank-throwers. Liz had sensed from Mrs. Bullock's letters the sort of woman she would probably be. One look and Liz knew. Nor had it taken extraordinary occult powers to peg Lou Ann as Trouble when it came to men. Purposely, purposefully, Liz led her troupe of Texas womanhood the long way around the swimming pool, past the table where Arthur Craine was regaling Bernice Potocki, Carolyn, and Bill.

"Arthur, darling," Liz said, patting the top of his head. "Order a gin and tonic for me. I'll be with you in just a moment."

"Righto, Liz, love."

"This way, ladies," Liz said.

"Was—was that *Arthur Craine*?" Susan asked, round-eyed once more. Liz had known that she would be the one to ask.

"Mm-hmm," Liz said, throwing it away. "A dear old friend—and a pet." That, for the time being, would settle Mrs. Bullock's hash. "And those young men arrived only this afternoon. Bachelors, both of them," she said, for Lou Ann's benefit. Lou Ann could learn the facts of life in her own sweet time. "This is Margaritas," Liz said, indicating the first cottage. "Dr. Craine is staying here with his sister and her *husband*." Lou Ann's glance at Bill Williams had not been lost on Liz. "Next comes Poincianas, where we have another celebrity of sorts—Rex Roman and *his* wife. But I'm sure you girls are all too young to remember him."

On cue, Susan squealed, "Tarzan? Oh, I've seen him on the 'Late Show' lots of times."

"Have you?" Liz said. "And here's Amapolas. Now if you'll just tell me how you want to divide up, I'll have the boys put the right luggage in the right rooms. Dinner is from eight on and we never dress."

"My girls *always* dress for dunnah," Mrs. Bullock said.

"Do they? Well, in that case, they'll be the only ones in Acapulco who do. If there's anything you want, please ring. *Hasta luego!*" So much for a woman who had stated in writing that the social distinction of herself and her traveling party should make ten dollars a day more than adequate compensation for accommodations and *three* meals.

"Which bed do you want?" Lou Ann said, lighting an illicit cigarette.

"I really don't care," Julie said. Julie Noyes knew that she would end up with whichever bed Lou Ann *didn't* want, anyhow, so there was no point in stating a preference. Almost as much as she hated sharing a room with Mrs. Bullock, with her steaming corset hanging like a dismembered torso in the closet, her upper plate grinning from a glass of water all night, Julie disliked sharing a room with Lou Ann. In a crowd, especially if there were boys around, Lou Ann McIver was the big personality kid. A laugh a minute—usually at someone else's expense. But alone in a room with just some girl she had gone to school with, Lou Ann was sullen, selfish, and sluttish. Julie knew now that she would never get used to the sight of Lou Ann's shoes, her clothes, her underwear scattered across the floor; Lou Ann's cosmetics, her contraceptive pills, her douche bag

57

cluttering up the bathroom; Lou Ann herself, slopping naked around the room, her small, underdeveloped bumps (you could never call them breasts), and her large, flaccid buttocks fish-belly white against the freckled tan of the rest of her skin. "I've had a better figure since I was twelve," Julie thought. "If the boys she's always grabbing at could see her this way, she'd still be a virgin. Like me."

Silly and stupid as she was, Susan made the best roommate of all. And now poor Sue—sweet Sue—was forced to endure Mrs. Bullock all night as well as all day. If Mrs. Bullock had any inkling of what Lou Ann was really like, what the duties of a chaperone really were, she'd keep Lou Ann handcuffed to her own thick wrist twenty-four hours a day.

All three of the girls were taking this dreary tour of Mexico for good reasons. Susan because she was so dull that her family hoped a bit of travel might be broadening. Lou Ann for exactly the opposite excuse; she was so lively that her mother and father wanted to get her out of Dallas to spare their becoming grandparents before they were even in-laws. Everybody knew about Lou Ann—everyone, that is, except Mrs. Bullock.

As for Julie herself, she had been living out of a series of suitcases ever since graduation day. Plans for her wandering had been drawn up on the day when she had come home from school announcing her intention to join the Peace Corps. What a scene! Mother in tears and Daddy pounding his left palm with his right fist and shouting that no daughter of Sam H. Noyes's was going to live with a lot of ignorant savages diseased from here to breakfast. Julie's plans to go into nursing had met with no more cordial reception. "But, Julie, darlin'," Mother had whined, "bein' around a lotta sick folks. Havin' to give baths to a lot of dirty men, seein' their"—the voice lowered confidentially—"privates." The answer was no to nursing, too. Shorthand and typing, then? Certainly not. Just *anything* so as to be doing something worthwhile? Again, no.

Last summer had been spent in the tonneau of the Noyes's huge air-conditioned limousine doing Europe with Mother and Daddy. It should have been interesting. It wasn't. London, to Julie, meant Claridge's and long nights in gambling clubs with Mother and

Daddy and other traveling Texans. Paris meant the penthouse suite in the Bristol, days of shopping with Mother, nights at the Folies-Bergère, the Casino de Paris, the Lido with Daddy, and overeating overpriced meals with other Texans in between. Italy was simply a succession of Excelsior Hotels so similar in their grandeur that even now Julie couldn't quite distinguish Rome from Naples, Florence from Venice. In any case, Julie was given to understand by Sam H. Noyes that no single thing in Europe compared at all favorably with its counterpart in Dallas, Texas.

But once back in that zenith of all cities, Julie was not permitted to benefit from its superior advantages. New clothes in new luggage and another grand tour. This time Mexico—*all* of it—with silly Susan, bitchy Lou Ann, and mean old Mrs. Bullock.

Mrs. Bullock, since the grateful departure of her late husband, had been making quite a good thing out of shepherding the daughters of the Dallas rich around the usual tourist attractions. She was basically nasty, stupid, and snobbish, with all the crust of the very rich and none of the money to justify it. On the strength of a family that had arrived in Dallas from Nowhere, Tennessee, four generations ago, she was able to intimidate the newly wealthy into entrusting their daughters to her for "finishing."

Julie would be "finished" at the end of the month. And then what? Back to Dallas for her eighteenth birthday and a party that, according to Daddy, would be "the biggest goddamned blowout Texas has ever seen or my name ain't Sam H. Noyes. And I'm doin' it all for my little princess." Daddy was doing it for Daddy, and the little princess knew it. Still, he thought that he was being kind; Mother, too. Just as they thought that they were being kind giving Julie "this lovely trip to Mexico with a really experienced lady like Miz Bullock." ("And to knock some of the nonsense out of her head," Julie overheard her father adding in a jovial aside.)

Mrs. Bullock was neither experienced nor a lady. Her gentility was put on and her dozen words of Spanish were mispronounced at that. Julie had learned more Spanish from the hands on her father's ranch than Mrs. Bullock would ever know. Maybe Mrs. Bullock could snow the Dallas parents with her "Hhhasta la vistas," her "Keen sobbies," her "Comma esta oos-teds," but she didn't fool their daughters for more than half an hour south of the border. Julie despised her, hated the female dogginess of Lou Ann, disliked the vapidity of Susan, and was revolted with herself for being here, wasting all this time, all this money.

Lou Ann came out of the bathroom, dropping a Kleenex on the floor. Dressed, wearing her padding, her eyelashes, her fall, she looked a lot better—almost attractive if you weren't going to be too analytical.

"Honey?" Lou Ann said. That meant that Lou Ann wanted something, that honey business. "What's the old bitch doing now?"

"I really don't know."

"I think she's on the potty. At least I heard her through the wall. I can always tell if it's her. Anyhow, I rang for a drink. You know the lingo, honey. When the waiter comes tell him I want a double bourbon and gin-ger ale and tell him to pass it through the windah so she won't find out about it. Now go on out to the front door and wait for him so he won't hafta knock. He's kinda cute, innyway. Both of 'em are."

That was Lou Ann for you. She'd get the drink and Julie would get the trouble if Mrs. Bullock found out about it. "Here he comes," Lou Ann whispered. "Go on out and tell him, honey."

It was Pablo, the tall mozo. He had changed into his lacy bridal shirt, his white trousers, and cummerbund. The evening uniform made him look even taller, broader-shouldered, narrower in the waist and hips.

"Sí, señorita? You . . . rang?"

"Oh? You speak English?"

Pablo broke into a dazzling smile. "Poco, señorita. Ai spik a lit-tle English. Muy poco."

"Y yo hablo el Español. Un poco, tambien."

Pablo beamed again. "You spik the Spanish perfeck, señorita. Beauty-fool."

Julie wasn't buying any of that. Mexicans were all alike. Any foreigner who could say "Una Coca-Cola," was accused of being a master linguist, of being a born madrileño, of having studied Spanish at the feet of Cervantes. Some of them, like Mrs. Bullock, even got to believing it. Julie knew enough Spanish to know that she didn't know any.

60

"*Gracias, pero no es verdad. Por favor, un* boor-bone *doble con ginger ale para mi* . . ." Here Julie's Spanish broke down. She didn't know the word for "roommate" and she would not describe Lou Ann as her *amiga* in any tongue. "*Para la Señorita Maqueyever.*"

"*Entonces, señorita, para usted?*"

"*Nada para mi, gracias* . . . uh . . ."

"*Pablo, señorita. Paul.*"

"Uh-huh. *Muchas gracias, Pablo.*"

"*Para servirle, señorita.*"

Mrs. Bullock had, indeed, gone to the bathroom, lengthily and explosively. She had sprinkled fresh Klutch on her upper plate, mopped herself down with the perpetually damp, slightly sour-smelling washcloth which, never quite dry, accompanied her on her travels. She had taken another Entero-Vioform, another large swig of Kaopectate and, just to be on the safe side, another laxative. She put on her acetate kimono, last of the spoils from a trip she had misguided through the Far East, unlocked the bathroom door and plodded out into the bedroom. Susan was asleep. Good.

That gave Mrs. Bullock a chance to do a really thorough search of the room. There must be something missing, something to complain about. She'd get that snippy Yankee woman to knock a few dollars off the rates or her name wasn't Lily Lee de Camp Bullock. It was. And what's more, Mrs. Bullock had faced down the managers of really big hotels in Paris, France, London, England, Rome, Italy, and . . .

Hangers? There were plenty of them. Too many. And wooden ones at that. Shelf paper? On every possible surface; clean, fresh, and cut to fit. Bottled water? Gallons of it, as well as a bucket of ice and a neatly printed notice stating that the water used for the ice cubes had been purified. The impertinence! Perhaps Mrs. Bullock could claim not to like ice. No. They would simply take it away. Extra blankets? Four of them. Brand new. Writing paper? Three quires of it in three different sizes and weights. Envelopes to match. Two ballpoint pens. Postcards showing an aerial view of Su Casa. Scratch pads. There was even a little sort of courtesy kit with pins, threaded needles, buttons, snaps, hooks and eyes. A fly swatter and insecticide stood at the ready.

Seething, Mrs. Bullock yanked up the spread on her bed and groped beneath at the sheets. Percale. Her pounding of the pillows proved them to be feather, not foam rubber. She plowed through the living room. Perfect—even fresh flowers arranged on every table. More ice. More bottled water. And the terrace? Wrought iron, soft cushions, even the candles in the hurricane lamps had been lit. Drat!

The sun had slid down below the surface of the Pacific. It was Acapulco's lavender hour. Lights appeared in the great hotels along the coast, in the villas up in the hills, on the yachts bobbing in the bay. From the main building, the dulcet, slightly falsetto singing of *mariaches* could be heard.

"Hon," Essie said from her balcony, "it's paradise. A real paradise."

"Susan," Mrs. Bullock barked. "Wake up. And I wantcha to lock up your jewelry good, hear? You know how light-fingered these Mexicans are."

I Saw That

Arthur waited until the two terry-cloth ponchos had drifted past their table, through the hall, and had started up the stairs. Then he began, "Will Jack and Jim find happiness and true love south of the border? Will Jack's new hair-setting lotion be sabotaged by jealous Antonio? Will Jim's bikini shrink at sinister Ho-Hum's Chinese laundry? Tune in tomorrow for the next thrilling episode of 'Small-Town Queen.'"

Bernice, a little tiddly on Coco-locos, whatever they were, threw back her head and laughed delightedly.

"Wha-a-at?" Bill said. And then he laughed, too.

"Hush, Arthur, darling," Carolyn said. "They'll hear you."

More pleased with himself than usual, Arthur pushed back from the table and lit a cigarette. Everyone said that Arthur Craine had such a perceptive eye, such a knack for sizing up people immediately, and for demolishing them with a word or two. Arthur should really be a novelist. Arthur agreed, or he had until, after attempting a few pages, he realized that he had nothing to say. "Shall we all have one more, loves, and then think about dinner? Perhaps we can even coax Liz back."

*

Fumbling with the enormous iron key to the door of Rosas, Roland said, "I wish you wouldn't stand just exactly in the light."

"Here," Chip said. "Let me do it."

"*I* can do it," Roland said. The door opened. He stood aside grandly waiting for the younger man to precede him. Struggling out of their ponchos, both men raced for the mirror.

"Think I got any color?" Chip asked.

"Mmm. Yes. A little. So did I."

"Yes. I think you did."

It was an armed neutrality. Chip and Roland hadn't exactly been bickering down at the pool, but then hadn't exactly *not* been bickering either. It had all started over Pablo or Florentino—one Mexican waiter looked pretty much like another to Roland—when the third pair of planter's punches had been ordered.

Roland had seen it with his own eyes, the look Chip had given to the waiter. He said as much. "I saw that."

"Saw what?" Chip had asked, all innocence.

"Never mind what. But it seems to me that three thousand miles is a long way to travel just to make eyes at another waiter. You could have stayed right back home at the Circlon instead of letting me spend all this money to bring you here."

That had got Chip where he lived, all right. It went without saying that Roland came from a far better background than Chip. It was obvious to everyone—especially to Roland himself. But only in rare moments of extreme annoyance did Roland allude, by word or gesture, to Chip's humble occupation as a busboy before their hands had touched over the *Apfelstrudel* and Chip had subsequently been installed in Roland's black-and-white apartment above the boutique.

"Well, I didn't ask him to come over here again. I don't even *want* another drink."

"Then don't drink it."

"If you ask me, you've had more than enough yourself."

"Well, I *didn't* ask you," Roland had snapped and flipped over to give his back fifteen minutes in the sun. Like slowly rolling logs, Roland and Chip sunned themselves systematically, evenly; fifteen minutes for the front, fifteen for the left side, fifteen for the back, fifteen for the right. Then repeat.

Slithering out of his bikini, Chip squinted over his shoulder at his reflection. "Whaddya know, I *did* get some color. See the difference?"

"Mm-hmm," Roland said. He might have known it. Chip would get darker sooner than he would. Damn him!

"Where's my bathrobe?" Chip asked.

"Your dressing gown? In the closet, I suppose." It was a slight improvement. Six months ago Chip would have said, "Where's my bathrobe *at?*" In fact, six months ago Chip hadn't even owned such a garment. Now he had four, all from Bronzini.

"I suppose you know who that was sitting down on the terrace with those other people?" Roland said, knowing perfectly well that Chip wouldn't.

"Who?"

"The one in the blue shirt. Gray hair. Mustache. That was Arthur Craine."

"Who's Arthur Craine?"

Well, really, Roland thought. "Well, really," Roland said. "Arthur Craine is just one of the most famous literary men in America." Roland had never read Arthur's book or anything else he had written. It was enough to know who celebrities were and why.

"Is he gay?"

"I'm sure that I neither know nor care," Roland said loftily. (As a matter of fact, Roland had wondered idly about Arthur.) "And I can't imagine why *you* would."

Chip stretched out on his bed, opened his gold cigarette case, lit a cigarette with his gold lighter. Go easy, Chip, he told himself. He was not unusually intelligent, but Chip was bright enough to realize that without Roland he would be back in the snows of Allentown working—if he were lucky enough to get a job—as a busboy, a bellhop, or a stock clerk at Hess Brothers. The robe he was wearing, the clothes in his closet, the little gold knickknacks, this fancy room in this ritzy joint would never be his at all. Of course there were guys richer than Roland, plenty of them, but Chip hadn't met any so far.

Slathering Après le Plage over his torso, Roland reconsidered the role of wounded hauteur he had been playing this afternoon. To begin with, it was largely wasted on someone as basic as Chip. It had always worked on Larry, who was musical and sensitive, but not Chip. And then what was the point of spending all this money to come to Acapulco and do nothing but fight? Roland certainly didn't want a repetition of that terrible dustup he'd had with Kurt in St. Thomas last winter. That had been just too degrading. He flashed Chip his little Giaconda smile. "I'll tell you what," he said.

"What?" Chip said. Was he going to tell him again that he, Roland, was an Allentown Preston and a Buchmacher and a Voorhees, a graduate of Muhlenberg College and a force in the artistic and social life of Allentown, while Chip was a nothing little hustler? Chip knew all that.

"Let's get dressed, go down and have a couple of cocktails, see what the food's like, and then go out on the town."

"Sure. Why not? What do we wear?"

"Well, I thought I'd try all black."

"With your pearls?" Chip hadn't much sense of humor but he'd picked up the patois of Roland's friends enough to get off a good one now and then. It didn't matter that it wasn't original. Roland's set loved to hear the same old funnies over and over again.

"No, silliness. But I don't see any point in wasting the whites until my tan gets deeper. You might try the yellow slacks and shirt. Do you want the first bath?"

"No. Help yourself."

As soon as the bathroom door closed behind Roland, Chip was off his bed and burrowing into his toilet kit—his nécessaire, as Roland called it. He snatched out a Hershey bar, with almonds, unwrapped it silently, and began wolfing it down. Of all the low tastes Roland had tried to cure him of, Chip's love for candy bars remained. It was bigger than the two of them. Besides, if he didn't eat the Hershey bars, they'd melt in all this heat. Anyhow, what the hell did he have to worry for? Chip was only twenty-four (he claimed twenty; most guys liked them young; not too young, but young) and hard as a rock. He could still eat and drink prodigious amounts without having to worry about his waistline. With Roland it was different. Roland was older. How old? Chip wondered. Roland had said thirty-nine when they met. But then at the surprise birthday party all those queens back in Allentown had thrown for him he was still thirty-nine. Shouldn't a guy be forty after he'd been thirty-nine?

Chip heard a rattling at the door and quickly stowed the half-eaten

Hershey bar into the drawer of the night table. No use getting Roland into a . . . But it wasn't the bathroom door. It was the door to the room.

In came Florentino, the waiter who'd caused all the trouble down at the pool. What the hell, he was kind of cute. He was wearing his white wedding shirt unbuttoned almost to the waist. He had had his trousers taken in so much that he could barely breathe. On the tray he carried were an ice bucket, a carafe, and some bottles of Garci-Crespo water. Florentino had assured the señora that they were in the room hours ago, when these two gringos checked in. But the last time Florentino had been in Rosas, he had been too busy going through the closets in the dressing room to remember about the ice and water. He'd never seen such silks! Silk shirts as light as smoke, silk robes so heavy that they stood by themselves. Florentino loved silk, planned someday to own nothing except clothes made of silk—underwear, shirts, suits, neckties, socks. They must be very rich, these two.

Florentino smiled down at Chip, who lay on the bed, "Con permiso," he said, placing the tray on the nightstand.

Chip could hear Roland splashing in the rose-colored bathtub, could hear him singing "Tenderly." Safe! No trouble this time. No accusations. No arguments. He smiled back at Florentino. Nothing wrong with that. If you didn't speak the language, you had to do something. He reached up and fingered the fabric of Florentino's wedding shirt. "Nice," he said, smiling again.

Florentino stood a little taller, a little slimmer. It brought him up to his full five-and-a-half feet. He smiled again and touched the sleeve of Chip's silk dressing gown. "Good," he said.

All of his life Florentino had slept crosswise in a bed with his four brothers. They were lucky to have a bed. But Florentino wanted a bed of his own. Failing that, he would be willing to share one with just one other male. It could be very profitable. Florentino only had to look around at some of his friends to realize how profitable. There was Javier, a bellboy until that old American gentleman had taken him back to California as his valet and at a salary that had made Florentino's eyes pop. Or Alejandro, who had merely been strolling past the old Colonial one evening and now had a house, swimming pool, and a car. Acapulco was full of such success stories. Look at

Carlitos, married now with his own business. He had started out as a beach boy. Think of Julio. . . .

Chip got off the bed. His robe negligently open. He stood before the mirror and let the robe slide off one shoulder, then the other. He pressed his fingers into his back and took them away, leaving four white marks on his back. "Hot," he said. He smiled again. He really didn't care much about this little Mex, but it was good to keep in practice.

Florentino touched Chip's shoulder gently, "Sí, mucho calor!" The silk robe slid to the floor. Florentino swept down and gathered it up. He was far more interested in the silk robe than in the American.

Might as well show him the works while I'm at it, Chip thought. Florentino held the robe for Chip. He wriggled back into it. Florentino tied the sash for him.

From the bathroom Chip could hear the gurgling of the drain, hear the water pouring off Roland as he hoisted himself out of the tub.

Moving to his suitcase, Chip beckoned to Florentino. Was the American going to give him something? A silk shirt? Money enough to buy one? Even two? Was it really as easy as this? Chip opened his toilet kit and handed Florentino a Hershey bar.

Mierda! Madre de Diós! What did that idiot gringo think Florentino was, a baby? Smiling beautifully, Florentino took the candy bar. "Muchisimas gracias, señor," he said. With a balletic little pirouette, he spun to the door and was out of the room. One lousy candy bar! Florentino wanted to throw it as hard and as far as he could. But then reason took over. He would give it to simple-minded Guadalupe after he'd had her on the beach tonight. And the American liked him. Obviously. Perhaps tomorrow . . .

When Roland came out of the bathroom, draped in a rose-colored towel, Chip was seated sedately on the edge of his bed drinking ice water.

"Where did that come from?" Roland asked.

"Where did what come from?"

"All of that. That water. The ice."

"The chambermaid brought it in while you were taking a bath."

67

Twice as Big and Full of Water

Liz stood in front of the bathroom mirror poking her hair into a turban. She could have done a better job at her dressing table, but she knew that if she once sat down she'd never be able to get up again. Anyhow, Salvador was napping and she didn't want to disturb him.

She had meant to shampoo her hair and do something interesting to it, for this, the first night. She had also meant to take a little siesta. No such luck. She had been on the go all day long and there wasn't a second to spare. Trouble.

From the guests' eye view, everything was wonderful at Su Casa. And it was nice to see them clustered around the candlelit tables on the terrace, ordering drinks, and saying flattering things about the place. Happily, they hadn't seen the kitchen. Liz had and, reeling unsteadily in the middle of it, that paragon among cooks, Aurelia. It had never occurred to Liz that a Mexican woman might have a drinking problem, but there was Aurelia, all woman (Liz calculated that Aurelia was in the sixth or seventh month of her eighth pregnancy) and half conscious. And there was the dinner, or what Liz had intended to become the dinner, some of it burned to a crisp, some of it untouched. Pablo was busy serving drinks on the terrace. Florentino was nowhere to be seen. Aurelia was just a little bit worse than useless. Liz thanked both her lucky and unlucky stars stars for the array of canned goods in the despensa. Shrimp cocktail or fruit cup: baked ham or chicken à la king. Just the kind of pooh-pooh menu Liz had sworn to avoid. But at least the crowd would eat. And that reminded Liz that the menus had to be rewritten.

"I look like a bull dike," Liz said, tucking her shirt into the waistband of her slacks. Of course she didn't. Liz was one of those lean, rangy women who could give themselves a pat and a shake and look as though they had spent the whole day getting dressed. She knew that this evening men would admire her curves and women would envy her lack of them. "Smart," they would all agree. But Liz didn't feel smart. She felt tired and dowdy and old.

She tiptoed on silent sandals into the bedroom. No need. Salvador was awake, propped up on a mountain of pillows and smoking.

"Are you awake?" Liz asked idiotically.

"Of course not, Elizabeth."

"Where were you all afternoon?" Oh dear! She should never have asked that. She could feel it coming now. In panic she wondered which course the storm would take. Would Salvador be bombastic or grandly sardonic?

"Forgive me, Elizabeth, but I did not realize that a new law had been passed stating that a grown man could not leave his own home without publishing an *itinerario*—a timetable—of his activities for the benefit . . ."

"Oh, Chavo, darling, do please come off it. I only asked because I missed you."

"Ah? Did you want me to scrub the kitchen floor? Or to carry bags? Or perhaps to make love to your charming guest, Señora Meyers?"

"Chavo, dearest. I simply asked a casual little question. But, speaking of Mrs. Meyers, we're a little long on women and a little short of men. I wonder if you could ask your cousin Ignacio if he'd like to have dinner here tonight. . . ."

"Aha! The *macho* American woman now gives orders. 'Send up a nice stud from one of Mexico's oldest families.' To entertain a lot of *cursi* Texas schoolgirls—the granddaughters of the men who stole Texas from . . ."

Dear God, don't let him get on to the Mexican war again! Liz agreed passionately with Abraham Lincoln, with Henry Thoreau, with Ulysses S. Grant; it had been one of the most unjust wars ever waged. But as it had been waged nearly a century before Liz was born, she felt little personal responsibility for the whole affair.

". . . gentlemen, not gigolos . . ." Salvador was saying.

"Darling, it doesn't really matter. But I thought that as long as Nacho has dinner here nearly every night, it might be nice to . . ."

"Ah, yes. And now the *gringa* Amazona thinks that she can buy a De la Vega y Martínez, a descendant of the viceroys of Mexico, a *licenciado*, a graduate of the law school of the University of Mexico, for the price of a dinner, well . . ."

There was a tapping at the door.

"*Pase,*" Liz sighed. Whatever trouble this was going to be, it was better than what was happening to her now.

It was Laddy. He looked young, immaculate, and just a tiny bit drunk. "Liz, that hole in the road. It's there again. But about twice as big and full of water. Your cousin Nacho's car is stuck in it, Salvador."

Simple, Pleasant and Sure

Pablo remained in the darkened swimming pool silently treading water. He was tired. Not from swimming; Pablo's family had lived in Acapulco ever since there had been an Acapulco, from the days of the conquistadores, Pablo believed. Pablo had been able to swim before he could walk. His people had been fishermen for three hundred years—even longer. But now it was two o'clock in the morning and Pablo had been up and working since six o'clock the morning before.

Still he stayed silently in the pool. In the first place, he was naked and could hardly emerge in front of the pretty young *gringa* who wore the beautiful fur. Imagine, wearing furs in Acapulco, where there was almost no difference between the temperature of noon and the temperature of midnight! These Americans! The second reason why Pablo stayed in the water was that Señor's cousin was with the young American lady. Señora had given Pablo permission to use the swimming pool when his work was finished, when none of the guests were swimming there. Señora was very kind, generous. Señor had forbidden Pablo to swim in the pool, told him to use the beach below. Pablo had been working as a servant half of his life. He knew how serious it was to disobey an employer—especially a Mexican employer. And yet Pablo had disobeyed. Pablo had been born here. He knew the ocean, knew that sharks came in close to shore—sometimes in as little as a meter of water—after dark. Pablo's father had been killed by a shark, so had one of his brothers; and a cousin of Pablo's dragged himself through the streets of Acapulco on one leg and two crutches

70

because of sharks. Now if *Señor's* elegant cousin, Ignacio de la Vega y Martínez, saw Pablo in the pool, he would certainly tell *Señor* and there would be trouble.

Pablo couldn't understand how he could have made such a mistake. He had waited at the front door until all of the guests were back from their nightclubs and dancing places. First had come the old *bruja* from Texas with her three pretty girls—could they be her daughters? Never! Then the man who lived alone in Alcatraz. He was very disagreeable. Then the two men who lived in Rosas. They were drunk and quarreling like two old *putas* in the red-light district. And last of all the gayest of the Americans—the fine gentleman who lived in Margaritas with his beautiful sister and her handsome husband. He, at least, spoke Spanish. Spanish Spanish. The Spanish of a Spanish king. "*Grrrathias, motho. Digame, a que hora es la thena?*" Pablo had had to fight back his smile. But when the elegant Don Arturo gave him a tip for just carrying the bags to Margaritas—well, who wouldn't smile? With them had been the beautiful young lady of the beautiful furs and *Señor's* cousin. All of them had gone off with the nice Americans who lived in Violetas in their big air-conditioned car, as cold as a *refrigerador*. And they had all come back. But somehow Pablo had lost track of the Señor Nacho, turned off the lights in the *sala*, and locked the doors. Now he and the American girl were back from their stroll in the garden.

Pablo had not really expected Señor Nacho to return from the garden. Pablo had been positive that Nacho would spend the night in the American girl's room, leaving very early in the morning, before the other guests were awake. Pablo knew the reputation of Licenciado Ignacio de la Vega y Martínez. If anything, it was even more sensational than the reputation of *Señor*. Of course he was very poor— poorer even than Pablo himself. But such a *caballero!* Grand. Beautiful clothes. Beautiful manners. Soft hands. Educated. The Señor Nacho could speak not only Spanish, but French and English, too. How Pablo envied him for that. No wonder that all the women loved Nacho. He could whisper words of love in English.

"Two o'clock," Bernice was saying. "I've been up for twenty hours."

"Just five minutes longer, Bernice," Nacho said.

It was much easier for Pablo to understand the English of Señor

Nacho. It was slower, each word separate from the others.

"No, Ignacio. Tomorrow, after I've slept and slept and slept. I can still hardly believe it."

"Believe?"

"Believe that I'm here—where it's warm. It was beginning to snow when I left Chicago this morning. And here I am in Acapulco wearing this silly fur jacket when the temperature must be . . ."

"It is a beautiful coat. It must have been very dear."

"I—I really don't remember," Bernice said. "But I know that I absolutely must go to bed. G-good night and thank you for—for everything."

If Pablo had been surprised that Ignacio de la Vega y Martínez had not spent the night in the girl's room, he would have died from shock if Nacho had not kissed her good night. Pablo was not to be disappointed. Nacho took Bernice's outstretched hand and pulled her to him. She remained in his arms for quite a long time before she drew away, stepped back, and clung to one of the terrace chairs for support.

"Oh, dear," Bernice said. "And on the first date!"

"I beg your pardon?"

"N-nothing. W-well, thanks again and . . ."

"Please don't say good-bye, my darling. I will call you on the telephone in the morning and then I will show you Acapulco—all of it. I'm leaving. Good night."

Pablo waited in the pool until he heard the great front door close, heard the girl's feet on the stairs, heard Señor Nacho starting his little car, saw the light go on in Hortensias, the American girl's room. She was a nice girl, very, very rich, like all North Americans, but Pablo sensed that she was different somehow. Vulnerable. Pablo wished that he knew enough English to shout out to her, to warn her against a man like Ignacio de la Vega. But that would not be his place. He was a servant, poor and unread. If the rich gringa wanted to share the blue bed in Hortensias with a famous seducer like the señor's cousin, that was not Pablo's concern.

Silently Pablo slid upward out of the swimming pool, then wrapped a towel around his waist. A sudden gust of wind set the towel to flapping against his wet thighs. That was strange. Acapulco always had a breeze, a céfiro. Yes, a zephyr. But not a wind like this. Not unless something was going to happen. A storm? Impossible. It never rained in Acapulco before June. An earthquake? Ah, perhaps. Acapulco often had little tremors. A quarter of a minute, half a minute—enough to set the chandeliers to swaying, to crack the plaster of the most badly built hotels, to send a few hysterical tourists shrieking out of the Hilton in their nightclothes and underwear. Droll! But nothing to worry about.

Pablo watched the wild flapping of the terrace awning. He hoped that the wind would die down, that nothing would happen to the new awning. Poor Señora had not even paid for it. Then Pablo thrust his square feet into his sandals and went into the house.

At the top of the spiral service stairs was Pablo's room. He had never slept in such a room before in his life. His bed was soft and it had sheets—sheets of the same quality the guests used. There were lamps and comfortable chairs, a rug on the floor, and pictures on the walls. The señora had done this and the señor had been furious. "Pigs," he had said in English. "Filthy Indians. You are throwing away money making a palace for pigs." The señor did not know that Pablo could understand a little English. Nor would he have cared. But the señor was in some ways correct. This neat, clean, beautiful room was, indeed, a palace to Pablo and he had to share it with a pig. Florentino.

It was as though a wall had been built down the center of the room. On Pablo's side all was in order, the bed made, the furniture dusted, a small crucifix tacked onto the wall. But Florentino's side! Ai! Florentino had never made his bed or changed his sheets since he had worked at Su Casa. His walls were covered with flyblown pages ripped out of girlie magazines. Girls? Sows! Sows in bikinis. Sows with pig snouts, pig eyes caked with paint, greasy lips, navels imbedded in fat and pig dugs in soiled brassieres. What kind of Mexican girl would pose for such photographs? Pablo knew. Pigs.

And the stinks! Florentino believed that he could cover his own stench with the lotions he splashed under his arms, into his crotch. There was the special stink he rubbed into his hair—lard and whore's perfume. And there was the worst stink of all, Florentino's jar of Machisimo. A hundred pesos for one miserable centilitro of the stuff! Florentino had read the advertisement in one of his sex magazines. "Men! Abandon shame forever! Deliver the girl of your dreams into

73

transports of ecstasy. Machisimo will make your organ longer, thicker, harder. Results guaranteed. Thousands of satisfied purchasers." Pablo had sniffed at the jar—lard. Lard and carbolic acid. The blubber of a hog massaged into the pork of a shoat. Florentino had gone through a dozen jars of the stuff, the idiot, actually believing that his little dark tassel was becoming the size of a bull's.

Florentino was out, God be thanked. He usually was. He had left Pablo to wash the dishes from dinner, rubbed himself with Machisimo, and walked down the beach with one of the señora's beautiful new blankets to find simple-minded Guadalupe. He was probably still waiting in line to have his moment between her legs.

Guadalupe was a simpleton, now showing the mean wear of time. The boys of Acapulco had lain with her for as long as Pablo could remember. Guadalupe had been Pablo's first sexual experience—and not a very rewarding one, at that. Pablo had rushed first to the priest for absolution, and next to the clinic for a blood test. Pablo had won out on both counts. It had been the last time with Guadalupe. But Florentino would come home at dawn pretending that he spent the night with a movie star in a suite at the Pierre Marqués.

Pablo dried himself, prayed, crossed himself, and got into bed. It was late and he was tired, but he would not sleep before he had mastered another lesson.

Fluent English in Ten Days. That was the title of the book that was further described as *Simple, Pleasant and Sure.*

"*Al Restaurante*—In the Restaurant." That was the lesson for tonight.

"Me Ai jaf e té-bel for tú?" Pablo read aloud. "Ai ouish tú spik tú th-i Mé-tra de Jo-tél. Ai oud laik e Cham-pén coktél, súp, e sték ouith mosh-rúms end e bék-d po-té-to end, for mai di-sert, ais crím." Pablo wondered what a restaurant was like. Even in the black suit that he wore to family weddings, christenings, funerals, and fifteenth birthday parties, would they allow him into such a magnificent place? How much would such a meal cost? Twenty pesos? More? Fifty? His eyes felt heavy, but still he plunged on.

"This oué-ter is ve-ry rúd end in-so-lent. Plíz sam-mon the pro-prai-e-tor im-mí-di-et-li. Mai co-fi is . . ." Pablo read no more. The book fell from his hands and Pablo slept.

A Telephone Call for You

"There!" Liz had never thought this could actually happen, but it had. She had shampooed her hair and set it, shaped and painted all twenty of her nails, creamed her face and her throat, and wallowed— absolutely wallowed—in a steaming tub with opalescent slicks of lemon verbena bath oil bobbing on the surface. She felt rich and pampered and even beautiful. The bills for the first week of Su Casa's existence had been delivered on the breakfast trays this morning and they had been paid—or most of them—by noon. With a gratifying stack of checks and traveler's checks and Mexican pesos and American dollars in the safe, Liz could look after a few of her own bills. She could finish paying for the swimming pool and the terrace awning; get that recurrent hole in the driveway fixed and fixed properly; even send the maestro a little something on account for the furniture in the sala.

There had been trouble—not really trouble, just a few moments of unpleasantness—with that horrid old Mrs. Bullock over her bill, which had been correct to the last centavo. And then Mr. Lee Goodwin hadn't been very nice about his bill, seeing no reason why it should be paid weekly instead of at the end of his visit. Frankly, Liz wished that his visit had ended on the day it began. Try as she would, she just couldn't force herself to like him. She hated the way he sat around the swimming pool, wet-lipped and raunchy, ogling the young Texas girls, darling Carolyn Williams, Bernice, even the parody of a figure that belonged to April May.

And Liz hated talking to Lee Goodwin. There was just something about him—she didn't know exactly what—that was too intimate, too personal. Every statement was an insinuation, double-edged, and rather cruel. "Quite the stud, your husband," he had said. "Young, too."

Well, Liz was just as modern and open-minded as any girl who'd ever graduated from Bennington, but there were just some things

75

that she didn't care to discuss with strangers. What business was it of Lee Goodwin's that Salvador was younger than she was? And the things he said to Roland Preston and his, uh, friend, Chip! "Don't you have the room named 'Pansies'?" Whatever it was that these men were to one another, it was no concern of Lee Goodwin's. Their clothes may have been a bit recherché, but they weren't bothering anyone. In fact, Liz rather liked Roland, had felt flattered by the compliments he paid to the appointments of Su Casa, had even gone down to the market with him to translate and to haggle for the bolts of Mexican pink manta he wanted for his boutique. It all sounded a little tatty to Liz—small-town faggotry—but it had been fun, too, to be back in the thick of decorating with one of the boys. And, needless to say, there hadn't been one jealous word out of Salvador.

And the place seemed to be running efficiently. Liz would know for sure when she added up the outgo and compared it to the income. Tomorrow. She had an uneasy feeling that Pablo was working too hard and Florentino not hard enough. But at least Aurelia hadn't got drunk again in the middle of the kitchen in the middle of dinner. Since their little heart-to-heart talk on the evils of drink, Aurelia had been a living saint. The gazpacho, the shrimp mousse, the individual chocolate soufflés today at Essie Dewlap's fortieth birthday luncheon had been sheer heaven. So ambrosial that Liz had gone out to the kitchen and kissed Aurelia. The tequila fumes had nearly knocked her flat, but she hadn't said anything about it.

Essie Dewlap was a darling and so was Walt. Imagine inviting the whole household to lunch for his wife's birthday! Two cases of champagne, imported and expensive, had been consumed. Why, the profit on the champagne alone . . . Not that Liz would ever dream of charging Walter the full price. Although, from the quality of the turquoise-and-diamond bracelet Walt had clasped around Essie's wrist, Liz couldn't imagine why not. Liz liked to think of the people at Su Casa—at least most of them—as her friends, rather than her paying guests.

And tonight, dear, generous Walt was giving another party for Essie. Just a few of them—Liz and Salvador, Laddy and Arthur, Bill and Carolyn, addled old Rex Roman and April May, and, unfortunately, Lee Goodwin, the older crowd—all going to La Perla to dine and dance and watch the divers. Liz's new dress was all ready. And now—and now Liz was going to lie down and sleep for at least two hours.

She wandered to the window to close the jalousies against the western sunlight and looked down. She liked what she saw. There were her guests—more like her children, really—cavorting about the pool, smiling and laughing like the people one saw in travel advertisements. It was the time of day Liz liked best, when everyone had come home to roost from their shopping forays at Lila Bath or Luis Estévez, from their golf and fishing, from their water skiing and parachute rides. They would have a swim and a drink and then drift off to their rooms for a siesta before dinner.

There was Rex Roman, slightly tipsy from the luncheon champagne, doing spectacular dives off the high board—jackknives, swan dives, half gainers. For a man who had let himself get so out of shape, he was still good. Better, even, than Salvador. And there was April May in her fishnet G-string and her pasties, gazing at her Tarzan in imbecilic awe.

There were the three girls from Texas. Happily, Mrs. Bullock avoided the sun, telling anyone who would listen how very delicate her skin was. Delicate? For all of her talk about her noble Southern lineage, her coy little hints about the aristocratic ailments to which she was constantly prey, Mrs. Bullock was about as delicate as a bulldozer. And if she was so damned well bred, why hadn't she had at least the common decency to thank Walter Dewlap for lunch? Not a word. She had simply summoned her three hapless charges, telephoned a taxi (not that she hadn't tried for the free services of Laddy and the Su Casa station wagon), and dragged her girls off to the cathedral—perhaps the ugliest house of worship in the world, noteworthy only for its Coney Island façade and the naked, hissing fluorescent lights of its interior. The girls would much rather have gone to the beach, met some boys, had some fun on their own.

With twenty-five years between them, Liz had little rapport with Mrs. Bullock's girls. Through the jalousies she studied them now for the first time. Rich and rotten spoiled, all of them, she supposed. Mrs. Bullock had allowed everyone to understand that they were from the finest families in Dallas. To someone like Mrs. Bullock, that would only mean money and lots of it. But they didn't seem bad—at least two of them didn't. Susan, the pretty blonde? Well, there just wasn't much message from her. The one they called Julie—Juliet Noyes? Yes, she really was an attractive girl, quiet, ladylike, and possibly even intelligent. But shy. Retiring. As for the other one, Lou Ann, well she was a total mess. With her really rotten figure—although the legs weren't bad—how could she wear a bathing suit like that? And her tacky accent—Texas with a few corny Southern-belle endearments tossed in for good measure. She was a comic Valentine. And yet she fancied herself as Helen of Troy, a menace. "Maybe she's lucky not to realize the awful truth," Liz said. "I'd have committed suicide."

And it didn't take a crystal ball to see what Lou Ann was up to or would like to be up to—with any male between the ages of fifteen and fifty. Liz had spotted a nymph-on-the-make the minute she had seen Lou Ann. And how badly Lou Ann did it all! Liz had been almost as amused as she had been annoyed when Laddy had come to her, blushing like a schoolboy, to say that Lou Ann was giving him trouble. Sticking her hand under his shirt as they danced, stroking his bare thigh as he lay in the sun, making up transparent little excuses for him to come to her room when Mrs. Bullock was out of earshot. Laddy was as susceptible to feminine blandishments as any other man. More so. But a gentleman—yes, gentleman—of forty falling for a teen-age hot pants with a figure like a Bartlett pear? Not damned likely! And Bill Williams, with a wife as beautiful, as sweet, as amusing as Carolyn—just what chance did Lou Ann think she had with him? Dear Walter Dewlap, who had eyes for no one but Essie, and had children older than Lou Ann herself, had been approached. Even Rex Roman, the once glorious King of the Apes, old enough to be the little brat's grandfather, and in the constant company of a real professional like April May, was not entirely safe from Lou Ann. As for poor, darling Salvador, with his prim Hispanic set of morals, he had simply fled. Liz didn't blame her husband for clearing out of Su Casa in the afternoons. Just sitting alone in the Zócalo was preferable to being pawed by Lou Ann McIver.

Roland and Chip. Liz had rather savored the two of them as her own private little joke on Lou Ann. God knew that they were unmarried and Chip was even the right age. It would have served the little strumpet right to try all of her silent-screen-siren blandishments on Chip and wonder forever why they hadn't produced results. But Lee Goodwin, with his nasty mouth, had taken care of that right away.

If the other men in Su Casa had the taste or the decency or simply the fastidiousness to steer clear of little Miss McIver, Lee Goodwin displayed none of these traits. He was down there at the poolside now, wearing his faintly vulgar slack suit and the jaunty jute hat that he couldn't quite carry off, a white, too manicured hand on Lou Ann's flabby bottom, leading the silly slut on and, at the same time, laughing at her, letting everyone else in on the joke. Liz fought down that good, old-fashioned word "cad." When you saw Lee Goodwin in the company of Arthur Craine, Bill Williams, Walter Dewlap, Laddy, there was such a difference. Liz snickered. It was almost—not quite, but almost—like seeing Flossie Meyers at tea with old Mrs. Twombly.

Flossie Meyers! She hadn't been seen all week. But this morning her breakfast tray had come back untouched, as usual, with the addition of a wad of dirty money—dollars, pound notes, and francs—to pay the bill for the eight bottles of vodka, fourteen bowls of milk, and two chicken sandwiches she had ordered during the week. Blowsy and boozy as she may have been, Mrs. Meyers didn't bother anybody.

But Lee Goodwin was all over the place, being just too matey with everyone. And now this cheap, cruel, public display with the little McIver slut. Liz supposed that she should pity Lou Ann. There must be some deep-rooted reason for her behavior. But Liz didn't pity Lou Ann and she didn't like Lee. She wanted the two of them out of the place and, please God, without an incident. Chaperoning the girl was Mrs. Bullock's problem, not Liz's. But Liz didn't want her house turned into a brothel, her guests revolted and—worst of all—a scene with Salvador on account of these two subhumans.

"Oh, my God!" Liz moaned. Now Mr. Goodwin had his hand *inside* her bathing suit. Except for Lou Ann, the reaction was not favorable. Even with her sunburn, the girl Susan blushed scarlet and turned away. Carolyn and Bill Williams made a hasty departure for Margaritas, saying something about writing letters. Arthur followed soon. Essie Dewlap, ill with mortification, suddenly found her finger-nails of unparalleled interest, while Walter colored and looked angry. There was the kind of man who would protect his wife from the passes of drunks, the bad language of oafs. A pity there were so few of them left. Laddy got to his feet, turned his back, and feigned a fascination with the sinking sun. Liz could tell by the set of her brother's shoulders how embarrassed Laddy was. But why didn't Laddy have the guts to say something?"

Julie got to her feet. "I think Mrs. Bullock's calling us, Lou Ann. Lou Ann?"

"Hmmmmm?"

"Coming Sue?"

Gratefully, Susan scrambled to her feet and scuttled after Julie, nearly falling flat on the tiles.

His audience dispersed, Rex Roman put on his old-fashioned toweling beach robe with the big R.R. emblazoned on the breast pocket like the insignia of a Rolls-Royce. "Bedtime, April," he said.

"Huh?"

"I said come on."

"Oh. Okay, Rexy." Breasts and buttocks bouncing, Tarzan's mate clattered off behind him on crystal mules.

"Hon?" Essie said.

"Yes, hon?"

"I think I'll lie down for a bit before dinner. Coming?"

Lou Ann and Lee were left alone. Like a cat in heat, Lou Ann rolled onto her back, her four paws waving in the air, her pitiable little breasts flattening like two poached eggs within the foam-rubber armor of her brassiere. "Oh, Gawd, Lee," she wailed.

Liz had had quite enough. Making as much noise as possible, she opened the jalousies. "Mr. Goodwin?" Liz called. "Mr. Goodwin? There's a telephone call for you. It's on the extension in the *sala*." There. That would get him a good long way from the pool.

"Da-yum!" Lou Ann spat. "Double Gawd da-yam!"

Liz went to the extension beside her bed, pressed the button to connect her to the *sala*, and waited. "Hello?" Lee said.

"Mr. Goodwin?" Liz said in the inanely cheery voice of a hotel operator. "Mr. Lee Goodwin?"

"Speaking."

"Listen you cheap little rat, any more of this behavior and you can pack up and get the hell out of my house!" Liz slammed down the telephone and bounced angrily onto her bed.

It Is Your House

"And so what do you expect me to do about it, Elizabeth? Shall I castrate your Señor Goodwin? Or should I sew up the little gringa ramera? In my family a girl like that would have been sent to the nuns. And no girl, until the day of her marriage, would be permitted outside the . . ."

"But, Salvador, it is your house and . . ."

Liz might as well not have spoken. Salvador was off on another of his tangents proving the absolute superiority of Hispanic culture, painting a quaint picture of a House of Bernarda Alba way of life— daughters imprisoned in the patio, the locking of lovelorn eyes through grilles, the marriages-by-arrangement—that had been dead long before he had been born. Liz knew, and Salvador knew even better, that Mexican girls of today lived and acted just like any others and that the higher they were on the social scale, the more liberty they enjoyed. If only Salvador could refrain from going back as far in Spanish history as Fernando and Isabel la Católica (pointedly detouring around Juana the Mad), she might still get an hour's nap before dressing for the party.

It wasn't Salvador's house. Oh, yes, when he was showing it off to his friends, when he was scolding the servants, it was Salvador's. It was also Salvador's on paper. But when there was work to be done, problems to be solved, the place belonged to Liz and no one else. Liz had told herself time after time that they were mature, sophisticated, intelligent people; that the difference in their ages, their cultures, their outlooks really didn't matter. But at moments like this, Liz couldn't avoid realizing that with Salvador she had a lord and master ten per cent of the time, a child the other ninety per cent.

81

Eventually Salvador came off it or, rather, ran down. Liz had learned that if there were no argument, no opposition, no voice of reason to push another button, flick another switch, turn another crank, his soliloquies could be mercifully short-lived. Salvador was saying something about the justice meted out to the Protestants of Seville in 1599—Liz didn't see the connection between Lee Goodwin and Lou Ann McIver, hadn't the faintest idea what creed either of them professed—when the tirade stopped as suddenly as it had started.

"We have been invited to La Perla tonight, no?"

"Yes, darling. For Essie's birthday."

"A-ha!" That was a good sign. When Salvador said "A-ha," it meant that he was pleased. When he said "A-ha," it meant trouble. Although Salvador didn't really like the company of Americans, he did like to be invited out to expensive places—the Rivoli, Cyrano's, Le Club, Le Dôme—to look well dressed and rich. It didn't hurt his standing in Acapulco.

Marriage to Elizabeth Hobson, née Parkhurst, had increased Salvador's status when it was widely believed that she was a rich gringa. Didn't she stay at the very best places? Didn't her brother own a yacht? But opening Su Casa had lowered that status. What were los Martínez, a family of innkeepers? And Salvador, inasmuch as he could like anyone else, was fond of Liz. She was almost as good as a young Mexican wife might have been; capable yet yielding. She took good care of him. There was a lot of money in the safe today. Nacho needed to borrow some for the care and feeding of his Polish countess and Salvador needed a little—"money for pins," they called it in English. Liz was very generous. Salvador hated those American women with balls as big as beer barrels. Liz wasn't like that.

But for the past six afternoons, Salvador had been forced to endure the attentions of a woman who was. The Princess-up-the-Hill. Ai! At first Salvador had been flattered. It was not every man attractive enough, talented enough in bed to be summoned by the Princess. Had his reputation as a lover truly traveled up the hill to the Moorish palace? Evidently. But she was old. Older even than Elizabeth. She was old and she was pinche. She had sent for him as though he, an heir to the kingdoms of Spain, were a common servant. And what had

82

she given him? Pills! With all of her millions or billions, she had given him pills and some ridiculous silver costumes to put on and take off at her bidding. Like a visiting barber or a room-service waiter, Salvador Martínez was called, given his instructions in writing. And such instructions! What kind of evil, perverted old witch was she that she, the woman, would tell the man what to do in her silver bed and then give him nothing, not even a pair of cuff links to commemorate his stellar performance? Fuck the Princess-up-the-Hill! No. Not that. Ignore her. Simply show her that with all of her money, which she showed no sign of sharing, she was still nothing but a woman—and an old one, at that—while Salvador was a man. This afternoon he would go to bed with his own wife. Thrill her. Have her gasping and groaning, stifling her shrieks of pleasure, beneath him. And then he would go out dancing with her tonight. People would turn and say, "Who is that distinguished young man with that handsome older woman?" There was something to be said for fidelity. Sometimes.

Salvador was expected at the Moorish palace up the hill at five. Expected to sit and wait until the Princess deigned to receive him. It was now five-thirty. Her anguish, her frustration at not being in his arms, must have reached the boiling point. Salvador would have his vengeance. A note. Casual but barbed with arrogance. "So sorry, but . . ."

"Liz?" Salvador began.

"Yes?" Liz said eagerly. It was a sign. When her husband called her Liz instead of the sedately formal Elizabeth, it meant that he was about to make love to her. It had been nearly a month since he had.

"Liz, amor, prepare the bed. I have to write a note to—to the man who makes my shirts. In about fifteen minutes?"

Take the Back Road Out

Florentino could hardly believe it. He was to deliver a note to the Princess-up-the-Hill and he was even allowed to drive the station wagon! Florentino couldn't drive very well, hadn't even a license.

But the palace of the Princess was directly above Su Casa. He would only have to look both left and right, before crossing the main road. By swerving sharply, driving through a flower bed, and just avoiding the telephone pole, Florentino missed—by several yards—that hole in the driveway with its gurgling spring of sea water. There! Oh, but wouldn't the Princess think he was a fine gentleman, driving right up to her door in this enormous automobile! She would undoubtedly say, "What manner of splendid *coche* is that, Don Florentino?" And he would answer, "It is my Mair-coo-ry Co-ló-ni Par-que, *princesa.*" Or did one call the Princess *Alteza?*

Florentino wished that he had been allowed time to change out of his uniform; put on the ravishing, sheer nylon shirt, printed with bull-fighters, which was *almost* as good as silk; rub some more of that sweet-smelling pomade onto his hair; scent himself again; possibly even apply another coat of Machisimo—every little bit helped, Florentino couldn't avoid noticing that. But the *señor* had said, "Leave immediately and return immediately. And say nothing about it." When the *señor* spoke, well . . . Anyhow, Florentino was wearing his tight, white evening livery. In the fading light, perhaps the Princess-up-the-Hill would not see the Su Casa embroidered on it. He undid his shirt another button, tightened the bright cummerbund.

It was really easier to enter the naval base, the National Palace itself, than the property of the Princess. An officer in a gray uniform with silver buttons and a silver revolver came to the silver gates to question Florentino. But when he saw that the station wagon was from Su Casa, heard that Florentino had been sent by *Señor,* he opened the gates and motioned the car through. Perhaps *Señor* was more important than Florentino had been led to believe by local gossip.

Up, up, up the car climbed, past gardens and grottoes where white peacocks with—yes—silver beaks and claws paraded. Almost at the summit of the hill, the car halted at another pair of silver gates even more elaborate than those on the road. There was a second interrogation, another opening and closing of the enormous lacy grillwork, and Florentino stopped the station wagon with a lurch at the entrance of the palace. In doing so, he struck his rib cage painfully on the steering wheel. *Frenos de potencia!* Power brakes!

The tinkle of silver chimes answered Florentino's touch. Immediately the last silver grilles were opened by not one, but *two* servants. They were enormous—each a full head taller than Florentino—and dressed in sheer silver pantaloons that made Florentino hot with embarrassment and envy. What with Machisimo costing a hundred pesos for a tiny jar, it would take years. Years! "*Sí?*" one of them asked. They were Mexicans, but Mexicans from the capital. Florentino could tell by their accents. He was glad that they were not locals who knew him. These two might mistake him for one of the Princess's social equals. It would be easier to get inside that way.

"I have a letter for the Princess from Se . . . from *Don* Salvador Martínez."

One of the servants thrust out his hand. "Give it here, kid."

Florentino was not known for his courage, but this evening he gave it a try. "Ah, but Señor, *Don* Salvador, has instructed me to give it to no one except the Princess herself."

The two servants exchanged a glance of surprise and scorn. "Wait." The silver gates clanged shut in Florentino's face. Should he slip the note through the grillwork and dash back down the hill? The *señor* had told him only to deliver the note to the gatekeeper at the road and to get right back to Su Casa. This journey upward to the palace doors had been Florentino's own idea. Now he was frightened.

The silver gates opened again. Florentino was confronted by a third man, taller, more imposing than even the two servants. He was dressed also in silver pantaloons, but fuller, thinner. He also wore a sort of silver *chaleco* that exposed his big, bare chest, his beefy arms. Could he be the Prince? The husband of the Princess? Or a king—her father?

"What is it you want, boy?" he asked Florentino. He spoke Spanish easily, but his accent was foreign—French?—like the owner of the restaurant where Florentino had been a dishwasher.

"I have a letter for the Princess, *caballero*. From Señor Martínez."

"Well, give it to me."

His watery courage failing fast, Florentino tried one last time.

"Señor, I have instructions to hand it to the Princess personally."

The foreign gentleman snorted, exchanged a glance with the two servants who had answered the door. "Very well. Follow me. Are your shoes clean?"

"Oh, yes, *caballero!*"

"Then come with me."

Blinded by the brilliance of the palace, Florentino followed the man—the prince? the king?—into the towering silver hall, through a silver patio where a silver fountain splashed and where two silver pumas, snarling and snapping, stalked on silver chains. They mounted a silver staircase and walked—how many kilometers?—down a corridor lined with silver mirrors, reflecting Florentino into infinity. Catching sight of his manifold selves, he tried to stand a little taller. He wondered now just what he would say in his conversation with the Princess.

Two men, even larger than the ones who had met him at the entrance, stood guard at the doors of the Princess's suite. They bowed as doors slid open. Florentino found himself trailing his escort through a huge silver room—larger even than the *sala* at Su Casa. But there was no place to sit. Only cushions and white fur rugs on the silver tile floors. Another pair of doors parted and there, directly ahead of him, lying in a silver bed with silver sheets, was the Princess.

The major-domo, who had led Florentino in, raised his chin and his eyebrows. It was a prearranged signal in a house of silence requesting permission to speak.

"Well?" the Princess said in English. The new sleeping pills made her grumpy as well as groggy. The servants couldn't wait until she found another new doctor. Even that Swiss who had given her baking soda for a barbiturate had been better than this one and the Princess had been easier to get along with.

Also in English, the major-domo said, "This boy has brought a note from Señor Martínez."

"Oh?" The Princess stretched out her hand. Trembling, Florentino advanced. Should he fall down on one knee? Grasp the hand and kiss it? The problem was solved when the Princess snatched the note from him and tore it open.

"All right, kid," the major-domo said in rapid, accented Spanish. "Out!"

The return trip covered a different route. Instead of being led through mirrored halls and Moorish courtyards, Florentino was prodded along a dim service corridor, down a clanging iron *caracol*, through a steaming hot kitchen, where a man in a chef's bonnet bawled orders in a strange language to people dressed in the white of hospital attendants. A final door opened and Florentino found himself out of doors in a cobbled service yard filled with garbage cans and drying laundry.

"How much is the maquereau paying you, kid?"

"Mande, señor?"

"Martínez. Her boy friend"—a gesture up toward the Princess's bedchamber. "How much is he paying you to work down in the pension?"

Florentino was almost confused enough to tell the truth. But Florentino was never quite that confused. He increased his salary by fifty per cent. "And then there are the tips, caballero."

"You have references?"

"Oh, yes, señor. Many." Many, indeed, the best of which had been written by Florentino himself.

"Can you pass a physical?"

"Physical, señor?"

"No syph, no clap, no skin diseases?"

"Oh, no, señor. I have nothing like that."

"If you're ever looking for a new job, come around on a Monday between ten and twelve, with the references, at the service door. And take the back road out."

Time to Get Dressed

"Hon?" Walt said.

"Yes, hon?"

"You know what, hon? I'm damned sorry I ever asked that Lee Goodwin to your party tonight." In twenty years of marriage Walter Dewlap had never withheld any information from his wife. Oh, pleasant things like surprising her with a luncheon this afternoon, Christmas presents, and unexpected treats, yes. And also unpleasant things, too; things that might worry Essie, like the time he nearly lost the Buick agency. Otherwise they talked things out.

"Why, Walter. It isn't your fault that he's a . . . well, that kind of man. There'll be so many people at La Perla tonight, we won't even notice him. And after tomorrow we can just sort of pretend that he isn't even here. I never liked him."

"But he seemed okay. A lot of big business connections. Interesting. From New York, too."

"Hm! Look at Bud Bagley. He's from New York and he's got a lot of big business connections and he's okay, too. Until he gets drunk at the club and starts making passes at everything in skirts. And remember, the girl—that Lou Ann—is to blame, too. Sometimes I wonder if we were wise to send Elspeth away to Wheaton when she's so young."

"Any girl who can get into trouble in Norton, Massachusetts, is a lot smarter than our Elspeth. But I still kind of wish I hadn't invited him."

As with everything he did for his wife, Walter Dewlap had planned this evening's dinner with only Essie's pleasure in mind. He would have Carolyn and Bill Williams because Bill was a hell of a nice guy and Carolyn had become Essie's good friend. He would have Liz and Salvador because Liz had always been so nice, knocking herself out to see that the Dewlaps had a good time. Laddy Parkhurst was a good guy, too, and you couldn't very well leave him out. As for Arthur Craine and Rex Roman, well it would be fun for Essie to tell the girls at the Crèche that she'd had celebrities at her fortieth birthday party. As for Rex's, uh, wife? Oh, well. Lee Goodwin had just been hanging around talking about some multimillion-dollar oil deal and so Walt had invited him, too.

"Walter, I'm having such a good time down here, I don't care if you've invited the devil himself. I feel more like it's my fourth birthday than my fortieth. And when I tell her who was there, hon, Madge will die."

"I hope so. Well, time to get dressed."

Poincianas was the smallest of the bungalows—a tool shed, really, that was now a bed-sitting room with bathroom and terrace added on. Had it been any larger, Rex Roman and April May would probably have got lost inside it and starved to death before finding their way out.

"Rex?" April wheezed through a cloud of hair spray.

"Huh?"

"What does Poy-na-can-a mean?"

"Huh?"

"It's the name of this house. Poy-na-ca-na. I just noticed.

"I dunno, uh, baby."

Since he had first swung through the trees to fame and fortune at the box office, Rex had been married four times and had had long relationships with a dozen other women. He wasn't terribly bright, but he had learned early on in his amatory adventures that to say "Claire" when you were talking to Jill or "Jill" when you were talking to Wanda could lead to nothing but trouble. "Baby" was always safe.

It probably wouldn't have made much difference with April May. Her real name had been something like Gertrude Mae Hassenpfeffer —something like that, Rex couldn't quite remember. Rex couldn't even recall his own real name. Raymond Rasmussen, Junior, he thought. He had written it down somewhere—his birth certificate, his passport, some kind of legal paper.

"Ya know what, Rexy?"

"What?"

"I think a Poy-na-can-a's some kinda ornj flower. I mean like didja ever notice that everything in here is all ornj flowers?"

"No. I never did. Well, whaddya know?" Rex reached out for the rum bottle and with trembling hand poured himself a drink.

"Aw, Rexy, whaddya wanna go an' do that for?"

"Huh?"

"C'mawn, Rexy, you don't need no new drink. You had all that stuff at lunch today, and more this aft and now we're goin' out to a party and have a lot more. You'll get sick, Rexy. Remember what doc said? Oasis of the liver. Doc says that can be very se-ri-ous."

"Ah. . ."

"C'mawn, Rexy, help me fasten this thing up the back."

Rex Roman stood six-four. His hands were the size of ham hocks and about as deft. A lot of people had said that April May wasn't bright enough to dress herself. This was true. Rex wasn't bright enough to dress her, either, but he bowed to no peer when it came to undressing her.

"Rex?"

"Huh?"

"Think I should ought to wear something under this? I mean like a bra?"

"You don't need no bra after all that stuff they pumped inta your knockers."

"I don't mean for that, Rex. I mean I wouldn't want they could see through my gownd like I wasn't nice or something."

"You're still nice enough for me," Rex said, patting her delectable little bottom.

"Aw, Rex, ya big chump!"

There was a pause while April May collected her thoughts, shifted her intellectual gears, and launched into a new subject—a serious subject. It was no simple task.

"Rex?"

"Huh?"

"This place? It's real nice, but isn't it awful ex-pen-sive? I mean about like the Beverly Hills or the Racquet Club?"

"Yeah. About the same. But nicer. Small-like."

"But, Rexy, you shouldn't ought to go spending all your savings on me. I never astcha to."

"That's okay, baby. I still got some left. And there's this guy wants me to make a TV commercial. Some kinda dog food. You getta lotta re-vi-suals from a commercial."

"An' maybe if you'd ask again at the studio I could get my screen test, Rexy. Then I could help out a little. An' if you was to lose a little weight, like doc says, maybe you could go back to makin' Tarzan again. Maybe even with me, after my test. Umajun, Rexy, you Tarzan, me Jane!" Visions of stardom danced beneath April's cotton-candy coiffure, while Rex pondered a comeback. This was a good life. Rex had April and sex and liquor and enough money to get by on. But to beat his massive chest again, to give forth with his famous simian bellow, to swing across the back lot on a steel-and-plastic vine, to dive into a heated jungle pool, swim it like a hydrofoil, and wrestle to the death a rubber crocodile—that was *really* the life. Once a star, always a star.

"Maybe, baby. Maybe," Rex said. He looked at his big, waterproof chronometer, with its dials of days and dates and phases of the moon, and tried to figure out what time it was. Pretty late. He gulped down his drink and poured another. "Well, baby, time to get dressed."

"Rex?"

"Huh?"

"I think I'll wear a Poy-na-can-a in my hair tonight. Ornj looks good with char-truce."

"Time to get dressed," Lee Goodwin thought. He got off his bed and was pleased to see that his shoes had left a dark streak across the spread. Serve her right, the goddamned society bitch! "Pack up and get out" was just what Lee would like to do. But to where and with what? He kicked the wastepaper basket across Alcatraz. It made him feel a little better, but not much.

No. What the hell was the French guff? *J'y suis, j'y reste*. I am here, I remain. He damned well had to. There was no place else to go in Acapulco, and if he left town he could chalk the whole season up as a total loss. Lee wasn't planning to take any more losses. He couldn't afford to. And, what's more, Lee didn't think he was going to have to.

Look at 'em, just waiting there, ripe for the picking. Bill Williams. Well, everybody knew about him. Arthur Craine. The old nance had bags of it. Bags! Walter Dewlap. Solid. Not sensational, but solid. As for the two fags, the older queen wasn't what you'd call flat on her ass, but it was small potatoes. The young one, Chip? All Lee had been able to learn about him was a little police record for illegal entry. Punk stuff. Lee wondered what his silence might be worth to the kid. Plenty if the kid had plenty. But the kid had nothing. Of course Lee didn't need much. Just enough to keep going until he landed a big one. There were big ones here. And the biggest one of all was a dame he'd never met—never even seen. Mrs. Florence Meyers, whoever she was. No. He'd stick around Su Casa for a little longer, even if it meant paying his bills in cash and being insulted by that Martínez broad, at least until he'd met Mrs. Meyers.

Lee hated women, but they made the best pigeons. They squawked the loudest later on, but they cooed the sweetest first. Just look at Lard-ass out by the pool today practically creaming herself until Martínez pulled her sneaking low trick with that phony phone call.

No, Lee would string along here, if he could. The old stolen wallet story—"all of my cash, my traveler's checks, my identification missing"—might work with Walter Dewlap, a square, a sucker, a check-grabber, a hick from the sticks if ever there was one. It was as old as God—older—but it was usually good for fifty, even a hundred. Lee would go to the Dewlaps' party tonight and really lay 'em in the aisles. People liked his sense of humor, the way he could cut other people down to size, make them squirm. Especially society types like these. "Well, time to get dressed."

Getting dressed, to Lee, was a matter of never getting undressed. Even in the heat of Acapulco, he slept in his underwear and pajamas. He had never gone into the pool, never appeared in a bathing suit. He put on and took off his clothes in dark or semidarkened rooms, the blinds drawn, the curtains pulled, avoiding all encounters with mirrors. Lee even changed his underwear in a dark closet, shrouded as often as was physically possible in a sweat-stained old robe. He even bathed in parts, in fits and starts, reaching under the folds of the robe with a soapy washcloth, with a towel, with his roll-on deodorant. Not looking.

Lee was in the midst of these monastic ablutions when he heard a tapping at his door. Damn! Maybe he'd pretend he was out or asleep. But it might be Lard-ass, the Yellow Nose of Texas, demanding an encore. She was a dog, but Lee talked a great lay; liked to demonstrate his superiority over women; lead 'em on. Men were supposed to.

Gathering his robe tightly around him, Lee moved through the soft darkness of his room, unlocked the door and opened it. Just some spick waiter with a lot of ice and bottled water.

Pablo entered the room. "*Permiso, señor?*"

"Okay, but make it snappy."

"*Sí, señor.* I will hasten."

Lee was impressed. No one had said "make it snappy" since before Pablo was born—even since before Lee was born.

"I see you talk the lingo."

"*Mande, señor?*"

"Speak English?"

Pablo beamed, "Oh, no, señor. *Un poco.* Only a little. I study." From the pocket of his trousers, Pablo pulled out his book, *Fluent English in Ten Days: Simple, Pleasant and Sure.* He displayed it proudly. "But it is not so simple or so pleasant or so sure. It is, for me, very dif-fi-cult."

Like a great, spreading cancer, an idea began to form in Lee's brain. The English course. He hated doing it. It was a nickel-and-dime business, chicken feed, like the ten-cents-a-week burial policies he'd peddled in Hoboken as a kid. Still, Lee needed money.

"*Un momento*," he said to Pablo. He took his attaché case down from the dark top shelf of the closet and spun the combination lock. Out came the last set extant of the *Oxford University Complete Home Study Course of Perfect English*, "bound in genuine Leatherette." With it came one of the last of the elaborate brochures, printed in English *and* Spanish. What luck!

Twenty years ago, when Lee was still a punk, the Oxford course had been on the up and up. Emanating from Oxford, New Jersey, it had been hastily compiled to appeal to the Puerto Rican market. To do it justice, it *had* attempted to teach English with lessons cribbed from McGuffy's *Readers*, free material from the Department of the Interior and, if the student lasted and kept on paying, snatches of Winston Churchill, George Bernard Shaw, William Shakespeare, and Geoffrey Chaucer culled from the public domain. Their names looked good on the brochure, almost as though they were fellows of the Oxford faculty. Lack of interest, payments, and results had killed off the English course, but, for some lucky reason, Lee had never thrown out his sales kit, even though the firm was defunct.

"Listen, señor," Lee said, "what an intelligent man like you needs isn't some little *caca fría* like this *libro de frases*." Man, even the lingo was coming back to him, the old spick sales pitch!

"A gentleman of your superior intellect, already advanced in the English language, should have a serious, thorough course in the speech of the kings and queens of England. Examine, if you will, the first illustrated lesson: 'John is a boy. *Juan es un muchacho.* Mary is a girl. *María es una muchacha.*' Et cetera. Why you can already read that with your eyes closed! But, see now, Lesson Fifteen: The *soliloquio* from *Hamlet*"—Lee obligingly pronounced it Om-let—"by the immortal Shock-es-pay-ar-ay. 'To be, or not to be. That is the question.' A man of your ability needs more than to speak with waiters and bus drivers . . ."

Pablo's mouth fell open. How did this Señor Guud-veen know what sort of thing was in *Fluent English in Ten Days*? He must be a famous authority, a professor. Reverently, Pablo fingered the dusty sham leather cover of Lesson Fifty: "*The Canterbury Tales*, by Geoffrey Chaucer. 'Whanne that Aprille with his shoures sote/the droghte of Marche hat perced to the rote. . . .'" Pablo couldn't understand a word of it and he wanted to—badly. To speak English like *Señor*; like *Señor*'s cousin, Nacho; to be something more than a servant all of his life. "Is—is it very expensive, señor?"

Lee thought fast. How much would he need? Or, more to the point, how much could this kid spend on a one-shot deal? Originally, the Oxford course had cost a dollar a week for a year, but everything was higher now. "If you were to pay for it every week, yes. Very expensive. *Muy caro*," he translated. "But I have recently been informed by the dean of the *Departamento del Inglés* that a saving of more than fifty per cent, imagine, *señor*, more than fifty per cent, can be made for those who buy the complete course in advance. In fact, this saving is so important, so advantageous, that the only way I would consider allowing you to enroll in the Oxford University is to have you pay for your course now, in advance. You understand, *señor*—may I call you Pablo?—that I am doing this only to save you money."

Pablo's mouth was dry. Imagine, learning to speak English like this fine professor and saving money at the same time!

"Furthermore, all students who pay in advance receive as a gift this beautifully illustrated atlas of the world without charge." Lee riffled the pages of an atlas that had gone out of print after World War I. Yugoslavia was a pastiche of Bosnia-Herzegovina, Serbia, Dalmatia, and Montenegro; England owned India; the capital of czarist Russia was St. Petersburg. "But only if you act now. This sensational offer is for a limited time only."

"H-how much?" Pablo breathed. "How much does it cost?" Lee thought fast. He was a fair judge of his victims. This kid was a hard worker, a saver, a scraper, a scrimper. He'd have something put by. But was he good for a hundred bucks? That would easily carry Lee for another couple of weeks.

"For those who pay in advance, the special price is five thousand pesos."

"Five *thousand* pesos?" Pablo's face fell. It was a fortune!

Oh-oh! Lee could feel the sucker slipping away. "*But!* But, as we are old friends and as I have special influence with the dean, I will try to arrange to get a special foreign student's scholarship reduction for you of an additional twenty per cent. Just think, an over-all saving of se-ven-ty per cent!"

"*Four* thousand? For these dusty old books?"

"Ah, no, my friend. Not *these* books. These are only the ones I use to enroll new students. New books, bound in genuine Leatherette, will be sent to you—once a week for the next year—upon receipt of your payment. Just think, is four thousand pesos much of a price to speak the tongue of the kings of England? To be as one with Churchill, Shakespeare—perdóname, Shock-es-pay-ar-ay— Shaw? Hurry, man, hurry! You're letting the opportunity of a lifetime slip by."

Frantic, Pablo gestured with thumb and forefinger. "Momentito, señor. The money is hidden in my room."

Lee sat down at the desk, filled in one of the yellowed receipts of the *Oxford University Complete Home Study Course* and signed it with a flourish—a *rubrica*, as the Spanish called it. Give the kid something for his money. What difference did it make? There wasn't any Oxford University in Oxford, New Jersey, any more than there was a Lee Goodwin.

Margaritas was the best of the bungalows. It had a terrace and two balconies banked with daisies, a living room, a study, three bathrooms, a downstairs and an upstairs. This was fortunate. In recent years not Carolyn, not Bill, not Arthur had been accustomed to existing on one level. Carolyn sometimes wondered why, wondered how many Everests she had scaled trudging up and down the curving staircase in their penthouse on Astor Street, in Arthur's bachelor duplex on State, in the multilayered houses and apartments and suites Arthur hired when he took them traveling—or, rather, allowed them to take him traveling.

Carolyn stepped out of her daisy-tiled bathroom at the same

time as Bill emerged from his. She was naked and so was Bill. Each crossed the big bedroom, passing one another like pedestrians on the street. Bill paused in front of the mirror. "Getting a little corporation," he said.

"What, darling?" Carolyn said "darling" as automatically as she said "please" and "thank you." Sometimes, when she wasn't thinking, she even slipped up and said it to her maids, to waiters, to salespeople in shops. She wasn't thinking this evening.

"I said I'm getting a little corporation."

"Oh? What corporation is that?"

"A stomach."

"Oh. Excuse me, darling. I was just thinking about something else. Yes. You are. That's a shame, Bill. You're only thirty."

"Twenty-nine."

"Well, it's still a shame. You should go to the club more. Exercise."

Still naked, they passed one another again, strangers in the night.

How long ago had it been—five years? more? less?—when the sight of one another's bodies had driven them to frenzies? When Bill would be an hour, two hours late to his office just because Carolyn had been slow about putting on her bed sacque? When they had been the last to appear at their own parties simply because Carolyn had asked Bill to clasp a necklace around her neck and, protesting happily, found herself without necklace or dress, being led to their bed? When weekend hostesses would sit downstairs, tapping impatient slippers, postponing dinner by the quarter hour, the half hour, just waiting for young Mr. and Mrs. Williams to dress? Once they had even done it on a tiger-skin rug in front of a roaring fire in a guest room. Shades of Elinor Glyn! A nettlebed would have hurt less than that tiger's hide, but it had been wonderful. One of the best.

And then it had stopped. Tacitly, each wondered exactly when and exactly why. Getting old, Bill supposed. Just a phase that married couples move into and out of, Carolyn guessed. Their relationship now was that of two passengers with little in common sharing a stateroom on an ocean liner.

Oh, they were civil—thoughtful and polite. Sometimes they were even chatty. Did Bill want to go to such-and-such a party? What would Carolyn like for Christmas? The new cook was awfully expensive and twice as grouchy; did Bill think that Carolyn should keep her? Bill had to entertain some out-of-town customers—bores, but big business—did Carolyn want to come along, or would she rather spend a quiet evening with Arthur? Arthur had suggested a quick trip to Bermuda that sounded like fun; could Bill get away from the office?

Everyone in Chicago envied Bill and Carolyn. And why not? They had youth, looks, money, position, possessions, and absolutely nothing to worry about. But Bill didn't envy Bill and Carolyn didn't envy Carolyn. In the small hours of the night, after their decorative appearance at this charity ball, that dinner dance, someone's supper party, they lay side by side in their mammoth bed, untouched and untouching, pretending to be asleep and wondering just what had happened to them.

Oh, it wasn't a life of absolute celibacy. When was the last time? Carolyn wondered. Yes! After the Bachelor and Benedict Ball in November. Bill had had a snoot full and Carolyn was a trifle tiddly herself. Arthur had been off lecturing in Champaign. Carolyn didn't remember it very well, and Bill probably not at all, but she *thought* that it had been fine. That was really the last time-and-a-half ago. On Christmas morning they had started a little something that held all the promise of the good old days, but they had been interrupted by Arthur pounding up the stairs in his new astrakhan coat, shouting, "God bless us all and Tiny Tim!"

Now Carolyn wished that Arthur *would* come in with his bright chitchat. Just someone to say *something*. The silence was really oppressive. There was Bill, stepping into his shorts—he really wasn't getting fat; he looked just fine. Next the trousers. Zip! Clip! All very nice and chesty. Finally the shirt, batiste and hanging like a maternity smock. Carolyn supposed that if Bill had some annoying personal idiosyncrasy—if he were less immaculate, suffered from falling dandruff, broke wind, had bad breath, or whistled between his teeth—she'd go stark, staring mad. But at least it would be something positive to drive her up the walls.

97

Now take Walt and Essie. Married for positive centuries and happy as clams—however happy clams were supposed to be. They were years older and they still enjoyed each other. And—yes, Carolyn could sense it, almost feel it—even as ancient as they were, they still had sex and enjoyed that, too.

Carolyn would have to say something, no matter how inane. The last fifteen minutes of shrieking silence had got on her nerves, like television with the sound shut off. "I bought Essie's birthday present this morning while she was shopping for shoes."

"Oh? What?"

"Oh, just some kooky junk earrings. Two pairs. One from you and one from me."

"That was nice of you. I'm no good at that kind of thing."

And it's pretty obvious that that's not all I'm no good at, Bill thought. Not a word, not a look since . . . since November. Not since the B & B Ball. And then she had to have a skinful to let me touch her! A shape like a starlet's, except Carolyn's is real. For two cents I'd . . . and what would that get me? A quick kiss and a "Darling, time to get dressed." Is it something I said? Something I did? Something I didn't do? Is it . . .

"Are you decent, loves?" Arthur roared through the door.

"Never more decent in my life, darling," Carolyn called. Thank God, at last and at least there'd be a little noise in the room.

"Come in, Arthur," Bill called. "We're not in flagrante delicto."

From outside they heard a slurring, unsteady voice. "Queenie. Queenie. Come to muvver, Queenie!"

And then the unmistakable voice of Mrs. Bullock. "Well! Ah nevah!"

For the second time that day Liz felt rich and pampered and even beautiful. She also felt adored. It wasn't long Liz Parkhurst who slid into that beautiful new dress, who touched her shimmering hair with perfume. It was the Duchess of Alba. She could hear Salvador singing in the shower and her heart sang with him. Life was . . . life was just perfect.

There was a rapping at her door. Rapping, hell. A pounding. Liz didn't mind, herself, but she hoped the servants didn't bring all the force of a battering ram to the doors of the guests.

"*Pase usted.*" Liz called. Even with the servants she spoke in the formal third person. They appreciated it from a foreigner.

"It's Miz Bullock," a voice shouted.

"*Sí. Pase usted.* Come in."

Mrs. Bullock puffed into the room and shut the door. "Miz Mártinez, Ah wish to speak to you about a very unpleasant matter."

"Oh?" The way Liz felt now, Mrs. Bullock could announce that the house was on fire, that Lee Goodwin had just had his will with her in the cactus garden, that Lou Ann had raped the standing army. Nothing made any difference to Liz at this lovely moment.

"Ah was sitting on my terrace, Miz Mártinez . . ."

"I hope you found it comfortable. No complaints?"

"Plentya complaints, but not about the terrace."

"Grand!"

"I was sitting on my terrace, minding my own business . . ."

"No?"

". . . minding my own business when out from the next cottage come this woman. This witch."

Liz refrained from saying anything as unworthy of herself as, "It takes one to tell one."

"She was whistling and calling for some kind of animal and, Miz Mártinez, she was so drunk she couldn't hardly stand."

"Well?"

"Well! Just that. I was nevah so horrified."

"Did she speak to you? Say something unpleasant?"

"Well, Ah should hope not!"

"But then of course you've never met. I'll introduce you tomorrow."

"There will not *be* any tomorrow, Miz Mártinez. I am in charge of three young girls, the daughters of the finest families in Dallas."

"And a grand job you've been doing, Mrs. Bullock. I couldn't help noticing this afternoon. You may not find it easy to get other accommodations on such short notice, but I'll have your bill made out and . . ."

"Well, of course we can't leave right now."

"I don't see why not."

"But surely you don't expect me to pay the kind of rates you're charging to live next door to a woman like that?"

"If you don't, Mrs. Bullock, someone else will."

"Why, her hair was hangin' down like I don't know what and she had on this dirty old lace nightgown that you could see clear through."

"Ah, yes, Van Raalte. 'Because she loves nice things.' "

"You do *not* seem to be taking this very serious matter very seriously."

"No. I'm not. She's paying her bills, minding her own business, and bothering nobody, Mrs. Bullock. I wish I had a dozen of her."

"You—you—you *what?* Tell me, just who is that woman, anyways?"

"That woman, Mrs. Bullock, is *my mother.* Salvador," Liz called happily, "time to get dressed."

We're Going to La Perla

Groping wildly for her glasses, the Princess-up-the-Hill read Salvador's note for the third time:

> Dining at La Perla. Can't see you tonight.
> In fact, busy all week.
> Salvador Martínez.

It wasn't even a proper note. Practically a telegram, and a damned insolent one at that. The Princess was not accustomed to having her orders disobeyed. And who was this insignificant little spick hotel manager—or whatever he was—to keep Her Serene Highness waiting for nearly an hour and then send a note flatly stating that he would not be there. No by-your-leave, no apology, no word of explanation.

The Princess flounced out of bed and kicked over her water pipe. "Shit!" she screamed, shattering the tranquillity of utter silence and higher thought. In a rage, she pressed all of the bells at the side of her bed.

Even through the soundproof walls she could hear the thunder of running feet pounding toward her room. The major-domo appeared; so did the Princess's maid, the secretary, the doctor, his nurse. The major-domo had seniority, having endured the Princess the longest. Sometimes the salary, the kickbacks, the bribes made it all seem worthwhile. This was not one of those times.

"*Altesse Serenissime* . . ." he began.

"Talk with your mouth like you were born, you mother-f—"

"Your Highness, what is the trouble?" His voice took on the honeyed coo of a nursemaid's, a psychiatrist's, a hypnotist's. Dulcet tones sometimes soothed the Princess. But not today. She was puffing like a grampus.

The new doctor—the Italian—said, "*Altezza* is distraught. *Signorina*, my hypodermic and . . ."

"Get your ass out of here, *guinzo*," the Princess snapped, "and take that dike nurse with you. When I want you, I'll ring."

"But *Altezza* did ring and . . ."

With a telling look at the doctor, the major-domo jerked his head toward the door. The doctor and his nurse retreated on white, gum-soled shoes.

The Princess had to get hold of herself, had to think clearly. She began now her search for serenity—one breath through the right nostril, one through the left. The major-domo, the maid, the secretary stood waiting.

At last the Princess was able to open her eyes, to smile, to feel utterly serene. "La Perla? Does anyone know about a place or a thing or a person called La Perla?"

"Yes, Your Highness," the major-domo said. "It is quite well known. It is a restaurant, a nightclub in the Hotel Mirador. The men who dive from the cliffs are internationally famous." Sometimes little travelogues, highly publicized facts well-known to anyone capable of reading a newspaper, had a calming effect on the Princess, attracted her fleeting attention momentarily.

"Book a table there," she said to her secretary.

"Call the car. Tell the boys I want them tonight," she said to the major-domo. "Also you. Get dressed."

The major-domo and the secretary bowed, began to back out of the room.

"Wait!" An eerie light came into the Princess's pale eyes.

"First draw a check," she said to the secretary. "A check for one million pesos to Salvador Martínez . . ."

"Is that spelled M-A-R . . ."

"How the hell would I know how you spell it? That's what you're paid for. Just make it out and bring it here. But first, wire the bank and tell them to stop payment on it."

"Does Your Highness wish to sign it now?"

"I'll sign it in my own good time."

The Princess lay back on her pillows and took a deep breath—with both nostrils. Men had tried, without much success, to cross her before, to disobey her, to try to extort money, even to attempt blackmail. Coincidentally, all of them had come to a bad end.

The Princess would show this cheeky little upstart, this little bantam rooster, who rejected whom or her name wasn't . . .

The Princess noticed her maid still standing in the room.

"Get me something to wear. Something decent. We're going to La Perla."

Toodle-oo

Bernice pulled the sheet up over her breasts, stroked Nacho's black hair, and sighed happily.

How easy it had all been! Easy and pleasant and fun. She wished that she had had the courage to do it years ago—to break away from the ugliness and the poorness that meant home and to come down here.

Nacho stirred in his sleep, turned in the bed beside her.

Easy and pleasant and fun. It hadn't hurt, the way Sis had always told her it would. Poor Sis, with her fat clod of an Ignatz! Ignatz and Ignacio; they were the same name, really—Ignatius—and yet the two were as different as they could be. One of them, hers, as slim and handsome and elegant and adroit as the other was oafish.

Bernice had always promised herself that she would wait for marriage. Now she was glad that she hadn't. It had been wonderful here this afternoon with Nacho. She hadn't taken any precautions —didn't know which ones to take—and she knew that Nacho hadn't. She didn't care. If she should be pregnant from only one time, she was glad. Delighted. Wasn't she practically Señora de la Vega y Martínez right now? As a matter of fact, she hoped she *would* have a baby—several. Nacho's sons would look like him: slim, dark, aristocratic.

Except for the date, everything was settled—well, practically everything. They had even gone out with an estate agent to look at the various houses and apartments for rent and for sale in Acapulco. Expensive, but that didn't seem to matter to Nacho. Bernice flushed, felt one of her scalding pangs of guilt. Would Nacho think that she was marrying him for money? She hoped not. She loved him. She really did. She hadn't come down here, throwing her weight around, talking big, talking social, talking rich. If she had falsified herself in any way, it was because she had said too little about herself, not too much. She had even tried to be honest. When Carolyn and Essie had decided to buy out Lila Bath's shop, Bernice had held herself down to a new bathing suit, a caftan, and a pair of slacks—what was right for Chicago wasn't necessarily right for Acapulco—and had said frankly that she couldn't afford to spend any more. Carolyn and Essie, dragging armloads of bright dresses to the fitting rooms, had laughed. "Poor Bernice, saving up for a sable bikini," they had teased. No! Bernice swore to herself that she had not put on any side, told any lies. Her only falsehood lay in being here, hobnobbing with the very rich, looking rich herself.

There was a discreet tap at the door. Bernice sat upright in bed, drew the sheet higher. Nacho stirred again, opened his eyes, grunted.

"Shhhhh," Bernice said. She had been of two minds about having Nacho come to her room. She didn't want Liz, or the other guests, to think that she was a tramp. But Nacho had been so persuasive, and after all that champagne at lunch . . . "Wh-who is it? Uh . . . *quién*, uh, *es?*" Bernice asked.

"Pablo, señorita. I have a—a letter for you."

Already Pablo felt that he was speaking English better. Tomorrow perhaps, the day after tomorrow surely, his English books would begin to arrive from the famous Oxford University. By the end of the season he would be speaking like an English gentleman. He could become a captain, a headwaiter, perhaps someday even the manager of one of the great glass hotels along the beach. Even now he could make out some of the English words on the envelope for the señorita. Haute Monde Society Resale Shoppe.

"Uh, could you put it under the door?" Bernice called,

Pablo smiled. Did the señorita think that he didn't know that Señor Nacho was in there with her? Did she think that Aurelia hadn't seen his car in the parking lot and remarked on it? That Florentino hadn't watched Señor Nacho hurry down the corridor and dart, without knocking, into the door of Hortensias? And could she really think that any of them cared? Of course a Mexican girl of good family would never behave so. But Americans were different. Look, if you could bear it, at that one from Texas. . . . Pablo stooped down and slid the letter under the door of Hortensias.

"Thank you," Bernice called.

"You are ou-el-come."

Bernice put on her robe, although it seemed silly to be so modest in front of Nacho after . . . well, after what had just happened and what she hoped would happen again and again and again. Nacho was sitting up in bed now, lighting a cigarette, smiling his beautiful, lazy smile.

Bernice picked up the envelope and tore it open, pulled out the sheet of rose-colored paper with Haute Monde Society Resale Shoppe printed at the top in Madam Kaye's high-class Olde Englyshe type.

She started reading. "Dear Bernice: Thanx for your postal. It looks pretty but . . ."

"No!" Bernice said aloud.

"What, my darling?" Nacho said.

"Nothing," Bernice said.

At a moment like this, when she was rising from—well, practically from—her bridal bed, the last thing Bernice wanted to be reminded of was Madam Kaye, secondhand clothes, and the life she had finally escaped. Bernice put the envelope down on the bedside table. "I'll read it later."

Nacho stretched out his arms. "Come here, my darling. My beautiful Bernice. My wife."

"In a moment, Nacho. But not right now. First let me attend to a couple of things."

"Later, my darling."

"No, Nacho. Right now." Darting away from his outstretched arms and blowing him a kiss, Bernice ran into the bathroom and locked the door.

Ignacio de la Vega y Martínez got out of bed and stretched. He heard the sound of the shower running. On narrow, bare feet, he strode casually around the room. It was attractive, that much he would grant Chavo's poor old wife. Cheap, but attractive. Poor Chavo! Impetuous, that was his trouble. Why did Chavo even ask Nacho, the lawyer in the family, for advice if he wasn't going to follow it? Marry in haste, repent at leisure. That's what Chavo was doing. Instead of investigating, allowing Nacho to draw up a proper marriage contract, Chavo had proposed to old Liz within a week. And where was he today? In the Ritz Hotel in Madrid? In a grand villa on the island of Majorca? In any of the places he expected to be? No! He was a little hotelkeeper right here in Mexico where he had started out, with a wife too old to give him sons, too poor to give him luxury.

With Nacho it was different. Of course Bernice was different to begin with. Young. Beautiful. Rich. She must be rich. She paid as much in one day for this room, furnished with junk from the Lagunilla, as Nacho paid a month at Señora García's. She needed him. Look how she had moaned and sobbed and clung to him in bed only an hour ago. A virgin, too! And she needed him for more than simply that. She was young, inexperienced, knew no Spanish. She would need a lawyer to look after her affairs, her investments. Nacho would speak to her at dinner tonight about the *dote*—the marriage settlement.

He sat down on the edge of the bed, flicked the ashes from his cigarette into the silly little *cazuela* painted with blue hydrangeas. His attention was caught by the pink envelope that Bernice had just opened. She had refused to read it. Had she a lover in the United States? Someone she hadn't told him about? Was she deceiving him?

The shower was still running. There would be time to read her letter. Why not? They were as good as married and a husband had the right to know what his wife was up to. If Bernice was innocent, all well and good. But if there should be another, someone she was keeping from him . . .

> Dear Bernice:
>
> Thanx for the postal. It looks pretty but *give me the old U.S. of A. anytime!!!*
>
> Sylvia is gone! *I* fired her! Better *I* should do your job and mine than pay a dummy like that! I sure wish you'd come back soon as I can't do both the buying and the selling. If you was to come back on rcpt. of this letter, before your 2 weeks was up, Bernice, you *would find $5 more in your pay envp. every week!*
>
> And Bernice, about the sable jacket I loaned you to wear down there . . .

Bernice stepped out of the shower and toweled herself briskly. She pulled off her shower cap and began to brush her hair until it glistened and crackled. Bernice often did some of her most serious thinking at this time. The hairbrush stimulated her brain, she supposed.

That old guilty feeling was beginning to spread over her again. Not about this afternoon and what she had done with Nacho. That was only natural for two people in love, two people who were going to be married. Bernice was thinking about the box— the little box from a West Side credit jeweler's with its purple plush covering, its sleazy sateen lining, like the coffin at a Polish funeral, and the pathetic little diamond ring that lay cold and fireless inside. She hadn't led Ralph on. She *hadn't!* But, on the other hand, she had never been courageous enough—decent enough —to tell him that there never would be a future for them, to send him on his way to a girl who would appreciate him. And even at the last possible moment, she hadn't had the courage to tell him the truth, to give back his ring, and to put him out of his misery. Even now the ring lay in the bottom of her suitcase under some totally useless sweaters she had brought along "just in case." Not once had she thought of Ralph since she had come here. Correction. Yes, once. Just once. She had sent Ralph a postcard, polished him off along with Sis and Ignatz, Momma and Poppa, Madam Kaye. "Having a wonderful time. Wish you were here. Love, Bernice."

Tonight—tomorrow morning at the very latest—she would have to sit down and write to Ralph, *try* to explain to him, let him down gently, kindly, and then somehow get his ring back to him.

But now was not the time to think about Ralph, not with Nacho lying in her bed just beyond the bathroom door. Tomorrow. She would do it tomorrow. She set her hairbrush down, tossed her head, smiled and, with glossy hair swinging across her shoulders, Bernice called, "Nacho, darling? Nacho? Would you like to have dinner here or . . ."

The bedroom was empty. Nacho's clothes were gone from the little slipper chair in the window alcove. But that was impossible. Bernice went to the chair. Through the window she saw Nacho striding—almost running—to his little car. Without looking back, he got in, started the motor. With a clashing of gears and a spray of gravel, he was gone.

"But what . . ."

Bernice turned. Lying on the unmade bed was one sheet of paper from the Haute Monde Society Resale Shoppe, on the floor, another.

Numbly, Bernice sat down and began to read:

> Dear Bernice:
> Thanx for the postal . . .

Madam Kaye's handwriting, like Madam Kaye herself, was large, florid, forceful; black with underscoring, it danced with exclamation points in ones and twos and threes.

Reading to the bottom of the first page, Bernice reached down blindly to sweep up the fallen sheet that lay on the floor.

. . . *please* try and get it back *as soon as possible!* A lady from Oak Park was hear this A.M. looking for a *high-class* garment. Sable and *nothing less!!!*

Wire me (*collect*) to say when your coming back! And do it *pronto* as I am *not* well.

Toodle-oo!!!
Madam Bella Kaye

Nacho had read the letter. Now he knew. And now he was gone.

"Toodle-oo," Bernice said, crumpling the letter in her hand. Then she fell forward onto the bed, still warm from their love-making, and cried as she had never cried before.

So Long

Roland lay sprawled naked in a deck chair on the secluded balcony of Rosas trying to even his suntan. He had spread Tan-Fastic on the narrow white strip which his bikini had covered. He had daubed his genitals with Elizabeth Arden's Sun-Pruf. (It would never do to be burned there.) Precariously he balanced a reflector beneath what were not quite yet jowls so that they, too, would tan. He had applied black Great Day to the hair of his chest and groin to disguise the silver that was appearing there, and had slathered Sun-Shield on the careful silver of his temples to discourage any tarnish the sun might induce. The bridge of his nose and his eyelids gleamed with Antoine's Bain de Soleil (tinted) to combat the paleness there from having worn sunglasses.

He was trying to read. It wasn't easy.

Roland had stormed home in a taxi from Condesa Beach at high noon, before he had finished his first planter's punch, before he had even ordered lunch to be brought out to the *palapa* he was paying for. That Chip! Chippie was more like it.

Roland had simply taken a little stroll down the beach. Of course he'd *asked* Chip if he wanted to come with him, and Miss Chip had said, "Oh, no, thanks." And Roland had happened to run into an awfully attractive designer from L.A. Well, they had fallen into conversation, both being creatives, and the time had simply flown. But he hadn't been gone much more than an hour— an hour and a half at the most—and when Roland got back to the *palapa*, what should be sitting in *his* chair and practically devouring Chip with his eyes but the fattest, nelliest old auntie you could ever hope *not* to see. "I *hope* you won't mind if I sit in *my* chair," Roland had said—just like that.

"Oh, not at all, *Grand-mère*," the revolting old bag of guts had said. "A *bientôt*, Chip. Give me a call. I'll be here all winter."

"So long, Harold. And thanks for the drinks," Chip had said. He hadn't even had the decency to *introduce* Roland to his—his pickup. Not that Roland had the *faintest* desire to know Harold or to exchange one, single, solitary word with anyone so repulsive. *Grand-mère* indeed! Roland would hate *to be hanging since that* numero had been fifty. "*Adieu, madame,*" he had said to Roland with a terrible twitch of one eye (even in his indignation, Roland had not missed noticing Harold's *nauseating* facial tic) and waddled —absolutely *waddled*—back to his own *palapa* and his gang of giggling little Mexican hustlers.

There had been words, plenty of them, hot and heavy on both sides, until Roland had risen with hauteur, striking his head painfully on the rustling palm-thatch roof of the *palapa*, and had stalked off Condesa Beach—*forever*.

Chip would be back soon, never fear. Roland regretted the five hundred pesos pocket money he had given Chip this morning. You could go a long way in a taxi on forty dollars. It would have served the little tease right if he'd had to *walk* back to Su Casa.

Roland squinted in the bright western sunlight. The type danced on the page in front of him. It would be much easier to read if he wore his dark glasses, but then he didn't want to go home to Allentown with pale eyelids. And considering what had happened at the beach this morning, it was a miracle that Roland could concentrate at all.

The book was one of Roland's favorites. It was entitled *The Call of the Goose* and it had created a perfect sensation in Roland's set when one of the boys had come across it at the Marché aux Paperbacks. Roland found it both rousing and soothing, depending on his mood. It was so manly—not a female character in it—and so sensitively written. *Basically*, Roland supposed, you'd call it a Western—cowboys and Indians, the kind of thing Roland usually hated. But this one—there were several in the series, each dishier than the last—was certainly different.

Damn Chip! Once a hustler, always a hustler.

Roland turned a page. The suntan oil on his thumb left a greasy, transparent oval on the cheap, pulp paper. Doggedly, he read on. ". . . untied the thong fastening of his breechcloth. It fell to the ground at Abraham's feet. . . ." A gold-digging little ingrate, that's what Chip was. ". . . firm columns of his copper thighs, the lean loins, the almond sliver of his navel . . ." Six months ago Chip wouldn't have known what to do with an oyster fork except toss it into the dishwasher. ". . . faint pulsation, the stirring, the rise of his throbbing maleness . . . " *I* gave Chip everything he has, taught him everything he knows. ". . . Abraham unbuckled his belt, felt his buckskin breeches spring free of the force from between his thighs. . . ." This is the thanks I get. ". . . quivering manhood soaring upward from curling copper tendrils . . . " Making eyes at everything that comes along—the waiters, Laddy, Señor Martínez, his cousin, Arthur Craine, anyone!

Roland heard the door of the room open and then close, very softly. So! Chip was back. Roland would say nothing. Chip could damned well come to him and apologize. If he were suitably contrite, Roland might even accept the apology and take him to El Patio tonight. Silently Roland waited, pretending to read. This was one of the best parts of *The Call of the Goose*. How that man could write! But Roland had no interest in Abraham and his Indian just now. Roland was interested in Roland and, of course, Chip.

His face arranged into a mask of wounded hauteur, Roland waited. Couldn't the ignorant little nobody see him sitting on the balcony? No. Of course not. The shutters were closed. Roland was about to signal his presence—cough, clear his throat—so that Chip would realize that he was here, patiently waiting for an apology. But then Roland heard Chip speak.

"He's not here"

"*Mande, señor?*"

"I say, other man not here. Gone."

"Ahhh. *Sí*, señor."

"You like Hershey bar? Candy?"

"*Mas tarde*, señor. Af-ter."

"Call me Chip, honey."

"*Cheep?*"

"Chip."

Soundlessly Roland rose from his chair. The scene that followed was the greatest one Roland had ever played.

Good-bye

It was a big night at La Perla, but then every night during the season was a big night there. Its setting—a steep cliff down which the nightclub meandered in tiers of tables to a stormy cove—and its famous divers plummeting downward at the split second when the waves were right had established La Perla as firmly as the Banco de Mexico. Furthermore, the food was good and the orchestra fair. La Perla had been a tourist mecca for decades.

The party from Su Casa left La Perla's cave of a bar and picked its way down, down, down to the front-row table which Walt had reserved for Essie's birthday party. In his bearlike way, Walt had done everything right, had forgotten nothing; place cards, corsages, candles, a centerpiece of tropical flora, medallions of beef, and champagne for all. As the ladies oh-ed and ah-ed over the beauty of the table, a sharp wind sent their long dresses fluttering, the candles flickering in their hurricane lamps. Tablecloths flapped, napkins tumbled, and fifty men rose to drape stoles and cardigans around the shoulders of their dinner partners.

"Odd," Liz said. "There's never a wind at this time of year."

"We always order something big for Essie's birthday," Walt said. Laughter. "Shall we have another round before they bring on the food?"

"Sure," Rex said, and stumbled into his chair between Essie and Carolyn.

The poinciana blossoms, perched precariously on the top story of April May's unyielding coiffure, rocked dangerously. "Ya don't suppose we're in fer a mon-soom or like that?" she asked. April had sat through enough reruns of Rex's old pictures to know all about monsoons. The big storm always came in the next-to-last reel, when Tarzan's mate was about to be sacrificed into the maw of a smoldering volcano. It meant that the gods were angry. The studio sprinkler system and the wind machines were turned on full blast and got the girl's sarong all wet and ruined her hair-do until Rex came swinging through the trees to carry her safely back to the make-up department.

"Never," Salvador said. "Look at the stars, the moon. Acapulco is always beautiful. Romantic." He treated April to a ravishing white smile. Halfheartedly, she flashed her caps back at Salvador, even if he was a foreigner. Salvador had no interest in April May. She looked like a stripper from the Teatro Blanquita, only older, and it would never do to seduce a guest of Su Casa. Too many complications.

"Yeah," April said after weighing Salvador's statement carefully. "Very ro-man-tic."

"I'll bet you could tell us a lot about romance," Lee Goodwin said, giving April's thigh a squeeze under the table. Get her warmed up. Then he tipped a conspiratorial wink to Carolyn sitting across the table from him. Carolyn smiled faintly, looked as though she might be quite sick quite soon.

"Ouch," April said, after considering carefully what Lee had done to her.

" 'S'matter, baby?" Rex asked.

"Noth-ing," April said. Now she knew who Lee reminded her of. Irving. That awful Irving who had said he was a talent scout and left her flat in Atlantic City with the hotel bill to pay. Irving was no gentleman and neither was Lee Goodwin. She smiled across the table at Rex. Rex was nice.

More cocktails arrived and Arthur Craine rose to propose a witty toast in Spanglish to Essie. While Essie blushed and giggled from the head of the table, Laddy, who had been able to follow the intricate plays on words, leapt to his feet and shouted "Hear! Hear!" Bill Williams, who had not, did the same. What fun! Liz thought. The darlings—all of them, with one glowing exception. I'm really having fun for the first time in . . . Oh, *now* what was Lee Goodwin saying?

"Runway?" April asked. "Whaddayuh mean runway? I was an ex-ot-ic dan-suce."

"Honey, I could swear I caught you swinging your tassels at the Old Howard in . . . "

"Look!" Essie said, her jaw hanging. "*Would you just look!*"

Essie Dewlap was not the only one who was looking. The babble of conversation stopped. Every eye in La Perla was focused on the stairway. Even the orchestra missed a beat.

"Why, it's the Princess," Liz said. "The Princess-up-the-Hill!"

The Princess rarely traveled light. Tonight was no exception. Wearing a silver sari and tinkling toe-rings, she made her way sedately downward, one claw clutching at the brawny, bare arm of her Negro attendant. The Caucasian, the Chinese, and the Indian followed, dressed alike in silver pantaloons. Behind them came servants bearing the silvered musharabia screens to be set up around the Princess's table. Last came her major-domo, wearing white tie and tails. Off the premises he was permitted to dress in usual butler's evening garb. It was perhaps a mistake as, in Acapulco, he was twice as conspicuous as the rest of the entourage.

"Make way for the daughter of the Caliph of Bagdad!" Arthur said.

"It's the floor show. It's jus' gotta be," April said. "Rexy, dint we see that magician at the hungry i?"

"Well," Walt said, "now I've seen everything."

"Nothing ostentatious about our poor little rich girl, is there?" Carolyn said.

"She's kinda cute," April said. "But old."

Salvador colored and studied the drink in front of him.

"So!" Liz said. "At last I've seen our famous neighbor. Unbelievable! Have you ever met her, Chavo?"

"No!" Salvador said, and took a great gulp of his drink.

Cringing, the Princess sank into her chair while the major-domo supervised the setting up of the silver screens. People were so cruel! Imagine! Staring at her. Positively gawking! Swine! If only they could realize how shy, how sensitive the Princess was. No wonder that she rarely ventured out in public. The ordeal was just too much. Ah! Now the screens surrounded her table, protected her from the inquisitive scrutiny of mankind. This was better. Much better. The Princess could not be seen through the filigree of the screens and yet she could see everything, everyone. The first person she saw was Salvador, seated with a large party of Americans. Had he a wife? And, if so, which of the women could she be? The tiny one at the head of the table? That common-looking blonde with poinciana blossoms in her hair? The Princess studied April May's astonishing breasts and wondered where she had had the work done. Angrily, she heard her four escorts babbling over the menu, talking of *ceviche* and *steak au poivre*. She snapped her fingers for silence. The major-domo hovered at her side. "Vichy water for everyone. Nothing more. And my pillbox." Then the Princess handed the major-domo an envelope and pointed to Salvador.

Arthur was regaling the table with an amusing anecdote concerning the concierge of the Gritti Palace in Venice and rather pointedly leaving Lee Goodwin out of the conversation. Lee had never been to Europe and he had made the mistake of allowing Arthur Craine to know it. Rapt, April gaped at Arthur, her scarlet lips parted. April assumed that he was talking about Venice, California, and "gritty" was sure the word for a dump like that. "What a vo-ca-brillary he's got!" April said in solemn wonder.

". . . and there, all but falling out of a gondola, was none other than dear Ernest, absolutely . . . " Arthur had a way of observing every member of his audience without actually seeming to look at anyone. It was a trick he had learned as a young instructor at Princeton, and woe betide any undergraduate who dozed in the back row, who used Arthur Craine's classroom to bone up on another subject or to write a surreptitious letter. A question having nothing to do with anything Arthur had been saying was always fired at the miscreant and, in the total confusion that followed, Arthur would treat the class and himself to a five-minute dressing down—actually a cutting down to size—so elegant, so exquisitely bitchy, that big, brawny football players were often reduced to blubbering, sobbing masses. Not for nothing had Arthur Craine been called "Old Rolling Eyes."

The eyes rolled slightly to the left and the anecdote—such an amusing one—died on Arthur's lips. Coming straight toward their table, impeccable tails fluttering in the breeze, was the Princess's major-domo.

"Zut a—" Arthur began, and then stopped.

The major-domo marched directly to Salvador and handed him a big, square, silver-bordered envelope. He bowed slightly, made a smart about-face, and returned to the table hidden behind the silver screens.

"Heavens!" Liz said. She tried to laugh, but it didn't quite come off. Something—nothing definite, nothing she could put her finger on—disturbed her.

"How they carried the news from Aix to Ghent," Arthur said. Before he finished, he realized that it wasn't one of his best. No one laughed.

"What is it, a summons?" Lee Goodwin asked. No one laughed at that, either.

Flushed, angry, embarrassed, Salvador fumbled with the envelope. How dared this rich old American hag mortify him in public? Him, a descendant of . . . "*Mierda!*" Salvador cut his index finger as he slit open the flap. A check fluttered and fell to his lap. Reading the check, Salvador gasped. One million pesos! But there was no signature. What kind of stupid joke was this? And then Salvador read the note in the Princess's tall, sloping hand:

> I will sign this tonight.
> Chez moi. Eleven o'clock.

Like the check, the note was unsigned. It didn't need to be.

Salvador was conscious of every eye. Embarrassed? Yes. But, then, one million pesos! Eighty thousand dollars!

"Chavo, what on earth . . . " Liz began.

"It's nothing, Elizabeth," Salvador said irritably. "Just a business matter."

"But what kind of business would we be having with her?" Would Elizabeth never shut up? "We don't even know her."

"I had the dubious pleasure of meeting Her Serene Highness at Cap d'Antibes in . . . " Arthur struggled valiantly to regain the conversational reins. It was hopeless. Everyone in the restaurant was gazing upward. The screens were being removed from the Princess's table. Her mission had been accomplished. There was no need to stay. Silver sari drifting in the breeze, the Princess and her cortege were making their way up the stairs to the exit. It just wasn't fair, Arthur fumed silently, to have a sight gag like the Princess and her gang upstaging a really accomplished raconteur. It was like—well, like bringing a trained seal onto the stage while Joan Sutherland was singing.

"Please go on with your story," Essie Dewlap was saying.

"What story?" Arthur snapped, hating himself for his bad temper. Arthur Craine was nothing if not urbane. Even William Buckley had been unable to shake him on that last panel show.

"Um-a-jun," April said, still staring after the Princess's party. "Comin' all the way here an' then not even staying to see the divers."

"Oh, shut up!" Arthur said.

There was a stunned pause and then Rex Roman said, "Hey!"

"Who's for another drink?" Walt roared genially. Celebrities Arthur and Rex might be—well, kind of celebrities—but they weren't going to louse up Essie's birthday dinner. Not even the President of the United States could get away with that—not if his name was still Walter Dewlap.

Nobody except Rex wanted another drink.

"Sure, Ape Man," Lee Goodwin called across the table. "Just what you need. Why not make it a double?" He tipped a lewd, face-distorting wink in Essie's direction. After all, she was the hostess. Give her a little thrill on her fortieth birthday. Appalled, Essie managed a smile that made her look as though she had been served alum. She supposed that she was just hopelessly provincial, but this Goodwin man was so—so echhh!

"Yeah," Rex said. "A double."

"Aw, Rexy, why yuh wanna go an' get smashed for? Remember what the doctor . . . "

"Pipe down," Rex said.

April was suddenly mute. Rex had hit her just three times. (Twice April had deserved it.) April did not want to repeat the experience. Out of shape Rex may have been, and closer to sixty than to fifty, but he could still pack a wallop that made April see stars, that loosened her caps, and set her empty head to ringing like a carillon. Better to do what Rex suggested. Two more drinks—three at the most—and he would be out on his feet; a big, lumbering docile baby to be taken home, undressed, and tucked into bed.

Salvador attempted a surreptitious glance at his wristwatch. A button popped off his cuff and landed with a clink on his dinner plate. Damn that cheap little tailor! He'd set the sleeves in all wrong, made the cuffs too tight, sewn the buttons on with inferior thread and not enough of it. Salvador could not help thinking that this would be his last Acapulco shirt. The next ones would come from Le Duc in Mexico. Le Duc, indeed! After tonight his shirts would come from Sulka's in New York, in London, in Paris. Salvador wondered if Sulka might not also have a branch in Madrid. Then he dismissed the subject of shirts and faced up to the problem at hand. It was half-past ten and time to get out of here. That he was going and going immediately was certain. But how? Salvador was a gentleman and a gentleman did not like scenes, not even those of his own creation. He would have to think of some excuse and think of it fast. The old wound? Yes! That would do.

From time to time Salvador had allowed it to be understood that he had done heroic and very hush-hush underground work against the Communists in Cuba. Even a decade and more after the revolution, Salvador did not care to go into specific details, except that he had suffered a near fatal wound. Having no scar on his body, other than a navel, the wound lay invisible beneath his lustrous blue-black hair. It was terribly convenient, really, causing severe migraine headaches at times when Liz asked him to do things like tot up the accounts, inventory the bottles in the bar, or talk to bores. Miraculously enough, it did not interfere with swimming, sunbathing, water skiing, tennis, riding, or drinking. Liz had implicit belief in Salvador's wound. Laddy, who had been cited for valor as the bridge-playing aide-de-camp of a daffy old general in Fort Sill, did not, although he was too polite to say so.

117

Salvador rose, swayed, clapped a slim hand to his brow, carefully avoiding contact with his perfectly combed hair.

"Chavo? What is it?" Liz asked.

"Nothing. Nothing really. Just the usual—a *dolor de cabeza*." With a wan, brave smile he snapped his fingers futilely. "How you say in English . . . it's no good. I can't even think." He bowed over Essie's hand. "If you will excuse me."

"I'm so sorry," the birthday girl began. Undoubtedly she and everyone else would have more to say, but Salvador did not wait to hear it. He reeled dramatically toward the stairs and then, feeling liberated and off stage, bounded up the steps two at a time.

"Chavo! Wait!"

Caramba! It was Liz, loping up the stairway behind him like a springbok. These *gringas!* Were they all Amazons? Hadn't they an ounce of the femininity of a Latin woman? Salvador pretended not to hear and charged on upward.

He had made it to a waiting taxicab when Liz caught up with him. "Chavo, darling, what's the matter?"

One million pesos as good as in his pocket and here was his great, gangling, Girl Guide of a wife getting in his way, trying to hold him back. Well, she couldn't. This was good-bye. Good-bye to being an innkeeper. Good-bye to Su Casa, with its silly rooms named for flowers. Good-bye to having to ask for every centavo he spent. Good-bye to "Darling, where are you going? Darling, what took you so long?" Good-bye to Laddy, bleeding Liz for everything he could get.

"*Por Diós, no me molestes!*" In moments of stress, Salvador's English deserted him. Understand it, yes. Speak it, no.

"But Chavo, darling. What's the matter?" In moments of stress, Liz's Spanish deserted her. Understand it, yes. Speak it, no.

"*Es nada. Un dolor de cabeza y nada más.*"

"Chavo, if it's one of your sick headaches, I'm coming with you." Although she had never quite wanted to, Liz had grudgingly entertained fleeting suspicions of Chavo's migraines. Tonight she was certain that Chavo was looking for more than an aspirin. She clutched at his sleeve.

With heroic effort Salvador got out a sentence in almost-English.

"For the mercy of God, Elizabeth, will you no more molest me! Return to your guests."

"But they're your guests, too, darling."

"*Chinga les!*" With a rending of cloth, Salvador tore himself free of his wife's grasp, fell into the taxicab, and slammed the door. The cab swung in a wide arc, throwing Salvador off balance in the back seat. As he pulled himself to an upright position, he saw his wife through the rear window. Standing there in the harsh lights of the driveway, she looked drained—drained and miserable and old. "Free!" Salvador said aloud. "Free and rich!"

"*Mande, señor?*"

"*A la casa de la princesa.*"

"*La princesa, señor?*" The respect in the driver's voice was almost tangible.

"*Sí. La princesa.*"

And Liz stood in the harsh lights of the driveway looking drained, feeling drained—drained and miserable and old. How wonderfully this day had started out, bringing love and fun and money; all that life could promise. And now . . .

"*Señorita?*" It was a cab driver. He pointed toward Liz's feet. Liz looked down. There was a large white square of paper, its silver border and crest glittering in the lights of the driveway. Stooping down, Liz picked up the note, holding it by one corner as though it were somehow unclean.

I will sign this tonight.
Chez moi. Eleven o'clock.

Sign what? Liz wondered absently. It didn't really matter. Nothing really mattered now. Liz crumpled the sheet of paper into a ball and dropped it. As she did so, she reflected that another woman—a smarter woman—would save it as a telling bit of testimony in a divorce hearing. Why bother? Liz knew that she would never leave Salvador. Salvador would leave her. He already had.

"I must think of my guests," Liz said aloud. She wondered why she always had to think about someone else; never about Liz. Other people, their comfort, their problems, their small talk could be therapy, like knitting or crewel work or modeling in clay. She took a deep breath, stood straighter, and strode back into the building. Picking her way down the meandering stone stairs of La Perla, she could hear the long, expectant roll of drums. "My entrance music," she said to herself. Then she realized that one of the divers was scrambling to the top of the promontory, was kneeling at the shrine before his one-hundred-and-sixty-foot plunge into waves below. "Tacky-looking shrine," Liz said to herself. "All those harsh, white light bulbs. It looks like a carnival concession. And the divers lack flair, too. I would have dressed them in lamé trunks with capes to match and lighted them. . . . Why do I think about those boring divers? Haven't I got real things to think about?" No. It was better this way. Trivialities would help. Liz could think about any number of inconsequentials: the place mats for lunch tomorrow, getting Mrs. Bullock and her girls out of Su Casa, planning a picnic on Laddy's leaking sailboat. It all helped. A splash. A thunder of applause. "For me?" Liz wondered. No. Of course not. It was for the diver. He had made it again. But then they always did.

". . . most thrilling thing I ever saw in my life!" It was Essie.

"I was scared to even look," April said.

Liz rejoined the table with a smile.

"Did you see it?" Carolyn asked.

"Yes," Liz murmured. "It was wonderful."

"And how is Salvador?" Essie asked.

"Oh, don't worry, please," Liz said. "He'll be all right." Of course he'd be all right. Everyone would be all right. Even Liz herself would be all right. She'd think about things—little things like doing over old dresses, running up a set of slip covers for the sala. She'd make everything all right.

". . . sent your meat back so it wouldn't get cold. Waiter!" It was Walt. How sweet he was. The kind of man every woman should have. Now all that Liz would have to do would be to eat the dinner.

Liz was conscious of Lee Goodwin's braying voice—yes, his common voice!—and of Rex Roman's thick, rumbling reply.

"I've got to pull myself together," Liz told herself. "Listen. Join in. Keep Essie's party going."

"Sure. Sure I done all those dives. Olympuck team. Eleanor Holm. Ever since I was a kid. Before I ever went into pictures."

"A *hundred* and sixty feet?" Lee was asking.

"Sixty. But it don't make that much difference. A good diver that can do ten feet can do a hundred easy."

"You mean you could do the same dive those Mex kids do?"

Oh, how Liz hated Lee Goodwin; the patronizing little half smile, the constant needling. Now what was he trying to do to poor old Rex Roman? Liz would have to force herself to listen. She might be called upon to make some comment.

". . . saw me this aft'noon, dincha?" Rex's eyes were red, his thick speech more blurred than ever.

"I'm not entirely sure that Mr. Goodman"—Arthur got the name wrong on purpose; he despised Lee Goodwin—"was noticing." He cast a feline smile at his sister. Carolyn smiled back dutifully.

"Off a ten-foot board into that bathtub at Su Casa? Hell, I'm talking about a cliff like this one with waves below."

"Listen, squirt," Rex said, "maybe you didn't hear my name right. It's Rex Roman, U. S. Olympuck team and number one box-office draw from . . ."

"Jus' ignore 'um, Rexy," April hissed. "He's only tryin' to get your dandruff up."

"Shut up."

"Speaking of swimming," Bill Williams said nervously, "there's this kid at the Chicago Athletic Club . . ."

Rex struggled to his feet and stood swaying. Through her misery, Liz hoped that Rex was going to ask Lee Goodwin outside and mop up the pavement with him.

"Another drink, Rex?" Walt barked, too sharply, too loudly, too quickly.

"When I get back."

"Back?" Liz whispered. But of course he meant from the men's room. He couldn't possibly mean . . .

Fumbling with the buttons of his shirt, Rex glared at Lee Goodwin. "Swimmin' is somethin' you never forget." the shirt flapped in the breeze and fell to the floor. Rex Roman stood at the table, diaphragm bulging, a roll of soft flesh hanging over his belt. "Think I can't still dive as good as them spicks?"

"Oh, now, Rex, come on." It was Laddy, flustered, embarrassed, and wheedling. Laddy was always said to have a winning way with drunks.

"Sure," Lee said with his whinnying little laugh. "Show us, Ape Man."

"Hang onna my watch," Rex said thickly. "I'll be right back."

"Rex! Sit down! Put on your shirt!" Walt was barking again. What kind of dear, old, faithful dog did he remind Liz of? And then Rex was gone, weaving unsteadily toward the parapet overhanging the inlet.

"Rex!" April screamed. She was out of her chair and clattering after him, curls bobbing, breasts and buttocks thrusting. April caught up with Rex just as he was stepping out of his trousers, kicking off his espadrilles. She was shrieking something to him, but with the wind, the hubbub of voices, the scurrying of waiters, Liz had no idea what it was. Then she heard a sharp crack, saw April reel backward on her ridiculous shoes. Liz saw Rex standing on the parapet in his shorts—rather baggy, it seemed to her, for a professional body beautiful to be wearing. Then Rex was out of sight. A moment later he was swimming across the inlet toward the soaring cliff. The divers were after him. No mistake about it, the old lush could still swim like a porpoise. April, clutching at her cheek, hung over the parapet screaming "Stop 'um, stop 'um! Rexy, come back!"

And now Rex had reached the other side, was out of the water and making his uncertain way upward. So had the two Mexican divers. Small and sleek and agile as lizards, they would surely overtake Rex before he lumbered to the top. Ah, good! Rex had lost his footing, had sprawled flat. Now the divers could stop him. But, no! Rex was up. With a well-placed kick, he sent the first of the divers over backward and continued his climb.

And now Rex was at the top, at the edge, arms outstretched. Old and drunk and fat and ludicrous. Stupid as an ox. And yet, even in her horror, Liz couldn't help thinking he possessed a certain wonderful dignity. But surely he wasn't going to . . .

"Oh, thank God," Liz said aloud. The second diver had scrambled up to the top. He darted forward and grasped Rex around the waist. "Poor little thing," Liz thought inanely, "his arms are hardly long enough to . . . "

"Rexxxxxxxx!" April screamed.

With a violent thrashing of meaty arms and shoulders, Rex struggled to break the diver's grip. Off balance, Rex stepped forward on to . . . on to nothing. Down, down, down he went, his body thrashing spasmodically.

"Rexxxxxxxxxxxxxxxx!"

The remains of Rex Roman, Olympic diver and motion-picture star, both arms and one leg removed by sharks, were discovered on the beach at Puerto Marqués four days later.

You Sent for Me

Salvador was trembling as he approached the silver doors of the Princess's bedroom. No. That would never do. By his cool indifference he had brought this imperious old hag to her knees. Now keep her there. Let her grovel a little more for what she wanted so desperately and what only Salvador could give her. There was only one nagging little question preying on his mind. It was a point of etiquette, really: Should he have the Princess sign her check before or after?

The major-domo pressed a button causing the doors to open. Salvador, drawing himself a bit taller, entered the bedroom. The doors closed behind him. By the flickering light of a single taper he saw the Princess seated in the lotus position on her silver bed. The old idiot! Did she think she was fooling him with her maharani masquerade? She was nothing more, nothing less than a rich, old American whore, stupid enough to pay . . . The Princess fixed him with a gaze as hard and sharp as a silver dagger.

"You sent for me, I believe?" Even as he said it, the statement sounded more pompous than dignified to Salvador. He was thinking more of the million pesos. Which should it be, business before pleasure? Or would that seem crass and commercial?

The Princess solved the problem nicely. "You have the check?"

Salvador moved toward the bed and handed it to her. She signed the check and returned it to him. Salvador glanced at the check and put it in his pocket. There it was. He was rich! And there might even be more to come. He managed what he hoped was a languorous smile. "And now?"

"Exactly," the Princess said. "Now." She clapped her hands twice. From the dim corners of the room the princess's four men approached. Salvador was aware of their oiled bodies glistening in the light of the single candle. "What sort of foolishness is . . . "

Salvador said no more. The Indian gave him a blow in the stomach that doubled him over. From behind him someone—the Swede, the Negro, the Chinese?—ripped Salvador's shirt down from his shoulders, pinning his arms to his sides. He was thrown to the floor. Through his shock and pain, he was conscious of hands grasping at his belt.

Sitting cross-legged on her silver bed, the Princess-up-the-Hill smiled.

II

PARADISE LOST

One-Two-Three

It was easy to remember the earthquake. It occurred at 1:23 in the morning and lasted for one minute and twenty-three seconds—rather a long time. Many visitors to Acapulco, in an outburst of originality, coined the phrase, "As simple as one, two, three."

Although the Departamento de Turismo, in its unflagging pursuit of the tourist dollar, rarely boasts of it, Mexico in general and Acapulco in particular are jiggled by numbers of vagrant earthquakes. While there has been nothing as sensational as, say, the destruction of Lisbon in 1775, San Francisco in 1906, or Tokyo in 1923, the "Pearl of the Pacific" has played host to countless smaller shakes. Acapulquenians have become almost blasé about them. At best, they have been so minor as to go almost unnoticed. At worst, they have registered 6.6 on the Richter Scale, toppled an unfinished beach hotel, finished forever a finished one, split a few jerrybuilt villas, and demolished quite a lot of squatters' hovels that should never have been where they were in the first place. Vital statistics are closely guarded, but it is piously believed that no human life has ever been lost in an Acapulco earthquake.

Anyone who has ever gone through a really good tremor can—and unfortunately will—tell you exactly where he was and what he was doing at the time of the shake. The stories emanating from this one, at 1:23 in the morning during the height of the season, are legion. Even those who slept through it have felt it their duty to tell the folks back home that they were thrown to the bedroom floor, pitched from a toilet seat or, with the more imaginative, pinioned beneath a toppled chest of drawers.

A Mrs. Humphrey Fargo, of Sedalia, Missouri, was unseated from

127

her bidet in Joie de Vivre (a hillside bungalow renting for $100 U.S. per diem) and suffered a minor concussion when her head struck the edge of the bathtub.

The mammoth crystal chandelier on the terrace of the Restaurant Rivoli, heretofore said to be "suspended by a moonbeam," crashed to the floor below, injuring no one as the dinner crowd had been gone for some time.

The psychedelic floor show at Tiberio was canceled and a number of customers escaped not only unscathed, but without paying their checks.

The seemingly impossible defloration of a little bride from Teaneck, New Jersey, was accomplished in nothing flat—but with shrieks of anguish—in the Roqueta Suite of the Hotel Caleta. The wedding night was memorable but not considered a success.

The grand piano at Armando's rolled wildly across the floor, tossing customers left and right, and crashed into the bar.

The much talked-about cantilevered swimming pool on the hillside property of Mr. and Mrs. Harrison Littlefield (formerly of Pawtucket, Rhode Island) was even more talked-about when it burst like a melon, sending a fifty-thousand-gallon deluge of water, turquoise tiles, and mud down into the garden and living room (white on white) of Marisol, the newly built retirement home of Mr. and Mrs. Bayard Ogilvie (late of Greenwich, Connecticut). The Ogilvies had never been very fond of the Littlefields to begin with.

On Calle Hidalgo a pink-and-white Jeep, driver unknown, careened through the plate-glass show window of Señorial, "Sports Clothes for the Man Who Cares," where it remained, abandoned, for the better part of two days.

Jean-Luc Dubois, cabin steward aboard the French cruise ship, Villefranche, sustained a broken rib and many painful bruises when catapulted from a bed at a brothel in la zona de tolerancia.

In her single bedroom at La Golondrina Family Hotel, Señora Ofelia Mendoza Vda. de Morales, aged seventy-nine, suffered a mild coronary occlusion while reading Lo que el viento se llevó. But as Doña Ofelia had just reached the part where Scarlett shot the Yankee soldier, it could not be definitely established whether excitement, the earthquake, or advanced age had brought about her seizure.

The Hilton Hotel, whose luck with earthquakes has never been good, got off lightly with a few cracked walls in rooms that were about to be done over anyhow, and a burst water pipe on the third floor.

Religious conversions were not uncommon. Although registered as "Mr. and Mrs. J. J. Johnson," a Mr. Alfred McNulty and a Mrs. Wilma Beemish (native cities unknown) dashed unclad from a room in the Pacificana Motel, fell to their bare knees in the gravel driveway, and became, quite independently, converts to Roman Catholicism on the following day. Four whores, unsuccessfully working the town square, raced headlong into the swaying cathedral screaming for absolution. As no priest was present, they felt pretty silly about it the next morning and avoided one another's society for a day or two. A Miss Gwenda-Lynne (she spelled it that way) Durkin, an almost certifiable nymphomaniac from the cruise ship *Villefranche*, rolled hysterically on the dance floor of Le Club, reverting noisily to the faith of her fathers (Baptist) to the chagrin of her escort, one Ignacio de la Vega y Martínez, who was planning to take Gwenda-Lynne and, possibly, her purse in his car a bit later on. Her redemption lasted for nearly three days until, within sight of her native state of California, she succumbed once again to cabin steward Jean-Luc Dubois who, cracked rib and all, managed one last wild, sweet coupling on her unmade berth.

Certain divorce proceedings were instituted during or because of the earthquake. A Mr. Clifford (Stud) Nesbitt, Junior, age twenty-seven, of New Algeria, Maryland, whose sexual prowess, as described by himself, was the gasp of the Eastern Shore, dashed to his bungalow from the men's bar of his hotel, where he had been telling an admiring· group how to keep a woman happy, to find his wife in bed with—not the sick headache she had claimed—but the chambermaid, who was not only female and almost coal black, but who had also allowed young Nesbitt to believe that he was as irresistible as he, himself, believed he was. Stud was speechless. Mrs. Nesbitt was not. Beginning with dimensions and ending with technique, Mrs. Nesbitt made Stud's inadequacies known in a voice that carried to the men's bar and beyond. She had, Mrs. Nesbitt said, married Stud only for his money and, except for fairly regular encounters with the masseuse at the New Algeria Country Club, the golf pro, Stud's partner, Stud's secretary, and Stud's own sister, it hadn't been worth it. What was more, Mrs. Nesbitt would be delighted to tell all—and possibly a bit more—in court if Stud felt like suing for divorce. Stud, his reputation to maintain, did not. So Mrs. Nesbitt got the divorce on grounds of adultery, settled for a million dollars and Stud's sister. Everyone on the Eastern Shore said that Stud was just oversexed.

A Mr. and Mrs. Cohn, of Sutton Place South, New York City, parted after thirty-four placid years of marriage. "Almost our ruby anniversary," Mrs. Cohn kept saying. At considerable expense, they had bought and decorated the penthouse atop the Playamar Condominium on the beach near Posada del Sol—two bedrooms, two and a half baths, a forty-by-twenty-foot living-dining area, a terrace, and twenty-four-hour room service. They were the first—the only—tenants to move into Playamar and also the first to move out; but not nearly soon enough. Although the sales prospectus had made much of Playamar's terrazzo floors, sliding glass walls, central air conditioning, purified water, and switchboard service—"Just like Sutton Place; and you can get a tan," Mrs. Cohn said—there had been no mention of the basic construction of the building. "A house built on sand," Mr. Cohn said later and often.

The noise, not the tremor, had awakened the Cohns. Mrs. Cohn arose, a vision in cold cream and curlers, to discover eight hundred square feet of living room ceiling on the terrazzo floor, and to find the building so out of plumb that the glass walls would not budge. "My drapes!" Mrs. Cohn cried.

Mr. Cohn, more concerned with the essentials, grabbed up the telephone to be greeted by utter silence. An outraged tugging at the knob proved the front door to be solidly wedged into its frame. The doorknob came off in his hands. "Just look at this mess!" Mrs. Cohn wailed. Mr. Cohn hadn't the chance because at that moment the lights went out.

During their many years of marriage, the Cohns had seen little of one another. She had been busy with their children, their grandchildren, mah-jongg, canasta, decorating courses, and Ethical Culture. His plant, poker, lodge meetings, the U.J.A., and an anonymous lady who was aging gracefully on Central Park West had kept him occupied. For the first time since their honeymoon, they spent three long days locked in each other's exclusive society, undisturbed by communication, ventilation, or food. There was, however, plenty of water in the penthouse as twin purified geysers—one hot, one cold—gushed constantly from the shattered washbasin in the half-bath. A number of terrible truths were exchanged and, by the time the Cohns were evacuated from the abandoned building, each was more than willing to go his own way.

As with every earthquake, the check-out rate in the large hotels ran to twenty per cent and there was an unprecendented demand for flights out of Acapulco when no airline was flying. The few planes for charter did a brisk business, at ten times the going rate, with tourists too hysterical to realize that they would have been much safer on the none-too-solid soil of Acapulco than braving the down drafts of the mountain ranges separating them from the capital.

All told, one-two-three was a rather blah little earthquake. Acapulco had gone through worse and would probably go through still worse. If only everybody would just shut up about one-two-three and *enjoy* themselves. . . .

Suddenly It's an Island

If comparisons could be made, the up-and-coming southern side of Acapulco near the naval station and the airport felt the tremor more than the fading-from-fashion northern end of town. The two hundred swimming pools of Las Brisas sloshed violently. Tall hotels, such as El Presidente, the Ritz, the Paraiso, the Maris, swayed and rattled like palm trees but remained standing. Hardest hit of all was Liz's little peninsula and Liz's Su Casa. But at one o'clock in the morning no one at Su Casa was thinking about an earthquake.

In Violetas, Essie Dewlap crawled wearily into bed, tried a warm, sweet smile, and abandoned the attempt. Now she was forty and she felt eighty. It wasn't easy to smile when a man had just got up from the dinner table and plunged to his death. Essie tried not to think about the noise, the confusion, the people crowding to the balustrade, the police, the reporters. She shuddered.

"Hon," Walt said, for perhaps the hundredth time, "I'm sorry."

"But it wasn't your fault, hon," Essie said, for perhaps the hundredth time. "You couldn't have any way of knowing that that poor old drunk . . ." Essie stopped. She felt that she was speaking ill of the dead, or at least the presumably dead. Essie changed her tack. "You had no way of knowing that Lee Goodwin—oh, that terrible, *terrible* man—would hound poor old Rex into . . . And April. *Poor* April!" Essie had never met anything quite like April May. She knew that, back home in Anthrax, April would never be considered Assembly material or a likely candidate for the Clara Kissinger Muggeridge Crèche. Essie hated to think what her friend Madge would have to say about anyone who looked or dressed or talked like April. But Essie's heart went out to women in love and, as unorthodox as April's relationship with Rex had been, Essie was sure that April had loved him.

"Poor little tramp," Walt said, struggling into his side of the bed. He felt old and tired and defeated. Essie's birthday had started out so well, and then that cheap loudmouth, Lee Goodwin . . .

"Hon?"

"What is it, hon?" Walt asked.

"Hon, I love it here. Really I do. Liz is an angel and there's an awfully nice crowd here. But, hon, after tonight . . . Well, I just don't feel like . . ."

"You mean you wanta go home, hon?"

"Well, home or someplace else. Someplace away from here. Like . . . *Walter!*" Estelle Dewlap was jolted into her husband's arms. She could hear the crashing of jars and bottles in the bathroom, hear the creak of beams over her head. And then the lights went out.

If Su Casa had any accommodation approaching a bridal suite, it was the bungalow Nubes. Nubes had once been a boathouse. Set off by itself in semi-isolation from the other outbuildings, it was an ideal romantic hideaway with vast views of the Pacific through its new sheet-glass windows, with its tiny green-and-white garden, with its own pocket handkerchief of private beach tucked into a secluded cove, and with the ocean lapping away beneath its random floorboards.

Liz, a bride herself when she tackled the renovation of Nubes, had gone all out on its decoration. Everything was heavenly blue and white, with masses of babies'-breath everywhere. Even as she planned Nubes, Liz knew that the place was impractical, with its thick white rugs, its shimmering Venetian mirrors, its fragile bits of blue opaline, its majestic bed canopied with acres of white organdy. Nubes was even a little silly. But Liz loved it and wanted it for Salvador and herself. Well, that was simply out of the question. Nubes was too large, too productive of revenue, and too far removed from the center of things to serve as the bridal bower of an innkeeper's wife. But Liz was so much in love and loved Nubes so much that she had privately earmarked it as a place for other lovers. A perfect spot for two. The two now in Nubes were Flossie Meyers and Queenie.

Mrs. Meyers was not a dirty guest; she was simply an untidy one. Flossie had lived out of suitcases for so long that hotel servants assumed she didn't know what to do with a chest of drawers. Flossie did know. A chest of drawers—or at least the top of it—was for the vodka, the bucket of ice, the glasses, her bottles of sedimenting Shocking perfume, and her diamonds. The drawers remained empty and so, as a rule, did the closets. Flossie always *meant* to hang her clothes, but somehow she rarely got around to it. Instead, her battered luggage overflowed with crumpled finery of the thirties and forties, "Garbo" suits by Adrian, snooded hats from Schiaparelli, the faded labels of defunct couture—Hattie Carnegie, Lucien Lelong.

Her cartwheel hat perched atop a lampshade. The light was too bright, anyhow. Her Paradise fox coat was sprawled over a luggage rack. You never knew when it might turn cold. Lank negligees, mostly in shades of what had once been pink, were draped over the most unlikely pieces of furniture. On the white chaise longue her rump-sprung old girdle lay dying. In the bathroom was Flossie's jumble of artifice—the cake mascara, the lip stencil, ten clotted bottles of "Mahogany" nail lacquer (Flossie shopped rarely and bought in wholesale lots; when she found something she fancied, she took the entire stock), the discs of Princess Pat rouge, the Lady Esther face powder, the Harper Method hairbrush.

The sitting room was taken over, more or less, by Queenie, her mange cure, her calomine lotion, her saucer of souring milk, her bowl of water, and her messes, not entirely off, but not quite on the newspapers which Flossie had spread over the white carpets.

Nubes was Pablo's despair. It had been so beautiful a week ago. He could clean it twice—ten times—a day and a moment later it looked like Carthage after a particularly unfriendly visit by the Romans. Nor was it easy to find a time to clean Nubes. When the other guests of Su Casa were up and about, Mrs. Meyers was likely to be snoring wetly beneath the wedding bed's white satin pouf. During the siesta hour or, say, at four in the morning, when everyone else was asleep, Flossie would be vivaciously at large, lurching about in grimy flounces, lisping baby talk to Queenie, or humming long-forgotten melodies to the rattling accompaniment of ice cubes.

Today had been a difficult one. Most days were difficult for Flossie, but some—about one a week—were worse than others. The really bad days were the ones when Flossie lived in the past, and this had been one of those. She had risen early, before the sun was fully up, bathed in the blue pool of a tub, dusted her blubber with Shocking powder, made up her face, and brushed her hair into a page-boy bob. She just loved staying here, high up in the Savoy-Plaza, with Hildegarde singing in the café downstairs, and the best shops in New York just a step away. Humming, "Darling, *je vous aime beaucoup*," Flossie had wriggled into her old gray girdle and had pondered what to wear—the lynx chubby or the Paradise fox? The Paradise fox. What was the point of owning one of the few ever made and not showing New York that Oklahoma got the latest fashions, too? Then she'd go out and buy a whole lot of new clothes just to please Daddy back home in Tulsa, and then . . .

and then she'd stop into F.A.O. Schwartz and buy a doll. Not some tacky WAC or WAVE or Red Cross nurse, but a big, old-fashioned doll with curls and ruffles and . . .

Flossie had stepped into her little private garden. The Savoy-Plaza sure knew how to do things right. Gardenias, camellias, white orchids just for the picking. And then Flossie had stopped. "What a nut!" Of course this wasn't New York. New York was winter and there was a war on. This was Paris, France, and Daddy said a war was coming. Yeah. Daddy was in a place called "Vitchy"—or maybe that town that sounded like "Aches and Pains"—taking the cure, and here was Flossie, twenty years old and the cutest trick in Tulsa, Oklahoma, turned loose in Paris with unlimited credit. "A-prull in Par-uss, la la la *la* la, holl-uh-day tables un-derr the treeeees." The Ritz Hotel with Schiaparelli—however you were supposed to say it—right next door, where they all spoke English. And just around the corner that big toy store. The Blue Nun? No. But something like that. Flossie would buy the doll there. A real French baby doll. Yes. It was Paris in 1939. Hitler was coming, and Daddy was going, and Flossie would show those high mucky-mucks back in Tulsa a thing or two. Flossie had stepped into her fuchsia sandals, fastening the ankle straps with a straining of leather. She had draped the two-toned wimple of her hat around soft wattles and hung the Paradise fox coat over her shoulders. Just like a movie star! Claudette Colbert in Paris.

In the blue-and-white sitting room, Queenie had whined and extended her stump of a leg. Odd. There had been no dog in the Paris Ritz—only a Labrador retriever back home in Tulsa. Folks had always said that Labradors were swell with kids.

Flossie had stepped out of the front door of Nubes and looked to the left for Schiaparelli's. But all this grass, tile roofs, palm trees, a swimming pool. No. It couldn't have been Paris, either. Maybe the Roney Plaza or the Los Angeles Biltmore. And there wasn't a toy store anywhere. Lost, confused, Flossie had swayed back into Nubes and poured her first drink of the morning as the cupid clock struck six.

And the clock had been striking six again when Flossie awoke. sometime, somehow, she had got back into—or onto—the bed and she was wearing a black lace nightgown. The nightgown had been part of her "hospital trousseau"—twenty-eight nightgowns with peignoirs to match. Two a day for a two-week stay. Her hospital wardrobe had run mainly to virtuous pinks and blues and ivories. She had included this black one just to give Daddy a thrill. Poor old poop! So proud that he had been downright pathetic. And treating Flossie like she'd been made of eggshells.

Flossie had focused her eyes up to the white organdy canopy. An oxygen tent? No! What would a big hulk like Flossie be needing with oxygen? She had turned her head on the pillow and her cheek touched something hard and cold. It was the heart-shaped picture frame. "Angel face!" Flossie had moaned. "Angel face!"

"Mande, señora?" Pablo had said. He had been surreptitiously cleaning the sitting room.

"Who?" And then it had all come clear. This was Mexico. Alcopulque. The place was called Su Casa and the boy—the good-looking one—was named Pedro.

"Uh, Peedro," Flossie had said. "Más vodka y más ice."

"Sí, señora, como no," Pablo had said. Then he had taken the heart-shaped silver frame and set it carefully on the night table.

"Nada para comer, señora? Nothing to eat? Camarones hindu. Curry of shrimp. Muy sabroso, Good." It always disturbed Pablo when people didn't eat.

Flossie hadn't wanted anything to eat, but supposed that she should order something if only for the sake of appearances.

"Yeah. Bring me a chicken san'wich. White meat."

"Sí, señora. Ahorita."

Pablo had reached for the half-finished drink on the night table, but Flossie had been too quick for him. Her hand had darted out to rescue the glass. "Más vodka, pronto, Peedro." The drink had tasted terrible; lukewarm and diluted by melted ice.

Flossie had struggled off the bed, breasts and buttocks straining against the black lace, and shuffled her bare feet into a pair of molting marabou mules. She had tottered to the chest of drawers and found an inch of vodka left in the bottle. No need for it to go to waste. Her drink replenished, she had splashed herself with Shocking and called for Queenie. "Come to muvver, poor li'l fing. You take a li'l walk wiv muvver?"

The warm vodka had struck fast; faster than usual. Flossie had been conscious of Queenie's leaping from her arms; conscious of candlelight in a garden; conscious of some sort of noisy old woman; conscious of Pablo's leading her across the lawn and back into Nubes. And then conscious of . . . nothing.

At 1:23 Flossie awoke again, this time on the floor beside her bed and tangled in the white satin pouf. The cupid clock was chiming again and would not stop chiming. More than once Flossie had come to in rooms that revolved. This room was pitching.

"Shouldn't of had that chicken san'wich," Flossie muttered. "Damn Mexican cooking." Except for a bit which Queenie had gummed, the chicken sandwich lay on the floor beside Flossie.

The room shuddered again. A fine powdering of plaster sifted down onto Flossie's face, into her hair. With a crash, the Venetian mirror above the chest of drawers fell, taking with it the vodka, the glasses, the bottles of Shocking, and a crystal lamp.

"Naughty Queenie," Flossie muttered. "Mustn't play so rough."

Whimpering and trembling, the dog burrowed under the pouf and quivered against one of Flossie's breasts. "Dat's a dood dirl. Come to muvver."

One final heave and the heart-shaped picture frame fell from the night table, striking one of Flossie's shoulders. Then the room stood still. Flossie reached out for the picture frame and held it. "Angel face," she whispered. "Angel face."

Mrs. Meyers wasn't the only drunk woman at Su Casa on the night of the earthquake. In Hortensias, Miss Bernice Potocki sprawled in her bed and groaned. There were certain differences between the two ladies' drinking patterns. Mrs. Meyers had gone to bed drunk every one of the nights Bernice had been alive—and perhaps a thousand nights more. Tonight was Bernice's first drunk.

Early in the evening Bernice had rung for Pablo and ordered a whole bottle of brandy. And then, carefully and systematically, she had drunk it, glass by glass, as she sobbed in her bed. The brandy hadn't made her happier—only sadder—but eventually it had knocked her out. And that was what Bernice had wanted.

At 1.23 in the morning Su Casa rocked and pitched. In Bernice's room a jagged fissure appeared in the plaster of the wall above her

137

bed, one of Bernice's suitcases tumbled off the luggage rack. A lamp and the empty brandy bottle fell from the bedside table and shattered on the tile floor. Bernice moaned. She was unaware that the earthquake was happening.

"Shit!" Lee Goodwin said. He felt like kicking the wastebasket across the room again; like picking up the urn of calla lilies—all right, *alcatrazes*—and smashing it into the wall. But his better judgment told him to be quiet, damned quiet. Attract no attention. Now was the time. Now, while all the commotion was going on. *Commotion?* Hell, hadn't there been enough at La Perla with all those spick divers plunging into the cove to dredge up Rex Roman; with the waiters, the police, the reporters, the mayor of Acapulco himself jabbering away in Spanish? And all over Rex Roman. How could Lee know that the old stumblebum would be so nutty as to do a Brodie off the cliff? Didn't these people have any sense of humor? "It was only a joke." "I was just kidding." "I didn't know he'd be such a fool as to . . ." "I tried to stop him but . . ." Lee had begun a dozen such apologies at least a dozen times. And how had these rich people—these so-called ladies and gentlemen—treated him? Like he wasn't even there.

Lee had started out with Essie Dewlap. "Believe me, Ess—Mrs. Dewlap—I had no idea that . . ." And what had Mrs. Hicktown done? Buried her head in her husband's big chest and sobbed like a baby, while Walt kept saying, "There, there, hon," and stared at something about three feet over Lee's head.

"Listen, Carolyn, Bill, if I'd thought for a minute that he'd take me seriously . . ." And what was the reaction from the Chicago Social Register? Carolyn had shuddered, shivered like it was ten below zero, and turned her back on him. "Bill, my wrap, please," she had murmured. And young Mr. Gold Coast had swirled some kind of fancy spick scarf around his wife's shoulders like it was a bullfighter's cape—practically hit Lee in the face with the fringe, that's what he'd done—and led her away without a word.

As for that big, blond Eagle Scout, Laddy, he had cut short Lee's preamble with a muttered something—it could have been "Screw you, Lee" or "Excuse me, please"—and gone striding off to where that stiff-assed Martínez broad was trying to control April May. April May, a smalltime call girl if Lee had ever seen one, and all these aristocratic types farting and fussing over her like she was the Queen of Heaven. If they were so bloody choosy, how could they choose a hooker like April?

Only Arthur Craine had spoken to him and no one—not even Lee—could put a favorable interpretation on what Arthur had said.

"Artie? Arthur? I . . ."

"My name, Mr. Goodwin," Arthur had said, "is Dr. Craine."

Doctor, yet! Should he call him "Doc"? Lee had begun again. "I hope you realize that I . . ."

Arthur Craine had drawn himself up like a palace guard, looked down his aquiline nose with frosty blue eyes, and said, "I realize that you are lewd and cruel and evil. I could forgive those qualities if you were not also loud, cheap, vulgar, and insufferably dull." Who did the old auntie think he was, some great English actor? "Lyewd . . . crewel . . . fawgive . . . vulgah . . . insuff-ra-bleh." And then Arthur had spat—yes, literally spat—his curtain line. "Now, get out of my sight!" On the word "sight" Arthur's rather liquid diction had caught Lee full in the eye. Lee had been wiping away the denunciation as Arthur did a full about-face and called, "Carolyn! Bill! Wait! I'm coming with you."

Having tangled with Mrs. Martínez before, Lee had seen little point in approaching her as she and Laddy supported the semiconscious April May up the stairs of La Perla.

Ladies and gentlemen, eh? Had any of them even so much as offered Lee a ride back to Su Casa as they piled into their big, fancy cars? Not on your life. Lee had taken a taxi, and it hadn't been easy to get one considering the way people were pouring out of La Perla.

"Shit," Lee said again. No two ways about it. He was a dead duck here at Su Casa. Pigeons like Walter Dewlap, Bill Williams, the Polish dame, Art Craine, and the unknown Mrs. Meyers, richer than the rest of them put together, had flown right out of his grasp. The season in Acapulco had just begun, and yet it was over for Lee Goodwin. There was only one thing to do; clear out. Go while the going was good. From across the garden, Lee could hear April's sobs and wails in Poincianas, hear Liz's steady, comforting voice, and Laddy's incoherent mumblings. Why wait to be kicked out? Why pay for another bar bill? Why be snubbed and insulted by these rich bastards? Fucking phonies! The thing to do was to pack up and get out unnoticed. Head for the airport. Buy a ticket to . . . buy a ticket to where? Well, it didn't matter, just so it was out of Acapulco—a long way out. But there wasn't much money left. Lee would have to watch every peso. Should he try his luck with other Yankee con men in Mexico City? The profession was certainly overcrowded there. Well, he'd see what was available when he got to the airport.

The thing to do was to pack and pack fast. Get out of this place without being seen. That problem had been taken care of, too. It had always been Lee's custom to find more than one means of egress from hotels, just in case. At Su Casa it had been easy. Alcatraz was on the ground floor facing the rear. It was an undesirable room. Undesirable to everyone but Lee. There were grilles on the windows, yes, but Lee had discovered that one of them was more than a little insecure. In his spare time, Lee had worked it quite loose. All that was needed was one good shove . . . and then Lee could pick up a taxi on the highway. Easier said than done, but Lee would worry about that later. He could always hitch a ride with some sucker; give out a hoked-up story about his car breaking down and having to catch a plane. Matter of life or death; sick daughter; blah blah blah. He'd get out of here or his name wasn't . . . well, what, exactly, was his name?

Drawing the curtains and covering the one lighted lamp with his dark blue sport shirt, Lee began hastily and systematically to pack. It was exactly 1:15.

Seven minutes later Lee and his bags were ready. The heat of the lamp had scorched the cheap rayon shirt that Lee had draped over the shade. Fuck it. He'd leave it for that dumb spick bellboy. A tip. Lee switched out the lamp, hoisted himself and his luggage to the window ledge. He grasped the grille. All that was needed was one good shove and . . .

Lee heard a roar, a rumble, a terrible cracking. He tried to cry out but no sound would come. He clung to the grille as he felt himself sway backward into the room and then, too fast for him to loosen his grip, the direction was reversed and Lee found himself falling headlong into the garden. With a screech, the grille came loose from the wall. Lee, still clinging to the grille, landed flat on his face in the shrubbery. "Mommy! Mommy! Mommy!" Lee whimpered. "Mommy, don't let 'em hurt me. Don't let 'em . . ." The ground heaved beneath him and something heavy struck Lee Goodwin on the head. He regained consciousness some minutes later, half buried beneath a pile of mossy tiles from the roof of Su Casa.

"This is the end," Roland said. He had said it several times since Chip and that cheap little Mexican servant had slammed out the room—been ordered out, rather—but it still sounded good. So final.

Roland rose, lit a cigarette, drifted to the railing of his balcony, and stared dramatically at the ocean. Should he leap from the balcony? Well, no. It hung a scant fifteen feet above the rose garden. A plunge would be painful, resulting possibly in a sprained ankle or a broken wrist, but hardly fatal.

The breeze whipped Roland's crepe-de-chine kimono around his bare legs. Chip! Took him out of the gutter. Well, the pantry, actually. Gave him everything he has. Taught him everything he knows. Now he'd grabbed it all and gone. Not entirely true. Chip was gone all right, but when he and Florentino had left it was with only the clothes on his back and what was left of the five hundred pesos Roland had given him. There had been neither the time nor the opportunity to reap the rewards of true love; not with Roland standing there in his various lotions and unguents like a well-larded avenging angel. True, Chip's severance pay had included a ring that matched Roland's, a gold cigarette case and lighter (plated), a gold identification bracelet, and a large St. Christopher medal. But the bulk of the investment hung in the dressing room of Rosas or remained securely under lock and key in Roland's apartment back in Allentown. It would have been no arduous task to have found a size thirty-six replacement, but Roland was enjoying his misery.

Slash his wrists with a razor and let his life gush gradually down the drain? It wasn't that simple. In the first place, Roland shaved electrically, and, in the second place, the sight of blood made him sick.

"This is the end," Roland sighed again. "Six months of my life gone. Gone, gone." It sounded so good that he said it again. "Gone."

Having performed—starred—in acrimonious leave-takings before, Roland knew all the lines, all the gestures, all the stage business. But for Roland, each violent parting was a new opening night. Forgotten now was last season's Grand Guignol with Kurt after seven stormy weeks of try-outs. Forgotten, the big renunciation scene with Larry in the black-and-white apartment above the boutique. (It had been tones of beige then.) Forgotten, too, the dramatic declamations to Leslie and Ernest and Victor and George and Johnny No. 1 and Johnny No. 2 and What-was-his-name and Bobby and Chris. These closet dramas, running pretty much to formula, had been played in bedrooms and living rooms or, quite publicly, in bars and restaurants, on ships and beaches, as well as that unforgettable name-calling episode with What-was-his-name in the Men's Department at Bloomingdale's.

"But this time it was the Real Thing," Roland whimpered. Each time—times ranging from three weeks to three years—had been the Real Thing. "I was so sure." And Roland should have been sure! Sure that he had picked another typical hustler; sure that the boy was more interested in getting than giving; sure that his own sense of superiority, his constant catechism of the chic, his nonstop nagging would eventually bring about rebellion.

Sleeping pills? "Damn!" There were just four left in Roland's toilet kit—his nécessaire. Not nearly enough to finish him off. "Damn, damn, damn!" Only yesterday Roland had been in a huge farmacia stocking up on orange sticks, hair spray, suntan lotion, and had noticed a great pyramid of Seconol displayed on the counter. Enough to lull a whole city. If only he'd . . . "But yesterday we were so happy. We'd never had an argument—not even a cross word. And now . . . now . . ."

Drowning? Roland looked out to sea. The Pacific was never

cold at Acapulco, but it looked a bit rough and Roland had heard that sharks lurked rather close to the shore at night. He'd always fancied Fredric March's suicide scene in *A Star Is Born*—the foulard robe dropping onto the wet sand, the bare feet stepping into the surf—but on the other hand . . . The swimming pool? No. Out of the question.

The bathtub? The bathtub in Rosas was a semicircular confection of sparkling pink mosaic overhanging the rose garden like an opera box. It had been constructed that way because, frankly, there wasn't enough space in the tiny bathroom to accommodate even a stall shower. But jutting out in its own glass bay, the tub had glamor. It offered the bather an unrestricted view of the rose garden and it offered anyone who happened to be in the rose garden an unrestricted view of the bather, albeit through pink net curtains.

Gradually the idea began to grow. Yes. Roland would take the four sleeping pills, fill the tub to the brim with warm water, and then get in. The pills wouldn't kill him, but they would knock him out and then gradually, gradually his head would sink beneath the surface. No pain. No fighting the water. Tomorrow they would discover him, poor Roland, at peace at last. And when Chip came crawling back, as Chip most assuredly would, he would find . . . he would find . . . Roland could almost see it now; the darkened *sala*, the white bier, four tall silver candlesticks, Señora Martínez in black with a lace mantilla, Carolyn Williams, the little Polish countess, Bill Williams and Arthur Craine, and in the middle of it all, Roland himself, laid out like a martyred monk in his white crepe-de-chine robe, his long hands crossed on his chest. Roland checked his nails. Glossy as pink pearls and a good length. Then Chip would realize what he'd lost. Then, when it was too late.

Roland put on the lights in the bathroom, approved of the flattering glow reflected from all that pink tile. He turned on the taps in the tub, tested the temperature of the water, and dumped in some bath essence. The tub was enormous—a perfect size for drowning—and would take some time to fill.

Back in the bedroom he glanced about with a practiced eye. He wanted to leave everything in order. He could almost hear Señora

Martínez now: "Such a fastidious guest!" With a slight shudder, Roland smoothed the spread on the bed where he had found Chip and that little Mexican hustler. The hotel bill had been paid this morning. There was more than enough in his wallet to cover another day—*single*, if you please. Funeral expenses would be deducted from his estate. He emptied the ashtrays into the fireplace. Was there anything in the drawer of the night table that should be disposed of? Yes, there was. That and his copy of *The Call of the Goose*. Great art or not, the book was pornographic and Roland didn't want anyone thinking . . . With his gold lighter he lit the kindling laid on the earth and, page by page, tore *The Call of the Goose* from its cheap binding. It burned beautifully. Anything else? Oh, yes. From his passport case Roland took the Polaroid photograph of Chip lying on that zebra rug, a tangible memento of happier nights. Roland looked at it for the last time. Chip's eyes always were too close together. "Serve him right if I sent it to the New York *Times*! Not that they'd dream of printing it." The photograph went up in a flash of yellow flame. Anything else? Yes! The plane tickets! Roland had them in his passport case. He wouldn't be needing his. As for Chip, let the little whore *walk* home! Traveler's checks? They all bore Roland's florid signature. Chip couldn't get his hands on a penny!

Chip's clothes! There were a couple of thousand dollars'— Roland's dollars—worth of resort things hanging in Chip's closet. Attempting to burn them would take all night and probably set fire to the whole house. Slicing them into ribbons might be effective, but Roland had only his nail scissors handy. Instead, Roland locked the sliding doors in the dressing room and pitched the keys out into the darkness. He had heard somewhere that in Mexico the quarters of the deceased were sealed and remained sealed until the rightful heirs appeared. That would be Roland's hulking sister, Harriet, who now stood guard over the boutique and who felt no iota of Roland's recent affection for Chip.

Roland snorted. Just let Chip flaunt his mahogany suntan through thong sandals and an eyelet shirt in the blizzards of Allentown! Assuming, of course, that Chip ever got back there.

A will? There was no need. Everything Roland had would go

automatically to Harriet. He supposed that she'd fill the boutique with a lot of Pennsylvania Dutch Kitsch, or close it entirely. But nothing could be done about that. Roland and Harriet had never seen eye to eye about anything. No point even to leaving her a note. Instead, he printed Harriet's name, address, area code, and telephone number on a sheet of writing paper and pinned it to his pillow. Then he hung out the Do Not Disturb sign and threw the bolt on the door.

In the bathroom the tub was full, but a trifle too hot. Roland plugged in his electric razor and shaved, brushed his hair and gave it a good going over with waterproof hair spray. He hardly expected people to say, "Goodness gracious, what a well-groomed cadaver!" But, on the other hand, Roland liked to look his best on all occasions. He took the last four sleeping pills and lowered himself into the tub. It was one o'clock. He guessed that it would take the pills about twenty minutes to do their work.

Roland gazed out through the semicircle of glass into the rose garden with its candles in hurricane lamps flickering dimly among the blooms. It looked almost like a solemn requiem mass. Chip would be sorry. Good and sorry.

The water was deliciously warm and soothing. It came right up to his chin. Soon Roland's head would slip under. He could almost see the front pages of the Allentown *Call* and the *Chronicle.* "SCION OF LOCAL FAMILY DIES IN MEXICO . . . last male survivor of the distinguished Preston, Voorhees, and Buchmacher families . . . age 44 . . ." Damn them, they would know his age to the minute! "My God, Zsa-Zsa!" Roland sat bolt upright in the tub. What would ever happen to his pet poodle, Zsa-Zsa, blind in one eye and due to come into heat next month? Ah, well, too late. Roland's sister Harriet, proud breeder of bull mastiffs, was specific in her dislike of Zsa-Zsa, but she would never let the poor little thing suffer. A trip to the vet's and it would all be over in a . . . all be over in a . . . the pills were working faster than Roland had supposed. He had never taken more than two before . . . more than two be—

The water rushing up Roland's nostrils roused him temporarily. Things surfaced in his mind—a set of Belter chairs on consignment to that woman in Emmaus, the cretonne for Mrs. Fenstermacher, Zsa-Zsa's estrogen shot. He tried to rise in the bathtub. As he did so, he was thrown down into the water. He felt himself being shaken and churned, felt the breaking of glass, felt a painful thud, the bursting of mosaic tiles. Then he felt nothing. A few minutes later Roland was more or less awake, more or less alive, stark naked and vomiting in a broken, empty bathtub in the middle of the rose garden.

". . . goaded him! Absolutely drove him into diving off that cliff," Carolyn Williams said, beating her fist on the arm of her chair.

"I know, Carolyn," Bill said. "But there's nothing we can do about it. Poor old Rex is gone now. Not a trace of him."

"Not even a Phi Beta Kappa key," Arthur said softly.

"What?" Carolyn asked sharply.

"Nothing," Arthur said. The witticism was perhaps ill-advised.

"But couldn't any of you men have stopped him? Or at least told that bastard Lee Goodwin to shut up? Did we all have to sit there like stones and watch poor Rex kill himself?"

"Carolyn, baby, relax," Bill said.

"*Relax?* My God, don't we ever do anything *but* relax? Can we just sit there in a nightclub and watch a man kill himself and then come home and relax? That's the trouble with us, Bill. With you and me and Arthur. All of us. We're too goddamned poised and pulled-together and *soigné* and, yes, too *relaxed* to even notice something as real as life or death."

Arthur was on the verge of saying something about split infinitives and then thought better of it.

"Carolyn, if you'll tell me what you think I can do about it," Bill said, "I'll sure as hell try. But I just don't feel . . ."

"That's the trouble, Bill. You don't feel. We don't feel. We're all so damned civilized and polite and sophisticated that by tomorrow we'll act as though this whole thing were some minor social gaffe, like passing out in a finger bowl. Tomorrow we'll all get into our city clothes and stand around at some sort of memorial service. We'll take poor old April to the plane—give her money if she needs it; what's money to any of us? Then we'll dine out on it for

146

a week or two, like we all did with the Fairbank divorce . . ."

As we all did, Arthur corrected mentally. As with all subjects that did not specifically concern him, Arthur was growing bored. He'd never seen Carolyn carry on this way. Ophelia!

"And then do you know what we'll do? We'll forget about it. Just as if we hadn't known Rex; as though he were some stranger who'd died in China."

"Hong Kong flu?" Arthur was about to suggest.

Carolyn got to her feet. So did Bill. "Bill, I tell you, I can't stand any more of this. This perfect life. This eating and sleeping and saying the . . . Bi-i-i-i-ll"

Carolyn was thrown into Bill's arms. The room lurched crazily, the candlesticks on the mantel fell with a crash. On the floor above, furniture rolled and toppled. The lights went out.

Arthur Craine was too frightened to move. He felt himself go gray and was grateful for the darkness. He gripped the arms of his chair for what seemed an hour while Margaritas swayed and heaved. And then it stopped. Arthur waited for a moment. Yes, it was really over. He felt for, then picked up a candlestick from where it had landed. Using both hands to steady his violent trembling, he began to light the candles. "Zut alors, Carolyn," Arthur said, "you take all the fun out of an earthquake."

Salvador came to in a ditch in front of—but not on—the property of the Princess-up-the-Hill. Was it possible that such pain could exist? He was battered and bloody and bruised and torn. He tried to get to his feet and fell into the weeds and nettles at the roadside. A car sped by and, in the glare of the headlights, Salvador saw a flash of white. It was himself. His clothes—such as they were— had been put back on him. The white lace shirt hung in shreds, the trousers were torn and stiff with his blood and excrement. . . . What time was it? The wristwatch had been snatched from his arm, he remembered that, but now he saw its dim golden glitter in the road a few feet away. Could he possibly crawl out and reach it? No. He lay face down, gasping for breath. . . . The check! Did he still have the check? He had put it in his pocket just before . . . just before . . . Was it still there? In trying to protect himself, his arms had been nearly torn from their sockets. Salvador felt that he would never be able to use them again. But the check. He had to find out. Inch by inch, he lowered his right arm to his pocket. The pain was so great that he had to stop halfway and rest. A pink-and-white Jeep jiggled by on its way to Las Brisas. He heard an angry American voice saying, "Fifty *bucks* for steaks you couldn't cut with an ax?" The Jeep ran over Salvador's watch. Sobbing like a baby, Salvador watched the red taillights disappear around a curve in the road. He began again to reach for his pocket. He tried not to scream with agony—but—yes! Yes! There it was! The check for a million pesos, signed by the Princess-up-the-Hill. Knowing that he had the money gave Salvador new strength. He inched the check from his pocket and held it in his hand.

One million pesos! Now he couldn't die here in a ditch like some vagrant. He was a rich man. A millionaire! There was Su Casa just across the road, floodlights illuminating the discreet sign above its wrought-iron gates. Could he possibly get to his feet and make it? Twenty yards, twenty-five. Could he do it? He would have to. Across the road was his own property, his home, his wife. Liz would take care of him, wash his wounds, put him to bed, order brandy, call a doctor. Liz!

Groaning with agony, Salvador rose to his feet. He felt that his guts were going to fall apart. Clutching himself, he staggered into the road. The pain was too much. He couldn't make it. He saw the carnival lights of a wildly decorated Acapulco taxicab rounding the curve, heard the scream of brakes. Heard the driver shout, "*Borracho!*" Drunk. If only he were. "Liz," he whimpered. He limped forward. Only a few more steps—nine, eight, seven, six. The pain was killing, but he had to get home. Five, four, three, two. Salvador fell headlong into the gravel of the driveway at Su Casa. Home! At last he was home.

It was a long way from the gate to the main house, but at least Salvador was home. He could crawl. Even if he couldn't make it, someone would find him—one of the servants, people coming back from the evening at La Perla. Perhaps it would be that American couple in their big, air-conditioned Buick, or Nacho and the *polaca*, or Laddy and Liz in the station wagon. He could tell them that he'd been beaten up and robbed by thugs, that he'd been in an accident. He'd think of something.

He looked at the check in the reflection of the floodlights. One million pesos! What he'd gone through to get it was another matter. But here it was. The check folded in his fist, he began to crawl along the side of the driveway.

Salvador's progress was slow and agonizing. Every few feet he would have to stop and lie prone in the flower beds that bordered the driveway. The pain was excruciating. He was bleeding again. Insects swarmed around him, droning, stinging. Would no one drive in and discover him? No. The parking lot was directly below him. In it were Walt's big Buick and the Su Casa station wagon. He had no idea of the time. Yet the windows were lighted, candles flickered in the garden. Salvador tried to call for help. It was hopeless. The roar of the ocean, the hiss of the breeze, the soughing of the palms drowned out his voice. He glanced again at the check in his fist, counting on it to give him strength, and struggled again to his hands and knees.

Halfway. More than halfway. Here was the hole in the driveway. Hole? By now it was a small lagoon. Salvador could hear the seawater lapping into it. Mexican servants were so lazy. Couldn't they ever do anything right? From his sickbed tomorrow he'd fire that indolent Pablo and . . . The earth heaved beneath Salvador, throwing him onto his back into the gravel. He screamed with pain. He was shaken and churned in the gravel. He heard the ground rumble, felt it beginning to split beneath him. Staring up in terror he saw the telephone pole above sway, rock, dance. He got to his feet, felt the water churning around his knees. He heard a sharp crack, the shriek of splitting wood. He fell on his face in the gravel, felt the sea swirling around his legs. "Mother of God forgive me for I have . . ." The telephone pole crashed down. The earth gave way beneath his feet. Salvador was silent.

Pablo sat waiting in the room he shared with Florentino. Save for the votive candles flickering in front of the figure of San Martín de Porres, the room was dark. That was the way Pablo wanted it. He was waiting. Waiting for Florentino. He would wait all night if necessary until Florentino came sneaking in, then Pablo would really let him have it. He'd tear the cheap nylon shirt off his back; grab him by his greasy hair and shake him until his teeth rattled loose; cuff him until his cheeks burned; rub his nose in his own stinking Machisimo to see if that would grow, too. Pablo had had enough.

Pablo didn't care what Florentino did after the work was finished; in fact, he preferred having Florentino away. But today Florentino had left before the sun was down; gone off in a taxicab with the pretty boy who lived in Rosas. Not a word, no "con su permiso." Florentino had simply gone, wearing his cursi nylon shirt and leaving his uniform in an untidy ball on the floor.

It had been Pablo, and Pablo alone, to light the dozens of candles, fill the water carafes, tidy the rooms, turn down the beds, tend the bar, and answer the bells. Ai, the bells! The old borracha out in Nubes wanted more ice, more vodka—as always—and this time even a chicken sandwich, which Pablo had known would remain untouched. And today, just to make Pablo's life a little harder, la condesa in Hortensias had ordered a whole bottle of brandy. After spending the afternoon with Don Ignacio, what she really needed was a strong ducha and a trip to the confessional. Pablo had felt a little sorry for her at the time, but he had been too busy to squander much sympathy.

The bruja from Texas had kept her bell ringing as though Su Casa were under an interdicto. More writing paper, more water, more ice. The dinner menu. Fresh shrimps or canned? From the Pacific or the Gulf of Mexico? How could one be sure that they weren't tainted? Naturally the Señora Bullock couldn't have said any of these things without the Señorita No-yes there to interpret. Even then it hadn't been easy. And just when it had seemed that there could be no more questions, no more problems from Amapolas, the borracha and her gozque had come reeling across the garden to be led back to Nubes and put to bed, while the bruja screamed as though she had seen Satan himself instead of a harmless old drunk.

And dinner! Dinner should have been simple with most of Su Casa going to La Perla; with la condesa weeping and guzzling brandy in Hortensias; with the *borracha* safely in bed in Nubes; and with *el señor Rolando* locked into Rosas because his *sodomita* had gone off with Florentino. But dinner had been the worst of all.

Pablo had found Aurelia drunk in the kitchen, weeping into a puddle of tequila. Nothing had been ready. Señora Bullock and her girls had appeared early. Mrs. Bullock had sent back the first plate of curry as being too strong; the second plate as being too mild— "Why it's no more'n cream sauce." She had grumbled constantly over the third. And when it had seemed that the meal had at last been accomplished, a carload of six *gringos* had appeared asking if Su Casa served dinner. It did. They had ordered impossible drinks—banana daiquiris and brandy Alexanders and Singapore slings. They had demanded dishes that had never been on the menu, while Aurelia had bumbled around the kitchen, alternately cursing and singing. Her songs had been viler than her curses.

They had demanded a tour of Su Casa, trying to force their way into the bedrooms—even the *señora's* quarters. They had complained about the prices and the service, and then had got their car stuck in the watery hole in the driveway, demanding that Pablo dig them out.

And when it had all been over, when the last dish had been washed and dried, what had happened? The others had come back from La Perla, the blonde *puta* crying and screaming like a *guacamaya*. It had meant that Pablo must rise, dress, mix drinks and, as the last straw, drive the station wagon to the open-all-night *farmacia* for a *sedativo*.

It was too much to be borne by one man. As for that Florentino . . . Pablo went to the window and squinted out. He saw—or thought he saw—something crawling. Could Florentino be too drunk to walk? Good! When Pablo finished with him, he wouldn't be able to . . .

Pablo clutched the bars of the window grille with all his might, lowered himself to his knees and commenced to pray. The beds skidded wildly across the room. The crucifix swung out from the wall, slapped back against it, and fell to the floor. The beams above his head groaned and screeched. The new brick-and-plaster partition separating this room from Aurelia's buckled and collapsed in a cloud

151

of dust. Pablo felt the new floor tiles beneath his knees shimmy loose from their mortar and clink together while, overhead, he heard the ancient tiles of the roof clash and rumble, rip free from their bed of moss. A rain of them fell past his window to thud heavily to the trembling earth below.

The top floor was no place to be during an earthquake, yet here he was. If it had been a really old house, Su Casa would have been safer. Buildings put up by Cortés and the conquistadores had stood firm for centuries. But this place had been built within Pablo's memory, thrown together quickly and cheaply with "seconds" and the demolitions of more substantial houses.

With earthquakes, familiarity does not breed contempt. Pablo had been through a dozen big ones before, and each was more terrifying than the last. The utter frailty of the strongest human, of the firmest building, of the stoutest tree, of the ground itself, was driven home in a message of sheer helplessness. Bracing himself in the window frame, which was supposed to be the safest place during a temblor, Pablo raced through half-a-dozen prayers.

With the wail of a banshee, Aurelia clambered over the pile of plaster, bricks, and girlie pictures that had once been a wall, her bulging belly in the flour-sacking nightgown leading like the prow of a galleon. An incoherent gurgle and she was upon Pablo, knocking him to the shuddering floor, where she lay on top of him blubbering and beseeching heaven for deliverance.

"Stop it, idiot!" Pablo shouted. "Stand in the window where you have a chance." Grasping the grille again, he rose to his feet, dragging Aurelia with him, where she clung to him, heaving and quaking.

"Look!" Pablo shouted. Out in the driveway, the figure in white had risen drunkenly. The telephone pole rocked and swayed. Pablo heard the splintering of wood, saw a blue-white flash of light, and saw the pole topple, pinning the figure to the ground. And then the earth behind him gave way. With a roar, what had been the driveway crumbled and disappeared into the churning ocean. The figure pinned beneath the fallen telephone pole raised both arms in supplication and then lay flat on the gravel.

"Madre de Diós! Es Florentino!" Pablo hated Florentino, but not that much. Not enough to want to see him dead.

"*No es Florentino*," Aurelia screamed. "*Es el señor!*"

And then it was over. The earthquake, with its rumbling and crashing, had ended. There was only darkness and, in an eerie stillness, the sound of the sea sucking the earth away. Pablo grabbed his flashlight and spun down the spiral iron staircase. Heedless of slashing his bare feet, he raced along the gravel driveway. There was Don Salvador, his torso flattened beneath the telephone pole, his legs hanging limply over the edge of a jagged precipice and, far below, the black, churning sea.

"*Señor! Señor!*" Pablo cried. Even as he said the words he knew that there would be no response.

Julie was awakened by the thud of a leaden body leaping onto her own, by a violent pawing and clawing of her coverlet, by a slobbery caterwauling in her ear. It was Lou Ann, a pulsing mountain of hysteria, her big, bare bottom bouncing obscenely beneath her nightgown.

"Julie! Julie! It's an earthquake! We're all bein' shook to kingdom come! We're gonna die, Julie! *Die!* I don't wanta die. I'm too young!"

With all of her strength, Julie grasped Lou Ann by her bare shoulders and flung her off the bed. A certain capricious pitch of the earth aided her effort immeasurably. Lou Ann landed on the floor between the beds with a gratifying plop and, over her, the carafe of ice water from the night table. Lou Ann squealed and then was silent.

"Now shut up," Julie said. "You're not helping things by acting like a baby."

"J-Julie. I'm scared."

"So am I, but . . ."

Amapolas rolled and rocked. Two poppy-red armchairs danced a wild fandango across the bedroom floor, collided with the dresser, and stopped dead in their tracks. Lou Ann began one of her better screams and then stopped. She had been hopelessly outclassed by a scream from the other bedroom.

The bulk of Mrs. Bullock shot through the sitting room of Amapolas through the front door into the garden, ripping her nightgown on the curlicues of the terrace furniture. It was the same Mrs. Bullock who, scant hours before, had been outraged by the sight of Flossie Meyers in deshabille. She charged onto the lawn, falling, crawling, rolling, rising, and falling yet again. To a woman who could rock the foundations of a hotel over mended sheets, cold toast, or a suspicion of mice, an earthquake presented a major challenge. In the tumult of her terror, Mrs. Bullock left nothing to be desired. With a final jolt, the earthquake subsided, leaving Mrs. Bullock sprawled on the lawn, her bunion pads and corn plasters thumping rhythmically against the turf, momentarily heedless that her upper plate in its bubbly glass was smiling encouragement at the terrified Susan.

"April, dear," Liz said again, "you must get to bed. Try to rest." Liz had forced her to drink a glass of hot milk laced with enough barbiturates to quiet a wild stallion. Still there was no reaction, no letup of April's tears. Her dry, racking sobs continued.

"April," Liz said firmly, changing tactics from doting mother to stern schoolmistress. "April!"

April lifted her ruined, tear-streaked face. Her stiffened, towering hair-do stood out from her head like the petals of a Fuji chrysanthemum, her reddened eyes burned dully from the smudges of black and iridescent blue that had earlier enhanced their lids. The double rows of false lashes, partially unstuck, drooped like sodden bunting.

"I lovedum," April said flatly. "Rex and me, we was gonna make pictures together. Now he's gone."

"May-maybe not," Laddy mumbled, speaking for the first time in half an hour. "The tides around here are tricky. And Rex is a strong swimmer. And maybe . . . maybe . . ."

Laddy gave it up. He didn't believe a word of his message of false cheer and didn't expect even an imbecile like April to believe it, either. Laddy's voice trailed off and he retreated into his embarrassment. Nothing could make Laddy as miserable as a woman's tears. His wives, every girl he had ever known, could reduce Laddy to a pulp by turning on the tears.

It was horrible, ghastly, gruesome, grisly; the most dreadful thing Liz had ever witnessed in her life. And yet it kept Liz's mind off her own problems. April had loved Rex and Liz's heart went out to all women in love.

"April?" Liz said again, this time the tone a little warmer, like that of a dedicated nurse trying to rouse a sleeping patient for middle-of-the-night medication. "A-pril?"

"Huh?" April said dully.

"Now, April, I'm going to help you into bed. If you need anything, you can always ring. Where's your nightgown?"

Silence.

"Where is your nightgown, April?"

"I don't have none. Rexy always liked to sleep rore." With that the sobbing renewed.

"All right, then," Liz said, raising her voice above the sobs. "Laddy? Would you mind getting the hell out of here while I . . ."

"Me?" Laddy shot to his feet. "Not at all." He had already reached the door and opened it. "Well, see you in the . . ." The little tool shed, now resplendently fitted out and called Poincianas, seemed to leap into the air. Helplessly Laddy stumbled and slid across its glossy tilework and sprawled over the back of a love seat. From her perch on the edge of the bed, Liz was thrown against April and onto the floor. Or, rather, the floor seemed to come up to receive Liz. "Laddy! It's an . . ." The lights went out. In silence the three of them pitched and rolled around the tiny bungalow. Would this never stop? Yes. Finally it did.

Laddy was the first to speak. "Are . . . are you all right?"

"Y-yes, thanks. I th-think so."

Bumping into the overturned furniture, Laddy hurried to the terrace and brought in the one hurricane lamp that had miraculously remained upright. "H-here's some light. I g-guess the electricity's off."

"Yes. I guess it is," Liz said.

In the dancing candlelight, April May sat like a statue on her bed, exactly as she had been before.

"It's nothing, April," Liz said, trying as much to convince herself. "Don't worry."

"I'm not worried," April said flatly. Systematically her sobs began again. Mrs. Bullock, trumpeting like a mastodon, could be heard pounding over the lawn in her bare feet. Her bleating was operatic. Attracted like a gypsy moth to the candle flame burning in Poincianas, she tripped over the brick floor of the terrace and fell, toothless, into the room. "It's an earthquake, hear? An *earthquake!*"

"Do tell," Liz said.

"I'm gettin' outta here right now. My girls and I."

"I thought you'd already gone," Liz said.

"You'll be hearing from me!"

"I can hardly wait."

"I'm gonna till iv'ryone I know just what kinda place this . . ."

"Get out," Liz said quietly.

"Wh-what?"

"I said get out. Go! Now." Liz turned to her brother. "Laddy. Have you got a cigarette?"

"Me? Sure. Here. April?"

"Thanks, but I don't smoke," April said flatly.

"That's very wise of you, I'm sure," Liz said. "Thanks, Laddy."

"Don't mention it."

In silence Liz and Laddy, smoking, sat with April. Once Liz got up to find an ashtray in the shambles of the bungalow. *Craig's Wife*, she thought. What difference could a few ashes possibly make? April was still now. Numb in her misery.

Laddy was deeply shaken emotionally, slightly battered physically.

Liz finished her cigarette and snuffed it out with ridiculous care into the ashtray. She rose. "Well, April, if you really think you'll be all right, I should go and check on the house. The lights. See if there's any serious . . ."

"Go ahead. I'm okay," April said.

"Well . . ." Liz began.

"*Señora! Señora!*" It was Pablo.

Oh dear, Liz thought, now do I have to deal with hysterical servants? She tried to compose a comforting sentence in Spanish and wished that Laddy would do it for her. "*No molestase, Pablo.*" No, she wasn't saying it right at all. "*Estaba no más que un . . . un tremolo . . .* " Tremolo? No, that was Italian, had something to do with music. "*Un temblor.*"

"*Señora! Señora! Es el señor!*"

Clutching Laddy's arm, Liz stared stupidly down at Salvador's broken body.

"Back broken, I'm afraid," Laddy mumbled.

"Yes," Liz said.

"And the whole causeway has gone," Laddy said. "I mean, suddenly it's an island."

"Yes," Liz said. "Suddenly it's an island."

"It's lucky that . . . well, I mean, if this telephone pole hadn't fallen on Salvador he'd have been swept away. I mean, you never would have known what happened to him."

"No, I never would, would I," Liz said flatly. It was neither a question nor a statement.

Laddy was speaking to Pablo in Spanish. Something about trying to lift the telephone pole so they could remove Salvador's body. There were, apparently, certain engineering problems involved. While the men stood aside discussing them in respectful *sotto voce*, Liz gazed down on her husband. Stooping, she removed a crumpled piece of paper from his hand. In the beam of Pablo's flashlight she examined it. It was a check for a million pesos, written in a secretarial hand, and signed by the Princess-up-the-Hill.

How very strange. Why would anyone give Chavo a check for a million pesos? Liz didn't want to answer her own question. Neatly and systematically, as she did everything, Liz tore the check first in halves, then in quarters, then in eighths, then in sixteenths, then in thirty-seconds. Standing at the edge of the washed-away land, she dropped the pieces into the wind and watched them blow away.

Desolation Might Be Fun

Even without the goddamned earthquake and that crazy spick kid going clear off his nut, Chip knew he was in trouble.

He didn't mind breaking off with Roland—always telling him

how to talk, what to wear, what to eat and what fork to eat it with. Chip had been planning to leave, anyhow. But he hadn't planned it quite like this.

Roland had given him five hundred pesos in the morning. That was like forty bucks. By the time Chip had bought lunch and a couple of drinks at the beach and taken a taxi back to Su Casa there was maybe thirty left; Kee-rist, this money confused him! Then there was the Big Scene with Roland, just like in the "cultural dramas" on TV which Roland forced him to watch. What crap!

So he'd left—escaped was the way he thought of it—with Florentino, the nutty spick, saying "Ai no go back!" That goes for me, too, Chip thought. Chip knew he couldn't face Roland again. Florentino couldn't either, and he had Señor and Señora Martínez to cut him apart, too. Chip hated to leave all those clothes; he sure could use them to hook someone new. Well, tough tit, he thought inappropriately. He'd better stick with the kid until he could figure out what to do next. For one thing, Chip didn't know enough Spanish to get very far. For another, he couldn't get that far on thirty bucks.

Time for figuring tomorrow. For a while he'd have some fun, but first he'd put a little distance between himself and Su Casa.

For dinner, Florentino had chosen a real dump. By ordering cheap Chip had got them out for a few dollars, including a tiny tip and a dirty look from the waiter. Well, the waiter could go screw himself!

Communication had been difficult: Florentino's English limited to "Yes," "No," "Good," and "No good." Even so, it had been more effective than Chip's Spanish. Florentino had hailed a taxi to take Chip to a place that was "Good. *Muy* good." "*Muy* good" had turned out to be a gay bar with a lot of young Mexican fairies screaming on the dance floor. And then this place—God alone knew where it was—for fifty pesos, cash, in advance. Chip watched a cockroach meander up the wall, listened to the drip of the tap in the rusty washbasin, felt the coarse manta sheet under him, the wafer-thin blanket over him. Kee-rist, he'd spent a lot of nights in a lot of crummy places, but nothing like this. Bowery time!

They'd hardly hit the sack when all hell broke loose. Chip had thought that the whole hotel would cave in. The bed had. And the kid carrying on like crazy.

Chip had been scared, too. Good and scared. After it was all over, Chip had gone to the toilet down the hall. When he had come back, the kid and his clothes were gone; that is to say, Chip's clothes were gone. Chip's now-empty wallet was on the beat-up little table. A quick search of the room disclosed only two of Chip's possessions left. His gold cigarette case and lighter were under the collapsed bed. Chip took his last cigarette from the case, lit it and got out of bed. It was either wear the kid's clothes or go naked.

What stuff! A cheap nylon shirt with bullfighters all over it, a pair of he-whore pants, and Jesus sandals. It was the kind of junk Chip used to wear—sateen bowling jackets and phosphorescent pants—before Roland came along.

Chip could barely get into the shirt and the trousers. Everything was too short and too tight. His heels overhung the sandals by an inch. In the pants pocket he found a dirty handkerchief and fifteen pesos. That would be like, say, a dollar twenty. Him, Chip, in a foreign country wearing some clown clothes and with a dollar twenty to his name. Kee-rist!

An idea began to grow. Chip would take a taxi back to Su Casa and lie low until Roland went out. Roland was always tracking down garbage for his junk shop back in Allentown. Then Chip would slip into the room. He'd pick up his plane ticket, his clothes, his bags, and any cash that happened to be around. Roland always kept a few American dollars in his passport case for emergencies. Then he'd decide what to do. It wasn't stealing—the stuff was his, wasn't it? And if Roland decided to make trouble . . . well, he never would, not with the stories Chip could tell. Nine o'clock. "Now," Chip said, with a disdainful glance at the room, "to get back to civilization."

Nine o'clock and the Princess-up-the-Hill was out on her terrace, her caftan flapping in the wind. She must speak to someone—or write to someone—about that. Acapulco wasn't supposed to have

159

wind. A breeze, yes. A gale, never! It was an ugly day, gray and blustery, with angry whitecaps on the ocean. But it had been such a beautiful night. *Exciting!* That Martínez had fought like a tiger trying to protect himself. Of course it had been hopeless from the start, but his struggles had made the performance all the more interesting.

And, for an encore, her first earthquake! It had been thrilling being tossed about on her big silver bed by no one at all. Actually, nothing had happened. Well, yes. The Princess had suffered an irreparable loss or two—that Persian bridal mirror in the cocktail room, a Chinese ceramic figurine of the K'ang Hsi period and, oh, yes, a rather good Venetian glass goblet, quite old she believed. Otherwise the house had stood firm. And why not? It was built on solid money. Nine o'clock and she hadn't gone to bed yet! Well, she was going. If *this* was the kind of beautiful Acapulco day her boys were always raving about, they were welcome to it.

That Martínez, the princess mused again. He'd put up such a fight that she almost regretted stopping payment on the check. No matter. Having learned his lesson, he'd come back. They usually did.

From force of habit, the Princess gazed over the parapet and down to Su Casa. "Good God!" she said, "they've turned it into an island!" She adjusted her telescope and peered through it. There were a lot of people standing around a mound of earth in the garden. Some sort of clambake, she supposed. Well, if that was their idea of fun on a vile day like this, let them have it.

But an *island!* What a wonderful idea. Of course the Princess had lived on islands—England, Bermuda, Capri, Haiti, and Japan, if you could count those. But an island of one's very own, away from crowds, away from tourist buses halted at the gate, away from people altogether. Deserted and desolate. Desolation might be fun.

The wind whipped the Princess's caftan around her legs. A filthy day. Time to turn in.

Cloudy, Windy, Humid, Cold

"Cloudy, windy, humid, cold," the hotel managers grumbled as they glared up at leaden skies, felt the breeze flap at their gaudy shirts and slacks, wiped the mist from their brows, watched the goose bumps rise between the hairs of their forearms. Just to make sure that it was cloudy, windy, humid, and cold, they all tuned in their radios to hear, as though God Himself had spoken, the official weather report that it was cloudy, windy, humid, and cold.

But this was impossible! Between October and June, the weather in Acapulco was guaranteed. Yes, *guaranteed!* A little earthquake, scaring the liver and lights out of everybody—that was one thing. Foundations could be shored up, roofs patched, rooms repaired. Other holiday-makers would arrive to replace those who had fled in terror, and the carnival would continue. But an inclement day —cloudy, windy, humid, cold—was a major disaster.

The trouble was that there was nothing to *do* in Acapulco when the weather was less than perfect. Fishing boats rocked unchartered in the bay; the beaches were bleak and deserted; golf courses and tennis courts were patronized by only an intrepid few, who soon abandoned sport and returned, shivering, to chilly bedrooms; excursion buses sat silent in the streets; even the ubiquitous peddlers of puppets, straw bags, beach hats, bark paintings, Chiclets, and pornography remained indoors. In the big hotels, recreation directors and public-relations men, who never had to do anything but smile and lay on weekly Fiestas Mejicanas, bustled through empty public rooms arranging bridge tournaments, canasta games, bingo parties, Charleston contests. A prize for the funniest hat? Nobody wanted to play. "We can do that back home." Among tourists the virtues of Miami, San Juan, and Nassau, heretofore loudly denigrated, were suddenly re-evaluated. Skiing in the snows of Aspen and Sugarbush became newly attractive. "At least it wouldn't be as cold there," more than one person said. Like a brood of convalescent children, housebound under quarantine, the visitors to Acapulco whined, bickered, and complained—noses all but pressed against the windowpanes. They wanted to go out and play; or at least to go.

Luckily for the hotels, no one was going. Fog and wind at the airport had grounded everything. But no one was coming, either. Three direct flights from the States had already been rerouted in midair and told to put down at Mexico City, where the sun was shining, the temperature a balmy 72 degrees, but where no passenger wanted to be. The change in Acapulco's weather amounted to a national scandal, and on the opposite coast there was jubilation in Vera Cruz where, for once, it was fair and mild and the allure of the beaches was marred only by sharks and oil slicks.

Executives of the large hotel chains had all telephoned the weather bureau. What was the meaning of this irregularity, this outrage, this double-cross? The blasé young Mexican, glancing at his charts, his dials, his needles, his radar screen, told them that today Acapulco would be cloudy, windy, humid, cold. He could have told them this the day before, as well as warning them of the earthquake, but no one had bothered to inquire. Now he took a savage delight in making as gloomy a prognostication as possible. But when would the sun burn all this off? Noon? During siesta? In time for the yacht races? No. No change indicated. Not today, not tomorrow, and not likely for the day after. They might even expect storms of gale velocity, torrential rains, and a massive cold front. Some unusual reaction from the earthquake. Sorry, the young man said, he only reported the weather; he didn't create it.

Standing there at the mound of earth, his index finger marking the proper place in The Book of Common Prayer, Arthur Craine recalled his sister's words of a few hours earlier. "Tomorrow we'll all get into our city clothes and stand around at some sort of memorial service." How perceptive he had taught Carolyn to be. Too perceptive! They were getting a big, double dose of memorial services. One for Rex, whereabouts unknown, another for Salvador, who lay at his feet.

Funeral first or general meeting? It had been an annoying

problem solved by Laddy. Everyone at Su Casa knew from looking that the peninsula was now an island. And everyone knew from trying that the lights and telephones had given out. Incommunicado was the word. What they did not know—what Laddy hadn't told even Liz—was that they would remain incommunicado for some time; that in the not-too-distant future there would be no water without the electric pump; that the bottled-gas company had promised to deliver today, now could not, and that hot coffee, soup, and cooked food would soon be memories.

In still voices, out of respect for the dead, the guests of Su Casa had predicted the imminent arrival of the Coast Guard, of a launch from the mainland, of a rackety helicopter to carry them and their belongings—and, of course, the remains of poor Salvador—back to the town of Acapulco. Laddy alone knew that nothing of the sort was going to happen, at least not for a while. For once, Laddy's sloop, the Sea Urchin, had proved useful. Using its ship-to-shore phone, he had called the yacht club, the Coast Guard, the police, the airport, the office of the mayor, everyone he could think of, to report the situation, adding that a dead man, a pregnant woman, and two seriously injured (Laddy saw no reason to underplay the painful, but superficial, wounds of Roland and Lee) were among those present. Everyone had clucked and cooed with Latin sympathy. Que lástima! But nothing could be done; not today, not tomorrow. Possibly the day after tomorrow; probably not. Yes, it was unusual, unheard of, but the weather bureau had spoken. Storm warnings were out. Planes were grounded, ships moored. No action for the time being. Keep in touch.

The funeral came first. Salvador would have to be put some place until rescue came. Save among the steaks and chops slowly thawing in the freezer, Laddy could suggest only a temporary grave.

"But, Laddy," Liz had said, "Chavo is a—was a—Catholic. I mean, don't we need consecrated ground and a priest and—well, I don't know what all? I think there's some sort of family mausoleum in Spain, but . . ."

"It's only temporary," Laddy had said. "He can be removed later when help comes. But now, as a precaution against the heat . . . " Laddy didn't want to describe the facts of life—and death.

"Heat?" Liz had said, through chattering teeth.

While Pablo had dug the shallow grave in a pretty, but seldom frequented, corner of the garden, Laddy and Walt had dealt—or tried to deal with—the mortal remains of Laddy's brother-in-law. As a boy, Laddy had once sent off for a mail-order course in taxidermy. Simply reading Lesson One had made him green with nausea. The years had not hardened him. Walter, if no less squeamish, had more bravado.

The corpse, unwieldy on the kitchen table, had been wrapped first in aluminum foil, twisted pertly at both ends. "To keep out the moisture," Walter had explained. Laddy could think of nothing but a kind of holiday turkey known as Oven-Ready. Would he throw up?

Next had come a blanket—cashmere. "For warmth?" Laddy had almost asked.

Last, a cocoon of tar paper. It had been the hardest task of all. Salvador, his back broken cleanly, had not been cooperative. His upper and nether regions had flopped grotesquely. He had nearly fallen to the floor. Finally, he had been rolled up and bound with cord. "There!" Walt had said, gray and ill.

"There!" The finished product had looked to Laddy like an untidily done-up package that would surely be refused by the post office.

Arthur had been chosen to read the services—nonsectarian—for a number of reasons. First, his doctor of philosophy degree had been the closest currently available to doctor of divinity. Second, the lecture series, the television appearances brought about by his best-sellerdom had made him accustomed to public speaking. And, third, Liz had known him for such a long time. "Not a sermon, Arthur. This isn't the real burial. Just a few words about Chavo and, of course, about Rex."

No simple assignment. Arthur hadn't known either of them well. He had privately considered Salvador a gigolo and Rex a nincompoop. Panegyrics would not come easily. And the *tone* of his eulogy bothered Arthur. Did one begin, "Dearly beloved, we are gathered . . ." No, that was something entirely different. Or should he strike a sort of chummy attitude, chin cocked toward heaven and the

"Bossman" upstairs: "Well, Sir, here we are to say so long to two old pals . . ." Never! It was unseemly, uncouth, un-Arthur. He'd have to think of some words, some style, and do it fast. Here came Pablo, changed from the coveralls of a gravedigger to the sable black of a pallbearer.

"Are we all here?" Arthur asked. Liz nodded and took Laddy's arm. "Oh, no! Wait, Arthur. Here comes Mrs. Meyers."

Arthur turned his head sedately and felt his jaw drop. Although largely unaware of the existence of Rex Roman, Salvador Martínez, or an earthquake, Flossie had somehow discerned that a ceremony was taking place and was careening across the lawn to join the bereaved. Out of a sense of decorum, she had hastily converted her cartwheel hat into a haphazard approximation of widow's weeds by the addition of a tattered veil that trailed limply down to the clocks of her black stockings. To ward off the cold, she put on the Paradise fox coat, but very little else. A gust of wind opened it, revealing the garters of Flossie's old pantie girdle. Queenie, cradled in her arms, yapped cheerfully. Reverently, Flossie took her place beside Mrs. Bullock. Mrs. Bullock snorted and moved aside, landing on Aurelia's instep. "*Ai, Diós!*" Aurelia cried. The impertinence! What was she, Lily Lee de Camp Bullock, doing here, standing between a drunken harlot and a greaser servant at a *Mexican's* funeral?

"Friends," Arthur began. Friends indeed! He eyed Lee Goodwin, his bound head, his blackened eyes, his arm in a sling. So, Lee had fallen out of a window. A *ground-floor* window? Odd. Perhaps he'd just let Lee have it, very subtly, right between those two black eyes.

"We are here to . . ." (To bid farewell? No. Keep it simple) ". . . to say good-bye to two other friends who met with tragic deaths last night. Both died heroically. One, trying to return to his wife, his home—to us." At least that's how the story went. But there was something fishy about it. If Salvador had taken a taxi directly home from La Perla, he and his migraine headache should have been tucked into bed hours before the earthquake. So what was he doing dead in the middle of the driveway at that time of the morning? Poor Liz! "The other, a famous athlete, a brilliant

165

actor . . ." Actor? ". . . the victim of a vicious practical joke." Arthur sensed veiled glances shot in Lee's direction. He sensed that Lee sensed them, too. Good!

Arthur continued in sonorous tones. "Juan José Salvador Felipe Martínez y Moya de Contreras . . . " He hoped he'd remembered all of Chavo's names and got them in the right order. ". . . was a young man, not yet forty, in whose veins flowed the noblest blood of the Hispanic worlds, both old and new . . ."

Mrs. Bullock started to listen. She'd always thought that young man, poor thing, was too good for that snippy Yankee woman he'd married. Noble, eh?

". . . descended on both sides from the grandees of Spain, the officers of Hernando Cortés, the viceroys of Mexico . . ."

Laddy stiffened. So, this beautiful fiction was following that little Indian *chulo* into the grave—albeit a temporary grave. Poor old Liz. Now she'd never have to find out the truth about him. He put a protective, brotherly arm around Liz's shoulder. Perhaps now —well, not right now, but in a few days—he could speak to her about the avocado ranch.

". . . in spite of his truly outstanding background . . ."

Outstanding background? Lou Ann thought. What about his outstanding foreground, if that bulge in his pants was any indication? She rolled her eyes in Lee's direction and wondered how soon he'd be ready for action.

". . . entire Martínez family known for its devotion to democracy . . ."

Bernice stiffened. Oh, yes! A democratic family, if they thought you were rich and aristocratic. Nacho! Bernice felt terrible. She supposed that she was experiencing her first hangover. She was correct. She felt ashamed of herself—so drunk that she hadn't even realized that there had been an earthquake until they told her about it. Waking up this morning, seeing the shambles of her room, broken glass and things overturned, she had felt just like some ignorant Polish clod. Like her brother-in-law, Ignatz, when he came back from a bender and wrecked the apartment. It had been almost a relief to know that the damage had been caused by an act of God. Everything had started out so beautifully and now . . . Helplessly,

Bernice burst into tears. Essie put an arm around her, gave her a comforting series of little pats. "There, there, dear." Essie was so sweet—*now*. Bernice wondered if Essie would be, and Carolyn and Bill and Arthur and all the rest of them, if they knew that Bernice was a little Polish nobody who sold secondhand clothes.

". . . internationally famous film star," Arthur was saying, "and an inspiration to youth all over the world . . ." Arthur considered that any youth whom Rex might inadvertently have inspired would now be well into his forties. Reruns of his old Tarzan movies had a certain vogue, but only as high camp; laughter after midnight.

Here's where I get it again, Lee Goodwin thought. Old Professor Zut Alors would let him have it for fair. What did Arthur Craine care that Lee Goodwin was suffering? Flat broke, stranded on an island where the natives were unfriendly, and all banged up besides? And then Lee began thinking. Hey! He could sue the ass off this Martínez bitch! He could claim terrible headaches, pains in his back. There was no sure way to check on either. Start at, say, a million bucks and settle out of court with the insurance company. Even if his stay in Acapulco hadn't produced anything, it wouldn't be a total loss. And then Arthur Craine and Bill Williams, who'd dug him out of the roof tiles, prodded him for broken bones, cleansed his cuts and abrasions, daubed on the iodine—Christ how that had stung!—bound his head. They weren't qualified. *Dr.* Craine. He could sue them for a pretty penny. And their pennies were both pretty and plentiful. Just in case anyone might be looking, Lee put his free hand to his brow and swayed unsteadily.

". . . brought excitement and pleasure to millions. A brilliant career suddenly ended . . ." Ended before the virile Tarzan could collect his first Social Security check, Arthur mused. But surely not by more than a year or so. Arthur cleared his throat and continued.

If it weren't for the earthquake, Roland thought, this might have been a *triple* funeral. For all the black coffee swilled last night, even for having been sick among the roses, Roland was still groggy. He could almost see the headlines in the *Call*, the *Chronicle*, the Sunday *Call-Chronicle*: "PROMINENT LEHIGH VALLEY MAN, STAR, GRANDEE—BENEFACTORS—MOURNED." And yet here he stood in

Arthur Craine's clothes, alive. At least Roland could always say, "Oh, yes, Arthur Craine. We wear exactly the same size. Even our shoes!" Roland suffered still, but not on account of Chip. His pain was far more specific. Roland's rump was as blue as a baboon's from landing in the rose garden in the pink mosaic tub. Roland had struck the back of his head hard. A concussion? A skull fracture? He was morally sure that his back and pelvis were broken. But would he be able to stand here at Salvador's grave if they were? Both shoulders and elbows were skinned and, in crawling on all fours over the shattered tiles, the broken glass, and the bristling roses, his hands, his knees, his shins, his feet were badly bruised. It would take days—weeks—to pluck out the thorns embedded in his flesh. Roland's heart was still broken, yes, but there were too many other places more immediately painful to the touch to worry about.

Nor did Roland feel that he had appeared at his very best stumbling dazed and naked around the garden until Arthur Craine had found him, swaddled him in a tablecloth, and led him whimpering incoherently to the candlelit Margaritas to administer first aid. No two ways about it, Arthur was a gentleman who would never cost another gentleman a nickel. More to the point, Arthur was attractive.

Attractive or not, Arthur was having the devil's own time with his impromptu funeral oration. Arthur always enjoyed being "on," but scarcely two minutes had elapsed and Arthur was running out of material. He had said everything he had known to be true, and a lot more things he had known to be untrue, about Salvador Martínez and Rex Roman, and now the well was running dry. Padding would be of the essence. But pad with what? This sort of thing simply wasn't Arthur's sort of thing. Walter Dewlap, with his bearlike gruffness, his locker-room joviality, his gift for finding—or trying to find—something good in everyone would have been better at conducting this particular service. Arthur glanced now at Walt, solemn in navy raw silk, as he put a large paw around Essie's small, black-linen waist. Walt, Essie, and the little Potocki standing there, arms entwined, looked as though they were about to burst into very close harmony. The picture supplied Arthur with a flash of inspiration. Perhaps the whole gathering should sing something. But what? The Lesser Doxology? It started "Praise God from Whom all blessings flow," but where did it go from there? Possessed of a pleasing baritone that had enlivened more than one Princeton Triangle show, Arthur had no objection to raising it in a simple Anglican hymn, key of B-flat Major. But one couldn't make up the lyrics. Now if it were anything ever written by Cole Porter or Lorenz Hart . . . No. Better forget the singing entirely. Do things right or don't do them at all.

Should there be any mention of heaven? Arthur doubted that such a place existed and, even if it did, that either Salvador or Rex would be eligible for resident membership. Arthur paused, stuck. He pressed his free hand to his brow, hoping to fob off his lapse as a seizure of emotion. Through his fingers, he glanced at the two—in a manner of speaking—widows. There they stood, long Liz, the eternal Bennington girl in her black cardigan, comforting the incredible April May. Arthur knew that April had been in no condition to dress herself, that Carolyn and Essie had done the job for her like two display assistants fitting clothes onto a department-store manikin. The task had not been light. April's wardrobe did not run to funerary outfits. There had been a black dress, but it was solid sequins. And there had been a white one, open to the coccyx in back, with a sort of rose window cut out over the abdomen. From his bedroom in Margaritas, Arthur had overheard the hurried consultations, had heard the Mesdames Williams and Dewlap saying, "Raise your arms, April," "Just let me get this zipper, dear," "I know I have a scarf somewhere," "A little lipstick, April?"

And now the final result of their handiwork stood there, lifeless, the impossible breasts straining at one of Carolyn's tennis dresses, the spun-sugar hair lank beneath a black-and-white-print scarf of Essie's. April May looked like a frightened little girl, abandoned, perhaps, at Ellis Island, pallid, mute, and numb with terror. "Silly little slut," Arthur thought. He saw Liz pat April's shoulder. Good old Liz; no matter what happened she was always calm, always collected, always pulled together. Breeding told.

Liz didn't feel very pulled together. She didn't know exactly what she felt. Nothing, she guessed. At least not at the moment. It would be something to think about after she finished thinking about all the other things she had to think about—this place, these people, how to feed them, how to get them to the mainland, how to cope with the physical problems of life and death. Then she'd have time to think about herself and what she felt.

". . . and we say now good-bye to our friend, our host, the beloved husband of our Liz . . ." Liz, slightly startled to hear her own name, was conscious that Arthur was running down. Now she would have to consider coffee for her guests, drinks, something for lunch, a general meeting to tell them what had happened, what was going to happen, although Liz wasn't entirely certain herself.

The Lord's Prayer was mumbled by all with marked discrepancies between the King James and Douay versions, a final confusion of "for ever" and "for ever and ever." A discreet, prearranged nod from Arthur, and Laddy and Pablo bent and hefted the lumpy tar-paper tube which contained Salvador Martínez. Arthur gazed at it with dismay. It looked more like a yule log than anything that had ever been human. As it was being lowered into the temporary grave, it buckled in the middle, slipped from Laddy's grasp, and plopped into the shallow hole like a felled tree. Arthur wondered whether he should murmur "Amen," or shout "Timber!"

Liz winced and shuddered. This black cylinder was her husband, her lover, her son. Chavo! Susan Holt burst into tears. "Hush, honey," Julie Noyes said, putting her arm around Susan. Flossie Meyers belched softly and was about to ask who it was who had just been buried. Aurelia, the cook, once more feeling life inside her, wailed loudly, clutching at her front. Carolyn Williams dabbed at her eyes. Arthur stepped back, allowed his noble head to sink, his shoulders to droop. It was a trick he had mastered as a sort of curtain call on the lecture circuit. It said eloquently to audiences "I've said it. I'm tired. That's all. Thank you. Good-bye." Mindful of his good black suit, Pablo began reverently spooning dirt into Salvador's grave.

"Shall we all go into the *sala?*" Liz asked. "We have several matters to discuss and I'm sure that everyone would like a cup of coffee."

A Natch for TV

"For, as religious a woman as you claim to be, Mrs. Bullock," Liz said evenly, "you should be able to understand that I am a mere mortal and in no way responsible for an act of God."

"That may be, Miz Már-tinez, but this *is* your place and we are your guests." Grim-jawed, Mrs. Bullock sat back on the sofa feeling that she had scored.

"*Some* of the people are my guests, Mrs. Bullock. You were released from your reservation yesterday—in fact, *told* to leave. If you are still here, trespassing on my property, you have no one to blame but yourself."

"But surely there is some kind of boat that could get me and my girls to shore?"

"Mrs. Bullock," Laddy said, "I've just explained that I've been in touch with the Coast Guard, the airport, the police—everybody. If the Mexican navy thinks it's too dangerous to come out, you can hardly expect . . ."

"Maybe you could swim it, honey." It had been Flossie Meyers's first statement of the day. By sitting very quietly and listening carefully, Flossie had deduced that there had been an earthquake that had turned this place—whatever it was called—into an island. Somebody or other had been killed and they were all stranded. Flossie was rather enjoying it. It had been a long time since she had known this much contact with anyone other than chambermaids and room-service waiters. And hadn't that blond fellow just said that there was plenty of liquor on hand?

"Common!" Mrs. Bullock said. "Nevertheless, Mrs. Már-tinez, I intend to report this matter to the authorities." It was one of Mrs. Bullock's favorite threats, which had always covered a multitude of contingencies.

"Which authorities and in what language?" Arthur asked.

"Mrs. Bullock," Carolyn said. "I wish you would try to remember that Liz's husband was killed here last night. We're all in this together. We're perfectly comfortable and it isn't going to last forever. So, instead of carping about a situation that no one can do anything about, I think it might be intelligent—not to mention decent—to stop complaining and to try to help Liz."

"Thank you, Carolyn," Liz murmured.

Temporarily, but only temporarily, deflated, Mrs. Bullock retreated farther into the sofa. She had traveled so far and so long through life on bluff and bluster that she almost believed in her own righteousness, her Christianity, her aristocracy. She was rarely aware of being outclassed. This was one of those times. But then, Mrs. Bullock had endured a difficult night.

"I don't see anything so terrible about this," Walter Dewlap said. "It can't last more than a day or two." Laddy glanced at the ceiling. A day or two or three or four. "In the meantime we've got plenty of food, plenty of drink, candles . . ."

"I think it sounds exciting," Essie added.

"It goes without saying that you won't be charged for however long you're marooned here," Liz said.

"Well, I should hope *not!*" Mrs. Bullock exploded. She was busily multiplying the day rate times four. As her cultural tours were always paid in advance, anything she could save went straight into her own pocket.

"But one thing I think we should all do," Carolyn said, "is pitch in and help. The earthquake did a lot of damage . . ."

"And Liz *is* shorthanded," Essie volunteered. "Only Pablo; and one *look* at the cook and you know that her time is coming at any minute."

Mrs. Bullock was about to say that she, a de Camp, had never soiled her hands at housework when Liz said, "That's awfully sweet of you, and it would only be little things like making your own beds until we get this mess cleared up. But I think we should put it to a vote. All in favor, please raise your hands."

As the hands were going up, Lee Goodwin shook his bandaged head and said, "Sorry, sorry; it's taking the messages a little longer to get through. Of course I'll do anything I can." He raised his right hand and winced with pain. It wouldn't do any harm to establish his infirmity right now in front of witnesses—brain not functioning correctly, trouble with his shoulder. It would also make his share of any work to be done a lot lighter.

Yes, it would be one hell of a legal case—*three* legal cases—Lee thought. He'd get the Martínez dame on neligence; an insecure window grille and the falling roof tiles damned near killing him. As for Arthur Craine and Bill Williams, he could nab them on improperly administered first aid.

"Well, to start with first things first," Liz said, "there's lunch. The freezer's full of things we ought to eat before they spoil. . . ."

"Villa Vera—here's where we turn off," the man said, with a glint of lenses, a flashing of white teeth. "Say good-bye, kidlees!" Chip got out of the car and closed the door with an expensive-sounding click.

Kee-rist, could he ever pick 'em! Well, it was better than walking, not that he hadn't walked almost halfway back from Su Casa.

Chip had felt pretty expansive, even in these cruddy clothes, three hours earlier. He'd hailed a cab, ridden out to Su Casa, got off at the gate, and given the driver the whole fifteen pesos. Smarter to go in on foot, keep out of sight, not attract any attention. Well, it hadn't been much of a walk—fifty yards, if that. And then what? A goddamned ocean and, off in the distance on the other side, Su Casa. Chip had just stood dumb at the water's edge and stared. Then he had turned around and headed back for town.

Hungry, no cigarettes, clothes so tight that they hurt, and not one red cent on him, he'd tried hitching rides, but cars on a day like this were few. Buses had roared along the road, but what good was a bus if you didn't have the fare? Finally a car had stopped. And what a car! A Rolls-Royce convertible—thirty thousand bucks if it cost a penny—with Connecticut plates and at the wheel, grinning like an ape, the nelliest old job of work Chip had seen in some time. Maybe busting up with Roland had been a good thing. Maybe these pants, so tight that no one could help noticing the merchandise, were a blessing in disguise. Maybe little old Chipper had fallen into a privy, but maybe, too, he could come out smelling like a rose. The driver had leaned out, tortoise-shell specs and a sweet simper showing

173

two hundred snowy teeth, "Heading for town?" Could Chip pick 'em! He'd given that old slow smile that had won him so many friends, thrust out his chest, and sort of undulated toward the Rolls. And what had he discovered in the back seat? Three brats who looked just like the driver.

"Y-your children?"

"The kidlees? My three youngest. The twins are in Rosemary Hall, Bryce Junior is in Putney, and Linda, our oldest, is in Sarah Lawrence." He hadn't had a cigarette—not in six years—and had told Chip of a sure way to quit smoking. For the rest of the trip he'd talked about Moral Rearmament and restoring a house in Guilford, Connecticut. Could Chip pick 'em! It was a relief to Chip when he was dropped off.

But now, coming out of Villa Vera was another, humbler, convertible—a Volkswagen with Mexican plates—and driving it, quite alone, a man about Chip's own age. The car stopped. "Going into el centro?"

"Uh, yeah." This one was a mystery. He looked Mexican, yet he spoke vernacular English without an accent.

"Hop in. You know Bryce? Bryce Goodfellow?"

Vague, misshapen pieces began to fall together in Chip's small brain. Bryce Goodfellow was some sort of big Broadway producer with a lot of money and a lot of children. Roland's chums were always talking about him. A closet queen, they said, but they said everyone was.

"Uh, yeah."

"I'm Jimmy Malvido. I'm in show biz, too."

"Yeah?" What was he? At least he was a smoker. Chip took out his badges of respectability, the gold cigarette case and the gold lighter. "Damn! Out of cigarettes!"

"Oh, here!" Jimmy produced another gold cigarette case and another gold lighter.

"Thanks." Jimmy's gold accoutrements had given Chip confidence. Chip decided that he had better establish himself as a gentleman in distress, not as a hustler. It wasn't easy. "That earthquake last night sure fucked up everything. These aren't even my clothes. I had to get dressed in such a hurry."

Jimmy was relieved. The clothes were beyond belief. Could the gold cigarette case belong to someone else as well? Jimmy was cautious. At least the boy knew Bryce Goodfellow, which was more than Jimmy could claim, even though they were staying at the same hotel. Hadn't Jimmy just seen him getting out of the Goodfellow Rolls-Royce? Perhaps he could arrange an introduction. Still, Jimmy was cautious. Ever since Jimmy had come into his own money, too many people had been after it—struggling, unknown young actors and actresses in both Hollywood and Mexico, outright hookers of both genders all over the world. Jimmy wasn't interested in going to bed with men. He wasn't much interested in going to bed with women, either. He did it occasionally because he felt it was good for him, like push-ups or jogging or a high colonic irrigation. What Jimmy was interested in was Jimmy and Jimmy's image as "Mr. Show Biz." Some very attractive bodies had been offered to Jimmy at the most reasonable rates only to be refused. But let any dubious impresario mention even inactive participation in an intimate little revue, an off-Broadway cycle of Czechoslovakian plays, a Spanish-language version of a flop American musical, and Jimmy was reaching for his checkbook. "I was born in show biz," Jimmy always said.

In a manner of speaking, this was true. Jimmy's mother had been Dixie Darling, a Wampus Baby Star, Class of '32. (Ginger Rogers' year.) While Dixie had made a lot of stills—coming out of a pumpkin on Halloween, straddling a prop rocket on July Fourth, posing with black cats and broken mirrors on various Fridays the thirteenth—she had never made a motion picture. However, after a decade of being fetching for the still photographers, Dixie *had* met Jimmy's father, a Mexican gentleman old enough to be *her* father, whose political connections during the stormy administrations of Presidents Calles, Portes Gil, and Ortiz Rubio had made him many times a millionaire, and almost respectable. Perhaps because neither spoke the other's language, they were married and, after some years of trying to avoid just such a fate, Dixie Darling de Malvido had given birth to little Jaime Sebastian Clark (for Gable) Malvido Darling—Jimmy.

As Dixie had never mastered Spanish, Jimmy grew up totally

bilingual, nurtured on Dixie's tales of the Good, the True, the Real Life of Hollywood. Dixie confided that a great career in pictures had been sacrificed to marriage and motherhood. Her bedtime stories, concerning as they did Clark Gable, Kay Francis, Dick Powell, Lupe Vélez, Jean Harlow, Robert Taylor, Tyrone Power, and other now-deceased luminaries, might today have the appeal of a guided tour through Forest Lawn. But Jimmy was bitten at an early age. When General Malvido was filed safely away on a marble shelf in the Panteón Español, Jimmy, with a mother's blessing, fled the Colegio Cristóbal Colón for the Pasadena Community Playhouse, where it was said that his command of Spanish was remarkable—but where he flunked, anyhow. A semester at the American Academy of Dramatic Arts in New York followed, and that by brief visits to the Actor's Studio and the Royal Academy in London. The opinion was unanimous: Jimmy lacked star quality.

Dixie confessed to disappointment that her own streak of genius was not inherent as with, say, the Kembles, the Coopers, the Booths, the Barrymores. But as she had settled down in Cuernavaca with a protégé not quite Jimmy's age, she was content to let her son seek fame elsewhere.

"Elsewhere" was in and around movie and television studios in Mexico, in Hollywood, and in New York, "of" but never quite "in" the performing arts, Jimmy was considered a sort of mild joke among the actors and directors and producers he worshiped. Too American for the Mexicans, too Mexican for the Americans, too social for show business, too show biz for society, Jimmy had never quite fitted in anywhere. It wasn't that they disliked him. How could they actually dislike a fawning rich boy probably good for a small loan and certainly good for the lunch check? He was even tossed a bone now and then—a walk-on in a crowd scene, a line of Spanish in an English picture, a line of English in a Spanish picture, or serving as interpreter for a director or a star unable to understand the other language. But Jimmy was too eager. He bubbled over with suggestions as to how the scene could be better, how the lines should be changed, how everything could be improved. It did not make him popular with harried producers. Jealous, Jimmy supposed. And so Jimmy had evolved a new plan. It wasn't an actor that Jimmy wanted to be. It was a producer. What's more, he had the money to do it. Not as much as people thought, but enough. Yes. Jimmy would produce. But what?

"Earthquake! Don't talk to me about the earthquake," Jimmy said. "I was supposed to come down here to have lunch with Merle—Merle Oberon," he explained, "and to go out on the yacht with Dolores—Dolores del Río, but now . . ." True, both great stars kept houses in Acapulco, but their association with Jaime Malvido was limited to a gracious smile and a nod of not-quite-recognition. Still, Jimmy liked to establish himself as established. "And tonight I was supposed to go to an opening back in Mexico City." Jimmy had been tossed another bone—two seats in the sixteenth row. For a thousand pesos he had also engaged a beautiful Austrian model to accompany him so that he might be noticed. "But no planes are flying, and I just don't feel like driving all the way back."

Chip wondered if Jimmy felt like bedding him down in Villa Vera after, of course, buying breakfast, lunch, dinner, cigarettes, and some halfway decent clothes. It wouldn't be much of a night for sleeping on the beach.

"That's tough," Chip said, "but at least you've got a place to sleep. Where I'm staying—where I was staying—the driveway's gone. The whole place is out in the middle of the goddamned ocean. They're stranded out there and I'm stranded here—my clothes, my plane ticket, my money."

"Really?" Jimmy asked. "Where's that?"

"It's the place called Su Casa. Nice."

"Su Casa? You mean out on the peninsula? Why, that used to be our home when my father"—pause—"the general"—pause—"was alive. My mother—you know, Dixie Darling, the star"—If Jimmy had said Sarah Siddons, the name couldn't have meant less to Chip. "My mother called it Villa Darmal, like Pickfair. How terrible!" Jimmy took on an air of noble suffering, like Prince Youssoupoff contemplating the shell of Tsarskoe-Selo. "Poor Dixie!" Both Dixie and Jimmy had jumped for joy and snatched the first offer—anything to get rid of the old dump. And just in the nick of time, Jimmy thought. If papá hadn't been so tacaño, pinching every last peso until it bent, maybe the old ark and the swamp it was built on would have lasted a few years. There had been trouble with it before Jimmy was old enough to say Barbara Stanwyck.

"Yeah, but what eats me is that everything I own is out there in . . ."

"Were there many people staying there?"

"Huh? Oh, yeah. There was this Polish countess, and some old broad from Texas, and a couple named Williams from Chicago . . ."

Jimmy began to lose interest. A lot of tourists ruining their lovely house!

". . . and their brother, this big author, Arthur Craine . . ."

The car swerved wildly. "Arthur Craine? You mean the Arthur Craine?" Jimmy had once been invited to sit in the sponsor's booth during a panel show on which Arthur Craine was a guest. He had even shaken hands with the great man.

"Yeah. I guess so. Is there more'n one? And this old Tarzan, Rex Roman . . ."

The car screeched to a stop, nearly throwing Chip through the windshield. "Rex Roman? Arthur Craine and Rex Roman?"

In the confusion of the earthquake, word of Rex Roman's death had not yet reached the outside world. As for Jimmy Malvido, he couldn't have been more excited if he'd heard that the College of Cardinals was locked into a burning brothel. And this had sentimental value. Hadn't Dixie herself told him that, but for studio politics, she, Dixie Darling, might have been Rex's original Jane? "Why didn't you tell me?"

"Maybe we could discuss it over lunch?"

"You're damn right we could, whatever your name is. And we're going to do it in my bungalow at Villa Vera, where there's a telephone and some privacy."

"But I already told you. I'm flat broke. Everything I own is out there in the . . ."

"But don't you see, man, this is a natch for TV."

Jaime Malvido, Producer

Jimmy was a fool, but not a moron. He was considered a joke in show business, but a nice joke, a sort of pet nuisance to be allowed inside studios, on to sets. In currying favor, Jimmy had been systematic; as pleasant to grips and gatekeepers as he had been to producers and stars. The boxes of candy, the paper cups of coffee and Coca-Colas he had bought for production assistants and secretaries were, today, paying off.

Yes, Jimmy was systematic. He first called Su Casa. The lines were down. Next he called the police. Yes. It was true. The causeway had fallen into the sea. Su Casa was an island. And, yes, somebody was dead, a couple of people were hurt, and somebody else was expecting a baby. Jimmy called the Coast Guard. No, indeed, no ships going out in weather like this. Not today, not tomorrow. And no planes, either. Jimmy called the weather bureau. No, there was no change in the foreseeable future.

Then Jimmy called his lawyer in Mexico City. In his machine-gun Spanish, he inquired as to the status of Su Casa and its land. Well, the new owner was a bit behind in payments, and Jimmy could reclaim it on a technicality if he was such a fool as to want it back from the idiot American who had bought it. The woman was most honorable and would surely send her check. . . . "No, let her hang on to it." Jimmy was merely interested in keeping out trespassers; trespassers with microphones and cameras. Next, Jimmy dictated a rough draft of his television idea. The lawyer was to put it into legal Spanish and send it by registered mail in a signature-sealed envelope to Jimmy at Villa Vera—and send another copy to himself. They would be opened only if and when there was any dispute as to whose idea this was. The postmark and registration would establish the date. Not the best legal protection in the world, but better than nothing.

And *then* Jimmy started calling the people in show business, both

Mexican and American, who had always found him such a joke. Jimmy telephoned Channel 3 in the capital and ordered outright the mobile color unit, its crew, extra lights, an extra generator and, of all things, a harpoon gun. Cash on the line and a bonus for the men if they got to Acapulco before dark. Everything Jimmy had said so far was in Spanish and wasted on Chip. Now Jimmy switched to his equally rapid English and got through to California.

After the necessary "dears" and "darlings" and "honeys" and "sweeties" in the outer offices, Jimmy hit bull's-eye with amazing speed. Yes, it was Jimmy Malvido and Jimmy had an idea that was worth a billion dollars. Not for next year, not for next season, but for now—tomorrow.

Chip was a moron, but not a fool. From room service, he ordered things that stick to the ribs: a thick soup, a thick steak, a baked potato—better make that two—lima beans, ice cream, and cake. He'd eat the ice cream now and take the cake with him. While Jimmy screamed bilingually over long distance, Chip wandered into the opulent bathroom, showered and shampooed, shaved with Jimmy's razor, splashed on Jimmy's cologne, rinsed his mouth with Jimmy's mouth wash, found a new toothbrush still in its wrappings and took it. In Jimmy's bedroom, Chip helped himself to under-wear—two pairs—and bathing trunks in case he'd have to work the beaches. He put them all on. Then he selected a pair of Jimmy's trousers, a shirt, a cashmere cardigan, socks, and espadrilles—all black so that they wouldn't show the dirt. Not a perfect fit, but better than Florentino's crap. He opened the top dresser drawer and helped himself to two handkerchiefs. And while he was at it, he also helped himself to the two hundred-peso bills that were there. Not much, fifteen, sixteen bucks. Further searching led to two packs of cigarettes and a pair of emerald cuff links. He took those, too. Just in case. If he'd given this Mexican nut something that was worth a billion dollars, the least the Mex could do . . .

Chip heard the clatter and clink of the room-service cart. Good! He was starved. He wondered how soon Jimmy would recognize his clothes, but as he entered the sitting room he realized that Jimmy wouldn't notice if he were wearing coronation robes.

"Okay, E. G.," Jimmy was saying, "then it's a firm offer? . . . I know you won't try to screw me, sweetheart. Not if you ever want to get so much as a Kodak or a crystal set into this country again. Let's see, it's one o'clock Acapulco time; eleven o'clock in L.A. You can telegraph your acceptance right now and do all the legal crap later. Send it to Jaime Malvido . . . No, not Hymie, *Jaime* Malvido, Villa Vera . . . No, v-i-double l-a, like Vil-la Vee-ra, Acapulco, Guerrero, Mexico. And I'm warning you, E. G., if it isn't here in two hours I'm offering this to NBC."

Word had already reached California of Rex Roman's death, but the details were not clear. In Acapulco, neither Chip nor Jimmy knew of it. But Jimmy was good at bluffing, and whenever that failed he could lapse into Spanish to stall for time.

"But I *told* you there were dead people on the place. Wounded ones too. All rich, all famous . . . E. G., please remember that Rex Roman is one of my mother's dearest friends . . . All right, then, *was*. Just a minute. Here comes my leg man." Covering the mouthpiece Jimmy said, "Is Rex Roman *dead*?"

"Search me," Chip said, buttering *bolillos* which he would wrap in his napkin and save for later. "He was dead drunk yesterday."

"Little drinking problem, E. G. Same old thing. And Arthur Craine . . . Yes, I know I've told you that a dozen times. You don't seem able to grasp the . . . Well, who the fuck do you expect to be out there, the goddamned Supreme Court? . . . Who else?"

Covering the mouthpiece, Jimmy hissed, "Who else, for God's sake?" Chip wasn't good with names, but he tried. Jimmy filled in and embroidered the rest.

"Well, there's this Mrs. Bullock from Dallas . . . Oh, stop being funny. No Bull-ock. Like the store. And these dames with her— real swingers—Julie—uh—Julie Noyes . . ." Now *Jimmy's* eyes popped. "*Samuel Houston Noyes?* Why, why, sure. Sure it's his daughter. And Mr. and Mrs. William Williams of Chicago . . ."

"The *steel* William Williamses?" Jimmy hissed again. Chip shrugged.

"Of course the steel family . . . And this Polish countess—uh— Potocki? . . . Excuse me, E. G., but my man here doesn't speak much English. After all, E. G., this is my family's house. What sort of guests do you suppose we'd . . . Just a minute.

181

"Who else? Come on, *think!*"

"Hello, E. G., well, there's a Miss April May . . . What's so funny? . . . Of course we don't have call girls! She's Rex Roman's traveling companion. They say she was found next to the body. Listen, E. G., we'll send the whole list—names, addresses, everything. But I sure as hell hope your secretary is on another line placing that telegram. You're wasting valuable time. I've got a camera crew out there shooting already . . . Who's going to narrate? Why, *I'm* going to narrate. Me on the shore, Arthur Craine on the island . . . Sure, sure, sure. Send Walter Cronkite. Just try to get a plane into Acapulco. Does he speak Spanish? Has he got Mexican working papers? Is he a member of A.N.D.A.? Sure, go ahead, E. G. While you're fucking around, this show's going to be on another network. I suppose my pal Arthur Craine isn't good enough for you. Who the hell do you want, Captain Kangaroo? . . . Okay, E. G., it had better be here. Oh, and don't forget that on the credits it says 'Jaime Malvido, Producer' . . . You can take that all up with my lawyer. He'll be in touch with you as soon as I get your telegram . . . Well, so long, E. G. You'll thank me for this . . . *Mister Dizzy Spick to you, schmuck! Muy buenas tardes.*"

Jimmy rang off and heaved a sigh. "Boy! Talk about shitting bricks, I thought I was going to conk out with the stuff I had to make up. I wish you'd get your facts straight."

"I *tolja*," Chip said, his mouth full, "I haven't got any facts. I don't know who's there and who isn't. I can't even get there myself. All my money . . ." Would Jimmy ever get the hint? No. Jimmy wasn't even listening.

"First we've got to pick up a bullhorn and a lot of rope. Here. Take this pad and write these things down."

"Huh?"

"Well, come on! Snap to it, man! I can't do this thing all by myself. I need some kind of secretarial assistance."

"A secretary?" Chip had just made it through the ninth grade, and that unwillingly. "What the hell dya think I am?"

"Well, a production assistant," Jimmy said impatiently. "You know, take notes, follow me around, see that things get done."

Jimmy meant work! "Man, you are plumb full of . . ." Chip

was aghast. He had known this Jimmy—what was his last name?—for exactly one hour, and had watched him change from a simple-minded Mexican playboy, who might just possibly be on the make, into a real, power-mad monster. And now this Jimmy expected him to *work!*

"Come on, we're wasting time. You can eat later. Now we'll pick up a few things and get out there before everybody finds out about it, and then . . ."

"Man, I tolja, you can't get anywheres near it. Kee-rist, I'm not goin' back out there!"

"All right then, don't come." Jimmy strode to the door and opened it, and stood there jingling his car keys impatiently. "I'll do this my own way. You'll have to go now. I want to lock up."

III

THIS SIDE OF
PARADISE

Help Is on the Way

"Well," Liz said to the little group at the water's edge, "there you see it with your own eyes. Help is on the way!"

Squinting through the mist, everyone had a different interpretation of what was happening on the mainland. They could see lights strung up in the trees, tents pitched, giant trucks with something painted on the sides, men dashing around. Over the rushing of the wind and the noise of the water between them, they could occasionally catch the drone of a big generator, the excited babble of Spanish. Walter Dewlap recalled boyhood dawns when Ringling Brothers' Circus set up tent on the fairgrounds outside Anthrax. Bernice thought of the time when there had been a disaster at the mines back home in Illinois and of waiting all night with Momma to find out if Poppa was dead or alive. Lee Goodwin was reminded, unpleasantly, of those big revival meetings his mother had dragged him to in the interests of being "saved" when he was a kid. To Julie Noyes, the sight across the water was like a roundup on one of her father's ranches. To April May, it looked like setting up television on location, like, maybe, for the Academy Awards. (For auld lang syne, Rex Roman had received an invitation to the last Academy Awards presentations and had escorted April. It had been the most thrilling night of her life.)

"Ya know what it looks like ta me?" April said. "It looks like TV."

"Television!" Mrs. Bullock spouted. "I've never been on television in all my born days."

"But I'll bet you've been deluged with offers," Arthur said.

Carolyn giggled helplessly and buried her face in Bill's shoulder. Then she said, "Excuse me," and drew away.

Television was exactly what it was, Jaime Malvido, Producer. But, so far, only Arthur Craine knew it for sure. Laddy had some sort of feeling that all the commotion across the way had more to do with television than with rescue, and that he had once met Jaime Something at some party or other. But Laddy wasn't certain.

"Well, shall we all go in and eat whatever there is to eat?" Liz asked.

"If you'll excuse me," Arthur said, "I'll forgo dinner."

"Oh, Arthur, darling," Liz said, "you must eat."

"Why?" Lee Goodwin asked. Lee regretted it immediately. He had spent the day building audience sympathy, impressing on them the slowing down of his thought processes. He hoped that no one had heard.

Lou Ann McIver had. "You're right, Lee, honey. He's nothing but a mean-mouthed ol' bitch." In the darkness she gave Lee an affectionate little squeeze on what she assumed was an erogenous zone. A day ago it might have been, but now it corresponded exactly with where one of the heaviest roof tiles had landed on Lee's backside. He yelped with pain.

Arthur groped his way across the dark garden, stepping, he thought with a shudder, on Salvador's grave. Of course they'd all know about this television thing tomorrow. But until everything was arranged—a *fait accompli*, as one might say—it would be better not to let on what was happening on the mainland. He stumbled along the dock and all but fell into Laddy's sloop. Striking a match, he found the ship-to-shore phone again. The boat had lights and probably couldn't be seen from the main house, but Arthur preferred not to use them—not until he got matters settled with this young upstart on the shore. Arthur got out his neat little notebook and gold pencil, struck another match, and memorized "Jaime Malvido" and his license number. Then he prepared his speech in Spanish for the operator and reached for the ship-to-shore phone.

For the first time since he had owned this car, Jimmy was grateful for its telephone. The telephone had been installed as a symbol of Jimmy's importance in the theatrical world and as a conversation piece. "Oh, yes, I have a phone in my car." Jimmy's telephone had been only the recipient of wrong numbers and had an annoying tendency to bounce off its cradle whenever the car hit a bump. But today Jimmy was getting calls from a Famous Personage and to-morrow even Hollywood would be clamoring to get through to the little Volkswagen. "*Bueno! Jaime Malvido hablando.*" And then, knowing who was calling, Jimmy switched to English. "Malvido here."

"Arthur Craine speaking." Arthur had no recollection of ever meeting Jimmy Malvido, although he had said. "Oh, yes," when Jimmy had reminded him of a dozen words exchanged in some television studio at some time in the past.

"How are they hangin', Artie?"

Artie, indeed! This was just the sort of smart-assed young man Arthur loathed most. On the other hand, this Jaime Malvido, who had spent the afternoon braying through a bullhorn across the water, had something to offer Arthur. Arthur had been dubious at first, but now, seeing really first-rate television equipment being set up, he realized that the young man was serious. Arthur was interested.

Although Arthur would deny it, he was impressed by the amount of money offered: two hundred and fifty thousand pesos, paid under the table and no bother about income taxes. That was twenty thousand dollars free and clear. Arthur always said that he had no need for money. Need, no. Greed, yes. Rich as he was, Arthur had no objection to growing richer. But of still more fascination was the opportunity offered to Arthur to present a new Arthur to ad-miring television audiences everywhere. Arthur Craine, authority on the English language, Arthur Craine, wit and raconteur, was known and loved. But Arthur Craine on an island, whipped by gales, surrounded by death and danger—and fully equipped with a complete ensemble of sports clothes—well, this would be a new Arthur Craine. Arthur Craine, adventurer!

"Artie?" Jimmy shouted again.

"Yes, Mr. Malvido, this is Dr. Craine."

"Just call me Jimmy, Art."

"Well, Mr. Malvido, I see that your equipment has arrived. Splendid. Now, as to my contract . . ."

"Hell, Artie"—did Arthur sense that this Artie was less hearty?—"hell, I haven't got time to fuck around with a lot of agents and all that crap. Neither have you . . ."

"Perhaps, Mr. Malvido, but I have more than enough time to

read and sign my name to some sort of written agreement—no matter how informal—concerning my, uh, fee for this particular appearance, or series of appearances. A simple letter will be sufficient."

"But we'll be ready to shoot at ten o'clock in the morning, Ar . . . Dr. Craine."

"Ah, yes. That will give you—let me see—just fourteen hours and twenty minutes to prepare your letter of agreement. As to getting it here . . ."

"Don't worry about that. We've got a harpoon gun and we're gonna shoot a rope over. With pulleys, see?" Arthur did not, but that was a technical problem that in no way concerned him. "That way we can send over mikes, a walkie-talkie, a hand camera—stuff like that."

"In that way couldn't you also evacuate this island?" Arthur asked.

"Well, maybe. I'm not sure. But if we did, where the hell would our show be? This is big business. Big for you."

"And even bigger for you, Mr. Malvido." Arthur let the questions drop. They were all perfectly comfortable here. It couldn't last more than a day or two. The people at Su Casa would probably even enjoy this television thing. There was a bit of ham in everyone, as Arthur knew only too well. Dared he be truly audacious? Yes, Arthur dared. "But with this—this rope contraption—you could probably send over a few vital supplies?"

"Surest thing in the world!"

"Then by all means send over a case of Moët-Chandon and a hundred pounds of ice. I'll let you know about other essentials tomorrow when the, uh, technical facilities have been set up. And, of course, my contract."

"Now, I'll be sending over a hand camera for you to work . . ."

"A camera? Not my union, I'm afraid."

"But Artie, we got zoomar lenses here for the distance shots, but we need other stuff—interiors, close-ups, and like that."

And like that! Really! The people one had to deal with in the interests of furthering the communicative arts! "Sorry, Mr. Malvido, but I'm not your man. I wouldn't know one end of a camera from the other."

"Well, in that case, I don't think we've got a deal." Jimmy was used to being stepped on, but not walked over.

"However," Arthur added—not too quickly, he hoped—"however, there is a Mr. Dewlap staying here who has a motion-picture camera. I suppose the techniques are roughly the same. I'll ask Mr. Dewlap. As to union difficulties, I really . . ."

"Leave the unions to me. Dewlap, eh? Oh, likewise, I'll need a list of the people stranded out there, names, home towns, stuff like that."

"Secretarial work, Mr. Malvido?"

"Oh, don't gimme that shit, Artie. We need publicity. Play this thing up big."

"Well, I'm here. There is my sister and her husband, Mr. and Mrs. William W. Williams."

"How do you spell that?"

"In the usual way. My brother-in-law is in steel in Chicago. My sister, Carolyn, came out at the New York Assemblies, at a private dance at the Merion Cricket Club, and also at a party in Princeton. Would you like their club affiliations, as well?" There. Keep this little Mexican nobody in line. Remind him that he wasn't dealing with an unemployed actor. "There is also a Miss Bernice Po-tot-ski, also of Chicago. It's a very distinguished Polish name. I'm sure you know it." Arthur was certain that Jimmy didn't. "But I'll spell it for you, anyhow. That's P-O-T-O-C-(as in contemptible) K . . ."

"Not so fast."

"In addition, we have some Texas people. There is a Mrs. T. B. Bullock of Dallas . . ."

"Bullock? What's the T. B. stand for?"

"Terribly Boorish . . ."

"What?"

Again Liz had thought about the "little things." It helped, yes. But even Liz recognized the silliness of her niceties and refinements. Considering the circumstances, her attention to detail was rather like dressing for dinner in the jungle, or the ship's band playing "Nearer, My God to Thee" (in first class, of course) as the *Titanic* went down. Luncheon had been pink with roses. Dinner was lavender with bougainvillea, with menus written in violet ink. As it was too cold and windy to eat on the terrace, the meals were served buffet style in the *sala* with a great blaze snapping and crackling in the fireplace.

But Liz had been practical, too. She had used up the last of the steaks from the tepid freezer for lunch. Dinner was made up of the things that would surely spoil if not cooked and served immediately. There was a soup made of leftovers and a great deal of sherry. A chafing dish offered up Swedish meatballs made from the perishable hamburger. There were filets of white fish from Pátzcuaro—delicious, expensive, and indigenous to only one lake in one state of Mexico. There was too much fish, and what wasn't consumed tonight would turn up in the bouillabaisse tomorrow. The frozen peas were swimming in the last of the butter. There was an enormous salad of limp, but valiant, lettuces and watercress. What was left of the fruit had been drenched in kirsch, garnished with mint and candied violets. Served with panache and a lot of wine, even Liz had to admit that dinner wasn't bad.

"Liz," Essie said, returning to the buffet table for a second helping, "I don't know how you do it!"

Neither did Liz. The bottled gas had given out with a sad little hiss just after the fish had been grilled. There was still plenty to eat in the larder—roasts of beef, legs of lamb, loins of pork and veal still fairly firmly frozen; there were hundreds of cans of things; there were noodles and rice and spaghetti enough to feed an army. But cooking them would be a problem. Liz was a resourceful and creative cook. From girlhood she had triumphed over the glowering, hooded range in the basement kitchen of her father's townhouse. During her first marriage she had coped with hotplates and electric broilers hidden away in Greenwich Village closets. As Mrs. Hobson of Duluth, Minnesota, she had presided over a sterile, stainless-steel laboratory of a kitchen to heat baby food for a moribund husband. But somehow she didn't quite see herself as the pioneer woman poking at open pots over a fireplace.

Like everyone else, Liz had assumed that the activity on the mainland was some sort of rescue squad. A private conversation with Laddy had disabused her of such an optimistic notion. Writhing with embarrassment, Laddy had told her, bit by bit, the bad news about the weather—that rescue was impossible today, would be impossible tomorrow, and probably the day after. "I see. Well, I think we won't say anything about it, Laddy. No point in upsetting everyone." In a way, Liz was almost glad. The present emergency effectively postponed the serious thinking she would have to do about the immediate past and the immediate future. Now encouraged by the ecstatic moans and happy coos of the well fed, Liz tapped her wine glass.

"First of all, let me say that I've never been stranded anywhere before, so I'm no authority. But I can't imagine being stranded with people who could be half as nice or as helpful or as understanding as you have been today."

"Hear! Hear!" Laddy roared.

It seemed to Liz that her brother was always roaring "Hear! Hear!" Although she fought the notion with all of her might, it often occurred to Liz that her brother wasn't quite bright. Sweet, yes, but not bright. Today he'd been useful as well as ornamental. Yes, really very helpful. But if he'd only break down and tell her the whole truth about their situation, Liz would be a lot more grateful. Of course he was trying to spare her feelings, and that was sweet of him, but whatever the troubles were, Liz would have to know them eventually. It would be easier to cope with them if she were told what they were right off.

"As you know, there's no light and no telephone. And you've gone all day without ice in your drinks."

"As long as we have meals like this one," Essie said, "Walt and I could live like this forever."

"Thank you, Essie," Liz said. "You bring up an interesting point. The very point, in fact, that I was just going to mention. We used the last of the gas on dinner tonight. Out here we buy it by the tankful. They were supposed to deliver more today. Obviously, they couldn't. We can always cook with charcoal and the fireplace. But I'm afraid that everyone's had his last hot bath."

"There's always the swimming pool," Susan said. "That's heated."

Bill Williams snickered. It was the cue for general laughter.

"Susan Holt," Lou Ann said, "if you aren't the damnedest jackass!"

"Lou Ann!" Mrs. Bullock said. "No lady . . ."

"Well, I'm afraid that the swimming pool won't be heated much longer," Liz said. "In fact, I think it's quite cold now."

"Uh, about the swimming pool," Laddy said, "I'm afraid we're going to have to use it as our water reservoir. You see, with the pump off, the water tanks will be empty pretty soon and there's no way of refilling them and . . ."

Now, right here in public, he's beginning to tell me, Liz thought. He couldn't have let me know, privately, at any time during the last twelve hours. Oh, no, not Laddy! Liz, herself, had been looking forward to a hot, deep bath in the unaccustomed solitude of the quarters which she had, until today, shared with Salvador. With dismay, it now dawned on her that her *grande cocotte's* tub, steaming and slick with bath oil, would be a bucket of water dipped out of the pool and warmed up in the fireplace.

"Well," Liz said, with an almost inane brightness, "as you've all seen, help *is* on the way. So I suggest that we all get to bed early, pack, and be ready to be evacuated as soon as they can manage. I *think* that's everything. Once more, you've all been perfectly wonderful and I thank you all more than I can say."

There was a spattering of applause.

"Laddy," Liz said, "could I have a word with you?"

We're in Color

Carolyn Williams awoke and opened her eyes very slowly. The bedroom in Margaritas was pitch dark. Why? Oh, yes. Bill had drawn the curtains last night trying to seal out the cold winds that roared across the island. Carolyn closed her eyes again and stretched. Her hand struck something warm, alive. She sat upright in bed, careless of her nudity. Bill! It was Bill, naked as the day he was born and sleeping silently beside her. Carolyn was shocked and then wondered why she was. Bill was her husband. What could be more natural? That was just it; it *wasn't* natural. Most unnatural.

Until last night, they hadn't made love since—"Let me think. Not since November. Two months ago. More." And here they lay, in their seventh year of marriage, like illicit lovers in some motel.

How had it been last night? Could she remember? Yes, Carolyn could. It had been fine. One of their best. But how had it all started?

Rubbing her eyes, Carolyn tried to think back to the night before. First, there had been a wonderful dinner, too much of it, and lots of wine. Then, afterward, heedless of Liz's instructions to go to bed early and prepare for rescue, the guests had sat around the big fireplace drinking and talking, rather pleased with the comfortable adventure they were sharing. Because there had been no ice and because the night was cold, Walt had experimented with some sort of hot drink made with rum and the remains of the fruit compote, mulled in a saucepan over the fire. The drink hadn't been exactly good, but there could be no doubt as to the wallop it delivered. Carolyn had been persuaded to take three of them.

Later, Liz and Laddy had organized the Dewlaps into a candlelit bridge game. April had sat alone in mute misery. Mrs. Bullock, summoning her gaggle of girls, had marched off into the night. Bernice, usually such good, quiet fun, had drifted off morosely. Lee Goodwin had risen, staggered, and said something about a blinding headache and bed. His deathbed, Carolyn hoped. Arthur had simply never appeared.

Carolyn and Bill had been left with that orchidaceous man, Ronald or Roland, and with the amazing Mrs. Meyers, who wore the most extraordinary coat Carolyn had ever seen. Carolyn realized that crazy furs were In, but was anyone really buying anything *that* crazy? The conversation had been crazy, too. Roland or Ronald had spoken exclusively of current trends in decoration, a topic that rather bored Carolyn and set Bill to stifling cavernous yawns. But Mrs. Meyers' staccato stream of *non sequiturs*, punctuated by bursts of baby talk to her revolting dog, had been the purest jabberwocky. Her conversation had leapt and darted from Tulsa, Oklahoma, to Paris, France, with perplexing side trips to long-gone hotels and restaurants, through the showrooms of dead dressmakers, and to ringside tables for the gala performances of "Morris Shevel-ear"

(Maurice Chevalier?) and "Miss Tin-gay" (Mistinguette?). Binding Flossie's trip through time and space into a runny amalgam was a mysterious cast of characters: there had been Queenie (the dog— Carolyn was sure of that). And then there had been "Daddy" (Flossie's father?), and "You, Jean" (Eugene?). Dazed, glazed, Carolyn had finally managed to rise and excuse herself.

Jostling Bill on their way across the garden, Carolyn had said, "Bill, darling, that woman is crazy."

"No, honey, she's just drunk."

"No, Bill. *I'm* drunk. *She's* crazy."

Carolyn remembered that their bedroom had been freezing, the sheets like dry ice. And then had she summoned Bill into her bed for animal warmth? But no! This was *Bill's* bed. Her own remained untouched. "Why, I'm practically a wanton woman," she giggled. And then she stopped giggling. "Am I so unattractive at twenty-seven, such a how you say lousy lay, that I have to thrust myself into Bill's bed? Does he make love to me because he feels sorry for me? Or is it because we're both too drunk to know the difference?"

Even in her self-dramatizing, Carolyn couldn't quite buy that one. She had little head for alcohol and less taste for it. Drink, to be sure, was an occupational hazard of the society in which she and Bill ran, but, as far as Carolyn was concerned, she would be perfectly content to live under the Volstead Act. One drink before lunch if she happened to be entertained or entertaining, two before dinner, and that was it. Bill drank more, but then Bill could. As long as Carolyn had known him, she had rarely seen Bill more than mellow. But it seemed to follow, now, that nights like last night, like the late, late, liquid evening of the Bachelor and Benedict Ball, were the only times when they could manage to be more to one another than roommates.

"A divorce," Carolyn said aloud. She amazed herself! She had never even considered such a thing before. Now, sitting up in Bill's bed, filled with his love, her bare, brown thigh touching his naked back, it occurred to Carolyn that divorce was their only answer. The state of Illinois was generous with its grounds for divorce: adultery, cruelty, desertion, alcoholism, impotence, bigamy, felonies, venereal disease, and some others Carolyn couldn't even recall; not that she or Bill could possibly qualify for any of them. They had never even had a real quarrel. Carolyn and Bill honestly liked each other, as once they had loved each other. But when love was gone, it was gone. And the only thing to do was to part, amicably and without regrets or recriminations, like intelligent adults. Surely there must be some state progressive enough, some judge sophisticated enough to realize that the only real reason for divorce was the death of love. Carolyn would ask no alimony, no settlement. Bill could keep his millions, the penthouse, everything he had ever given her. Carolyn would get a job—doing exactly *what* she wasn't sure. Other women managed. If she had been a flop as Mrs. William W. Williams, housewife, she might be a success as Carolyn Craine, career girl.

Carolyn slid gently out of Bill's bed. She would brush her teeth, comb her hair, put on a modicum of make-up before she faced Bill. No need to make him grateful to be parting company with a frump. Drawing her robe around her, Carolyn considered which of the two bathrooms was hers. Ah, yes. The one near the hall. Carolyn opened the bathroom door and gave a little gasp. There stood her brother, Arthur, a ruche of Kleenex around his collar, skillfully applying Carolyn's cosmetics.

"Arthur! What . . ."

"*Zut alors*, dear girl, now you've made me smudge my eye. I hope I didn't disturb you and Bill. Run along now, do. I'll explain later."

Carolyn closed the bathroom door and sat down on the edge of her bed. Had the Craine family finally gone to seed? Would it die of its own decadence with a nymphomaniac and a transvestite as its sole survivors? Shivering, she wanted now to crawl back into bed with Bill, but with Arthur doing his face in her bathroom, such a notion was naturally out of the question.

Arthur repaired the damage to his lower lid. Arthur had never applied make-up before, but it had been done so often for him by the experts in television studios that he knew exactly what to do. He had watched their work in the big, light-framed mirrors and had been gratified by the results. Put on a little, take off a lot, powder it, and what was left? A face younger, sharper, more photogenic. Dispassionately, the make-up men could look, analyze, and set to

197

work, emphasizing the good points, playing down the bad ones.

Arthur lightened his splendid suntan. It was good for personal appearances, but on color television it would go either burnt orange or the unappetising purple of raw liver. He remembered to do his throat, his ears, the back of his neck and his hands and wrists. Arthur was famished, but glad that he had forgone dinner last night. Mindful of an embryonic weight problem, Arthur had worn his waist-cincher under dark, slimming slacks and a pale jacket with vertical stripes worked into a sort of V-formation. There! Thank God his teeth were straight and white and his own—mostly—so that he needn't bother with painting them or, worse, wearing one of those disgusting plastic bits in his mouth. Now to tone down the whole paint job and Arthur was ready.

When Arthur emerged from Carolyn's bathroom, the curtains were open, the room filled with an anemic sunlight. Bill was propped up on his pillows smoking a cigarette, and Carolyn, seated at the dressing table, was directing her attention—too much attention?—to the filing of her nails. Damn them! If Arthur had wanted them to get up early to do something amusing, they would have slept until noon. But today, when Arthur had a rather personal errand to perform, and one that necessitated passing through their bedroom, they were as wide awake as barnyard fowl.

Arthur decided to brazen it out. "Well, how do I look?"

"Why, you look divine, Daphne!" Carolyn said. "Would you like to borrow my lilac chiffon?" And then Carolyn dropped her attempt at badinage. She had heard of men—especially men like Arthur, who were always under the sternest self-control—cracking up in emergencies. "Arthur . . ."

Bill interrupted. "Arthur, are you wearing *make-up?*"

"Yes," Arthur said.

"Well, you'd never guess it," Bill said.

"Arthur," Carolyn said, "just—just what *is* all this?"

"Perfectly simple, my dears; it's for television."

"*Television?* The electricity doesn't even work." This was more serious than Carolyn had feared.

"Not to *watch* it, silly. God forbid! To be *on* it.'

"What are you talking about, Arthur?" Bill said.

"Well, my dears, I wanted to save it as a surprise, but in less than half an hour Su Casa and its dramatis personae—you, me, all of us —will be thrilling the world at large with our dramatic plight."

"I don't know what's so dramatic about it, Arthur," Carolyn said. "We're all here, safe, sound, and comfortable. No lights, no water . . ."

"Just be grateful that your audience can't smell us," Bill said.

"It hardly matters, anyhow," Carolyn said. "We'll all be taken ashore today. You heard Liz."

"Don't be too sure," Arthur said with an annoying inscrutability. "I'll see you down in the parking lot. Oh, and try to avoid wearing black or white. We're in color." Good at entrances, better at exits, Arthur was gone.

Whatever it was that Carolyn had meant to say or do to Bill, Arthur had effectively driven it from her mind.

On the Air

Like most amateur undertakings, the televising of the plight of Su Casa got off to a bad start. Disorganization was rampant on both sides of the water. The weather, while somewhat improved, remained uncooperative; cold, windy, and with the sun appearing intermittently and only pallidly.

The harpoon gun that was meant to carry a lifeline across to Su Casa missed killing Arthur Craine by a matter of inches. To disguise his genuine terror, his counterfeit fury put to shame the temperamental rampages of the late Tallulah Bankhead, albeit a full octave higher. Pablo, Bill Williams, and Walter Dewlap securely anchored the guy rope from the mainland. When it was tautened, its pulleys tested, an interesting array of equipment bobbed and jiggled across the waters. First came a walkie-talkie so that Jimmy Malvido could bark bilingual instructions. It was followed by a hand television camera that fascinated Walt, and then a color television monitor that fascinated everyone.

Taped to the monitor was an envelope containing Arthur's contract. Once opened, studied, and signed, the letter of agreement worked wonders at soothing the star's outrage. With restored calm, Arthur returned to Margaritas, relieved himself, tightened his waist-cincher, powdered, and permitted Pablo to serve him a pot of coffee heavily laced with brandy. Considering that Arthur had eaten nothing for more than twenty hours, the addition of brandy was perhaps unwise.

Since daybreak, Jimmy had been pounding around the television encampment in pale desert boots, gnawing on a long, black cigar, which he detested and could not keep lighted. He was trailed by his Girl Friday. As a production assistant, Jimmy had too hastily acquired an intense Lesbian drama student, the alumna of forty dollars' worth of Berlitz Spanish lessons, who was terribly interested in television as an art form, but whose only experience with the medium consisted of switching her set from one channel to another. The camera crew found their boss and his executive secretary funnier than Cantínflas.

At Su Casa reactions to the intrusion of television were mixed. Walter Dewlap, who doted on things mechanical, fell in love at first sight with the hand camera, which he, without previous experience, was expected to operate. Essie was happy that Walt was happy. She beamed at the sight of him toting the camera on his shoulder like St. Christopher with the Infant Jesus, the wires of his headset trailing in his wake.

Pablo was entranced with the walkie-talkie and in hog heaven when eventually a set of earphones and a mouthpiece jounced over the water for his more or less exclusive use. He now became unaccountably sullen when he had to surrender his new toys to Laddy in order to be a hewer of wood and drawer of water—the jobs he was paid to perform.

Bill Williams was enjoying a number of new sensations. He was by nature affable, willing, helpful, and oddly knowledgeable about a number of things. He had spent the earlier part of the morning helping Carolyn make their own and Arthur's beds, tidying Margaritas, dipping up buckets of water from the swimming pool to flush the toilets and swab down the tiles of their three bathrooms, then warming still more buckets of water at the fireplace for bathing and shaving—tasks he had not performed since the Spartan New England boarding school and the hairy-chested Canadian summer camp of his adolescence. On the whole, he rather liked it. Carolyn was not so sure. Oh, she had enjoyed playing Swiss Family Robinson with Bill, so much so that she had quite forgotten to tell him that she wanted a divorce. It was Arthur who had disturbed her—first the sight of him in her bathroom, tongue lolling out like a hydrocephalic's as he outlined his eyes. And then the tantrum he had staged down at the water's edge. It was so unlike the suave, urbane, self-contained brother she had always admired. The experience left Carolyn slightly shaken for the second time that morning.

Liz was of two minds about the television when Laddy told her what was going on. "Arthur? Arthur is broadcasting a television show? From *here?*" Laddy, sensing that his sister was not entirely pleased, blushed, mumbled, and nodded. "Of course Arthur is a very old friend. I'm devoted to him and I know you are, too, Laddy. But doesn't it seem just a little as though he were dancing on Chavo's grave?"

"H-he said that he thought the pub-publicity would be good for you," Laddy stammered.

"Why, of course, Laddy! By all means let's show the world this bankrupt, crumbling old ruin falling apart at every seam—stranded all by itself out in the Pacific, no gas, electricity, telephone, or water."

"Liz, I only . . ."

"And the interviews should be a barrel of laughs. Do bring on Mrs. Meyers to convey the impression that Su Casa is really a retreat for alcoholics. Or vivacious Lou Ann McIver, so they'll think it's a home for fallen girls, as well. Or what about April and Roland—something for everyone. I have a feeling that Mrs. Bullock probably sings and, even if she doesn't, she's so charming she'll bowl them over. Or Lee Goodwin. He could really add tone to any place. And be sure to have Arthur point out the spot where Chavo was k-killed. That should bring them in droves. Oh, Laddy, how *could* you?"

"How could I?"

In suspecting her brother of any complicity in Arthur's television venture, Liz was incorrect. Laddy had simply heeded the mating call of Jaime Malvido's bullhorn on the previous afternoon, rescued the note addressed to Arthur and fired through the mist by the harpoon gun, summoned Arthur, taken him to the *Sea Urchin*, and shown him how to operate the ship-to-shore telephone.

"Oh, hell," Liz concluded, "what difference does it make anyway? If it keeps the guests amused it can't be all bad."

Amuse it did. Amapolas was in full twitter over the opportunity to appear on television. Naturally, Mrs. Bullock had been as unpleasant as possible. "Fools' names and fools' faces . . ." she quoted to Laddy. Publicity was vulgar. "A *lady's* name appears in print only three times: at her birth, her marriage, and her death."

"I'm only telling you, Mrs. Bullock," Laddy said. "Nobody's *required* to appear."

And nobody was surprised when Mrs. Bullock appeared, earlier than any of the others, hair frizzed, nose powdered a blinding blue-white, wearing her best print, her cameo earrings, and a sixty-inch rope of Pop-it pearls.

"I vow I'm so nervous I won't know what to do or what to say and I'll just stand there like some big old idiot," Susan Holt said, wriggling into her dress.

"Which is exactly what you will do because it's exactly what you are," Lou Ann said. "Here, move out of the way. I want to see if I put on enough foundation." She had. Too much. It made her look older than she was and nearly as hard. "You just stand there and stick out your titties, Susan. *I'll* do the talkin'."

"S'pose they'll see us in Big D?"

"Course they'll see it back home, fool," Lou Ann said. "First thing I'm gonna say is 'Piss on Hockaday School.'"

"Oh, Lou Ann, you *wouldn't!*"

"Oh, Lord," Julie sighed, "I never thought of that! And there'll be my mother in hysterics and Daddy calling out the state troopers and chartering ships and planes and trying to buy Mexico. If they see this, I'll *never* get away again."

"Hey!" Lou Ann said, her small eyes lighted as though by divine inspiration. "Ya think I oughta wear my new hip-huggers? Would they look all right?"

"They'll look all right if you don't turn around," Julie said.

Back in Rosas again by means of a stepladder, the door unbolted, the locks on his clothes closet broken open, Roland felt better. It was scary to go into the bathroom with one whole wall out. Why bother to go there anyway? There was no water. Roland was glad that he'd had the foresight—the luck, really—to take a shower in Laddy's bathroom yesterday just before the last of the water gave out. It hadn't been hot. Barely tepid. But at least he was clean.

This morning Roland had walked over to Margaritas to return Arthur Craine's borrowed clothing. The Williamses—Bill and Carolyn—had received him, given him a cup of instant coffee brewed in their fireplace. And then Bill had been nice enough to lend him his razor, his badger shaving brush, his wonderful, old-fashioned English soap, and enough hot water to do a proper job. What nice people they were and what lovely things they had, Carolyn and Bill and Arthur. Say what you would about the momentary delights of an ignorant little toughie like Chip, it was nice to be back among one's own kind again. Hadn't Carolyn hung on his every word last night? Roland actually liked women if they were chic and decorative and sophisticated. Carolyn was.

And now Roland was going to be on television—*with Arthur Craine!* Wouldn't they positively die back in Allentown when they saw him! But what to wear? Yellow with an orange sling? Roland didn't actually need a sling, but he had so many bright silk squares, and a sling would add a touch of color, interest, drama. Lime with the henna paisley? Or white with . . . no, Arthur had said not to wear black or white on color TV. And what else had Arthur said? Oh, yes, he had said, "And for Christ's sake, don't let your slip show!" What on earth could Arthur have meant by that?

Flossie Meyers felt strange and oddly exhilarated. She had been awake all day yesterday and asleep all last night. She had rung for room service and a bottle of vodka and ice this morning before she recalled that there was no electricity, no bells, and no ice. Flossie felt very proud to have remembered that. She had been perplexed to turn the golden swan taps of her bathtub and have nothing happen. But then the reason for that came back to her, too. In fact, for the first time in some years, Flossie was able to remember everything—well, almost everything.

She was in Mexico. She couldn't recall the name of the hotel, but her cottage was called Babies'-Breath. Sweet! There had been a hurricane or something, and also a funeral. For some reason they all had to stay here. That suited Flossie just fine. She had been invited to two parties. There was a luncheon with steak and pink napkins yesterday, and then someone gave a buffet supper. (There! How was that?) And then some guy had given her a hot toddy, and she'd sat around a big fire having an interesting talk with a nice American girl named Carrie or something like that. (Yes, by jinks, Flossie was having what amounted to a social season and *remembering* it.)

And whaddayuh know, here came a visitor! Not a waiter or maid, but a real gent. Good-looking, too. Blondish. Like Nelson Eddy or Gene Raymond or Douglass Montgomery—some of the big stars. It was Laddy, glistening with apprehension. He bore gifts—a pot of coffee, a fifth of vodka, and a bucket of hot water.

"Top of the morning!" Flossie brayed. Hospitably she brushed Queenie off the white sofa and patted the cushion beside her. "Siddown. Drink?"

"I-I'm afraid I can't," Laddy said. "I just came to bring you some water for washing and—and coffee and . . ."

"You sure know what Flossie likes, doncha, good-looking?"

Laddy leapt to his feet. "I—I also came to tell you that we're going to be on television. In color. Arthur Craine, you know."

Flossie didn't. But she brightened anyhow. Show folks! That's what these people were. No wonder she was having such a good time. "Swell!" Flossie decided.

"I mean, you don't have to be interviewed. Not if you don't want to be. I mean, you'd probably rather not."

"I don't mind, honey." Flossie could be generous.

"I mean, Liz—that's my sister—Liz said that maybe you'd just prefer to watch. Or maybe you don't even want to bother. The point is, we've got plenty of vodka, and if you'd rather, uh, just stay here in your bungalow . . . well, whatever you prefer to do. Lunch is at two. We can send it out if you like. Hey! Look at the time! Well, thanks ever so much."

"Likewise, handsome. Abyssinia!"

Cute!

Flossie took the bottle of vodka to her bathroom, opened it, and poured a generous three glugs into a glass. She tasted it and didn't really like it. Odd. It was Smirnoff's 100 proof. Nothing wrong with that. Maybe it was because there was no ice. Flossie's eye caught her bottle of mouthwash. Something called Micrin. It looked a little like laundry blueing. Boldly she tipped the bottle of Micrin into the glass of vodka and stirred it with her index finger. She sipped. Not bad. Sorta minty. And the color! Ice blue! Flossie carried the drink into her bedroom.

In no time at all Flossie was feeling just wonderful. From the bottom of a suitcase she had dredged up a dress she hadn't thought of for years—ice-blue satin, damned expensive, and designed just for Flossie by some fancy French dressmaker in 1939. It had a smart, triple peplum, a slit back, sleeves tight from the shoulder pads to the elbows and then cascading in ruffles to her knuckles. There were also twelve rhinestone buttons, nine still attached. They sure didn't make clothes like this nowadays! With the Carmen Miranda platform sandals dyed to match, Flossie felt like a queen. She put on her diamonds—all of them—and threw the Paradise fox over her shoulders. Arranging her black cartwheel hat at a rakish angle, Flossie emerged into the garden, ready to live life to the hilt. Just imagine! They wanted her, little Flossie Meyers, to be on TV.

A treasure trove of theatrical clichés had lodged themselves somewhere under April May's hair spray throughout the years. "Born in a trunk backstage at the Palace," "the show must go on," and "greasepaint in my veins" were the few she could remember most easily.

Actually April had been born above a bakery in Cleveland. Except for stripping to enthusiastic cheers at a number of stag parties, she had never appeared professionally. If there was greasepaint in her

205

ans, it was purely by osmosis from the layers and layers of panchromatic make-up she had slathered on daily since the age of twelve. Still, April liked to think of herself as a part of show business, and her fondest dream was to be really *in* it.

She had gone hungry to enroll in all the courses offered by the "La Mildred Ecole de Danse—Tap, Acrobatic, Ballet, Jazz, and Spanish," where it was decided that, in spite of promptly paid tuition, April had no sense of rhythm. Her earnings as a call girl, after commissions, had been cheerfully offered to the "Pucini Academy of Voice Culture—Popular, Operatic, Stage, Concert, Nite Club." Although two months behind in the rent, the one-man faculty was forced to confess that April was tone deaf. And April had kept her vigil—sheet music and leotards at hand—through hundreds of auditions, only too willing to sing her own particular version of "Night and Day," perform her "danse exotique" to "Mood Indigo." Never, in ten years of trying, had April been permitted to finish either number. Her liaison with Rex Roman had been April's sole contact with the glamor, the glory that was show business.

And now show business was coming to her! Liz had visited Poincianas to tell April that there was going to be some sort of television thing. They wanted April to appear!

Clutching Rex's chronometer, the last thing he had given her, April gazed through crimson eyes at the eleven-by-fourteen studio portrait taken of him thirty-five years ago, leopard loincloth, chest and armpits sleekly depilated. "It's for us, Rexy. For you an' I. The show must go on." Heaving with dry sobs, April reached for her wiglet, her teasing brush, and began to spray more lacquer into her rigid hair.

Arthur had been correct in his cynical estimate of people. When it was known that the inmates of Su Casa were to appear on television, that the cameras on the shore were equipped with long-range lenses, and that Walter Dewlap was manning a hand camera for close-ups, everyone became, almost magically, better dressed, better groomed. They seemed to stand straighter, smile more, speak with a new and mysterious vivacity. Even those who had feigned indignation or indifference were suddenly slicked up and never too far out of reach of Arthur and the hand microphone.

Pablo, in a moment snatched from his never-ending chores, had changed into a fresh uniform and heightened the luster of his blue-black hair with a few pungent drops of the absent Florentino's brilliantine. Aurelia applied lipstick, skewered her braid into a towering topknot, jammed her square, bare feet into a pair of the Señora's narrow, cast-off pumps, screwed dangling earrings into her lobes, and, after a pitched battle, managed to fit her best dress over the kicking, pummeling lump that was her unborn child. Even Liz, while thinking about what to give her household for lunch, and trying not to think about more serious matters, devised a sort of spur-of-the-moment mourning and decided, after an appraising glance in the mirror, that she didn't look too bad. If she had to go through with this television of Arthur's she might just as well appear at her best in case someone who knew her when might be watching.

Bernice Potocki also tried to pull herself together. She didn't want to be on television. She didn't even want to be here. She wanted to be dead, and she cursed the cracked wall in Hortensias for not collapsing on her and killing her outright. But still Bernice had her pride. None of the people here—her new, and oh, so temporary, friends—knew that Ignacio had spent an afternoon in her bed and had fled when he had discovered the truth about her. Essie had gently teased her about her lovelorn swain on the opposite bank and made a feeble joke about Leander swimming the Hellespont. Well, they never would find out! As soon as she could get out of this place, she'd go someplace where no one knew her, start over again.

Bernice began dressing without even thinking of what she was putting on. There was no need to. The finished product would be ineffably smart. Smartness was her knack; now it would be her life. She stepped into trim, tailored slacks, formerly the property of that horsy size ten in the suburbs; put on the monogrammed silk shirt bought from that girl with the same initials as hers—Barbara Penfield? Bianca Pignatelli?—and expertly knotted a French scarf snapped up by Madam Kaye from a bankruptcy sale. She threw the sable jacket over one arm. Now, at least, Acapulco was cold enough to wear it. If this television nightmare ever got as far as Chicago, of course Madam Kaye would be watching. What else had she to do with her evenings? Yes, Madam Kaye would be sitting in her cheap, furnished apartment that stank of cigarettes, Shalimar, TV dinners, and Madam herself, blunt hands folded across her satin stomach. Madam would nod lugubriously and say, "I told her so. I was right." No doubt about it, Madam Kaye was right. Helplessly, Bernice threw herself down on her bed and cried. Miss Potocki arrived late, but wonderfully smart, for Arthur's program.

The only guest who did not appear on television that day was Lee Goodwin. True, no one had exactly urged him to join the others, the stuck-up bastards! Lee was just naturally camera-shy. He had good reason to believe that various arms of the law held photographs of him. Not in post offices. Lee had never used the mails to defraud. He preferred the personal touch. Nevertheless, in a handful of states where Lee no longer chose to visit, it was likely that snapshots affectionately taken by wealthy widows being wooed to invest in the Happy Ending Retirement Fund or some of Lee's other projects were now enlarged and in the hands of local police chiefs.

Naturally, Lee's name—or names—kept changing. There were Leonard Goodrich, Lewis Goode, Lenox Goodhue, and others. And Lee, himself, kept changing. He was sometimes fair, sometimes dark, sometimes redhaired, with coming-and-going mustaches dyed to match. A collection of windowpane spectacles in a variety of frames traveled with him. But there was something about Lee's face, the pale eyes, perhaps, or the small twitching mouth, that defied the subtleties of masquerade. And, once heard, his voice was unforgettable. Why flirt with fate?

It was boring as hell to be holed up in Alcatraz all day, but to be out with the others, appearing on television, might engender just too much excitement for Lee. Anyhow, he had turned his refusal to appear into a good thing. "Not up to it, sorry. . . . Kinda groggy today . . . eyesight going bad on me. . . . Dizzy. . . . Better not chance it." Little seizures such as this one, spoken and acted out for the benefit of that Park Avenue idiot, Laddy, would prove extremely valuable in the series of lawsuits Lee was planning.

"All dressed up and nowhere to go," Carolyn murmured to Essie. There they all stood, a spectrum of scarlet and pink and yellow and lime, in broad stripes, bold plaids, splashy floral prints, and polka dots, ready to appear in color. By contrast, Liz, in her bereaved black, shone like a beacon. It was already three hours past starting time. What the inexperienced residents of Su Casa did not know was that show business, like the military life, was largely a matter of hurry up and wait. "But then, dears," as Arthur explained, "I'm accustomed to working with professionals."

Placing Pablo's headset gingerly against a well-powered ear, Arthur rapped out some sharp inquiries to the shore and, to his dismay, recognized Jaime Malvido and the Girl Friday as rank amateurs, and, worse, hysterics.

While waiting for Arthur's tantrum to subside and for things to be set up at Su Casa, Jimmy had trained his guns and also his cameras on the silver palace of the Princess-up-the-Hill. The Princess had been press copy for more years than she cared to count. Her proximity to Su Casa gave the place a certain cachet, and if her palace was anything like as outlandish on the inside as it was on the outside, it would be good for a lot of footage.

Jimmy was stunned that his boyish charm had not worked on the Princess, had not even been demonstrated to her. At pistol point, the eager producer, the grim Girl Friday, and the unit manager were dismissed from the silver gates. The Princess had received all the publicity—none of it good—she cared to have. Nor did Jimmy's sunny, but somewhat garbled, news bulletins concerning the death of Salvador Martínez do anything to encourage her hospitality. After putting on a black caftan (trimmed with silver), the Princess went into one of her best declines. *Crise de nerfs* they called her performance. Between siren shrieks and oboe moans, before the injection had time to take effect, the princess wondered if Salvador had spoken to anyone before his mysterious death.

In the early afternoon everyone on both sides of the water was ready simultaneously. Walter Dewlap *thought* that he understood the workings of the hand camera. The zoomar lenses from the shore were trained on the little band lined up in the parking lot of Su Casa. Instructions and counterinstructions were barked through the bull-horn, the walkie-talkie, and the headsets. At last Su Casa was on the air.

Standing well to the fore, elegant and manly, the hand mike clutched in his made-up hand, Arthur Craine—the new Arthur Craine—opened his mouth to speak, and for the first time realized that he hadn't a blessed thing to say.

It had all been so easy before, seated in a mocked-up library with other erudite celebrities discussing the difference between "further" and "farther," upbraiding brash but terrified young novelists for their use and misuse of four-letter words, trading risqué badinage with columnists, commentators, and the gabbier film stars. Arthur's panels had always been conducted under the beady eye of a well-oiled moderator, a sort of combination cruise director and nursery governess, who kept things going, encouraged what was lively, cut in on what was dull, and suavely blue-penciled what was blue. Arthur had always looked down on the moderator as a network windbag, barely literate, and probably unemployable at anything more demanding than shooting off his mouth.

Now Arthur was the moderator, an amateur among amateurs. In his efficient daydreams he had planned the new Arthur Craine down to the last aquiline profile shot, the last frosty blue twinkle. He had neglected only to plan the first word. The new Arthur was on the air and he was suddenly caught with nothing to say.

In Trouble

"What the eff-you-see-kay do you call this mishmash?" E. G. d'Enker said softly.

"E. G., if you'll only wait a minute," Jimmy said.

"I've only been waiting three hours. Three hours of that old Craine nance making like Margaret Rutherford."

"Arthur Craine's a big star," Jimmy Malvido said, knowing that Arthur was not.

"So's Tiny Tim. But he don't narrate prize fights yet."

"I—I thought there was some pretty interesting footage," Jimmy said, knowing that there hadn't been.

"Oh, sure kid. The lunch scene was great. Really roughing it. Bouillabaisse. Ninety per cent of the American population don't even know what it is. What is it anyways? Bouillabaisse and French bread and camemberry cheese and "—here E. G. stopped to do a horrid imitation of Liz's rather "social" voice—"and 'some Pösian melons we were fawtunate enough to plahnt in the garden.' Shit! Ya know what the average viewer is sitting down to tonight? Top round. Top round and macaroni. And they can't afford to buy that. This is drama? This is hardship? Finger bowls, yet!"

"But, E. G. these are classy people. Famous."

"Famous for what? Their table manners?" Again, Mr. d'Enker lapsed into mimicry. He was not good, but Jimmy had no difficulty recognizing E. G.'s target. "My sistah, Carolyn, Mrs. William Williams of Chicago. Her husband, Bill, is in steel. And Mr. and Mrs. Dewlap of Pessary, Pennsylvania.' What the fuck's he think he's covering, the Junior League Ball? And that fagola wearing the sling! 'My boutique.' My tokus!"

"But, E. G.," Jimmy wailed, his eyes filling with tears from emotion, from disappointment, and from the miasma of blue smoke caused by E. G.'s cigar, "we've got some real folksy types, too. What about the servants? What about . . ."

"Yeah, kid, and what about that old lush in the blue dress and the cat's ass coat. It's Phyllis Diller's mother. And April What's-her-name, Rex Roman's old flop. Kid, I was banging her in the Astor ten, fifteen years ago for twenty bucks a trick."

"E. G., listen . . ."

"No, kid, you listen to me. You're in trouble."

Jimmy Malvido had committed an error in judgment. He had stumbled across an interesting situation, and had bought and sold the idea without pausing to consider what its dramatic possibilities might or might not be, and whether it contained such bare essentials as a beginning, a middle, and an end. Jimmy had sighted a spark. Now where was the bonfire?

True, far more important events—things like flights to the moon, congressional hearings, and Olympiads—had their dull moments; moments to be filled with inconsequential hot air or with commercials for floor waxes, detergents, and toothpaste. They had now watched three solid hours of tapes of Su Casa, environs, and inhabitants. *Dull, dull, dull.* And Walter Dewlap's film writhing through the processing tank like a sea serpent, was no more interesting—only closer. Yes, it was true that big happenings had their dull moments, but the Su Casa story had no other kind. "I'm in trouble," Jimmy told himself.

What E. G. d'Enker actually meant was not you are in trouble, but *I* am in trouble. The Mex had nothing to lose. E. G. had everything to lose. Mr. d'Enker had been in big jobs—various vice-presidencies of three motion picture studios and the two other networks. Before that he had been high up in two different talent agencies. He'd come one hell of a long way from those ancient days when he had been a minor press agent in New York. This job was as close to the top as he could ever hope to get. It was also the end of the line. And the very end was in view. E. G. d'Enker, Vice-President in Charge of Programming, had, within the last six months, personally rejected a highbrow "talk show" that was now big on NBC. Worse, he had personally selected a ruinously expensive situation comedy that had been lopped off the air after thirteen weeks at a loss of as many millions. Nor had he come up with anything good to replace it. None of the big brass had said anything. The big brass never did—until "Good-bye. Good luck. Keep in touch." Then, yesterday, this smart-assed Hymie—*Jaime*—Malvido had caught E. G. in a weak moment, with a bad hangover, and a worse case of desperation after he had examined the rating sheets. And this slick little Mex had given him a real snow job over long distance, forced his hand, and demanded a confirming telegram naming facts and figures. And E. G. had been dumb enough to fall for it. (The telegram now sat snugly in Jimmy's new safe deposit box in the Banco del Sur.) It wasn't until that Harvard Law School goy from the legal department came into E. G.'s office to take notes for the formal contract that E. G. d'Enker, Vice-President in Charge of Programming, began to suspect what he had let himself—and the network—in for.

"Arthur *Craine*? Oh, yes. We were in prep school together. Is this *his* sort of thing?" Mr. Harvard Law stuck to his booklined office, never questioned artistic policy, never commented on the quality of the programs, in fact, never watched television. But he felt it only polite to show an interest. Yesterday, with his innocuous, businesslike questions, he had shown much more. Quite unintentionally, he had shown E. G. a vision of a pig in a poke growing into a huge white elephant.

"Have we a name for this program, just a tentative title to use on the contract? . . . Copyright clearance? . . . Half hour, one hour, ninety minutes? . . . Will it be a one-shot? . . . Well, about how many? Just a rough estimate . . . Is this show to pre-empt our regular sponsored programs? . . . What time slot, more or less? . . . How much did you say? . . . Golly! That *is* a lot of money . . . *Who* did you say was producing it?" E. G., with an uncommonly quiet voice, confessed. "Oh, yes," said Mr. Harvard Law, sociably, "that little Mexican. I've met him. Quite a practical joker."

Practical joker? Had he, E. G. d'Enker, wheeler-dealer par excellence, been hornswoggled into signing away a fortune, on no one's authority but his own, to a practical joker? He was silent for a minute, then, jabbing the key of his squawk box, he had bellowed, "Debbie? When's the next plane to Mexico?"

Mr. d'Enker never traveled alone. Mass movements were more impressive, complicated, and wasteful. On this trip, his entourage included his secretary, whom he was hoping to bed down, and his sharp, young assistant, who had been doing just that with Debbie ever since the Christmas party. They had flown to Mexico City and had taken a limousine direct to Acapulco. Seated in the rear of one of the mobile unit's trucks, they had watched the first three interminable hours of Jimmy's show of shows. Worse than a practical joke, it was the real thing—trucks, cameras, generators, a mobile processing lab, electricians, cameramen, sound men, cutters —costing God only knew how much for every boring minute.

Now, fully aware of his unlimited limitations as a television impresario, Jimmy fell back on the only resources he had ever had— bluff and bluster. "For Christ's sake, E. G., I thought you *knew* something about telly. You don't think I'm planning to air all this crap, do you?"

"You couldn't. Even the 'Sermonette' is more exciting."

"What I plan to do is to shoot everything. Everything! And then edit down to just the interesting parts."

"What interesting parts? Listen, kid, you can shoot a million miles of nothing and cut it down to an inch. And what have you got? An inch of nothing. Kid, let's face it: it's Zerotime, Dullsville. Now why don't we just . . ."

"Jimmy! Jimmy!" the Girl Friday bawled, lunging into the truck, "Did you see it? A whole house just fell into the ocean!"

Into the Ocean

"Did you see it?" Susan whinnied, charging gracelessly out of Amapolas. "A whole house just fell into the ocean! I was in the bathroom and I heard this kind of rumbling and felt . . ."

"Did I see it, honey?" Walter Dewlap said. "I got it! Right here on film." He patted his portable camera. "I was just coming out and I felt the whole earth kind of buckle and then, like you, I heard this rumbling. And then I saw that house—it was swaying like, well, I don't know what. But I had the camera and just in time for the whole goddamned—excuse me—the whole house to topple right into the water. Jesus, what a splash! Which house was it?"

"Nubes—Mrs. Meyers' cottage."

"Oh, my God! You don't suppose she was in there? That old drunk with the coat and the dog."

"Oh, how awful!" Susan wailed.

Together they ran to the jagged lip of land that had once been the doorstep of Nubes, honeymoon bower in heavenly blue. The sea beneath them thrashed and churned. Walt aimed his camera downward. He was just in time to focus on a spindly bamboo chair draped with something that looked like drenched pink feathers. It spun and bobbed crazily in the eye of a whirlpool and then was sucked down into the roiling sea. Susan screamed. She was gibber-

214

ing senselessly, weeping, and flailing her arms. It was more expression than she had shown in any of her seventeen years and Walter filmed every second of it. "The poor old woman," Susan cried. "And her little dog. Miz Bullock hated her, but she wasn't doing anybody any . . . oh God, oh God, oh God! Now she's dead!"

Walt wheeled just in time. Half the population of Su Casa was racing across the garden and right into the camera's eye. Liz, Laddy, Bill and Carolyn, Pablo, Mrs. Bullock, Lou Ann, and Julie. More casually, Arthur sauntered out of Margaritas, freshly dressed and made-up, the cable of his hand mike trailing behind him.

Liz was the first to speak—or to try to speak. "What was that? My God! Laddy! Nubes! It's gone! Oh, poor Mrs. Meyers!"

"Jesus," Laddy breathed.

"Good riddance, I say," Mrs. Bullock said.

"How dare you?" Carolyn snapped. "Oh, Bill!" Carolyn threw her arms around her husband and burst into tears.

"Well," Arthur said, angling for position in front of the camera, "here is a bit of excitement. It seems, ladies and gentlemen, that one of Su Casa's loveliest bungalows has just been swept away."

"I got it on film," Walt said proudly. "It's right here."

"Don't interrupt," Arthur said. "Yes, ladies and gentlemen, an entire house, occupied by Mrs.—uh, what was her name—has just fallen into the Pacific Ocean. Mrs. Martínez, would you tell our audience a little something about the bungalow. It was called, if I'm not mis . . ."

"Arthur, will you please take that goddamned microphone out of my face and try to get it through your head that another human being has just been killed?"

"Poor old lush," Laddy said softly, but not so softly as to escape the microphone.

"Oh, Arthur . . ." Carolyn said, turning her tear-streaked face to her brother and, quite inadvertently, Walt's hand camera.

"See here, Arthur," Bill said, "this television crap is getting to be . . ."

Walter Dewlap's face lit up as though a message from Mars were coming through his headset. Knowing none of the standard studio hand gestures, he shouted, "Mr. Malvido asks that you *please* watch your language. The television code . . ."

"To hell with Mr. Malvido!" Liz roared. "Whoever he is. Now listen to me, all of you. While you're all having fun playing in front of that damned camera, a woman has just been killed. Can't any of you realize that we . . ."

"Dass a dood dirl, Queenie. Oo had a dood lunchie, din you?"

Everyone and the camera wheeled around. There was Flossie teetering across the lawn on her platform soles, Queenie and a dirty suède purse that might once have been ice blue on one arm. In her free hand a glass of vodka sloshed gaily. "Where you all been? I was in the kitchen feeding Queenie some of that fish stew. She loved it. Then we heard this noise like the world was coming to an end and . . . well, what's the matter with everybody? You look like you seen a ghost."

"It can't be true, ladies and gentlemen," Arthur said with a sudden urgency, "but it *is* true. Instead of perishing with her bungalow, Mrs.—uh—Mrs.—"

"Meyers," Julie prompted.

"Yes, thank you, dear girl; Mrs. Meyers is safe and sound!"

"And drunk, as usual," Mrs. Bullock said.

"Would you please say a few words to the people out there, Mrs. Meyers," Arthur said, extending his hand microphone.

"Jus' call me Flossie, honey. Everybody does." Into the mike she said, "Ish kabible." Then she laughed heartily and took a great swig of her drink. "Well, cry-yi, what's everybody standing around for like it was a funeral? Oh, pardon me, honey," she said to Liz. "Queenie and me was coming to take a see-esther, a li'l lay down, and . . . well, for Christ's sweet sake!"

Walt's camera got Flossie's raddled face as she stared, slack-jawed, into the emptiness that had once been Nubes.

"Mrs. Meyers—uh, Flossie," Liz said, her words tumbling on top of one another, "I can't tell you what a relief it is to find you— and the little dog—alive. But your bungalow just—just now fell into the ocean. Thank God you weren't . . ."

"Jeest," Flossie said. "Whuddya know! Babies'-Breath."

"Mrs. Meyers is speaking of the name of her bungalow, Nubes, or 'clouds' in Spanish," Arthur droned on. "It is also the colloquial term applied to a small white flower known in English as babies'-breath. As I may or may not have told you, each of the accommodations at Su Casa is named for a flower and decorated accordingly. My own bungalow, for example . . ."

"I'm afraid that your things, everything," Liz said, "went with the house. Everything but the clothes on your back."

"But they sure Lord are chic," Lou Ann said. Susan, now recovered, giggled.

"Oh, that don't matter," Flossie said generously. "Easy come, easy go. Anyways I had some of them ever since . . ." She paused. "Angel face," she murmured. "Angel Face." And now she screamed it. "*Angel Face!*" Flossie's knees buckled. She sank to the lawn, a great heaving mound of fox fur. "Angel face." In front of the stunned circle, Flossie Meyers lay weeping on the grass.

Just Maybe

E. G. d'Enker sat stunned, his eyes bulging toward the television monitor in the darkened truck. Jaime Malvido, seated beside him, was almost, but not entirely, speechless with astonishment. He heaved a sigh, lit a cigar, coughed, and said, "Well, E. G., what did I tell you?"

"Shit, kid, that's the real stuff!"

"It's *life!* Raw emotions," the Girl Friday breathed. "Marvelous facial planes on that woman in the fur coat! And that tragic little dog. Fantastic camera angles. James Wong Howe . . ."

"Don't that dike know how to turn off?" E. G. muttered.

"Could we just see—*and hear*—the rest of this, Priscilla?" Jimmy said.

"Sorry, I'm sure. I was merely trying to convey . . ."

"Shhhhhh!"

Liz appeared on the monitor. She was standing beside the swimming pool, the guests of Su Casa seated tensely around her.

"Ex-quis-ite colors," the Girl Friday said. "The blue of the pool, the hot, hot pink of the . . . "

"For fuck's sake, Mac, will ya can it?"

"Sorry, I'm sure. I was merely . . . "

"Shhhhhh!"

"Now listen, everyone," Liz was saying, "and listen carefully. In five minutes' time I want every bungalow empty. You just saw what happened to Flossie's house . . . "

"Angel Face," Flossie whimpered.

"What's with this angel face bit?" E. G. said.

"Shhhhh," the Girl Friday hissed.

"I don't know anything about earthquakes or what comes later, but if it could happen to Nubes it can happen to all the rest of the bungalows. Until they can get us away from here, we'll all have to double up in the rooms of the main house."

"It was clearly understood that I am paying for a suite of rooms consisting of . . . "

"You are paying for nothing, Mrs. Bullock," Liz said. "But you may be paying *with* your life. If you don't care about your own, at least you might consider the girls."

"From the finest families in Dallas."

"Exactly. And unless Dallas is to declare an official state of mourning, you and your girls will have your bags packed and be up here immediately. The married couples can have rooms to themselves and . . . "

"We're already in Violetas," Essie said, "but if it would be more convenient for you, Walt and I could . . . "

"Thanks, Essie, but it's better that you stay put. That leaves Bill and Carolyn. The people who booked Claveles obviously aren't coming, so you can move in there. The single men will have to bunk together . . . "

"There's an extra bed in Rosas," Roland said, smiling at Arthur.

"It's *The Well of Loneliness* in drag," E. G. said. The Girl Friday tossed her lank hair indignantly, contemplated Debbie through the dimness of the truck, saw the hand of E. G.'s assistant on Debbie's thigh, and tossed her hair back in the direction of the monitor.

"Rosas has got to be vacated," Liz said. "With one whole wall of the bathroom out, it's too dangerous. And so, Roland, if you don't mind moving to Alcatraz with Mr. Goodwin . . . " Roland's face was a study.

"Well, sister, maybe Mr. Goodwin minds. Ever thought of that?" It was Lee Goodwin's first appearance, first words on camera. He had been forced to leave his room and come to this meeting.

"Oh, what mean eyes!" the Girl Friday said.

"In that case, I have the perfect solution, Lee," Liz said. "Start swimming! Arthur, you can move in with Laddy."

"Going back to Nassau Hall," Arthur quipped. Then, aware of his audience, "Mr. Parkhurst was one of my students at Princeton, ladies and gentlemen."

"Maybe you could complete his education," Lee said.

Liz cleared her throat and waved the microphone away. "Arthur, I've told you that we have more important things to think about than your damned television show."

"Debbie, make a note to edit that out."

"Yes, Mr. d'Enker."

"Now that leaves Flossie and April and Mrs. Bullock and . . . "

"I'm sure I don't want to share a room with any of . . . "

"And I'm sure that they don't want to share a room with you, Mrs. Bullock. And so I'll move Bernice out of Hortensias. You don't mind sharing, do you, Bernice?"

"Of course not, Liz," Bernice said.

"Isn't she darling!" the Girl Friday said.

"Hortensias is a single. It's all yours, Mrs. Bullock."

"I'd like to see it first."

"You will be seeing a good deal of it, I'm afraid."

"Well, if I don't like it . . . "

"Mrs. Bullock, if you don't like it, you can nest in a tree. I don't mean to throw my weight around, but this is a state of emergency. It's my house and as long as you're here, you'll do as I say. Is that quite clear?"

"Man, if that Liz broad ain't careful she'll cop an Emmy for herself!" E. G. was lost in admiration. So was the Girl Friday.

"Wonderfully plastic face. Such an air of . . . "

"Oh, pipe down!"

"Sorry, I'm sure. I merely . . . "

"Shhhhhhhh."

"Gladiolas has twin beds and a little sitting room with a sofa Will that be all right for you three girls?"

"Of course, Mrs. Martínez," Julie said. "Whatever you say."

"Yessum," Susan said.

Lou Ann simply sniffed. She had her own notions as to the idea bedding arrangements.

"Thank you. I'll put Bernice and April in the big room at the head of the stairs. That leaves Mrs. Meyers—uh, Flossie. And now that Salvador is . . . well, now that I'm alone, there's plenty of space in my room. So Flossie can move in with me."

"And don't forget about Queenie," Flossie said.

"How could I?"

E. G. got out of his canvas chair and snapped off the monitor. "Well, kid, I think maybe you got a show. At least half an hour of one."

"Half an hour?" Jimmy said indignantly.

"Not more. It wants a lot of editing. Start out, maybe with that Texas kid doing the crazy bit—say like thirty seconds. Drag the viewers in at least. Then back to you doing a narration. A new one. Short. Lenny, he'll write it for you." With a thumb, E. G. indicated his assistant. "Then we go to Mother Craine and the social bit. You know. Introduce the folks. Then maybe the lunch scene."

"I thought you hated the luncheon," Jimmy said sulkily.

"Okay, okay, okay. I gotta new idea. These people are pretty much class—how America would like to live. As for Arthur Craine, they couldn't give him balls at the Mayo Clinic. I mean, Tony Quinn he ain't. In fact, none of the guys out there are very ballsy, except maybe that spick servant and he don't count."

"They happen to be *gentlemen*," the Girl Friday said. Her loathing of Mr. d'Enker was growing great and hot.

"Sure they are, Mac. And you try to sell that in Hicksville. So we'll play it like it is: class with its ass in a sling. You know, the social register doing its own laundry. A *nafka* like April May moved in with a Polish countess. She *is* a countess?"

"She's lovely," the Girl Friday said.

"Tell you the truth, E. G., I don't really know," Jimmy said.

"Well, you know it now. She's Countess Potocki. Shit, man, we gotta have some angles. Sell this package. Then we got this Liz, the only one out there knows her ass from her elbow, bunking with the alky and that miserable mutt. You know, real guts under that Park Avenue voice . . . "

"Mrs. Martínez happens to speak as *educated* people do," the Girl Friday said. She was elaborately ignored.

"So there she is with the rummy. You know. Contrast. So right after the lunch scene we do the house falling down bit, the Texas kid again with Mr. Squaresville. Then the mob scene. Gotta tone down their language, fuckin' slobs! So we play it for real drama. Then the meeting with Liz in the driver's seat. . . . Now if only something else could happen—I mean like the roof falling in."

"You might call the naval base and ask them to shell the house," the Girl Friday said. Her mordant wit was famous the length and breadth of Sharon, Connecticut.

"Debbie, call L.A. and get an editor down here."

"*I'll* do the editing," Jimmy Malvido said. He wondered, as he said it, how editing was done. He was relieved to have at least *some* sort of show, but he felt its control slipping rapidly from his hands.

"Kid, what you know from editing I could lose in my belly button. Get Marvin Barouch, Debbie."

The young assistant now spoke, eager to be a cog in what might turn into something big. "Marv's working on . . . "

"I don't give a shit if he's working on the Last Supper. Tell him to hop the first plane to Mexico City and hire a car. I want him here tomorrow noon at the latest. It's a chance we gotta take. Maybe—I say *maybe*—we got a show. Now, if only something else could happen, like, maybe, they're starving. Hey! Carolyn Williams and that old Bullock bitch fighting over a Ritz cracker . . . "

"That reminds me, I told Arthur Craine that I'd send out champagne and ice on the guy rope and . . . "

"*Champagne?* What the . . . Hey! I'm beginning to see an angle. Look, we'll play it like it is. We'll say 'You ordinary folks would be happy with a loaf of Wonder Bread, but these aristocrats want caviar even in the face of . . . ' Hey, think we could gettum to dress for dinner? It's a good shot; cases of champagne, chopped liver, filet mignons going over on the rope. And we'll have to send some lights out, too."

"But, E. G., we've already said that they don't have lights or gas or . . . "

"Man, who hasta see the lights? We get a great shot of this Liz broad wearing like a chinchilla coat cooking beef Wellington in the fireplace. And there's this countess in like long gloves washing dishes in the hopper. Or maybe . . . "

"Honestly," the Girl Friday erupted in her best drama-school outrage, "here you have real people in a real situation saying real things and showing real emotions. Why do you have to hoke it up with a lot of vulgar, one-dimensional trumpery stunts from the wasteland of . . . "

"Uh, Priscilla . . . " Jimmy began.

"Listen, Mac," E. G. said, "I'm a very patient man. I also been in the business since before you was born. There's more money riding on this half-assed hunka nothing than you'll prolly ever see in your life. I'm not selling facial planes, I'm selling excitement. And if we ain't got it, we make it. So unless you want a one-way ticket back to the Actor's Studio, you'll button your lip and listen to Daddy. Right?"

"Oh!"

"Now, you got a list of who they are and where they come from? Good. Debbie, get on long distance to the public-relations department. Find out everything about these people. Tellum to plant stories in the home-town papers. Get it on the wire services. Get the boys to play it up on tonight's newscasts. Gettum to break into that deadhead panel show and the afternoon soaps with a flash. They all know there's been an earthquake here, but what they *don't* know is that Arthur Craine, famous blah blah blah, and blah, blah, blah, distinguished leaders of society, are trapped on an island that's crumbling away like a halvah. Get some good stills off the tape. Get interviews with the folks at home—the families— fly 'em down here if you can."

"Yes, Mr. d'Enker," Debbie said, scribbling away in her note-book.

"Sure, E. G.," the assistant said.

"And you, Malvido, work up some local interest. Nobody in Acapulco even knows what's going on out there. It's cold as a polar bear's ass and they got nothing else to do. Bring 'em out here to watch the filming. Set up bleachers if you can. Drag out the local celebrities, you knowum all."

Jimmy blanched. "Well, E. G., I'm not sure that . . . What I mean is they may be, uh, reticent to . . . "

"Kid, you show me an actor that's reticent and I'll show you a pig on the Mayo Diet. Check and see who's in town."

"W-well, there's Bryce Goodfellow. He's staying at . . ."

"To talk about what? Religion or Planned Parenthood? Man, we need *names*."

Seething, the Girl Friday said, "Bryce Goodfellow only happens to be one of the most dis-*ting*-guished producers in . . ."

"Sure, honey, and a household word in Fargo, North Dakota."

"Or there's Darryl Zanuck's daughter," Jimmy tried. "A friend of mine knows . . . "

"Great! And then get Whistler's mother and Bess Truman's third cousin. Now try to read me and read me right: I want *names*. I want news coverage. I wasn't a PR flack on Broadway for ten years without learning *something*. We gotta put this over big—or *else*. This ain't the campus frolic, kids. This is real. This means pre-empting, bouncing sponsored shows off prime time. Maybe one night, maybe two, maybe all week. Any idea how many millions of bucks that involves, kids? I thought not. That don't matter. We get other sponsors. We make it up in ratings, *if* we givem something to watch. Action. Excitement. Names. Otherwise it's Death Valley time. Dig?"

Mr. d'Enker was beginning to feel a little better. Not much, but a little. At least now he had a chance. Smelling smoke, the war horse inside him began pawing the ground. Maybe he could turn this nothing fiasco into something big, an hour spectacular, ninety minutes, maybe more. Maybe a whole goddamned week. If he could, he'd have the whole industry eating out of his hand!

"Now, listen, it's like three o'clock in L.A. Debbie, you get on the horn to the press department. Lenny, you gettum to start breaking in on every mothering program—the soaps, the panel shows, the 'Kiddies' Kartoon Karnival,' everything."

"Right, E. G., but what should they say?"

"Shit, I don't care what they say. Make it up. But make it good. Plentya drama—stormy seas, people dying, no hope of rescue, plague, starvation. The works. And maybe we'll get a show outa this. Just maybe."

IV

THE OTHER SIDE OF
PARADISE

Delivery

Trying to keep her temper and her sanity, Liz stood in the parking lot shouting over Pablo's headset to Jaime Malvido. The wind whipped her hair and her skirt. She was unaware that she was being filmed through a telescopic lens or that every word she said was being recorded. And she wouldn't have cared anyhow.

"We're very grateful, Mr. Malvido, for the supplies you've been sending over. But among the things we *don't* need are champagne and Rock Cornish hens and a case of caviar. By the way, the case was empty. I suppose we can always use it for firewood."

"You getting all this down, Debbie?" E. G. asked.

"I mean, these things are all frightfully amusing. But what we really need is stuff like bread and butter and vegetables."

"Cut that last bit," E. G. grunted.

"Mr. Malvido, you'll have to forgive my ignorance, but if you can send over these lights all hooked up to your generator, couldn't you send over an electric wire or something so that we could get our own lights going, the water pump? I mean it would help a lot."

"Cut all that, too," E. G. said.

"My *what?*" Liz said. "My chinchilla coat? I'm afraid I don't own such an animal. Only an old beaver jacket and it's in storage. What's that? Naturally I'm going to prepare dinner. The cook is about ten months pregnant and feeling rotten. I'm awfully worried about her. Champagne is one thing, Mr. Malvido, but I think you're being just a little *too* campy. I feel responsible for the people here and they are in danger. And so if you can manage to send over all those heavy lights and tons of other equipment, don't you think that you might be able to rig up some sort of harness and get the people off here, one at a time?"

227

"Tell her you don't know. You'll try. Too dangerous at night. Maybe in the morning," E. G. muttered. Jimmy repeated the message.

"I see," Liz sighed wearily. "Okay. Simply thought I'd ask. If you'll forgive me now, I've got to go in and get the meal going. What am I going to wear? Who gives a damn what anyone's going to wear? Pants and a sweater, I suppose. This dress is just too cold for dinner." Liz put down the headset and strode up to the main house.

"Okay, kid," E. G. said, handing over the typewritten transcript of what Liz had been saying, "here's how it cuts down. Liz: 'We're very grateful, Mr. Malvido, for the supplies you've been sending over . . . champagne, Rock Cornish game hens, and a case of caviar . . . these things are all frightfully amusing . . . My chinchilla coat? . . . It's in storage . . . I'm going to prepare dinner. The cook is . . . feeling . . . her . . . champagne . . . *Too* campy . . . If you'll forgive me now, I've got to go in and . . . dress . . . for dinner.' Howzat?"

"*Hombre!*" Jimmy Malvido said.

"Do you think you're being entirely honest," the Girl Friday fumed, "not to mention . . . "

"Get the tape spliced, kid. We focus on this Liz for the long parts and on you, Jimmy, with voice over, where there's a lot of cutting."

Dinner was finished and so was Liz. She felt a thousand years old, was certain that she looked it, and didn't really care. Through Arthur's headset, some idiot from the television encampment told her that dinner looked lovely—"marvelous colors!"—with the gay parade of hibiscus blossoms meandering along the top of the buffet table. Liz snapped out an unpardonable word and then said, "But can they *taste* it?" The Rock Cornish hens had been a frivolous disaster, charred on the outside and bleeding on the inside, a burned offering snatched from a roasting pan perched atop a bed of coals that was either too hot or totally extinguished. In transferring the last of the black, shriveled little birds from the fireplace to a platter, Liz had burned her hand badly and she nearly burst into tears when someone from the mainland asked if she didn't intend to garnish the platter.

Sheer irritation had carried Liz through dinner. But she nearly exploded when the meal was finished and Arthur said, "Liz, dear girl, they're asking from the control truck if you and the other ladies would mind washing the dishes."

"They're asking *what?*"

"They want you and Carolyn and Bernice and one or two of the others out in the kitchen washing up. You know, the incongruity of it all—pampered American women all dressed up and . . . "

"What's so incongruous about it, Arthur?" Essie asked. "And just what century do they think we're living in? You can't find a decent maid for love or money back in Anthrax. I've been putting dishes through the machine ever since . . . "

"It might be fun," Carolyn said.

"I certainly don't mind," Bernice said. Her days in Acapulco had been the only ones of her life when she hadn't washed dishes. It would be a good idea to get back into the routine.

"Well, I certainly *do* mind," Liz said. "Just who the hell are these television people, invading my house, telling me what to wear, what to eat, where to sit, what to say? I'm sorry to disappoint your audience, Arthur, but as long as there are servants in the kitchen to tidy up after meals, my guests are not going to do KP duty."

"E-liz-a-beth Parkhurst! You're not losing your temper?"

"Yes, Arthur, I am. I consider this intrusion one big, bloody nuisance. We have problems enough without having to change our clothes and say 'cheese' every time we turn around. It was also damned cheeky of you, Arthur, to spring this television thing without asking me. If you had, you know that I would have refused. I suspect that's why you didn't bother. But you can just get on that Princess telephone thing right now and tell them that the show is over. There isn't going to be any dishwashing scene or any other scene. Here's Pablo now and he and Aurelia will be more than adequate for cleaning up—without champagne or chinchilla coats or any of the rest of this cheap nonsense. O, *Pablo, por favor, diga Aurelia que* . . . What's the matter? I mean, *Pablo, que pasa?*"

"Señora, es Aurelia. Está muy enferma. Creo que es su tiempo!" Pablo, always calm, always collected, always aware of his dignity, was ashen, wild-eyed, the slow, precise Spanish he usually spoke to foreigners tumbled out of his mouth incoherently. His English was forgotten.

"Lentamente, por favor, Pablo. Yo no comprendo. Laddy! For God's sake please tell me what he's . . . Where is Laddy?"

"It's something about your paragon of a handmaiden, Liz," Arthur said.

"Oh, God, don't tell me she's gone and got plastered again! Aurelia está borracha, Pablo?"

"No, señora, no! Mira, usted." Pablo plucked at Liz's sleeve. His staccato Spanish fell like hailstones around her ears.

"For God's sake," Liz said, "will somebody please find Laddy!"

"Mrs. Martinez," Julie Noyes said, "I think I understand what he's saying. It's about your cook. Pablo says it's her time. She must be starting to have her baby."

"Oh, my God!" Liz said. "Pablo, a donde está Aurelia?"

"Arriba, señora, en su cama. Y está enferma!"

As though to verify his words, a wild, shrill shriek reverberated through the house, echoing, clanging, ricocheting off the stone walls and the tile floors.

"Listen, everyone. You all heard. Poor Aurelia's up there going into labor. Does anybody know anything about delivering a baby?"

" 'Lan' sakes, Miz Katy Scarlett, I don't know nothin' about birthin' no babies,' " Arthur said.

"Arthur!" Carolyn gasped.

Ignoring him, not even hearing him, Liz went on. "I've never had a baby. But you, Essie, you've had two. Do you . . . "

"Oh, Liz, both Elspeth and LeRoy were caesarean sections. I didn't know a thing until it was over. Of course I'll help, but . . ."

"You, Mrs. Bullock?"

"I certainly have not!"

April May spoke. "In the movies they boil water and tear up a lotta sheets."

"Yes, I suppose that's a beginning," Liz said.

"I've helped a lot of mares in foal," Julie said. "It must be about the same."

"Thank you, Julie," Liz said. "We'll need all the help we can get."

Again the house rang with a scream.

"I had a baby," Flossie said. "Not only that, honey, but I brought nine others inta the world back in Oklahoma." Flossie rose unsteadily, the ice rattling in her glass of vodka. "I was just a kid myself."

"You mean you actually *know* how to deliver a child?"

"Well, it's been a long time, honey, but I guess it's about the same as it always was."

Liz glanced quickly at Flossie, wondered how much she'd had to drink. Plenty, but beggars couldn't be choosers. "All right. Come with me. And anyone else who can help."

"If you don't mind, Miz Mártinez," Mrs. Bullock said, "I'd prefer that my girls do not witness any such . . ."

"Except for me," Julie said. "I'm sorry, Mrs. Bullock, but I can help. I want to."

"Juliet Noyes, I forbid . . ."

"No, you don't, Mrs. Bullock. I've been waiting nearly eighteen years to do something useful. Here's my chance."

"Come on, Carolyn, Bernice," Essie said. "We can at least give moral support."

"You want I should start boiling water and ripping up the sheets?" April asked.

"Yes, please. Anything you think will help," Liz said. "But first we've got to bring her downstairs. She can't stay up in that dark little room with the wall caved in and bricks and plaster all over the place."

"And down here, at least you've got the television lights," Arthur said suavely.

"And the boiling water," April said.

"That's true," Liz said. "We'll need a couple of able-bodied men to carry her down the stairs. She weighs a ton."

"I'll come," Walt said.

"You can stay right where you are," Arthur said. "Bill, you and Roland can lift her."

Laddy appeared from his bedroom. "Anyone for a rubber of bridge?"

Another scream tore through the house.

"Oh, Laddy, thank God! It's Aurelia. She's having her baby."

"Up there in that little maid's room?"

"No. We'll bring her down to my room. Come on. At least you can translate. Come on, whoever's coming."

"Arthur, I ought to get up there and help out," Walter said.

"You stay right where you are, Walter Dewlap. I'll need you on the camera."

"On the . . ."

"Yes. Now, let's get these lights into Liz's room. It isn't every little television show that features the birth of a baby." Arthur whistled into the mouthpiece of his headset. "Malvido? Arthur Craine here. I suppose you heard that last passage? Good! You'd better send over a lot more film, dear boy. I'm planning a little serendipity for the show."

"Hey, camera!" E. G. d'Enker bellowed through his headset from the control truck. "Remember now, don't focus on her snatch. This ain't no stag film."

"Yes, Walt," Jaime Malvido said smoothly, patronizingly, "please bear in mind that this is coast-to-coast *family* documentary."

"And don't use your zoomar until the kid starts comin' out," E. G. added.

"When will that be?" Walt asked. "I've been shooting for more than two hours and . . . oh, God, she's screaming again. I can't stand it."

"*Hijo*, hear that scream, E. G.?" Jimmy said.

"Great!"

Liz paced back and forth in her bedroom. She was certain that if she heard one more shriek she would go stark, staring mad. How long did it take to have a baby, anyhow? Carolyn squeezed Bernice's hand and shuddered.

"Here's more coffee, everyone," Essie said, bustling into the room. "April's boiled enough water to drown us all. How's Aurelia?"

"Not good," Liz said.

"God's got to be a man," Carolyn said. "A woman would have thought of an easier way."

"Oh, *pobrecita*," Essie said in her halting Spanish. "*Un poco de—uh—café?*"

In reply, Aurelia screamed again. Her flailing arms knocked the cup of coffee from Essie's hands and sent it crashing, splashing to the floor.

"She don't want coffee, Essie. Get her a good belta tequila. An' me, I could use another vodka. Jus' bring the bottle."

"Do you really think that's wise, Flossie?" Liz asked tensely. How many vodkas would this one make?

"Yer darn tootin' I do. Honey, we got no anesthetics or like Twilight Sleep. Booze is the best thing we got. For her and for me, too."

"I'll get some right away," Essie said.

"But she's already thrown up three times," Bernice said.

"Honey, if that was all she done we'd be lucky. We oughta change the bed again. Got more sheets?"

"Twelve dozen pairs," Liz said, "if April hasn't ripped them to shreds. Laddy, please say something to Aurelia."

Gray beneath his tan, Laddy bent down over the bed. "Uh, *como siente usted*, Aurelia?" In reply Aurelia shrieked and pitched and tore at her sweat-drenched hair. "Not very good, I'm afraid," Laddy said.

"Oh, Laddy, really! We *know* how the poor thing's feeling. Pablo, *por favor, diga* something helpful to Aurelia. But in Spanish, of course."

Pablo leaned down and whispered into Aurelia's ear. She moaned and groaned, gazed up at him with glassy, unseeing eyes. He wiped the sweat from her brow.

"How long is it between pains, honey?" Flossie asked.

"It's hard to tell, Mrs. Meyers," Julie said. "I was able to time them until about fifteen minutes ago. Now it just seems to be one big, terrible spasm."

"The poor darling," Essie said. "If only there were something we could do. I mean, couldn't we at least get word to her husband!"

"It sure beats me," Flossie said, slapping back her drink. "Now you take those Indian squaws back home—big, rawboned, wide hips. This one's no different and she's already had seven. This oughta be like shelling peas. I can't figure it out."

Again a congealing scream, louder and longer than any of the others. Aurelia heaved and shuddered, tore at the sheets, called upon God, Christ and the Virgin of Guadalupe.

April popped her head through the door. "Has she had the baby yet?"

"Not quite yet, April," Carolyn said.

Again the scream.

"Nothin' wrong with her lungs and that's for sure," Flossie said. "I'm goin' have another look-see.

"Okay, now, honey. I'll try not ta hurt," Flossie said.

Pablo translated gently into Aurelia's ear. Aurelia looked up through glazed eyes and breathed, "*Gracias.*"

Liz looked on with a sense of awe. What divine providence had sent Flossie Meyers to Su Casa? What would they have done without her? There she was, old, drunk, and vulgar, none too steady on her feet, her hennaed head tied up in Bernice's Hermès scarf, her incredible ice-blue satin dress stained with sweat, splattered with blood, a fortune in dirty diamonds crammed into the pocket of the old kitchen apron she wore. Yet here she was in a roomful of allegedly educated, superior women, the only one who knew or understood about woman's primary function.

"Now bear down, honey," Flossie said. "Pee-dro, you talk the lingo. Tell 'er."

Aurelia gazed up again. This time the scream tore through everyone in the room.

Carolyn threw her arms around Bernice and burst into tears. "Oh!" Essie said. There was a loud thump and Laddy lay in a dead faint on the floor. Pablo stared wide-eyed. A tiny, tan leg protruded from Aurelia.

"Oh, sweet Jesus!" Flossie moaned. "A breach delivery."

The room was still. Had Aurelia fainted again? Was she dead? If anything, the silence was more terrifying than her screams. "Aurelia? Aurelia?" Liz said again, advancing toward the bloody bed.

"Liz," Arthur's voice called, "please. You're right in the way of the camera."

Liz wheeled. Standing on the other side of the French window was Arthur Craine. With him, Walt and the hand camera.

"Arthur!"

"Arthur!" Carolyn cried. "This is unspeakable!"

"Walter!" Essie whimpered and burst into tears.

"Aw, Essie . . . "

"Did I startle you, Liz?"

"No, Arthur, you shock me. I've always thought you had at least a scrap of human decency. Now listen, Arthur, I want you to get this television stuff out of my house and off my property. I don't give a damn if you dump it into the . . . No, wait! Give me that thing!" Liz grabbed the hand microphone. "Hello? Mr. Malvido, whatever your name is? We're in desperate trouble. Flossie's doing everything she can, but the baby's coming out wrong. Can you hear me?"

Arthur nodded from within the halo of his headset. "Yes, Liz, he hears you . . . "

"This is a matter of life or death," Liz shouted. "Isn't there some way we could get Aurelia over to your side? Tie her to a stretcher? However it's done. We've got to get her to a hospital."

"What'll I say?" Jaime Malvido muttered to E. G. d'Enker.

"Stall 'er."

"How can I? We could maybe do it. The wind's died down and . . . "

"Tell 'er it's too dangerous."

"Arthur, tell Mrs. Martínez it's too dangerous. It might kill the cook."

"Get rid of her. Some of the first footage is comin' through the tank."

"But Mr. Malvido, if we don't get Aurelia to some place where she can be taken care of, she'll die anyhow. Please, Mr. Malvido, couldn't we take a chance? I don't know anything about obstetrics. No one here does, except Flossie. And this is a job that needs doctors and nurses and instruments and anesthetics. . . . Please try to help us. We have no equipment—nothing. If you could just put a doctor who speaks English on that telephone thing and . . . "

Aurelia screamed again. It was a sound that came from some prehistoric jungle. And she kept on screaming and screaming and screaming. Liz dropped the hand mike and rushed to the bedside. Aurelia's screams kept coming. Flossie, steady and intense, the years momentarily pushed away, was acutely aware that she must not pull on the emerging baby and she must get the mouth clear without delay. "Aw, for Pete's sake, honey, pipe down. This won't hurt."

"Aurelia," Liz began in a shaken voice, "*la señora diga que* . . ."

"Don't bother to tell 'er, honey. It's gonna hurt."

"Okay, givum a crack on the bottom an' he's as good as new." The baby howled with outrage and fury. "It's a boy, okay."

"He looks awfully red," Carolyn murmured.

"Cleanum up an' he won't look so bad. I betchoo didn't look like any movie queen when you came out. But I wanta fix him a pretty belly button. Good an' flat. We boil up one of those eight-cent pieces and tape it down good. Anything I hate's one of those bubble-bellies."

Bloody, battered, and bruised, the baby squalled with indignation. "Boy, he's a mean one," Flossie said amiably. "Well, washum good. That'll help. Couple weeks an' he'll be handsome as Pee-dro here. Hey, Blondie, remember all that water you been cooking? Maybe you'd like to give the kid a bath."

"Ya mean in the boiling water?" April asked.

"I'll do it," Julie said quickly.

"I thinkya better, honey. Blondie, I tellya whatcha can do. Tear up a sheet inta squares about so big, see? We'll make some nice didies."

"And . . . and Aurelia?" Liz whispered. It was a foolish question. Liz already knew the answer.

"She's gone, honey. What could I do?"

Tears starting in her eyes, Liz said, "Nothing, Flossie. You were wonderful. Without you, we . . . "

"Come on, Carolyn," Essie whispered, "help me cover the poor thing." Another sheet was unfurled, laid gently over Aurelia's dead body.

"Liz, Flossie," Bernice said, "you must be about to drop. It's time you went to bed."

"Bed?" Liz said, gesturing toward Aurelia.

"We'll clean up your room in the morning. Tonight you and Flossie move in with April and me."

"Thank you, darling," Liz said, "but it's practically daylight and I wouldn't be able to sleep, anyhow. I'll just take a blanket and stretch out on a sofa in the *sala*. But Flossie must be . . ."

"Flossie's damned thirsty, that's what Flossie is," Flossie said. "You girls get your beauty rest. I'm about ready for a real drink."

"You know, Flossie," Liz said, "I am, too."

Baby Talk

"Well, here goes," Julie said.

"Pardon, *señorita*," Pablo said, "but the water is possibly too hot."

"It's exactly the temperature I like my bath—if I could remember back to the last one."

"*Vamos a ver*," Pablo said, pushing up his sleeve. He dunked his elbow in the water. "*Está demasiado caliente para un esquincle*. It is too hot for a baby. Wait." Pablo added a dipper of cold water and tested it again. "Is okay."

"Pablo, what does a great, big *macho* Mexican man like you know about babies?"

"Everything, *señorita*. I have younger brothers and sisters, *sobrinos* . . ."

"*Sobrinos*? Ah, yes. Nieces and nephews."

"*Primos*—cou-sins. Yes. I have experience."

"Oh, Pablo! Be careful with him!"

"He won't break, *señorita*. He is a Mexican and we are very—uh—*dura*."

"*Dura*? Durable? Tough?"

"Exactly. If we were not, there wouldn't be any Mexicans."

"He's no beauty, is he?"

"He had a difficult na-ti-vi-ty. Wait. He will soon be beauti-ful."

237

You certainly made it, Julie thought. Instead she said, "Yes. Puppies and kittens—*perritos y gatitos no estan muy hermosos. Como ratas.*"

Pablo laughed. "You are *bery* beauti-ful, *señorita*, but on the day of your na-ti-vi-ty? *Nunca!*"

Julie felt herself blushing. Beautiful? "Here," she said, "give him to me before you drown him."

Pablo handed Julie the wet, wriggling, furious baby. "Careful," he said.

"He won't break. Remember, you Mexicans are tough. *Dura.*" She laid the baby on a soft, fluffy bath towel and began to blot him dry. "I have some oil and talcum powder. Do you suppose we should put any on him?"

"Why not? He will smell better."

"If only he'd stop yelling. Maybe it's good for his lungs. His *respiración.* And I'm sure he's hungry. But, with his mother dead, who can feed him?"

"First, *señorita*, water. For to clean his interior."

"And how do you plan for him to drink it—from a highball glass?"

"*Mira usted,*" Pablo said. He took a clean washcloth, dipped it into hot water, waved it in the air until he had cooled it a bit, and rolled it into a cone shape. Then, carefully, he put the tip of it into the baby's mouth. Instantly the baby stopped squealing and began to suck.

"You're going to make a wonderful husband for some lucky girl."

"Oh, no, *señorita.* Not for long time. To marry, a man needs education, money, decent employment. Not to be like my family, always poor, too many children, no future."

"Well, there's my family—always rich, not enough children, and no future, either."

"*Mande, señorita?*"

"Nothing. Now that we've got this baby clean, what are we going to do with him?"

"Here is his *servilleta.*" Pablo flapped open a large damask dinner napkin, folded it expertly, and handed it to Julie with two big safety pins. "You compre-hend?"

"Yes, I comprehend. I used to have a doll that wet itself on schedule—*una muñeca qui pi-pi*. It was supposed to bring out the mother in spoiled little American girls. Maybe it did." Surprised by her own competence, Julie slid the diaper under the baby's bottom and pinned it snugly at the sides. "Do you think that big silver peso taped over his navel is really a good idea?"

"*Mande, señorita?*"

"Uh, *es una idea buena idea*, uh, *este peso encima de su*, uh, *umbilico?*"

"Ah! *El ombligo! Sí, señorita. Mira.*" Pablo lifted his shirt and showed her his own slit of a navel. Julie felt herself coloring again. "Very pretty," she said. "And now that he's all ready for bed, where do we put him?"

"*La cama está preparada.*"

As the plastic dishpan had made a perfect bathtub for Aurelia's baby, so did the champagne case make an ideal bassinet. Pablo had lined it with towels, had fitted a pillow into the bottom, had torn sheets and a clean blanket to fit the baby's first resting place.

"Why, Pablo, that's adorable!"

"*Gusta?*"

"Oh, I *gusto* it very much! Now, let me tuck the baby in."

"*Momentito,*" Pablo said. He pulled back the coverlet and quickly removed three hot bricks. He tested the temperature of the bed and said, "Now."

"Hot bricks! You *do* think of everything. But where did you find them?"

"Very simple, *señorita.*" Pablo pointed upward. "My room. After the *temblor* my room is full of them."

Julie put the baby into his improvised bed and Pablo carried the champagne case to the hearth of the kitchen fireplace, where the glowing coals gave off an enveloping warmth—not too hot, simply pleasant. Kneeling over the baby at Pablo's side, Julie suddenly realized things she had never even thought about. She felt a happy aching in her breast, as though the baby were hers—hers and Pablo's. So this was what it was all about! She turned and faced Pablo in the rosy light. Then she felt his arms around her, his lips on hers.

Pablo leapt to his feet. What had he done? He had touched a guest of his employer, had taken her in his arms and kissed her! Not a *golfa* like the Señorita Lu-an Maqueyever or the idiotic April May, but a young lady, a Norteamericana, rich and remote and educated and untouchable. "*Señorita! Perdóname! Yo no intendé . . .*"

Julie reached up and grasped Pablo's arm. It was warm, nearly hairless, ivory smooth. Something to do with Indian blood, she thought. And then she drew him firmly down to the floor. "Am I any different from Lou Ann?" she wondered. She felt his arms around her again, his lips on hers once more, and she stopped wondering or even caring.

Angel Face

From her corner of the sofa, Liz looked at Flossie and then back into the crackling fire. She's got to be stinking drunk—sozzled, boiled, swacked, blotto. She had eight drinks while she was delivering the baby, God only knows how many before, and now she's pouring her fourth! And yet she's able to stand and walk and she's even fairly coherent, for a change. How does she do it?

Flossie shuffled across the tile floor of the *sala* in her stocking feet and sat down heavily at the other end of the sofa. Flossie was wearing a woolen robe that had been Salvador's, pinned at the throat with an enormous diamond brooch, dimly lustrous in the firelight. Her ice-blue satin dress, haphazardly laundered of its bloodstains, hung from the back of a chair drying in the warmth of the fire. The dress was so terrible that Liz had been stunned to see its workmanship, its Paquin label. If Flossie had to be left with only one dress, why that one?

Flossie tucked her feet under her, pulled the Paradise fox coat over her lap and stroked it maternally. Queenie dozed at her side. "They don't make clothes like that any more," she said.

"No, they certainly don't. Of course, I carry insurance, but as to replacing your actual wardrobe . . ."

"Oh, don't worry about that, honey. I got nowheres to wear those old glad rags. I don't hardly buy anything anymore. Fer what? Paruss."

"Paris?"

"Yeah, back before the war. Believe you me, honey, I was some punkins in those days."

And she very probably had been, Liz considered. One of those magnolia-skinned redheads, comfortably upholstered, with lovely hands and feet. Despite the oceans of alcohol Flossie had drunk, the signs of a long-lost beauty were unmistakable.

"Daddy was still alive then—not very, but still warm."

"Your father?"

"My *father*? Hell, no, honey! Oh, he was old enough to be my grampa, even. No, honey. His name was Abner Meyers, but everybody yoosta callum Dry Hole Daddy."

"Dry *Hole*?"

"Yeah. Daddy was an oil wildcatter. He yoosta pick up dead claims—you know, oil wells that hadn't come in—an' get a strike every time. Rich as God an' even older. I was only seventeen when I nabbed 'um."

"Nabbed him?"

"Yeah. Tricked him into marryin' me. He liked 'um young. He couldn't do anything, poor old poop, but I toldum he'd got me in the family way an' he believed ut."

"But I think you said that you did have a baby."

"Angel Face?"

"I don't think you mentioned, uh, the name."

"That was later, honey. When I was twenty."

"Oh. Then, uh, Daddy was able to, uh, function?"

"Him? Never! Oh, he tried. He tried everything. I sat around his big old house in Tulsa while he took every kinda shot an' pill there was."

"Didn't he wonder why his, uh, baby took so long in coming?"

"After we got married I pretended I had a miscarriage. Nearly killed poor ol' Daddy, he wanted a kid so bad."

"But then you finally *did* have a baby?"

"Yeah, but it wasn't Daddy's."

"Oh, I see."

"Daddy heard about this place in France where they give yuh some kinda glands. All kindsa old men acting like they was stud stallions after they been there. So off we go—Daddy to the hospital and li'l Flossie to Paruss. So there I am, all dressed up and cute as a bug's ear, all by my lonesome in the Ritz bar. And along comes You-Jean."

"Eugene?"

"Yeah. French. From some big, fancy family. At least that's what he said. Honey, he was nothing more'n a cheap French gigolo—and not so cheap, either. And me? I was nothing but a hash-house waitress from the oil fields that had lied and cheated into a big bankroll. We was made for each other, him an' me."

"Well, I suppose if your husband was impotent and quite old . . ."

"An' decent. . . . So there's You-Jean showing the li'l hick from Oklahoma all over Paruss on Daddy's dough an' up in my hotel suite every night. So the next thing I know, I really am expecting, and there's Daddy, out of the hospital, still limp as a necktie, but thinkin' it's his. Talk about proud! You'd of thought I was made of glass the way the ol' goat actud. A big hulk like me! Half a deck on the boat goin' home fer just Daddy an' I and a nurse that didn't know near as much about havin' babies as I did. A private car on the train back to Tulsa, and then layin' around on a chase-lounge until my time come."

"And the baby?" Liz asked.

"It was a li'l girl. We named her Eugenia. That was kinda private, just for me. But I always called her Angel Face. Honey, she was the prettiest li'l thing you ever saw in yer life. Hair that was so blonde it was almost white, an' big blue eyes."

"Did she look like, uh, Eugene?"

"No. But he was her father. He was the only one."

"And what about, uh, Daddy?"

"Honey, he was so pleased he like ta bust. After I givum a baby there wasn't nothing good enough for me. Anything I wanted. Clothes, joolry, shopping trips to New York on my own. That poor ol' man jus' wanted to stay home and watch Angel Face. An' I loved her even more'n he did—but in a healthy way, not so smothering, like. I says, 'Daddy, let Angel Face grow up like any other kid. She don't haveta have some English nurse follow 'er around like a shadow. Let 'er run barefoot if she wantsta. Let 'er play with other kids. Tell 'er no once in a while.' I says, 'You'll spoil 'er rotten this way.' I says, 'Lookiter, three years old an' she don't even use the potty yet. She don't talk. She don't even try to.' Daddy says, 'Shut up. She's perfect.' I says, 'If she could play with some other kids, she'd see what they were like. Try ta copy 'um.' But Daddy wouldn't hear a word against Angel Face."

"But surely some nice nursery school . . ."

"Honey, she never went no place. When she was four years old she started havin' these temper tantrums, bangin' her head on the marble floors in Daddy's house until her beautiful hair was all blood. And over nothin'. It wasn't like we'd crossed 'er. An' the doctor came an' he tells us that Angel Face is re-tarded. Was from the very beginning. That she'll never get any better."

"Oh, Flossie!"

"Well, that nearly finished Daddy. But he was a tough ol' cuss. Stubborn. So then we start the round of specialists. Chicago, Philly, New York, Boston." The tears were flowing now. "An' they all tell us the same thing. Hopeless. Our li'l girl's a idiot."

Liz grasped Flossie's plump, boneless hand. "Flossie, darling, you don't have to tell me if it hurts you too much."

"It hurts all the time. That's why I wanna tell yuh. I never told nobody before—unless it was sometimes I can't remember. All those high mucky-mucks in Tulsa. They knew what I was an' they hated me. They hated poor ol' Daddy, too. But he was so rich they was all scared of him. I got no friends—never did have."

"Flossie, that's not true! Everyone here is your friend. Those women tonight, they admired you more than . . ."

"That's not the same. A year from now—next week—they won't even know my name. I'm not their kind."

"You're my kind," Liz said.

"Well, anyways, we're in L.A. to see this other big kid specialist. By now Angel Face got two nurses, a coupla big Swedes built like wrasslers. We need 'um, see, for when the baby gets these fits. But Daddy still don't believe anything the doctors tellum. So he's stretched out in his chair an' he says, 'Hi, there, Angel Face! How's Daddy's li'l doll?' An' then she attacksum. She's only five years old but she's like a tiger when she's havin' a fit. Before anybody could stop 'er, she's all overum, clawin' an' bitin'. The nurses get 'er off okay, but poor ole Daddy just lays there dead. Oh, sure, the doctors said he died of a stroke. He was sevenny-seven. But that poor ol' man died of a broken heart. Ya could almos' hear it break."

"How dreadful."

"After that it was the home."

"Home?"

"This instatution. The doc made me put 'er there. What else could I do? After she done that to Daddy not even the nurses'd stay. Oh, it's a real fancy place. She's got 'er own li'l house there on the grounds, her own nurses. Fat lotta good all that does. They can't even keep clothes on 'er. An' I always dressed 'er like a li'l French doll."

"Do you . . . do you ever see her?"

"I yoosta. I sold Daddy's big place in Tulsa an' took a li'l apartmunt right near the home. I yoosta go ta see 'er every day. It was no good. After about six months the head of the home comes ta my li'l place an' tells me to stop goin' ta see 'er. He says she's never gonna be any diffrunt an' my visits only make 'er worse. I mean he wasn't snotty er anything. He was only tryin' ta help. . . ."

"Of course."

"So, when he leaves, I don't bawl my eyes out er anything like that. I jus' go to the kitchen an' get out this bottle. Gin it was. Six months it sat there an' I swear I never even open it. Well, I opened it then, an' I finished it. An' then I phone to the licker store for another. I come to in the Savoy-Plaza Hotel in New York a week later, an' I been on the go ever since. It's God's punishment for what I done."

Flossie got to her feet and shuffled toward the bar.

"And your daughter?" Liz said gently.

"Search me. They send a report every month along with the bill. I haven't seen 'er since."

It occurred to Liz that the girl would be about thirty by now.

"And . . . what do you plan to do after we all get out of here?"

"What's the diff? Hawaii, maybe. Someplace where it's warm an' there's booze." Flossie lurched back to the sofa and plumped down.

"But, Flossie," Liz said. "It isn't too late for you to make something of your life. I saw you tonight. I know you could do it. You can't be much older than I am."

"Pushin' fifty, dearie, an' I feel it. No, honey, He's got the finger on me."

"But, Flossie, with all of your money. The way you feel about children. There's so much good you could do."

"Ha! Know what I just been thinkin'?"

"What?"

"Ya know that kid tonight?"

"Aurelia's baby?"

"Yeah. Him. I got ta thinkin' I maybe could adopt 'um. Raise 'um like my own. Like get a li'l house someplace and see that he gets educated an' all that. Hell, I got kind of a claim on 'um, an' who else wants the poor li'l bastard?"

"Flossie! That's marvelous. It would be wonderful. Wonderful for him and wonderful for you, too."

And now Flossie's tears poured out anew. "Jesus, who'm I kiddin'? Angel Face," she sobbed, "Angel Face."

Rest in Peace

Arthur had risen early, given himself a sponge bath, shaved, applied his make-up, and now stalked about Laddy's room selecting his costume. It would have to be something not black, but rather somber. Arthur sensed that he would be doing another funeral oration today, and for a bigger congregation than just the people at Su Casa. In addition to his waist-cincher, he chose slim gray slacks, a snug cashmere sweater, and knotted a navy-blue scarf at his throat. He could go back to brighter plumage as soon as this Mexican was buried. Satisfied with himself, Arthur shook Laddy gently. "Laddy, dear boy, time to get up. *Zut alors!* Poor Liz! She'll be needing all the help she can get."

Putting on his headset, Arthur went down to the parking lot, where there was no danger of being overheard. Today, like the others, was cold, windy, and gray, but he could see clearly to the shore, where the television crew was already stirring. Jaime Malvido's car was parked next to the control truck. Good!

Arthur spoke perfunctorily to the little Malvido, accepting his noisy compliments. Then, more deferentially, Arthur spoke to E. G. d'Enker. Arthur knew that Mr. d'Enker wasn't the sort whom one would invite to lunch at one's club, but he was a big voice in the industry. If there were to be a new Arthur Craine on a new network, the Vice-President in Charge of Programming would be an essential ally.

"That's very kind of you, Mr. d'Enker. And I'm glad that Walt's footage turned out so well . . . The baby? As well as can be expected, as they say." Arthur supposed that the baby was alive. "Well, yes, I'm sure that we will be needing some things for it. I'll get a list and read it to you a bit later . . . That unfortunate Mexican woman will have to be buried this morning. I'll do the oration, brief and dignified. You know, short but sweet. She was Roman Catholic, so my service is only a gesture. But I feel that something serious like that might really grip the audience, don't you?" Arthur had shown several facets of the new Arthur Craine, and he was damned if those yokels were going to miss Pious Arthur, Simple Servant of Our Lord. For Aurelia's burial, he had in mind something along the lines of *Our Town*.

"Sex? Really, Mr. d'Enker, are you suggesting that I come on naked? . . . Well, my sister, Carolyn, is hardly the 'boojums' type, nor is Miss Potocki. As for Liz and Estelle Dewlap, there's no need to point out that they, too, are ladies. The Texas girls are a bit *jeune fille*. As for Mrs. Meyers or Mrs. Bullock . . . April May?" What, please, did anyone with a vestige of intelligence say to April May? Arthur thought fast and decided that he could cope. No point in arguing with E. G. d'Enker or seeming uncooperative. He could simply stand April in front of the microphone and confound her so rapidly and so thoroughly that they'd be begging him to get rid of her. The face on the cutting-room floor! "You may have an interesting idea there. At least we can try it. If it doesn't work, you can always edit the poor girl out, can't you? Oh, by the way, is there any word on when they might be able to evacuate this place?" Arthur hoped that there was and that the word was no. "I see. Oh, we're perfectly comfortable. Just wondering. Since that's the situation, there's a small, but delicate matter in which I'll need your, uh, cooperation. . . ."

"Yes, Arthur," Liz said. "Naturally we're going to bury Aurelia. They're getting her ready now. But it's going to be just us, Arthur. No lights, no camera, no running commentary. Interment private. I believe that's the expression. I wasn't kidding about getting this television stuff out of here. The comedy hour is over, Arthur."

"And the baby, dear girl?"

"He's in there yelling his head off. Can't you hear him? Hungry, I suppose."

"And of course you're going to nurse him at your own shapely breast?"

"Why, no, but . . ."

"Zut alors! How stupid of me. I'd quite forgotten that you have a full stock of bottles and nipples and sterilizers and infant formula on hand."

"Oh, my God!"

"Sweet Essie was kind enough to make up a list of what a newborn baby needs. Look, Liz, dear, it comes to quite an inventory. I know that a word to the television people on the other side would have the whole thing coming over on the rope within an hour."

"I never thought of that."

"And something else you never thought of, my dear, is that you are in a very weak position to be ordering those fatherly television people away from here. Unless, Liz, you're the unusual type who enjoys seeing a muling and puking infant starve to death."

"Arthur, you are . . ."

"I am a very practical person. I suggest that you be, too."

"Arthur, you are a first-class, Grade-A son of a bitch!"

"Thank you, Elizabeth. I enjoy being first in everything."

Liz turned on her heel and stomped back to the house.

"Malvido?" Arthur barked into his mouthpiece. "All right. You can start sending over those things for the baby."

While Flossie and Essie cooed and fluttered over the baby, feeding him, dressing him in the new clothes that had come over from the mainland, Carolyn and Bernice shudderingly attended the remains of his mother. They washed her and got her into her Sunday dress.

Bernice studied her hair, then said, "She liked to wear it up."

"Bernice," Carolyn said, "I hate to be such a sissy, but if I don't get out of this room for just a minute or two I think I'm going to faint or be sick or . . ."

"Sure, Carolyn," Bernice said. "We'll have a cup of coffee. I can do her hair by myself."

"I feel such a fool," Carolyn said, cuddling her coffee cup. "I'm not afraid of dead people. There's nothing to be afraid of. It's simply that . . ."

"Don't worry about it," Bernice said. "I understand. Laying out bodies is no fun. I know. I've done it before."

"In Poland?" Carolyn wondered if there might have been some quaint local custom whereby the ladies of the manor house descended to minister to the corpses of their serfs. Noblesse oblige. Like kings washing the feet of twelve beggars on Maundy Thursday.

"No," Bernice said. "In Colliery, Illinois, where I was born. My grandmother was an old Polish immigrant, a lot like Aurelia, but older. When she died we didn't have enough money to use the local undertaker. So my dad made the coffin and I helped Momma lay her out. I was fifteen. You look surprised."

"I am, a little. From what Arthur said, I thought . . ."

"Remember, Arthur said it. I didn't. There are lots of Potockis; rich counts and poor coal miners. I'm from the mining branch." She set down her coffee cup. "Well, back to poor Aurelia."

"Wait," Carolyn said, "I'll help you." Slipping an arm around Bernice's waist, she went bravely back to Aurelia.

Arthur had been equipped with a lavaliere mike for Aurelia's burial. It afforded him a splendid opportunity to hold *The Book of Common Prayer* in his left hand and to perform a few fluid, but manly, gestures with his right.

He felt—he *knew*—that he was doing beautifully. But Arthur was a little put out with the others. Liz, Essie, Bernice, even his own Carolyn, all of them seemed to be drooping. April May, always a stand-out in any crowd, had taken on the look of an albino Dolores del Río, her tow hair pulled straight back, her head swathed in what appeared to be a mantilla. Where had she found such a thing? Could it be that black lace jump suit of hers, so tight that it gave every appearance of being stenciled on? Yes, by God, that's exactly what it was! Mrs. Bullock, refreshed by a long night's sleep, had taken the usual disastrous pains with her toilette, but who wanted to look at her? The other men were glum and haggard save for Roland who, shaken by another death, wore stark white with a black jerkin and looked as if he were about to dance *Les Sylphides*. Only Flossie showed any true sense of theater as she stood there in her fur coat and the cartwheel hat proudly holding the baby. The baby, thank God, was asleep. One yip out of that little bastard, Arthur thought, and I'll chloroform him.

". . . this hapless woman, who gave her own life while bringing a new life into the world . . ." Pause. Gesture.

"From the long shots they're beginning to look right," E. G. said. "Kinda fucked-out an' fouled-up—not like they were on some kinda picnic." Bleary-eyed, he sat in the control truck contemplating the monitor.

"Uh-huh," Jaime Malvido said, stifling a yawn. He'd give his soul to get some sleep.

"I can see Walt gettin' a close-up of the kid. Good!"

"He's darling," the Girl Friday said.

"Ugly as a panful of ass-holes, if you ask me."

"Well, I *didn't* ask you!" She thought she'd be fired this very minute. It didn't matter. She was too tired to care. Mr. d'Enker said nothing. He, too, was too tired to care.

A few especially hardy and especially bored tourists had come out to watch the show. Desperate hotel managers and recreation directors were admitting it was something to do. Bleachers had been set up to accommodate the live audience. At an improvised altar in front of the bleachers, a Benedictine priest sang a requiem mass to a parish of mourners dressed in bright slacks, sweaters, and rebozos. The cleric, too, was being televised. This had been Jaime Malvido's idea. "She was a Catholic. We all are. Do it this way, with Arthur out there and a priest here, and there won't be any trouble with the Catholic audience."

"That's a great idea, kid. How'dja get permission so fast?"

"I didn't. Everyone in the bishop's office will think somebody else okayed it."

"And dramatically it's extremely effective," the Girl Friday had said, placing her imprimatur on Jimmy's lapse of taste and ethics. "The pomp and circumstance of the ancient Roman ritual in juxtaposition with Arthur Craine's few simple heartfelt words. . . ."

At his vast console, the camera director was artistically mixing shots of Arthur, the priest, and the baby. He had just pulled off a stunning effect of the baby in an aura of Paradise fox placed in a neat little circle square at the center of the priest's stomach, as though in utero. The Girl Friday thrilled.

"This is gettin' dull as duckshit," E. G. yawned. "Tell Craine ta cut it short. Fulton J. Sheen he ain't."

"All right, E. G.!" Jimmy snapped. "They're getting ready to put the body in the grave."

"Good. Tell Walt ta get a close-up of the stiff."

On the monitor, they watched Pablo, Roland, Bill, and Laddy each take a corner of the blanket on which Aurelia lay and lower it gently into the garden grave. The men stepped back. To everyone's surprise, Arthur simply said, "Aurelia María Guadalupe Sierra, may you rest in peace."

"Well, that's more like it. We can cut the . . ."

"Look!" The Girl Friday screamed.

Two of the outbuildings at Su Casa—Amapolas and the larger Margaritas—swayed and rocked drunkenly. Even without the microphones, the grinding and shrieking of their timbers and masonry could be heard plainly on the mainland. The crowd in the bleachers set up a cry.

"Run, everybody!" Liz shouted. "Run!"

Stumbling and falling, the band of mourners raced toward the main house. There was a long, low rumble and then the two bungalows slid slowly, almost gracefully, into the sea. A tremendous curtain of white spume rose like a geyser. When it finally settled, a large section of the garden was gone, and with it Aurelia in her fresh grave.

Ratings

On the third morning after the earthquake, Su Casa was *the* entertainment of Acapulco, not because any of the visitors to Acapulco gave a damn about Su Casa, but because there was nothing else to do and practically no way to get out of the town short of walking. To the disbelief and despair of hoteliers, the skies were still gray, the winds still howled, the planes were still grounded. By now, any tourist with a car had driven it to sunnier climes—Taxco or Cuernavaca or Mexico City—and nobody was driving in. Taxicabs were doing a land-office business evacuating the town, first at a hundred dollars for a trip to the capital and, later, at a hundred dollars a passenger. Tickets on the buses were suddenly sold out and were being scalped by entrepreneurs at ten times the usual price. It was thus that many a tourist who had never traveled anywhere by bus was able to visit some of Mexico's most obscure and unpronounceable communities in the colorful company of a dozen chickens and a genial Mexican drunk. "We really got to *know* the people."

To watch the televising of Su Casa became the thing to do. Word traveled quickly and inaccurately in Acapulco. Wasn't that amusing Arthur Craine out there? Hadn't someone had a baby or killed a baby? Wasn't a famous murderer marooned there, and hadn't Rex Roman been murdered by that famous murderer, or was it the other way round? And now it became downright chic to dress warmly, pay a dollar, and watch what was going on from the bleachers.

Yes, Su Casa was In. Jaime Malvido was in show business. E. G.

d'Enker was in clover. The show was officially entitled "This Is It" and "This Is It" was really it. But Acapulco, despite what Acapulco thinks, is not the world. Although Jaime Malvido had done well on a local basis, the East and West Coast offices of the network had performed miracles.

As disasters go, the huge catastrophes are too disastrous, involving too many millions of people for the average mind to grasp. Six million Jews liquidated in World War II is an impossible figure to comprehend, but if the synagogue roof caves in killing six guests during Melvin Plotnik's bar mitzvah, it is a tragedy. In the language of the press this is called "human interest." And human interest is what makes the world care—and care passionately—about a kitten caught in a tree on the corner of Main and Maple Streets; about a baby born in a taxicab on Mosholu Parkway; about two Cub Scouts lost overnight in Starved Rock State Park; about an unknown child trapped in a well in an unheard-of hamlet in West Virginia.

During the time when a handful of not terribly important people were stranded at Su Casa, wars were being waged and young men killed; elder statesmen were dying and governments toppling; planes and trains crashed; there were floods, fires, famine, and flu epidemics; biochemists were discovering new ways to keep man alive and other biochemists were discovering new ways to wipe him out. Naturally these humdrum events were given full press *coverage*, but what got full press *readership* was Su Casa and its inhabitants.

"Talk about luck!" E. G. d'Enker said contentedly over long distance to the head of the public relations.

"You talk about luck, E. G. *I'll* talk about working our asses off. You think it's easy for us to plant this crap?"

But planted it had been—on the network's newscasts, on the wire services, and on the front page of every newspaper in the United States. The Su Casa story was now so big that even the other networks had to mention it, although somewhat disparagingly, on their own news programs.

Public relations had done its job well. Arthur Craine had been easy. His publishers had obligingly released wildly inflated sales figures for his book. *Who's Who* had yielded quite a lot of boring misinformation, supplied by Arthur, couched in incomprehensible abbreviations. And the old tapes of Arthur on various panel shows provided buckets of useful guff.

Rex Roman had been simpler still, and no circulation-conscious daily had been able to resist digging an ancient glossy of Tarzan (48–28–35) from its morgue to adorn a still somewhat garbled account of his death.

Mr. and Mrs. William W. Williams arrived on a number of front pages outside Chicago by virtue of being rich, social, and damned photogenic.

The state of Texas, and especially the city of Dallas, went wild over Mrs. Bullock, whom no one had ever much heard of, and Juliet Noyes, Susan Holt, and Lou Ann McIver, whose fathers everyone had heard of. "Fort Worth papers please copy."

The net worth of Mrs. Florence Meyers had made a number of blasé editors sit up and take notice. Although hitherto unknown beyond Tulsa, Oklahoma, and a number of service bars, Flossie was suddenly billed as "the eccentric widow of multimillionaire Oklahoma oil speculator Abner ('Dry Hole Daddy') Meyers." The word "eccentric" could mean almost anything and was, if discreetly used, libel-proof.

April May would be thrilled to hear herself described as a starlet; the Dewlaps would be pleasantly surprised to discover that Walt was a "prominent Pennsylvania businessman"; and Roland, the dilettante proprietor of a failing gift shop, would tremble with delight to find himself called the "well-known decorator."

Although Liz and Laddy had never caught the public eye, New York editors were glad to remember that they were East Seventieth Street Parkhursts, had gone to the Right Schools and to the Right Dances with the Right People. Liz's first marriage to Norman—now a Name—and her second marriage to Mr. Hobson, "Minnesota tycoon," were duly described. Fulsome accounts of his two marriages were disinterred from yellowed society pages and both of the former Mrs. John Benedict Nicholas ("Laddy") Parkhursts were interviewed. Diane obligingly said, "Laddy was always a lamb." Barbara said, "Who?" But then Barbara, who had been married once before Laddy and had collected enough men afterward to justify her sometimes losing track, was a bitch.

Even Salvador would have been gratified by the ducal quarterings allotted him, first by the chivalrous Spanish-language press, and then by a totally uninformed North American press convinced that a martyred grandee makes for better reading than a dead nobody.

Titles still sell papers. Hence, Bernice was thoroughly entrenched as "Countess" Potocki. It was impossible to uncover anything about Bernice, so she was established as the fragile aristocrat who had fled the Iron Curtain, wolves in her wake, muffled in sable and carrying the crown jewels of King Stanislaus I in the glove compartment of the troika. It made for livelier reportage.

But who had the real glamor? The press was not long in discovering it. Lee Goodwin, alias Leonard Goodrich, Lewis Goode, Lenox Goodhue, etc. Lee offered the one indispensable item—a *criminal at large!* Within fifteen minutes after his name (as Lee Goodwin) had been mentioned on the network, there had been three telephone calls to local television stations. By the following day there had been thirty, and all of them legitimate, from various victims, from vigilant police chiefs, and from hotels, banks, and credit-card firms which Lee had honored with his patronage.

The hands of a dozen headline writers at a dozen metropolitan dailies were poised to print the ultimate attention grabber: "A KILLER IN THEIR MIDST!" It sounded good. It sounded great. What reader could resist it? Take a dozen people with whom the average reader could identify. See? They're all stranded on this island. See? And they've got this murderer stalking them. See? Print an extra fifty thousand copies!

There was only one problem. Lee Goodwin hadn't killed anyone. Or at least there was no proof that he had. No question about it, he was a crook. Plenty of police wanted a word with Lee-Leonard-Lewis-Lenox, etc. But such a shabby little crook! Sad, really. Pathetic. And no criminal record. Lee wasn't even a reformatory graduate. Never been caught. Oh, he would be. No question there. "Famous Confidence Man," "Master Thief," "Cat Burglar," "Gentleman Cracksman," "Society Swindler," all of the favorite clichés were tasted, tested, and found wanting. They weren't good enough. "But, look," one enterprising reporter said, "if he's got this many names and he's in this much trouble, how do we know he *isn't* a killer? And wasn't there something about his throwing Rex Roman into the ocean? Maybe if we wrote it like a question . . . 'A KILLER IN THEIR MIDST?' "

An extra hundred thousand copies were sold that afternoon.

Yes, the network's public relations department had done its work well. Su Casa was on the front pages. Su Casa was human interest. And now, deeper into the daily newspapers, the advertising department took self-congratulatory full-page advertisements announcing that "as a public service" this evening "Our Miss Jukes" and the "Murph Muffin Variety Hour" would be pre-empted by the "Su Casa Story" on "This Is It." Furthermore, and as a further public service, sponsored programs appearing between eight and nine (EST) on subsequent evenings would be pre-empted until the Su Casa calamity had been terminated.

The network was eternally conscious of its function as servant and savant to the public. Every year it polluted the air for seven thousand three hundred hours. Of these, just seven thousand were devoted to audience participation shows, situation comedies, panel shows, soap operas, old movies, older cartoons, and their incessant reruns. The other three hundred hours were generously given over to reporting the news, to unheard Sunday-morning sermons, to a few lugubrious minutes of Shakespeare, Marlowe, Miller, and Ionesco and, under governmental pressure, to unsponsored political debates. Now the network, as a public service, was offering its helpless viewers something big—real, live people in a real mess. And what's more, the network owned it exclusively. "This Is It!" And already bought and paid for by a mouthwash, a deodorant, a hair rinse, and an oil company—with plenty more sponsors lined up and begging to buy in.

"Shit, kid," E. G. d'Enker said, dropping fifty pounds of day-old American newspapers on the floor between the twin beds, "I would never of believed it. Never in a million years."

At the expense of the U.S. taxpayer, Mr. d'Enker and Debbie had moved into the bungalow adjoining Jaime Malvido's at Villa Vera. It was double the size and the price of Jimmy's, as befitted the Vice-President in Charge of Programming of a major television network.

But for business purposes, E. G. preferred to use Jimmy's place. It was cozier.

Realizing how useful each was to the other, the two men had developed a sort of guarded fondness, a cautious mutual respect.

"Imagine," Jimmy sighed from where he lay stretched out on the other bed, "New York, Chicago, L.A., Washington, Dallas . . ."

"And, kid, this stack is just the top twenty cities. But you can betcher sweet ass that if the big time is giving us this kind of play, they're eating it like herring in the tank towns."

"I suppose we oughta send these out to Su Casa," Jimmy said charitably. "Let 'um see how really big they are."

"Man, are you outta yer box? We're just now beginning to gettum forgetting about the camera and acting natural. You showum their press and next thing you know they're all believing their own publicity and making like the Gabors. Keepum innocent, keepum intense, keepum wondering. Kinda like Method acting. Ain't that right, Mac?" E. G. said, tossing a bone to the Girl Friday.

The Girl Friday, exuding hatred for E. G. d'Enker, sat sullenly picking her toenails in a chair placed as far from Mr. d'Enker as possible. Torn now between humanitarian instincts and the opportunity to speak as an expert on the drama, she said, "What you say has some basis of fact, Mr. d'Enker. The lack of consciousness of the camera's eye; the mystique of . . ."

"Maybe E. G.'s right, Priscilla," Jimmy said.

"You betcher sweet ass I'm right, kid. But listen, the one we gotta concentrate on now is the con man, Lee Whatsisname."

"It seems to me that he has a good many," the Girl Friday said.

"Right, Mac. Now you're the big drama specialist while I'm just a dumb slob." The Girl Friday was in violent agreement, but not entirely averse to airing her considerable views before an audience. "But don't that tell ya something, honey? Like you've got a whole pack of decent, respectable, God-fearing people—ladies and gents—trapped out there. Good kids, but all pure vanilla. And right in the middle of 'em a criminal. Like it says in the tabloids. 'A Killer in Their Midst?' Now how does that grab yuh?"

"Well," the Girl Friday said, "it is certainly not without theatrical values. Ra-ther old fashioned, of the genre, perhaps, of *Alias Jimmy Valentine, Outward Bound, One-Way Passage,* or . . ." She had already exhausted a meager stock of criminal-cum-gentry plays all produced long before her mother's birth. "Uh, yes. The formula is dramatically sound, although trite. Now, placed in the hands of Tennessee Williams . . ."

"Placed in the hands of Tennessee Williams he'd have a fag and a nympho fighting for three acts over which one gets to wear Momma's old hoopskirt. Butcha got it, Mac, first crack outa the box. I'm real proud. *Conflict!* The good guys and the bad guy. So we tell Arthur to concentrate on this Goodwin character . . ."

"Supposing this Lee doesn't want to play, E. G.?" Jimmy said. "He hasn't been what you'd call hogging the camera very much."

"So where can he go? All right already, he can hide in the biffy all day, but he's gotta come out for meals, don't he? We got one helluva cameraman out there in that Walter whatever he's called. Dja see how he handled getting that baby born—right through an open window? Blood and gore all over the place, but not so much as one pubic hair to get the show canned."

"Oh, yes," the Girl Friday said eagerly, "and shot through Liz's perfume bottles and that one perfect hibiscus. The juxtaposition of two cultures—the chic, frivolous Anglo-Saxon and the primitive Indian servant. But both *women* beneath it all. Federico Fellini or Michelangelo Antonioni would have . . ."

"Hang up, Mac, for the lova God; I'm tryin' ta think."

"Uh, *Priscilla*," Jimmy said meaningfully.

Now human values overpowered dramatic values. "But then all you think of is a cheap hour's entertainment . . ."

"Cheap?"

"It means nothing to you that a human being lost her life, died in agony, left a motherless child, was buried out there in . . . and that poor woman's life *could* have been saved! Somehow, some way we could have rigged up a stretcher to get her across to land and . . ."

"And if we had, Mac, ya know where we'd be today? You'd be back on the football team and *I'd* be sending résumés all over the TV industry. That Mex havin' a baby was the ironclad, brassbound clincher. Four fuckin' hours before the poor spick croaked and I hate to cut a second of it. Of course we have to . . ."

"I couldn't look," Jimmy said.

"Well, you can betcher sweet ass that about fifty million viewers up in the States can. Jesus, the ratings!"

"Ratings! That's all you think of," the Girl Friday spat. "It turns my stomach!"

"*Priscilla!*" Jimmy said. Really, this girl was too much.

"Yer two hundred per cent correct, Mac," E. G. said. "Ratings is all I think of. Breakfast, lunch, dinner, in the sack, on the can, all day and all night. Ratings is what pays my salary, and yours, too. This ain't the Ibsen Festival and it ain't amateur night, either. You start thinking about ratings, just like yer old Uncle E. G. d'Enker, and you might wind up with a pretty fair job on the network. We can use broads like you with a little know-how and a lot of chutz-pah."

"Well, if I thought I could do something to raise the standards of television, turn it into a vital art form . . ."

"Sure ya could, honey, in just about two centuries. In the meantime, let's think about *this show*, that's what *I'm* tryin' ta convey. Now, get on to Art Craine and tell him about this Lee Goodwin character. But strictly confidential, see? Tell him not to let on that he knows about Lee, or that we do. Just tell Artie to keep buggin' him. Keep him on camera as much as he can. Tell him to stick the needle in an' leave it there. Who knows, maybe we can get some footage out of the con man that may be a whole new art form. Ya read me?"

"I read you." The Girl Friday was reading more than that. She was reading her name lettered in discreet gold on the door of a private office with a cute secretary—something along the lines of Debbie, but more sensitive—coiled in the anteroom; she was reading her name in the gossip columns—". . . lunching at 21 with Katharine Hepburn . . ." ". . . brings Chekhov to telly . . ." ". . . wonder woman signs Garbo . . ." She was even reading her name on the screen: "As conceived, directed and produced by . . ."

"Stout fellah," E. G. said.

The Man in the Blue Suit

The big Greyhound bus stood panting at the side of the customs shed in Nuevo Laredo. Its passengers, their tourist cards duly checked, their luggage given a cursory examination and sealed with Mexican stamps, piled wearily aboard.

It had been a long trip: Chicago, St. Louis, Joplin, Tulsa, Dallas, San Antonio, Laredo, across the International Bridge, and now this miserable Mexican border town. It was about half over. What next? Monterrey, Saltillo, San Luís Potosí, Querétaro, Mexico City. And after that Cuernavaca, Chilpancingo, Acapulco.

"All aboard everybody!" the driver called. "Mexico City next stop." If he didn't scare 'em, they'd scatter like ants buying up every paper flower and plastic sombrero in sight. "Bo-ard! Hey, you! The man in the blue suit. Comin' er arncha?"

"Hold it, I'm just gettin' a paper."

The man in the blue suit plowed back onto the bus and took his seat behind some hippies who smelled like old mackerel. The door sighed closed, the motor sputtered. The bus was off.

The newspaper was printed in Spanish but, with a lot of effort, he could make out most of the words—at least the ones he wanted to understand. There were the big front-page pictures; Arthur Craine, some Chicago society folks from Astor Street, a crazy old dame in a haystack fur coat holding a baby and there, more beautiful than ever, was Countess Potocki.

The man in the blue suit shook his head. "Countess Potocki? Countess Potocki?" Was Bernice off her rocker? Had she got hit on the head in that earthquake?

Well, the man in the blue suit would soon find out or his name wasn't Ralph Przybylski.

Or My Name Ain't Sam H. Noyes

"Sam, you jackass," Mrs. Noyes whimpered from the frosty tonneau of the Continental, "you nearly hit that jackass."

"Don't worry your pretty head, Punkin. We're almost there."

As Mr. Noyes drove on the flat, straight highways of Texas at a steady one hundred miles an hour, so did he drive on the circuitous mountain passes of Mexico. They could make them flat and straight if they really wanted to. The chauffeur snored softly at Mr. Noyes's side. They were driving nonstop from Dallas to Acapulco. The chauffeur was useful for speaking Spanish, for running errands, for taking over the wheel when Mr. Noyes simply had to catch forty winks. But in the long run, no one drove as well as Mr. Noyes. In fact, no one did anything as well as Mr. Noyes.

He had been overseeing one of his many ranches when Mrs. Noyes telephoned hysterically from their perfect copy of the Petit Trianon in Dallas to wail that Julie was more dead than alive on a volcanic island in the middle of the Pacific. He had driven the thousand miles that separated the ranch from the Petit Trianon in just eight hours (including lunch and urination), and before he had even taken off his hat or kissed Mrs. Noyes he was telephoning the twelve richest men in Mexico—summoning them from board meetings and business luncheons, from fairways and steamrooms, from quarrels with their wives and trysts with their mistresses—barking at them as he did at the wetbacks who worked for illegal wages on his many rural holdings. Lazy greasers! They were all unable or unwilling to stop the wind, lift the fog, or calm the sea. No wonder they were poor!

Then he telephoned the airport and told his pilot to get the Lear jet ready for a trip to Acapulco—now. Outraged to learn that no one, not even Samuel Houston Noyes, could take off or land at Acapulco, he rang for the big Continental limousine. "Punkin," he said, "if you want a thang done right, do it yourself."

The parents of Lou Ann McIver were on a safari, the parents of Susan Holt on a cruise of the Orient. But Martha (Punkin) Noyes had been in constant telephonic communication. With remarkable speed, she had found the McIvers perched in a tree in Kenya and the Holts submerged in a tub in Osaka. Within a few traumatic seconds, she had one family scrambling down from its nest, the other beached on the bathhouse floor. All were heading home forthwith. But the Noyeses, as the closest and the richest, were to have carte blanche as their ambassadors. Spare no expense! In a sort of secretarial capacity, Mrs. Noyes had been receiving calls in the back seat of the Continental ever since they had left Dallas. Waiting at the airport. Grounded in Addis Ababa. A layover in Bangkok. Engine trouble in Tunis. Missed connection in Honolulu. Snowbound in New York.

Following in a second Noyes car, being driven rapidly but at a less hazardous speed, were Sam's secretary (bilingual), a doctor, and a nurse. Sam was taking no chances. The invitations to Julie's eighteenth birthday-cum-debut party were already in the mail. Miss Purdy, the bilingual secretary, had addressed all the envelopes herself.

"Sam," Mrs. Noyes said, "there's a sign. At least, there was a sign. It said Acapulco, ten. Ya s'pose that meant ten miles or kilometers? They have such funny ways down here."

"We'll soon see, Punkin."

"We're stayin' at the Peer Marqués. It's the only place had enough rooms for us all, you, me, the Holts, the McIvers, the girls, Miz Bullock, Miz Purdy, the doctor, the nurse, the help. Miz Purdy made an open reservation 'cause I didn't know how long we'd be stayin'."

"Don't you worry your pretty head about it, Punkin. I'll git our little girl outa that place tonight or my name ain't Sam H. Noyes!"

Horns blaring, telephone ringing, air conditioning on at full blast, the big Continental soared down the last hill on the road to Acapulco.

A Woman Just Knows

The presence of the baby created a certain amicable rivalry among the ladies of Su Casa. Flossie and Essie, as mothers, took precedence over the others, speaking with tongues of wisdom about formulas, burping, bathing, powdering, the consistency of stools, the colors of urine. Feeling decidedly inferior, Carolyn, Bernice, and Julie were content to serve as handmaidens, rinsing, hanging, and fluffing diapers, sterilizing bottles, doing the groundwork for such epic events as baths and feedings. If their labors had been found fault-less, they were sometimes rewarded by being allowed to feed the baby—"But, carefully, Carolyn. Not too fast. No, he's getting too much air. Here. Better let me do it, dear"—or at least to hold him.

Liz would probably have been an excellent mother had nature seen fit to endow her with children. But she was frankly a little afraid of the baby, as though he might shatter if ever she held him. His every cry, belch, and scowl presaged disaster to Liz; she was, on the whole, glad that braver women than she had taken over.

April May was rather disappointed in the baby. From her constant perusal of late-night movies, she had expected something with golden ringlets, a peach-blossom complexion, cooing, gurgling, and just about ready to go into an adorable song-and-dance routine. This wrinkled, little, brown creature fell far short of the mark. Anyhow, April was too busy with her new television career to waste time with anything or anyone else. A great actress must be dedicated.

As the baby was Mexican—oh, unmistakably Mexican!—Mrs. Bullock regarded him as a sort of subspecies of human, if that, and probably diseased. She had warned her girls to stay away from him. Lou Ann, unlikely ever to be willingly maternal, was glad to comply. Susan, although rebellious enough to speak of the baby as "cute," obeyed out of docility. Julie now quietly and firmly ignored Mrs. Bullock. Here, where life was happening, where she felt useful, and where she felt loved, she was simply too busy to bother with the dreary woman's nonsense. Mrs. Bullock, obtuse as she was, kept sullenly silent. She had the bully's uneasy fear of the defiant: Liz was one, Carolyn another, and now Julie.

Julie was spending every night with Pablo. She supposed that she ought to feel like a slut, like Lou Ann. Somehow she didn't. Each night she waited until her roommates were asleep. Then, noiselessly, she stole out of the room and wound her way up the *caracol* to Pablo's little room at the top of the house. Here the two of them found the only love they had ever known. He had been horrified at first, protesting that he was a servant, poor and barely literate, while she was a rich Norteamericana, too fine to touch him. Primly purposeful, Julie had simply drawn him down to his bed. The rest had been simple. If this was love, she was all for it.

Julie was fairly sure that no one else knew about it. And she didn't really care. A certain latent sense of mischief even made her imagine a mythical confrontation with her chaperone in which Julie, quite naturally, had all the best lines.

MRS. B: Juliet Noyes, I have never been so shocked in my life!

JULIE: Well, don't let it carry you off, Mrs. Bullock.

MRS. R: Those Mixicun min want just one thang from a white woman.

JULIE: And Pablo's getting it. Sometimes two and three times a night.

MRS. B: I could have the law on him, seducing a young girl like you.

JULIE: Ah, but you see, *I* seduced *him*.

MRS. B: What would your mother and daddy say?

JULIE: Just about what you're saying. Who listens?

MRS. B: Julie Noyes, I forbid you to so much as speak to that dirty Mixicun man again.

JULIE: We don't have time to do much talking. Which reminds me, I'm already late. Don't wait up, Mrs. Bullock.

Carolyn still thought about a divorce in odd moments, but she had been too busy to work out any of the details. And now that sex had returned to the lives of Mr. and Mrs. William W. Williams, it seemed inappropriate to say, "Darling, I'd like a divorce," in mid-orgasm. But shut away by themselves, away from Arthur, sex was indeed back on the agenda as it had not been for some years. Carolyn told herself that it was because the nights were cold, that there was nothing else to do. At home in Chicago the Williamses were much in demand—cocktail parties, dinner parties, sports, and a modicum of theater. There were endless steel moguls and visiting firemen to be entertained. On rare lone evenings, say Mondays or the cook's night out, there was always Arthur just around the corner to dispel their solitude.

And now Carolyn asked herself a question: Could I possibly be pregnant? She had never been regular, had never worried about it or even thought about it very much. In the last couple of years there hadn't been anything to think about. She had even stopped using contraceptives. Now, gazing at the neat package of tampons she had brought to Mexico, it occurred to her that she hadn't needed them for better than three months. That *was* unusual. And there had been that night in November. It was probably just some psychological thing brought on by Aurelia's baby—seeing him born, hearing him cry, waiting on him. Anyhow, Carolyn felt that she wanted to talk to someone.

"Ah, Essie?" Carolyn said. "Are you frightfully busy at the moment?"

"Why, no, dear. Flossie's just fed him and now she's putting him to bed. Really, the change that precious little thing has made in Flossie! She's a different woman."

"Well, Essie, I think he may have made a change in me, too. Essie, how do you know if you're pregnant?"

"Why, darling, you miss a period. Of course you know that. But, if you think it happened just since we've been here, it's much too soon to tell. Not even a doctor could be sure this early."

"No, Essie, I've missed about three."

"*Three?* Why, Carolyn!"

"Clockwork isn't exactly my middle name, but I've never gone this long."

"That *is* a long time, dear. Any morning sickness?"

"What *is* this morning sickness you keep hearing about?"

"Frankly, Carolyn, I think it's more up in the attic than it is down in the furnace. One of those old wives' tales. Although when I was first pregnant with Elspeth I'll admit there were some mornings I couldn't even look at Walt, let alone breakfast."

"Well, now that you mention it, I haven't felt just great. Oh, nothing like swooning and throwing up. Just a little blah, if you know what I mean."

"Mm-hmm. That's the way I was with our second. Of course every pregnancy is slightly different. Any pains in your breasts?"

"Yes! Is that a sign?"

"Sometimes. I had it with both of my children. Swelling?"

"Just a little."

"It's still very early. Uh, tell me, dear, do you feel a kind of unusual craving for—well, for sex?"

"Yes, I guess I do. But that's being satisfied nicely, thank you."

"Walter was always most obliging about that, too," Essie said, blushing girlishly. "Although at first he acted as though I were going to miscarry if he so much as kissed me good night. But, tell me, Carolyn, how do you feel?"

"Why, fine."

"No, dear, I don't mean physically. I mean how do you *feel?* It seems to me that a woman can have every test in the world to find out whether she's going to have a baby or not. But when she really is, a woman just *knows.* At least I did with both of mine."

"Well, I guess I just know, too."

"Oh, Carolyn! I'm so happy for you! What does Bill say?"

"Bill doesn't know anything about it. I didn't myself until right now."

"Well, you'd better tell him. And Arthur, too."

"Bill, yes. Arthur? No."

"I just can't think of anything lovelier than the baby you and Bill will have. But don't tell anyone else, dear. I made that mistake when I was having Elspeth. Of course she was my first and I was thrilled, beyond sense. But once people find out, they never stop staring at your middle until the baby's born. And the way they leap up to offer you chairs you don't want to sit in! Just don't say anything to anyone. The baby will make its presence known in its own good time."

"I wonder if I should even tell Bill?"

"But of course you should. You must! Nothing in the world brings a couple closer together than a beautiful secret like having a baby. *I know.*" Essie sniffled. "Oh, now I'm getting all soppy, like some maudlin old *hausfrau.* Listen, dear, Bill's out in the parking lot helping Walter rig up something to our car that will make the water pump work. Walt doesn't need any help. He loves to tinker. So you call Bill right now, take him up to your room, and tell him. He'll be the happiest man alive, and you'll be the happiest girl."

"I guess you're right," Carolyn said. "Well, here goes."

Easier said than done. Carolyn picked up a basket of freshly washed diapers to give her an excuse for wandering out toward the parking lot at all. Keep it casual. But just what, exactly, did one say casually? "Bill, guess what? The Armageddon has just been announced for two o'clock local time." "Oh, Bill, it just occurred to me. Martians have landed at the yacht club!" "Bill, guess who's having a baby." Now Carolyn understood. It was hard for her and Bill to talk because they had been given precious little opportunity to do so. Except to sleep or make love, they were hardly ever alone together. True, they were treated like royalty—and had just about as much privacy. Even their honeymoon had been a sort of royal progression, spent mostly in the country houses of Arthur's foreign friends, and with Arthur himself turning up at various points along the route to launch them in London, present them to Paris, pave the Via Appia for their entrance into Rome. Carolyn had learned small talk at her brother's knee. Now she was such a glib master of it that, drained daily of banalities, there was no large talk left for Bill—not even a stack-blowing, air-clearing row over capping the toothpaste. Yes, Carolyn could talk to anyone about anything, except Bill. "But we've never had a chance."

The sight of Bill made her feel a little better. She liked the way he looked—dirty hands and a smudge of black grease on his nose as he bent over the open hood of Walt's car.

"Well, by God, *that's* done," Walt was saying. "Now I just back up the car a couple of inches to tighten the belt and we've got running water again."

"Ah, Bill," Carolyn said in a high, false voice of cheer. No. She'd

266

have to tone that down. It made her sound like one of those idiots about to give a recipe for cheese fondue. "Bill?" There. That was better. "Could I, uh, have a word with you?"

Grab Your Spear, Kid, You're On

Essie had been right. Learning that his child just possibly might be inside Carolyn had a profound effect on Bill. Now he was to be seen stripped to the waist, splitting firewood with Pablo's ax as though he were not only going to make the cradle, but build the log cabin for the birth of some future President. Carolyn called herself "Nancy Hanks Lincoln" and giggled helplessly with Essie over the imbecility of men.

Now Bill and Carolyn talked—actually talked—to one another. She was amazed by how nice he was. No, not quite. She'd always known that. But by how deeply concerned he was, how much he loved her, how much she loved him. Of course he was driving her quite crazy with his attentions. Every time she tried to do the simplest thing for herself—open a door, bend down to find a pair of shoes, pick up a book—he raced to her side like a czarist serf to perform the onerous task. "But, Carolyn," Essie said, "they always do. I was ready to kill Walter. He wouldn't let me play golf, drive a car, swim—anything. He even tried to make me leave the bathroom door open in case I miscarried on the toilet! Well, I put my foot down there. Even pregnant, you've got to have some mystery. They're all alike, dear. Idiots! But sweet."

The first night that he knew of his impending fatherhood, Bill said, "From now on I'll sleep on the chaise longue."

"Well, you'll do no such thing, William Williams. In the first place, it's too cold. I want you here if only for body heat."

"Yes, but suppose I get—uh—ideas?"

"Which I sincerely hope you will."

"Yes, Carolyn, but the baby."

"Bill, if there's a baby there at all—I'm pretty sure there is—it's no bigger than the tip of my finger. I promise that you won't hurt it. Now stop this foolishness and come to bed."

Maybe it's what they'd always needed: a little baby and a lot of privacy.

As thrilling as the television adventure had been, its novelty palled rapidly. Where all had been smiling lips, twinkling eyes, and straightened spines when the camera hove into view, the attitude was now "Oh, that!" Even Walter Dewlap, for whom the hand camera had been like a boy's first electric train, now growled audibly when asked to shoulder it. On the opposite shore the pressure was easing. "As a public service," the most carefully edited moments of life at Su Casa appeared for an hour every night on "This Is it." The show was a smash, its ratings astronomical. There was talk of making E. G. d'Enker president of the network. Jaime Malvido was receiving eager letters asking for future dramatic-documentary works. Only the evening before, when he had dined with E. G. at Coyuca 22, no less than *six* famous personages had hopped right over to his table. They *knew* him! Of course, they all remembered meeting him at a party in Mexico, an opening in New York, a discotheque in London, a *vernissage* in Beverly Hills. In! He was Mr. Show Biz! It made him almost indifferent to the show itself.

The work was getting lighter, anyhow. The basic shots had all been taken—people eating, the women cooking, Flossie changing the baby. It was pointless to repeat them. Audiences had a low threshold of boredom. Except for a camera constantly trained on Su Casa in case anything good happened, such as the whole place collapsing into the Pacific, the shooting was now cut down to two or three hours a day around noon when the light was brightest, the weather warmest, and the grandstand filled.

"Kid," E. G. said, "unless something really big happens over there, I think we can milk about two more days outa this. A week is about all the audience'll take, although I'd like ta stretch it inta Sunday night justa ram our rating up Ed Sullivan's keester. Then we'll wrap it up with a big rescue scene."

"How do you plan to do that, E. G.? There are still no boats out and no planes taking off."

"That's your problem, kid. You're the producer."

Even E. G. was getting bored. He liked to think of himself as a kickoff man. Get a great idea, launch it, and then let some underling take over while the genius retired to create another masterpiece. "This Is It" had hit so big that it more than made up for some of the costly clangers Mr. d'Enker had perpetrated. After five days it was still front-page copy and Aurelia's baby had started a perfect cult. Unofficial contests to name the baby had sprung up. The network mailroom, local television stations, and Mexican customs were deluged with blankets and booties, every-stitch-a-stitch-of-love sweaters and soakers. Manufacturers of cribs, bassinets, high chairs, baby food, and toys had selflessly sent samples of their wares thinking only of the poor orphan and a possible plug on the show. Nearly twenty-six thousand dollars in checks, money orders, and dirty dollar bills had been mailed in. It was an outburst of public sentimentality that stunned even E. G., although he modestly accepted the credit for the movement. Short of blowing up Su Casa, there was nothing now that he could do to make the show any bigger. He was restive here in Acapulco. He wanted to get back to Los Angeles to bask in the adulation of really important people.

Mr. d'Enker was not the only one who was restive. Dr. Craine was seething. Dr. Craine was too angry to speak, and couldn't have spoken if he'd wanted to. Dr. Craine, on the threshold of a new career, was suddenly bedridden.

It had all happened yesterday when Arthur's mirror and infallible judgment had told him that then was the time for the world to see almost all of Arthur Craine, sage, wit, raconteur, and body beautiful. Oh, he had plotted it so cleverly! If Mr. d'Enker wanted sex in the form of April May's silicone mammaries, why not let the dizzy tramp wear one of her glass bikinis? But wouldn't it look odd to have April nine-tenths naked and Arthur fully dressed? Of course it would, and so Arthur had consented to appear in what he called "bathing dress." The scene would be staged on the dock at the far side of Su Casa, where Laddy's boat, the *Sea Urchin*, was moored. That would be a nice change, and the audience could see with its own eyes how violent the ocean was, as well as what a flawless figure lurked beneath Arthur's flawless tailoring.

The maquillage had taken nearly two hours. Arthur had shaved his torso, leaving only a narrow and slimming line of hair running from his crotch to the sparse fur on his chest. Enough there to look like a man but not like an ape. The numerous white hairs had been darkened with mascara. The "bathing dress," which he had reluctantly agreed to wear, consisted of a minuscule knit-elastic romper ("one size fits all") purchased in an indiscreet moment at José, Artículos para Caballeros, and just slightly padded with Kleenex. Over it all, "for concealment," Arthur wore a fishnet shirt, open to the navel, through whose inch-square mesh winked Arthur's subtly rouged nipples. Thong sandals displayed his elegant feet, his dimly burnished toenails. By comparison, April in her lace pasties and G-string looked almost overdressed.

As Arthur appeared on the dock, chest up, buttocks clenched, stomach sucked in nearly to his spine, Mrs. Bullock's jaw dropped. "Well," she gasped, "I never!"

"Well, I have," Lou Ann muttered to Susan, "and maybe I'll just try it again with that old goat. He ain't half bad." Susan went scarlet and emitted a strangulated giggle.

"Arthur, you'll catch your death!" Essie said.

And it *had* been cold, raising goose flesh and contracting his roseate nipples beneath the flapping fishnet shirt. But the effect of the wind and the waves surrounding Adonis had been irresistible— to Arthur. "When do I come on?" April asked, with chattering teeth. "I'll tell you," Arthur said.

But first Arthur had been alone on camera, pacing up and down the dock to display long, leanly muscled legs, indicating, with a splendid twist of his shapely waist, the turbulence of the seas, standing like a naked Ulysses beside Laddy's sloop, and explaining why no one could hope to sail ashore in a sea like this one.

"Fer Christ's sake," Mr. d'Enker growled from the control truck, "tellum to stop flashin' his shwantz and bring on the tits!" Walt colored and began to make all of the frantic television hand signs he had learned.

At last Arthur, feeling that he had given his all, said, "And now see what lovely water sprite is coming down to the ocean! Why, it's talented, glamorous April May, everyone's favorite starlet." His sarcasm was delicious. "Coming down for a dip, April?"

270

"Huh? Oh, no. It's too cold. Anyways, I can't swim."

"*Zut alors*, dear girl, don't you find it a little chilly to be wearing that—ah—you *do* call that a bathing suit?"

"Yeah. Whaddayuh call that thing you're wearin'?" Oblivious of Arthur's displeasure, April had gone right on. "Rex yoosta callum . . ." Wide-eyed, April leapt backward. And just in time.

A tremendous wave rose high above the dock and knocked Arthur flat. Coughing and sputtering, hair hanging into his eyes, he tried to struggle to his feet. And then he fell again. His tiny elastic trunks had been washed down to his knees, locking them together. His Kleenex floated along the planking in a sodden wad. "Cut!" Arthur roared, tugging and yanking at his trunks. "Cut, goddamn it!" Stomach limp, buttocks sagging, one testicle not quite back in its nest, Arthur achieved his footing, slipped on the wet new wood of the dock and went down again. "Cut, I tell you! Cut!"

"Keep right on grindin', Walt," E. G. shouted into his mouth-piece. "Is that the broad I hear?"

It was. For the first time since Rex Roman's death, April was laughing. April was howling, clutching at her stomach, stamping her crystal clogs on the dock, her coiffure rocking, her turgid breasts bouncing.

"What the fuck's goin' on out there?" E. G. roared. "It sounds like 'Laugh-In.' "

"It is," Walt said. "I can hardly hold the camera still."

"Cut, I tell you, you son of a bitch!" Arthur shouted. He was sprawled on the dock, a large splinter piercing the rear of his swim-ming suit, his fishnet shirt hanging like kelp, and salt water coursing in little rivulets through the mascara and rouge on what had been, until just a moment before, television's newest great physique.

"Arthur! Let me help you," Roland said, slipping and sliding to his side.

"Take your hands off me, you tatty little faggot!"

Arthur got to his feet and charged furiously to his room.

Carolyn had ministered tea and sympathy, Essie aspirin and hot lemonade. When she got over laughing, Liz had tendered scalding rum, extra blankets, and ascorbic acid. Crimson, Laddy had removed the splinter from his roommate's rear with sterile tweezers and, with the best intentions in the world, daubed the site with iodine. Arthur's bellow of anguish had frozen the household.

Arthur suffered his first chill at midnight. Since then, Laddy had served as a dedicated, if inept nurse, piling on blankets, offering Contac and Bufferin, and mixing mugs of rum and boiling water. At daybreak he had fallen asleep in a chair. "How like Laddy!" Arthur thought. But when Arthur tried to call Laddy to adjust the curtains, no sound came out. Arthur's golden voice was gone. Only his violent sneeze stirred Laddy from slumber.

Arthur's rasping and gasping, his frenzied pointing to his lips and larynx frightened Laddy thoroughly. "Wait till I get my thermometer," Laddy said.

"It isn't my temperature, it's my voice," Arthur whispered. "Call Liz."

Liz came in from the kitchen, where she had planned to scramble eggs over the fireplace. "Good morning, Arthur," she said with a maddening brightness. It pleased her just a little to see him like this. "I'm boiling some water to make a nice hot honey lemonade for you."

"That's sweet of you, dear girl," Arthur whispered, "but this is more important. My voice. It's gone. I can't speak."

"Poor Arthur," Liz said.

"Now this is what I want you to do. Take my headset and get in touch with Jaime Malvido on the other side. I want you to tell him two things: First, we'll have to suspend shooting until my voice is back . . ."

"Oh, that *is* a crying shame," Liz said, trying to repress a smile.

"And the second thing—and this is really important—is that I want yesterday's footage destroyed."

"You mean when that little old tidal wave hit you? I rather liked that. So Captain Ahab! If only there'd been a whale. And you certainly showed the audience the whole man. We all admired it."

Laddy blushed and sniggered into the back of his hand.

"Goddamn it!" Arthur's voice rose to a piteous squeak. "Stop camping and do as I tell you. This is important. I want that footage cut. And do it right now!"

"Yes, sir! Certainly, sir! Whatever you say, sir! But do you mind if I call him from the kitchen? Flossie's trying to feed the baby and I'm trying to feed the grownups, including even you." Liz grabbed up the headset and went back to her ham and eggs. Arthur groaned and gazed mournfully at the ceiling. Fate, the fickle bitch!

Fitting on the headset, Liz felt a little like the brave Bell Telephone girl saving Johnstown from the flood. Today it was even the Voice With a Smile. After a little basic Spanish with a Mexican technician in the control truck, Liz got through to Jaime Malvido. Jimmy was, once again, feeling very big-time producer.

"Mr. Malvido? This is Mrs. Martínez. I have a message for you from Dr. Craine. He asks me to tell you that he has lost his voice and that shooting will have to be suspended for today at least . . . But, Mr. Malvido, Dr. Craine *can't* speak to you. He can't speak at all. He can barely whisper. That's why I'm . . . Really, Mr. Malvido, there is no need to use that sort of language. I am merely telling you what . . ."

Liz's jaw dropped, hitting the mouthpiece. "Uh, excuse me, Mr. Malvido, I didn't quite hear that. Would you please say it again? . . . Did I understand you to say that you are paying Arthur *twen-ty thou-sand dol-lars* to broadcast this—this *thing* from my house? . . . Tax free? . . . Dear me, yes! That *is* an added inducement! . . . Oh, I can readily understand your wish to protect your investment. However, Dr. Craine's voice is . . . No, Mr. Malvido, I would *not* be interested in narrating your program. Nor would anyone else here. . . ." Liz paused. Her eyes slid toward the kitchen door. April May had just entered wearing a short, short nightgown. "However, Mr. Malvido, there *is* our Miss April May, the actress, you know . . . Yes, a truly remarkable figure. But it's her intellect that interests me even more, Mr. Malvido. I feel that her running commentary would be perfectly keyed to a program of this caliber. A little coaching from you, Mr. Malvido, and, well, the mind boggles! . . . Salary? Well, you'd really have to ask Miss May, but I can't imagine that it would be a fraction of what you're paying my dear old friend, Dr. Craine . . . Yes! She's right here!"

An uncanny glitter came into Liz's eyes. "But before I put Miss May on this contraption, Mr. Malvido, Dr. Craine was rather inter-

273

ested in yesterday's shooting. You know, when that wave hit the dock? . . . Yes, it was amusing . . . Mr. d'Enker did? So hard that he fell out of his chair? Fancy! Did he break anything?" Liz asked eagerly. "Nothing. Pity . . . Yes, dear Arthur has always had a great flair for comedy . . . *All* of it? . . . Yes, I suppose you would have to cut *that* part in the interests of public decency, although I understand that all men have them . . . And it's going on the air tonight? How I *wish* I could see it! Dr. Craine will be so pleased. Well, enough of my idle chitchat, Mr. Malvido. I know that you're busy and that you'll want to talk to Miss May about replacing poor Arthur . . . Yes, I certainly will tell him. Now here's Miss May."

Handing the headset to April, Liz said, "Grab your spear, kid, you're on!"

"Huh?"

Steam curled from the spout of the kettle. The water for Arthur's hot lemonade was boiling. Liz lifted the kettle from the fireplace, carried it to the sink, and poured the water down the drain.

His throat swathed in scarves, Arthur rose and tottered to the window. There was April May, breasts barely contained in their hammock of silver mesh—cheap little exhibitionist! Arthur couldn't hear what she was prattling into the the mike, but everyone was laughing. And now she was interviewing people, Essie and Flossie with the baby, and—yes!—even Liz. The perfidy of one's old friends! Of course they were all laughing at—not *with*—April. How could a nitwit like that one ever even hope to compete with an Arthur Craine? But April was on and Arthur was here, sick and mute. He shivered and plodded back to his bed. Of all times to fall ill—and with only laryngitis. It would draw about as much public concern as a sunburn or hemorrhoids. Arthur Craine stoically wasting away with a rare and fatal disease—that would be something. Even a broken bone: Arthur Craine, virile and visually interesting with his arm in a silk sling like that aging pansy, Roland. Or Arthur in . . .

Roland! Arthur's attempts to draw out Lee Goodwin, in accordance with Mr. d'Enker's orders, had met with less than no success. But now that Roland was sharing Lee's room, the two of them would certainly have to talk—say *something*. Arthur clanged away at the silver bell that had been placed on his night table. Where was that lazy Mexican servant?

Roland was of mixed emotions when Pablo told him that Don Arturo wished to speak to him. "I think he said quite enough yesterday," Roland said with a sniff. Roland had never been so humiliated in his life, and he'd only been trying to help.

"*Mande, señor?*"

Roland's prickly retort was wholly wasted on Pablo. Too bad. Anyhow, his curiosity was piqued. Arthur undoubtedly wanted to apologize.

"Yes?" Roland said coldly, standing like an obelisk in Arthur's doorway. He had taken time to change his clothes and fix his hair. Old bitch-mouth could damned well wait for *Roland!* Roland's tardiness had given Arthur the opportunity to put on fresh pajamas and wrap his throat in a more becoming scarf. No harm in looking one's best with that type.

"Come in, dear boy," Arthur whispered. "And close the door, please."

Roland closed the door and stalked to a chair in the corner of the room. He sat stiffly, the picture of wounded sensitivity. He would accept Arthur's apology, but in his own good time.

"Closer, dear boy," Arthur croaked. "*Zut alors!* I can barely whisper." Arthur nudged over in his bed and patted the coverlet hospitably. Roland crossed the room and perched primly on the edge of Arthur's bed. All was *not* forgiven. Not yet.

"You're looking splendid, Roland. Stunning shirt!"

"Th-thank you," Roland said, warming just a little. "And those are lovely pajamas. Bronzini?"

"Charvet. Tell me, Roland, how do you enjoy sharing a room with our Mr. Goodwin?"

The question was so unexpected that Roland forgot his wounded feelings, the words bubbling and sizzling on his tongue. "Oh! How can you even mention his name? I'd rather move in with *anyone* else —even Pablo."

"One could do a great deal worse than Pablo," Arthur whispered, with just a flicker of a wink.

"Yes. He *is* nice-looking. But, oh, Arthur, living with *Lee!* I don't know if you ever noticed it—*I* never got close enough to him; certainly didn't want to—but there's such an awful odor about Lee. It isn't like BO. I mean, he washes and uses a deodorant. But it's like, well, I don't know *what* it is. Sort of like mildew, kind of clammy. *Ugh!* And the way he never takes his clothes off! You'd think he had something I wanted to see."

"Not our sort, eh?" Again a tiny half wink. Now what did Arthur mean by that?

"He's certainly not *my* sort. And the way he just lies there on his bed all day, following me around with those cold little eyes. He made me so nervous yesterday I dropped a whole bottle of Canoe. At least it makes the room smell better.

"Maybe he's developing an interest in you, dear boy," Arthur whispered with a secretive smile.

"Well, I certainly have none in *him*."

"Does he talk much?"

"Hardly a word. Oh, things like 'Do you want to use the bathroom?' or 'Is it dinner time?' Nothing else. And I don't *want* to say anything to *him*."

Arthur's hand reached across the coverlet and patted Roland's knee. "Dear boy, how would you like to do me a very great favor?"

"Well, uh, *what?*"

"Talk to Lee. Try to make a friend of him."

"*Me?* That'll be the day! No, thank *you!* I can't stand him."

"Come closer," Arthur whispered. "If I tell you a secret—a very important secret—do you swear that it will never go beyond this room?"

"Yes, Arthur. But what?" The proximity, the excitement, the contagion of Arthur's whisper was forcing Roland to whisper, too.

"Lee Goodwin is a crook."

"A what?"

"A crook. A confidence man. He's wanted by the law."

"*No!*"

"Yesssss. There are agents on the shore just waiting to nab him. That's why they've asked us—you and me—to help." The story was as implausible as it was untrue, but Arthur guessed correctly that by this time Roland would question nothing.

"But how? I mean, what can *I* do?"

"Everything, my dear. That's why I want you to make friends with Lee. Lead him on."

"You *can't* mean . . ."

"No! Not that. I meant lead him on financially. Tell him you've come into some money—a biggish inheritance, say—which you want to invest." Arthur's hand now rested on Roland's leg. "Don't worry. He'll do all the rest of the talking. And then I want you to tell me everything he says." Slight squeeze.

"But suppose he has a gun or something?"

"*Zut alors!* Never! Con men don't resort to violence."

"Well, Arthur, if you think . . ."

"I *know.*" Squeeze, pat, pat. "And I know that you can do it, *if* you will."

"Of course I'll do it, Arthur. For you."

'Thank you, Roland. You're the only one here I could count on. I knew that the minute I laid eyes on you." Stroke, squeeze.

"Did you, Arthur?"

"The very instant. We'll have some good times together when we get out of this place."

Nearly faint with excitement, Roland already envisioned the future. Arthur Craine and Roland Preston, buddies! Together they would go to the White House to accept the President's heartfelt thanks and matching medals. Together they would share a stateroom on a world cruise. Together they would arrive at the smartest restaurants, the choicest parties. *Who are those two distinguished older men? Why, my dear, don't you know? Arthur Craine and Roland Preston. They've been inseparable for years. Well, do you suppose they're, uh . . . My dear, with men that attractive who could possibly care? Would you like to meet them? Oh, yes!*

"You must go, dear Roland. We can't be seen together too much —just now." Like a languid French general, Arthur drew Roland's face to his own and planted a quick little kiss on each cheek, lightly chaste, but heavy with promise.

Roland reeled from the room.

Pillow Talk

Feeling like Mata Hari, Roland splashed on a superabundance of Brut, as much in self-defense against Lee's pervasive sour reek as in the hope that its come-hither scent would drive his roommate into orgies of confession. He opened his kimono to show off the big St. Christopher medal, plumped his pillows, and slid into bed, waiting for Lee to finish doing whatever he did in the bathroom. Thanks to Walt's hooking up the pump to his car, there was at least running water—cold. But with Lee it didn't help very much.

Roland was nervous. In the little theater group, of which he was a leading light, he had not only designed the costumes and sets, but had played major roles in such resounding successes as *The Admirable Crichton, Peer Gynt, The Importance of Being Earnest, Blythe Spirit,* and *Ghosts* without a moment's stage fright. But this was different. This was real. Roland heard the toilet flush. He quivered with anticipation. Now was the time and he simply couldn't let Arthur down.

The bathroom door opened and Lee appeared wearing his robe and pajamas and, under them, Roland knew, underwear and socks. "Ready to blow out the candle?" Lee asked.

No! Roland wanted to see Lee's face so that he could report everything to Arthur. He'd have to invent an excuse. "Uh, wait just a minute, I want to wind my little traveling clock."

"Suit yourself." Lee got into bed.

"Uh, Lee?"

"Yeah?"

"I, uh, wonder if you could give me some advice."

"What about?"

"Money."

"Money?" From what Lee had learned in his routine check, Roland had some money, but not much. There was enough in trust to keep him in food, clothing, and boys; nothing more.

"Yes. This is some money I just inherited from this, this great-aunt of mine. Oh, it's rather a lot."

"About how much?"

"Uh, well, it's just over a million dollars." Had he seen Lee's cold little eyes open wider? "After taxes," he added for a touch of realism.

"Nothin' to sneeze at." Lee attempted an indifference he did not feel.

Now Roland tried a master thrust. "Yes, uh, Aunt, uh, Gertrude left everything to my sister and me."

"A million between you or each?"

"Each." Oh, how audacious! "It takes forever to get these wills through the courts. But I just got a letter from Harriet—that's my sister—saying that we finally had the money."

"How could you get a letter out here?" Lee asked flatly.

Oh, dear! "I don't mean just now—*today*. It came before the earthquake. That afternoon." Another touch of realism? Yes! "It's in my bag. The letter. Wait, I'll get it." Roland even started to get out of bed. A lovely bit. It was like the time he sewed black sequins on his umbrella in *Ghosts* to make it look wet, as though he'd just come to Mrs. Alving's house through the rain. Then he stopped. "Oh, I'll never find it in the dark. It doesn't say anything anyway—just news about the weather and that the money's been deposited in the bank." Letting his kimono fly open alluringly, Roland got back into bed. Tomorrow, with Arthur's help, he'd even forge a letter in Harriet's bold, black scrawl.

Lee remained silent, but Roland could almost feel an electrical current in the room. Now, that little self-deprecating giggle that he'd done so effectively in *The Importance of Being Earnest*. "I'm such a fool about investments and things like that. And Harriet's no better." Hah! If Lee could just see Harriet; barking at her broker, ticking them off at the bank, totting up her bull mastiffs' meat bills. "And I know that you're an expert in these things."

"Who told you that?"

Roland thought fast. "Uh, I don't really remember. I think it was Walt. Walter Dewlap."

Lee thought back. Yeah. That made sense. Lee looked across the candle flame at Roland propped up on his pillows, limpid eyes demurely lowered. (Lowered indeed, but open enough to observe Lee's face reflected in the mirror opposite.) One million bucks! Two, counting Sister Harriet. Candy from a baby! Jesus, for half that amount he'd pile into bed with the crazy queen, if that's what he wanted—and sister, too. Lee had done much worse for lots less.

Play it cool. "Well, uh, Roland, there are a few pretty good investments around. They're not open to everybody, but . . ."

"Oh, you can tell me!" No! Don't be too eager. Revise. Do the *Blithe Spirit* offhand thing. "Unless you'd rather not. I just thought that maybe you could . . ."

"Oh, that's okay, Roly . . ."

Roly, really! Wouldn't Arthur rock with laughter when he heard that one!

"Only, uh, Roly, these are corporations that don't want a lot of two-bit investors. A million dollars is about as small an ante as they'll consider, if that. But then you say your sister . . ."

"Oh, yes! Harriet's very anxious to invest. She said so in her letter." Roland was already drafting the letter from a never-never Harriet, a feminine bit of fluff concerned only with fashion and frivolity, the kind of sister Roland would have enjoyed. She would own a poodle like Roland's Zsa-Zsa, and write a chic backhand as Roland did.

"Wait till I get my attaché case, Roly. I've got some things to show you." I've got plenty to show you, you big fruit! Maybe without actually *doing* anything he could even warm the poor fag up a little; let him think that in the not too far distant future . . .

"Here," he said, putting the case on Roland's bed.

Roland was even able to memorize the combination—15, 33, 24. He tingled with the thrill of this grand intrigue. Arthur would be so proud!

"Now there's Texokla Petroleum. That's good because of the depletion allowance. Or Royal Canadian . . . Hey! It's cold! Shove over and I'll crawl in with you. We can put the candle here so you can see and . . ."

How ghastly! To be in the same bed with this awful, awful, creepy man. Shuddering, Roland moved over. He felt like Floria Tosca yielding to the odious advances of Scarpia for the sake of true love. Trying not to breathe, drawing himself as far from Lee as possible, Roland sent a fervent telepathic message across Su Casa. "I'm doing this for you, Arthur. Only for you!" Aloud he said, "Tell me about Texokla, uh, Lee."

Julie tapped softly at Pablo's door, opened it, and slipped inside. Pablo was in bed studying *Fluent English in Ten Days—Simple, Pleasant and Sure*. He had forged ahead to "Amor y Cortejo—Love and Courtship." "Iu ar mai su-it-jart. Ai lav iu." If only he could get to the post office where his *Oxford University Complete Home Study Course of Perfect English* would surely be waiting. There was so much he wanted to say to Julie. But now she was in his arms.

"Pablo! Pablo! I waited so long. I thought Lou Ann would never go to sleep."

"An' I wait for you, Julie. I read. Study. The English."

Julie took the book from him, glanced at it, and closed it. "Pablo, I can teach you English. And you can teach me Spanish."

"Me? A servant? Teach you Spanish? You would talk like a bootblacker."

"Bootblack, Pablo."

"Bootblack. Julie! No! Is impossible. I love you. You love me. But is impossible."

"If you love me and I love you, anything is possible, Pablo. Everything. Hold me."

"Julie."

Julie stroked the glossy head buried in her breast and blew out the candle.

Liz lay in her bed watching Flossie feed the baby. "That's a good fellah. Now let's have a li'l burp." Expertly, Flossie hoisted the baby over her shoulder and patted his back. He belched magnificently. "Good boy! Any more?" The baby obliged with a halfhearted encore. "Okay, kiddo, time ta hit the hay."

Except for state occasions, Flossie had abandoned her ice-blue satin and was dressed mostly in the shirts and slacks and sweaters that had been Salvador's. Worn with all of her diamonds, Flossie looked a little like Tugboat Annie played by Magda Lupescu.

But still, Liz thought, she's healthy and happy and useful and alive. It's amazing. The drinking—well, she's still putting away enough vodka to floor two men, but . . . "Tired, Flossie?" she asked.

"Me? Hell, no! I done enough two o'clock feedings in my day. This is ol' stuff ta me. Well, time fer a li'l nightcap. Move over, Queenie." Flossie plumped herself down on her bed and filled her glass with vodka.

"Liz?"

"Yes, Flossie?"

" 'Member what I was sayin' the other night? The night Junior, here, was born. About maybe tryin' ta doptum?"

"Yes, Flossie."

"Aw, hell, it's just some kinda pipe dream. Cantcha jus' see that social worker givin' me the once-over? One look an' that'd be the enda that."

"Flossie, dear, in Mexico, it's not quite that difficult. The supply of babies far exceeds the demand. This poor little thing is up for grabs. Illegitimate, mother dead, father unknown. As for his brothers and sisters, well, the oldest isn't more than ten."

"Hell, I'd be willing ta takem all. Keepum right here in Acapulco. I could maybe try ta learn the lingo, or I could teachum to talk English. Ha! Who's gonna teach me?"

"Eight children are a big burden, Flossie."

"So what? I got more 'n enough money. Hire somebody like Peedro ta give a hand. Oh, honey, don't think I'd try to swipe yer help. What kinda pal'd that be?"

"Flossie, if we ever get out of this place alive, the least of my problems will be the servant problem. Pablo's a wonderful boy, and he even knows a little English. But there won't be any Su Casa for him to work in, or any money to pay him."

"Maybe I could buy it off ya. Plentya rooms."

"Flossie! You are the sweetest, kindest, most generous woman alive. But the answer is no. It would be like selling you an acre of quicksand. But, as for taking over Aurelia's children—or just this one—a cousin of—of—my husband's is a lawyer. He speaks English. He could arrange . . ."

Liz felt the room lurch. The candle at her bedside rocked and then righted itself. Flossie was on the floor, the glass of vodka still in her hand.

"My God! What was that?"

"Didn't spill a drop," Flossie said, getting to her feet.

Liz could hear excited voices echoing through the house.

"But what was it?"

Throwing a robe around herself, Liz hurried out of the room. "Laddy! Laddy! What on earth . . ."

"It's the parking lot, Liz. The whole thing just caved in—the station wagon, Walt's car. It even dragged the water pump in with it."

"Je-zuz!" Flossie said, taking a great gulp of her drink.

"Still interested in buying the place, Flossie?"

Beddy-bye

Almost everyone at Su Casa had been very good—even brave— about the series of catastrophes that were slowly eating the place away. They had mostly accepted the first earthquake as a spiteful caprice of mother nature and their subsequent isolation as a short-lived inconvenience, fraught with excitement and novelty—something interesting, amusing, to talk about when safely back at home.

The collapse of Nubes had been jarring, but at least the house had been empty. No one had been hurt, and it gave everyone a chance to know—really know—the earthy, the fantastic, the fabulous Flossie Meyers, who had been its recluse of a tenant.

The third jolt, sweeping away Margaritas, Amapolas, half the garden, and poor Aurelia's body seconds after she had been placed in her grave, had been truly terrifying. There, but for the grace of God and the highhandedness of Elizabeth Parkhurst de Martínez . . . For the most part, they were speechless with gratitude for Liz's obstinate insistence that they vacate the bungalows and double up in less comfortable quarters. Tacitly, they avoided looking out at the ruined garden, the flowering frangipani tree that leaned tipsily over the Pacific, clinging by half its roots to the edge of the earth, or the chimney of Margaritas protruding at an angle from the water. There were some things better left unseen, better left unsaid. They had held themselves in rigid control, all very chin up, stiff upper lip.

But this last shock, coming in the blackness of the night at half past two on the morning of the sixth day, carrying off the gravel parking lot just behind the kitchen, the Su Casa station wagon, the Dewlaps' new Buick, and yanking out by the roots the water pump that had been attached to it . . . Well, it was just—what would one say? It was just too close to home.

At the very edge of his bed in Alcatraz, quivering with distaste as the obnoxious Lee was explaining how he could be fleeced of a mythical fortune, Roland felt the house lunge. Then he felt Lee's arms lock around him, felt Lee tremble and sob, felt Lee's wet lips saying something—could it be "Mommy"?—into his neck.

Roland didn't feel like Mata Hari and he didn't feel like Floria Tosca. Roland felt like throwing up. Thrusting himself loose from Lee, he ran to the window of Alcatraz. "Oh, my God!" Roland said. "The parking lot. The cars! They're gone!"

Now Lee was stretched full length on Roland's bed, the attaché case with its cargo of bogus stock certificates fallen to the floor. Like a child having a tantrum, Lee was pounding the pillows with his fists, kicking his stocking feet. "Mommy!" Lee sobbed. "Mommy, get me outa here! Fer Christ's sake, get me outa here!"

Roland stumbled to the bathroom and vomited.

"Laddy?" Arthur croaked, trying to prop himself up on his elbows. "Laddy, what was that?" With a palsied hand, Arthur located a box of matches and lit the candle. Laddy's bed was empty. Arthur heard excited voices outside his door. He tried to rise from his bed, but could not. He was overcome with a paroxysm of trembling. His teeth chattered. Arthur was terrified. "I really am sick," Arthur told himself. With great effort, he lit a cigarette in the candle's flame and was racked by a spasm of coughing.

"Arthur, dear," he whispered. Arthur always addressed himself in terms of the warmest affection. "Arthur, dear, you've got to get hold of yourself." He lay back on the pillows trying to pluck a word or two from the babble of voices outside. The crisis, whatever it may have been, had passed. Arthur's fear subsided. A leaden depression replaced it. This had all seemed such a lark—and such a *practical* lark—the fame, the prestige, the on-staginess, not to mention the money. And it *had* been. Right up until yesterday. And where was Arthur now? Sick and old and alone! Would no one trouble to come in and see how he was? Whether he was dead or alive? Carolyn?

Arthur sighed and coughed. Then he coughed louder, longer. It hurt. And why bother? They were talking so loudly in the *sala* that they wouldn't hear a thunderclap. He'd just lie here until the noise outside abated, until everyone calmed down, then, staggering just a little, make his haggard appearance in their midst—possibly even clutch at the back of a chair for support. *Then* they'd all be sorry.

It was a pathetic little group huddled in the *sala*. Laddy had lit a fire and the gathering in assorted nightclothes looked surrealistic in the dancing light of the flames. Susan Holt whimpered. "Shut up, Sue!" Lou Ann snapped. Lou Ann had put on her own mad scene upstairs. With that out of her system, she took a grim delight in being unpleasant to Susan. It made her feel better, braver. Estelle Dewlap, manikin-neat awake or asleep, glanced at Lou Ann and breathed a little prayer of thanks that her own daughter had nothing in common with Miss McIver. In gratitude, she moved closer to Walt. Flossie stood, grotesque in Salvador's clothes and her diamonds, the squawling baby on one hip, yapping Queenie on the other. Now, if she only had a third hand for her drink . . . Bill helped Carolyn down the staircase as though she were crippled. "Please, darling, I'm just fine." Tensely, he permitted her to manage the last two steps unaided and then stood with a protective arm around her. Carolyn liked that. April, her face clean of make-up, looked like a frightened baby. It made Bernice stop regretting that once more her life had been spared to look after this poor, dumb girl, to lead her like an automaton to a chair, seat her in it, tug the indecent itty-bitty nightie down over the ink-black hair of April's much frequented, but still childlike, pudendum. "Jeest," April kept saying.

Kimono flying, Roland soared into the *sala*, so anxious was he to escape his room. Escape it he had, leaving Lee blubbering on his bed. Roland had barely made it to the bathroom. Groping for mouthwash in the lightless bathroom to cleanse his mouth of the stench, he had inadvertently used cologne—about fourteen dollars' worth, he realized now, and worth every penny. With Lee still sobbing "Mommy" into his—into Roland's—pillows, Roland had fled.

Julie slipped into the room through the pantry door. She hoped that she had not been noticed. She had been. So had Pablo.

Laddy was pale and Laddy was perplexed. Laddy was at a loss. Since Laddy could first remember, Liz, the big sister, had been on hand to protect him through every crisis. Now he felt that *he* should do something. But what? The starch had suddenly gone out of Liz. She clung to Laddy, sharp nails digging into his arm. This was all wrong. Liz had always been the mother hen, clucking over the fuzzy chick. Now the positions were reversed and Laddy was helpless. Liz, the brain, the tower of strength, simply stood there, still and white, the tears pouring down her face.

Mrs. Bullock could be heard before she was seen. A crashing of glass, the thud of an overturned chair, the slamming of a door, the cloppety-clop of sensible heels on the tiles above, the splat of a canvas airlines bag as she missed her footing on the last step and clutched at the stone balustrade.

The sight was worth waiting for. Over her nightgown, Mrs. Bullock wore a bright blue plastic raincoat. Her bare, mottled feet were thrust into tie oxfords (untied) and, for some occult reason, she wore a straw hat with "Acapulco" stitched over the brow.

Frightened out of her wits, Mrs. Bullock had packed by braille in her dark room. Her selection of emergency gear was interesting for all to see—and all could see it as it tumbled out of the burst zipper opening of her flight bag. The Pop-it pearls came first, followed by the cameo earrings, then the Kaopectate, then the laxatives. Next came an extra upper plate and, hot on its molars, Mrs. Bullock's Klutch. The Lily of France one-piece corset was thrust out of the bag by two ashtrays and a dinner plate marked Su Casa. Last of all came Mrs. Bullock's passport, her tourist card, her airline ticket, a dozen sheets of Su Casa writing paper, and quite a lot of money.

"Excuse me," Carolyn said, "you dropped something." She went to her knees and began retrieving Mrs. Bullock's escape kit.

"Careful dear," Bill said.

Carolyn piled the writing paper and the ashtrays on top of the dinner plate and handed the stack to Pablo. Then, thrusting the last of Mrs. Bullock's belongings into the flight bag, she said, "Here are your *thangs.* Leaving us?"

Mortification cured Mrs. Bullock of the worst of her hysteria. Now the sight of Liz's white, tear-streaked face restored her to her usual even nature. Here, at last, was the enemy—on her knees.

"Yes! Ah'm gittin' outa this hell hole if ah hafta walk!"

"Like Our Lord," Carolyn breathed.

Now Mrs. Bullock advanced on Liz and began screaming into her lifeless face, pellets of spittle flying into Liz's eyes. "An' let me till you, you damn, uppity, New Yawk niggah lover—livin' with a Mixicun, actin' like yore so high an' mighty when yore no bitter than a common border hoor—Ah'm tillin' you that . . ."

There was the sound of a sharp crack. Mrs. Bullock reeled and stumbled backward. Her jaw dropped, followed instantly by her upper plate.

"Shut up and stop acting like a braying bitch for once in your life!"

"*Wal-ter!*" Essie gasped.

"Shut up, Essie. I mean it. I've had enough." He turned on Mrs. Bullock again. "We've been working our asses off while you haven't done a fucking thing but sit on yours and give Liz a hard time."

"*Wal-*ter *Dew-*lap!" Essie's lips moved, but no sound would come forth.

"You're nobody from nowhere. You wouldn't know the Mona Lisa from the menopause, but you've got the gall to drag these poor kids around Mexico and run out on 'em when things get rough. Hell, you're not fit to lead pigs through shit!"

"Walter," Essie whimpered.

"If you want to leave, sister, I'll be happy to kick you right over the edge. Otherwise, haul ass up those stairs and don't let me hear another word out of you or, by Christ, I'll break your goddamned neck!"

Transfixed, Mrs. Bullock started slowly up the stairs. At the landing she turned and gaped at Walter. He took a menacing step forward. Mrs. Bullock fairly flew the rest of the way up.

The room was silent.

Essie was a hopeless romantic. She realized that such words existed. Not for nothing had she read nearly half of *Portnoy's Complaint*, talked to other Wheaton College mothers, found that horrid paperback hidden under her son's socks. And naturally Walter would know those words. Walt was a man—all man. But for Walt to *use* them!

"W-Walter," Essie said, not much believing herself, "you've got to go up and apologize to Mrs. Bullock."

"In a pig's ass I will, hon. I meant every word."

"Don't," Julie said. She came forward and kissed Walt.

Liz began to speak like a medium in trance. "Darling Walter, thank you. I—I just don't know w-what to say. Your lovely new car . . ."

"It's insured, Liz. Hell, I'm insured, too. But the way things are going, it doesn't look like Essie's going to be around to enjoy the money."

"Walt! I wouldn't *want* to be!"

The door of Laddy's ground-floor bedroom opened. Arthur appeared, slightly bent, hair most carefully disarranged. No one noticed him.

"But what I mean, Liz," Walt said, "is that I'm getting scared. We all are."

"That's right, Liz," Bill said. "If it were only us, it wouldn't matter. But Carolyn's pregnant and . . ."

"You and your big mouth!" Carolyn sighed.

"*What did* you say?" Arthur hissed.

"Oh, Arthur," Liz said, turning. "It's only you."

Only you? Only Arthur Craine? Arthur was about to whisper a stinging rebuke, but Liz turned back to face the others. "I know. We've got to do something. We must. There has to be some way out of here."

"Hell," Bill said. "You can see the shore. It's not more than a hundred yards."

"Yes, you're right, Bill," Liz sighed. "Tomorrow we'll figure something. But now . . ."

"But now it's beddy-bye, honey," Flossie said, thrusting the baby at Bernice, Queenie at April, and taking Liz by the arm. "C'mawn, honey, an' let Flossie fix you'n I a li'l drink. An' maybe not such a li'l one at that."

"Comin' ta bed, Julie?' Lou Ann asked.

"Naturally."

"Well, it's up the front stairs—*not* the back ones."

Liz tried to pull herself back into her role of the light-hearted hostess. "Well, if we're all going to die tonight, we might as well do it comfortably in bed instead of standing around here. Good night everyone."

In Violetas, Walt sank onto the edge of the bed, a shattered man. Never in his life—not even in the army—had he said such things aloud. Essie regarded him in the candlelight. So this was her knight in shining armor.

"Walter."

"Okay, Essie, I deserve it. Let's have it."

"Very well, Walter. Here it is." She put her arms around him and said, "I love you, I love you, I love you, I love you!" Then she snuffed out the candle.

Lou Ann McIver had no very good excuse, ever, to behave as she did. If she needed to blackmail Julie Noyes, that would have at least given her a logical motive. But the McIvers were almost as rich as the Noyses. If Julie were more popular, a frustrated envy might account for Lou Ann's performance but, for reasons well known to the *jeunesse dorée* of Dallas, Lou Ann's evenings were booked far in advance. No. Lou Ann was simply a rotten human being who found it necessary—essential—to give vent to her rottenness as often as possible. Without doing so, she would have exploded in her cradle.

Lou Ann had had an inkling. Just that and no more. But tonight, when she had vaulted in terror from her own bed to Julie's and found it empty, she had been almost sure. And when Julie slid into the *sala* by way of the pantry door, well, you didn't have to be a genius to put one and one together and get two.

"So!" Lou Ann said, closing the door.

"So what?" Julie said. She knew what was coming. She didn't care.

"So, you been shackin' up with a Mixicun!"

"Have I?"

"You know good an' damn well you have. Lookatcha nightie! Ya got it on inside out! I oughta till Miz Bullock."

"Hasn't she been told enough for one night?"

"An' I always thought you were a *lady*."

"Really? I never thought you were."

Heedless, Lou Ann raced on. "Sneakin' off to spind the night with a Mixicun bellboy. Julie Noyes, what kin you be thinkin' of?"

"Something you've never thought of and never will. I'm thinking of getting married to someone I really love and taking care of him and having his children and making something out of my life."

"Married? Are you outa yer cotton-pickin' mind? Married to a greaser? I'd sooner sleep with a nigger."

"Do you mean to say that you haven't?"

"You can't insult me like that, Julie Noyes!"

"No, I can't. No one could. The right words haven't been invented."

Lou Ann raised a long, simian arm. "I . . . I . . ."

"No, you won't, Lou Ann. Lift one finger and I'll mop up the floor with you. And you know I can. Now go to bed."

"You . . . you thank I'd sleep in the same room with a . . ."

"No. You're sleeping here. I'm going back to Pablo. Good night, Lou Ann."

As Julie hurried out through the little sitting room Susan's head popped up from the sofa. "Julie. I didn't mean to listen, but I couldn't help hearin'. Are you truly gettin' married to . . ."

"Exactly, Susan. He's a boy from Houston with thirteen ranches and fourteen oil wells."

"Oh, that's jus' wonderful, Julie! But, Julie?"

"Yes, Susan?"

"Julie, couldn'tch've found a boy from *home*?"

A Star Is Born

"Well, it sounds like the end of the world, butcha can't see much," Mr. d'Enker said, watching for the third time the rerun of the collapse of the parking lot.

A vigilant cameraman had returned from his coffee break just in time to catch last night's disaster through a camera that was barely warmed up. Su Casa was floodlit from the shore, but not very effectively, and the drifting mists, while adding drama and atmosphere, took away a good deal from nighttime visibility. Try as they would to see the sensational deterioration of Su Casa, the picture remained a couple of candlelit windows and a grayish blur falling into the sea.

"It was one hell of a splash," Jaime Malvido said.

"Oh, yes!" the Girl Friday added enthusiastically. "Marvelous spume rising like a . . ." While she still found Mr. d'Enker—she now called him E.G.—grossly male and unspeakably coarse, she had come almost to like him. The job at the network was as good as hers. She was already planning the decoration of her office—blue tweed.

"So even if it looks like a cheesecake falling apart, we run it with Jimmy here doin' the narration. Make'm *think* they're seein' it. Shit, with the splash it makes, they'll swear they seen it. Jimmy'll do it in pajamas and a robe. No, make that a raincoat. We shoot him in the shade so it looks like night, holding, maybe, a flashlight. An' Jimmy says, 'Oh, oh, folks, it's after midnight an' it looks like there's gonna be trouble out there.' Are ya gettin' this, Debbie?"

Debbie was getting it. Debbie was getting it all night from Mr. d'Enker, and every afternoon from Mr. d'Enker's aide-de-camp, Lennie. Debbie was also getting sick and tired of the whole thing. She'd packed a suitcase full of pretty things for Acapulco and she hadn't worn any of them. It was only sweater and slacks here on the television lot, and Orthofoam in one or another bed. And they called it a glamor job.

"Then we follow it up today with interviews. You know, 'Where were you when the land fell in? What didja think? How did it feel?' But tell Craine to let some of the others talk for a change."

"Arthur still can't speak," Jimmy said. "I just checked."

"Good! We'll use the broad again."

"April May?"

"Sure. The kid's a natural. If I'd known it ten years back, I'd be a rich agent today. She's a scream."

"But such an obvious little tramp," Debbie said virtuously.

"And rather sad, too," the Girl Friday began. "There's a pathetic, Chaplinesque quality . . ."

"Yask me," E. G. said, "I think she's a kinda small Dagmar."

"Small?" Jimmy said.

"I don't mean the boobs. I mean . . ."

"Yes, Jimmy," the Girl Friday said. "I know exactly what E.G. means. Exactly. April has the pathos of Giulietta Messina combined with the touching naïveté of a Marilyn Monroe and the comedic *je ne sais quoi* of . . ."

The people in the control truck didn't know it, wouldn't realize it for another day or two, but at that moment a star was being born. "This Is It," with Miss April May narrating the "Su Casa Story" in the place of a voiceless Arthur Craine, had been broadcast the night before. April, her outlandish clothes, her astonishing poitrine, her inane comments lisped with her little baby voice were already being talked about across the United States. "But did you see that dumb blonde on 'This Is It'?" Yes, they had all seen April—and April had come into her own.

Deciding to strive for a more intellectual performance, April had, today, borrowed one of Bernice's good little suits, some of Carolyn's conservative jewelry, and knocked the lenses out of a pair of her own enormous sunglasses. "Ta be more like Arthur," April explained. Arthur moaned in his bed. In her eagerness to explain natural phenomena to her audience, April had consulted with Walt and had even taken notes. The result was epic. The word "seismographic" had issued from April's lips as "stenographic," "psychiatric," and, finally as "circumcise" before Mr. d'Enker chortled "Cut!" and lay his head down on the console to heave with laughter. "Oh, Christ, she's too much! They'll shit! Fifty million bucks in the kip with me at the Astor an' I was such a horse's ass I couldn't see anything but gash!"

E. G. could see a lot more now. He could see a weekly variety show with April—buoyed up by a lot of *real* talent—as its bumbling hostess. During a break, he dictated a nicely binding letter of agreement, pending a three-year contract with the network, and shot it over to Su Casa with the harpoon gun. As the guy line from the shore to the house had to be replaced, it made for some interesting footage. And, just to show the other networks that E. G. d'Enker could sight a star without a telescope, he had Jaime Malvido announce that it was April's papers of indenture to E. G. d'Enker.

"What is ut?" April asked.

"Why, darling, it seems to be some sort of contract," Liz said.

"Contract?" Arthur croaked from his bedroom. "It must be for me."

"No, Arthur, it quite clearly says April May. It's for three years at five thousand dollars."

"On'y fi' thousan' dollars for three whole years? Gee, Liz, I wu'n't be able to live on . . ."

"No, April. Five thousand dollars a *week*."

"Oh! Ya think I should sign?"

"Yes, if you know how."

Dearest Roland

A study in despondency, Arthur yanked shut the curtains of his room so as not to witness the triumph of this cretinous little ignoramus, and bounced angrily into his bed. How the tide had turned! First, his humiliation on the dock; then the loss of his voice; frightened out of his wits last night; forgotten and ignored by the others at Su Casa; nonplused by Bill's general announcement that Carolyn was pregnant when she, his own sister, hadn't even hinted it to Arthur; and now this—replaced by an illiterate little hustler.

293

There was a soft tapping at Arthur's door. "My God, won't they leave me *alone?*" Arthur fumed.

"Arthur? It's Roland."

Arthur was about to rasp "Go away," when Roland said, "I have something for you." Roland opened the door, wriggled into the room, and closed the door softly behind him. The *nerve!*

Roland came directly to Arthur's bed and sat on it. Well, *really!* "How are you feeling, Arthur?"

"Terrible. In fact I think that you'd better go."

Roland looked hurt. "Oh, well, if you don't want to hear about Lee Goodwin . . ."

Arthur recalled his blatant flirtation of the day before. Had this dismal fag really found out anything? With a bombshell to drop, Arthur would be back on the air with a bang!

"I meant that I didn't want you to catch whatever it is I've got, dear boy."

"Oh, don't worry about me. I'm a Christian Scientist."

"But did you actually get him talking?"

"Didn't I just! He even tried to get in bed with me." No harm in making Arthur a little jealous.

"How nice for you!" Arthur hissed.

But not *too* jealous! "Oh, Arthur! He gives me the shivers."

"What did you find out?"

"Puh-lenty! I even took notes."

"Was that wise?"

"Well, after I told him that my sister and I had two million dollars to invest, he even jotted down a few facts and figures himself. Look. I've got it right here—and the combination to his briefcase! Now, this is the way Lee operates . . ."

Reluctant to return to the room and the hysterical Lee Goodwin, Roland had tactfully borrowed a sheet of Carolyn's letter paper. He had admired it earlier: Wedgwood blue with a white border, engraved in white with the Williams crest, watermarked "Cartier," and no telltale monogram to explain away. It was just the sort of paper his fancied and fun-loving Harriet would use. Chic.

"Darling, darling Roland," he had written in the candlelight of the *sala*. "Aunt Gertie's will has finally gone through probate and the checks are in the bank. Isn't that divine! Now the question is, what do we do with it? Darling, you know what an ass I am about money, so please help me before I go out and spend it all. . . .'" Roland had added trivia about the weather, about Harriet's nutria coat (mink was too obvious), about a shopping spree in New York, and wound up with another plea for financial advice. Roland considered it a masterpiece and tried to hide his smile this morning as Lee rapidly ran a thumb over the engraved crest and casually held the sheet up to the light to see the watermark. Lee had even licked his lips while reading the letter.

As terrified as he had been, the prospect of two million dollars had worked like magic in curing Lee's fright. He had even shaken Roland awake this morning in order to renew his sales pitch, "Mind if I write some of this down?" Roland had asked. "I have a terrible head for money matters."

"Here, I'll do it for yuh," Lee had said.

"And here it all is, Arthur. *In his own handwriting!*"

"Roland, my dear," Arthur whispered. "You are a genius!" There should be some reward beyond mere flattery for Roland's work, and so Arthur gave him a quick little hug and, lips moving against Roland's ear, repeated, "A genius!" There. That was enough. Roland's services could be dispensed with as of now.

With his heart pounding, Roland rose to his feet. "Uh, Arthur?"

"Mmmmmmm?"

"Arthur, where are you going when we get out of here?"

Really, the cheek! What business was it of Roland's where . . . Then Arthur thought again. Roland had been damned useful. He might still be useful. "Where would you like to go . . . Roland?"

"I don't care," Roland panted. "Wherever you want, Arthur."

"Well, we'll think about it," Arthur whispered. "There's always Greece." Imagine trying to explain Roland to his friends in Athens! "Now, Roland, you must go. Laddy could come charging in at any moment."

"I'll bring your lunch to you," Roland gasped.

"No need, dear boy. I think I'll get up for lunch." Arthur would

get up from his coffin to avoid another second of what was beginning to look like a very sticky situation.

"Oh, Arthur, I . . ."

"Dear Roland! Now go."

The Sun

To E. G. d'Enker's practiced eye, the signs were unmistakable.
"This Is It" was a hit—but it was beginning to peter out. They
were running low on material.

The three sets of Texas parents, now hysterically congregated on
the television lot, had made for a bit of variety as they bleated messages of love and anguish to Julie, Susan, and Lou Ann. And seeing
the three girls happy, healthy, and well fed on the television monitor had made them even more hysterical. But the blustering of the
fathers and the bathos of the mothers had been more ludicrous than
touching, and the editor had been hard put to cut their unconscious
comedy out of the tapes. "One more word outa Sam Houston Noyes
an' I'm gonna bulieve all the stories I been hearin' about rich
Texans," E. G. said.

Walt and Essie had politely but firmly refused permission to have
their children removed from school and flown to Mexico to wait
anxiously on the opposite shore. It was a blow to E. G. d'Enker. A
wholesome daughter from a good girls' college and a clean-cut
Culver cadet, preferably in uniform, would have added a lot.

Mr. d'Enker received another blow in the arrival of Ralph
Przybylski in his blazing blue suit. Ralph was more than willing to
talk to Bernice. He was downright insistent. Technical difficulties
mysteriously developed.

One look at Ralph's suit, his blunt mechanic's hands, one falter-
ing sentence spoken in Ralph's West Side Chicago accent, and Mr.
d'Enker was in a rage. "A Polish *countess* engaged to a rube like
that?"

"It's incredible," the Girl Friday said. "A lovely delicate thing

296

like Bernice and that big brute. How could she even touch him?"

"Well, Mac," E. G. said, "you're gonna do a lot more'n touch him. You're gonna getum off this lot an' keepum off. You're gonna keep yer eye on um twenty-four hours a day. See that he don't talk to reporters. We got this broad set up as a Countess Potocki an' she's gonna stay a countess until we getum rescued or the whole motherin' island sinks right through to hell, which I sincerely wish it would do. We can't stretch this show out much longer. I wanta wrap it up fast."

"Cheer up," Jaime Malvido said. "The weather's about to clear. Tomorrow. Next day at the latest. I got it straight from the weather bureau. Then we send a boat over, rescue everybody, and the show's over."

"Cheer up," Laddy said, beaming at Liz. "The weather's about to clear. Tomorrow. Next day at the latest. I got it straight from the weather bureau." The credulous Laddy had suddenly stopped believing anything the television people told him and had taken to making hourly calls to the weather bureau over the ship-to-shore phone aboard the Sea Urchin.

"Oh, Laddy, how wonderful!" Liz cried. "Did you hear that everyone? This weather's going to break. That means that tomorrow or the day after we'll all be on dry land."

"I'll believe that when I see it," Mrs. Bullock said. It was the first complete sentence she had uttered since she had been put to flight by Walt.

"Look!" Essie called. "The sun!" Mrs. Bullock slumped in her chair.

The reappearance of the sun for the first time in a week was like a magic wand waved over Su Casa. The winds were still strong, the waves still wild, but there was the sun, blazing hot and bright. Vivacity overcame the luncheon table, wine was poured and repoured, the logs in the fireplace allowed to smolder and die. Jackets and sweaters were peeled off.

Carolyn and Bill retired to their bedroom to make love in the warmth that poured through their windows. Carolyn was sure about the baby now. If she had ever been anything like regular, the day before yesterday should have been the beginning of the fourth period she had missed. And even if, by some wild fluke, she wasn't pregnant, she soon would be at the rate she and Bill were going.

April, the lensless spectacles slipping down her little bobbed nose, lay on her bed trying to read a collection of plays she had come across in the sala: *Heroines of George Bernard Shaw*. With her letter of agreement signed, April was preparing herself for stardom— Ellen Terry, Mrs. Patrick Campbell, Katharine Cornell, Wendy Hiller, *April May!* She could quite see herself as St. Joan, Candida, and Major Barbara. As for Eliza Doolittle, she had serious reservations. That word "cockney" distressed her—there wasn't going to be any more dirty stuff from now on.

At the desk, Bernice covered sheets of Su Casa's stylish letter paper with her neat, businesslike writing. They were letters of application for work in California—Los Angeles, San Francisco, she didn't care which just as long as it was away from Chicago and Madam Kaye. If she had to be shopgirl, she was going to be a damned good one. And if love and marriage happened her way, it would have to come looking for her. Bernice had been ashamed of herself, but after a conversation with Liz, she felt better and limp with relief. So, the aristocratic Ignacio, who was to place her into a life of ease and sire his noble sons on her, was the poorest relation of a poor family, a fortune hunter. It would have been almost funny if they *had* married. Bernice would go back to Chicago just long enough to return the sable coat to Madam Kaye, break off decently with Ralph, and then go on to some place that was new, warm, different.

Drying the luncheon dishes, Julie and Pablo came to a definite decision. They would be married immediately. Pablo would enroll in the government hotel employees' school. Julie would find a job teaching English. The idea in no way horrified Pablo. Everyone in his family had always worked. What he did not know, and what would have horrified him, was that the traveler's checks in Julie's purse amounted to more than three years of his present salary, that

298

the balance in her personal checking account was about ten times that much, and that her expectations as the only child of an immensely rich man would be unfathomable. Julie promised herself that he would never find out. Of all the things Julie could afford, the most priceless was Pablo's pride. Julie was young and Julie was patient. Let him start out as a desk clerk, then an assistant manager. Later on . . .Why worry about it now? They had all the time in the world.

Flashing with diamonds and bulging out of an old cotton robe of Salvador's, Flossie carried the naked baby and her drink out to the lawn. "C'mawn, kiddo. Time fer yer first sun bath." It was as good as done. There were plenty of houses for rent in Acapulco—big ones. Liz would help her to move the baby's brothers and sisters and the cousin of Pablo's who had looked after them while Aurelia worked. As long as the children were being sheltered, fed, and educated, the Mexican government wouldn't interfere. Later on, legal adoption would be simply a matter of paperwork. After all these footloose years, a home and a baby. "A baby, hell! A whole ready-to-wear fam'ly! Okey-dokey, honey, over yuh go! Let's take a look at the belly button. Flat as a dime!"

The worst of it was over. After tomorrow there would be no more splitting firewood, no more lugging buckets of hot water to people's rooms, no more calls to the weather bureau. Laddy stretched out in the shade of an avocado tree and gazed up at its ripening fruit. He could almost see this tree multiplied by ten thousand, by a hundred thousand, on that avocado ranch where the money literally grew on trees. Laddy wondered what Liz's insurance would amount to; or if Salvador had taken a policy on his own worthless life. Anyhow, Liz ought to realize *something* out of this insane investment. Enough for a down payment on the avocado ranch? Well, whatever happened, Laddy wouldn't leave Liz. A gentleman always took care of his sister.

Lee hummed a tuneless little tune as the door closed on Roland's brown back. Lee had wanted Roland to stay right here in the room and talk turkey about certified checks for how much and when. But Roland wanted to get into the sun. It had all been too easy. Lee hadn't even had to play house with Roland. Two million beautiful dollars for nothing! "Brazil," Lee sang, "where hearts are serenading June . . ."

Earlier in the day, Arthur had whispered and rasped his information concerning Lee Goodwin to the television control truck. A con man, just as they told Arthur. There was no Texokla, no Royal Canadian—not even a Lee Goodwin. But he was remembered by a lot of his victims. "Send me everything you have on him," Arthur had croaked. "And I think that possibly I can catch him right in the act."

A fat packet, sealed, and marked "Personal and Confidential," had come over on the guy rope. It contained Lee's press clippings from the major newspapers, and there was enough there to hang him. Figuratively, of course.

With the banner headline, "A KILLER IN THEIR MIDST?" Arthur heard himself saying "Zut alors!" His voice had been shocked back into full cry. Not the golden baritone, but a usable voice withal.

But how perfect! The weather was clearing. Tomorrow Su Casa would almost surely be evacuated. What better way to wind up the show than to have the Real Star return to trap a thief? And as for April May . . .

Arthur whispered—this time on purpose—once again over the headset to Jaime Malvido. Yes, yes, yes. They had all the equipment if only Walter Dewlap knew how to use it. It was delicate stuff. Sensitive. But it was worth a chance.

Arthur began dressing—or, rather, undressing—with great care. There was one more service that Roland could perform. Once again in his elastic romper and his fishnet shirt, Arthur spread two towels —not too close—on the patio tiles. Then he called Roland.

Gleaming in his lotions and salves and unguents, Roland unfurled his towel and lay down. His tan had faded during the cold, dark days following the earthquake and he simply had to work on it.

Roland wanted to think and think carefully about his future with Arthur and exactly how he would be able to pay his own share. Now he would have to be very realistic and face the fact that his capital was much, much less. Enough to live comfortably, especially if he closed the boutique. But could he afford to keep the lavish pace Arthur set?

"Roland!" Arthur called. "Dear boy, you'll freeze to death out there in the wind. If you want to sun yourself, at least do it here where there's some shelter. I want to talk to you anyhow."

"Arthur!" Roland said beaming at Arthur. "Your voice! It's back."

"A miracle."

Poor Man

Essie was nervous. "I don't care, Walter, I just don't like it."

Walt was more nervous and inclined to be irritable. "Do you like Lee Goodwin?"

"You know I can't stand him. But that has nothing to do with it. I mean we're not the CIA or G-Men or 'Gangbusters' or anything like that. We're plain ordinary people and catching crooks just isn't our sort of thing. You could be *killed*, Walt. Suppose he's got a gun."

"But he hasn't, my dear," Arthur said. "Roland shares a room with him and Roland *knows* that he hasn't a gun. *Don't* you, Roland?" Arthur gave Roland a telling look. Arthur was nervous, too.

"Y-yes," Roland said. Roland knew no such thing and he was the most nervous of all. The sun-kissed idyll in Arthur's patio had come to nothing. Roland had planned to speak frankly about their future, tell Arthur exactly what income he had, what he could afford. But Roland never had a chance to say a word. Arthur had done all the talking. Arthur had talked about trapping Lee Goodwin. Arthur had talked *sotto voce* to those television people, whoever they were, on the shore. Arthur had summoned Walter Dewlap and talked in the most mystifying language about "bugs" and "muffles" and "baffles" and other technical matters. And then Arthur had talked to Roland, telling him exactly what he must say and do.

Now they were standing around in Violetas, with the curtains drawn, with Walt's hand camera swathed in a blanket so that its faint whirring could not be heard, with Arthur's noble head hooded like an Eskimo's in Essie's mink cape so that his voice would be inaudible except to his hand mike. A tiny microphone no bigger than Roland's thumbnail—the "bug" they had been talking about and said to be so sensitive that it could pick up the sound of a real bug—dangled down from the balcony and was concealed in the vines that grew up the wall. A tape recorder sat on Essie's dressing table.

"I *still* don't like it," Essie said. Neither did Roland. If there were to be any real danger, he would be the one meeting it face to face.

Arthur spoke through his headset to the television people once more. "All right, Malvido, we're ready . . . The bug works and we've got at least an hour of daylight . . . No, I can't promise anything," Arthur said waspishly. "We can hardly hogtie him and command him to swindle Roland for the benefit of the television audience. We can only try."

"W-well, I guess if everything's ready . . ." Roland began.

"Now, remember everything I told you—the sunshine, the certified check, drinks? It's watertight."

"I hope so, Arthur," Roland said.

As usual, Lee was stretched out on his bed when Roland let himself into Alcatraz. "Enjoy your sun bath, Roly?" Lee tried to sound pleasant.

"Oh, yes!" Roland said eagerly. "It's glorious. Why don't you come out, Lee? It's so lovely and warm."

"Nah. Not with that old Craine fart"—Roland bridled—"pussyfooting around with his TV camera. He bugs me." Roland gaped, but then he understood what Lee meant.

"But that's all over," Roland said quickly. "They're sending the equipment back. We're definitely being taken ashore tomorrow."

"Yeah?"

"Yes! Things have been flying back and forth on the rope all afternoon." Roland paused dramatically. "Including the check from my sister Harriet."

Lee sat up and darted a reptilian glance in Roland's direction. "Whaddayuh mean, a check from your sister?"

"Well, I mean she sent it."

"How?"

"Why, by registered mail." Oh God, please don't let me panic! "It's made out to you. Lee Goodwin."

"How'd she know my name? How'd she even know about the deal?"

"Why, I dictated a cable to her over that, that *thing* the television people use for talking, and, well, they sent Harriet the cable, and Harriet sent the certified check."

"Certified? Let's see it."

"Lee, I don't have it here. I left it downstairs. Outside."

"You left a check for *two million bucks* layin' around downstairs?"

"It's certified. Only you can cash it."

Lee tried to hide his look of wonderment. The story was so screwy that it had to be true. "That's pretty fast postal service. Two days from the States."

"It comes from Mexico City. Our bank has a branch there."

"What bank is that?"

Could Roland remember the name on that scrap of pink paper which an Acapulco printer had struck off under Jaime Malvido's guidance less than an hour ago? "Why, it's the Pennsylvania Fidelity and Trust Company." He hoped that was right. It lay in a plain white envelope on a table just beneath the balcony of Violetas.

"Get it," Lee said. Then he added, "please." For two million dollars, Lee could say a lot more than "please." He stood up and smiled at Roland. "You run down an' get the check, Roly, an' I'll start makin' out the certificates and the receipt."

"Oh, not up here in this cold, gloomy room. I'm so sick of it I could scream. . . ."

"Sorry, but I'm kinda camera-shy."

"But I told you—they've all been sent back."

"Anyways, I don't want a lot of people hanging around. This is a very confidential deal and . . ."

"No one *is* around. They're all taking naps or packing to leave tomorrow."

"That Lou Ann dog was sniffin' around outside the door not so long ago."

"Oh, her!"

"Pain in the ass, ain't she?" Lee flashed his buddy-buddy smile toward Roland. Roland recoiled, checked himself, and smiled wanly back.

"So we can sit out in the sun and have a drink. I made two. Scotch." He attempted a self-deprecating little laugh. "It's the only time in my life I'll ever have this much money, and I think the least we can do is have a drink to celebrate." Roland felt that he'd read that line pretty well.

"Okay," Lee said slowly. He didn't like to complete his deals in anything but total privacy. Nor did he especially like Scotch. Well, for two million dollars he'd drink cyanide. And what could he lose? A certified check was as good as gold anywhere. Tomorrow they'd be out of this dump, and the day after tomorrow, thank God and Varig Airlines, Lee Goodwin would be safely in Brazil. Two million dollars were a lot of cruzeiros! "Wait till I get my attaché case."

"Here comes the dizzy faggot now," Arthur muttered, turning from the closed window curtains at the windows of Violetas.

"But a very courageous 'dizzy faggot,' isn't he?" Essie said. "Braver than anyone in this room, which you happen to be using against my wishes."

"Shhhhh."

And it occurred to Essie that the room wasn't all that Arthur was using. He was using poor Roland as a decoy, her own husband as an unpaid servant, and even Essie herself. Essie did not like to be used.

"Here they come, Malvido," Arthur grunted into the mouthpiece of his headset. "Turn on the tape recorder," he said to Essie.

"What's the magic word, Arthur?"

Arthur ignored her. Essie turned on the tape recorder. Then she said, "You're welcome."

"Shhhhhh! All right, Walt. Start shooting."

Walt put his blanket-swaddled camera into the hole Arthur had cut in the curtains and began noiselessly photographing the terrace below. Arthur covered his head with Essie's cape and began his narration of what was happening. Essie sat on the edge of the bed, nervous, angry, and unhappy.

*

"S-sit down," Roland said.

"Why here?"

"Because here's where the drinks are. *See?*"

"Yeah."

Roland quickly sank into the chair Arthur had told him to use, leaving Lee the one opposite, facing the camera and brightly lighted by the late afternoon sun.

"And here's the envelope," Roland said, snatching it up as he had been instructed to do.

"You said it came by registered mail. That's just a plain envelope."

Roland's heart sank. He thought fast. "This was inside the other one. Now, where did I leave it? In the *sala*, I think."

In the television control truck, Jaime Malvido said, "It's coming over like a bell, isn't it?"

"Yeah, I wish we could see it," E. G. said. "The fagola's a pretty cool article, ain't he? He'll be lucky if he don't get his balls beat—or worse. An' fer Christ's sakes tell Craine to shut up. We don't need him to butt in when the con man's makin' it clear enough."

"He must be filling out the stock certificates now," the Girl Friday said. "You can even hear the sound of the pen."

Roland took a gulp of his drink. He was terrified. It was frightening enough to deal with Lee in the privacy of their room. But now, in front of the camera . . .

"Okay, Roly. Here's number one. One million smackerinos for Roland Preston of Allentown, Pee-Yay. Now for baby sister."

The thought of "baby sister" in the Pennsylvania Dutch farmhouse she had remodeled with her own hands, glowering at the television set a few hours hence, enormous thighs bulging through homespun slacks, half a dozen bull mastiffs snoring at her feet, made Roland wince. Harriet had absolutely no sense of humor.

"Whatsamatter, Roly? Yer tremblin'."

"Wouldn't you tremble to be spending all this money?"

"Nickels an' dimes, Roly. Wait till ya see yer return on it. Now, how do we fill in your sister's?"

"It's Harriet Eleanora Preston, Miss, also of Allentown."

"Okay, Roly. Here's for sister Hattie. And now, the check."

Roland slit open the envelope and handed Lee the slip of pink paper. Lee's hands shook as he held it. *Two million dollars!* Lee almost fainted. Roland almost fainted, too.

"And now for that little drink, Roly," Lee said, lifting his glass. "Here's to small vices and big dividends! And may you and your . . ."

On the balcony above them the curtains flew open. Arthur stepped into view, followed by Walt and the camera.

"Thank you, Mr. Goodwin, Goode, Goodhue, et cetera! You have just been photographed and recorded in the act of swindling another innocent victim out of a fortune!" Arthur was in his element. He felt like John Barrymore, Douglas Fairbanks, Errol Flynn. He almost wanted to leap over the railing. "Yes, ladies and gentlemen, you have just seen one of our slickest confidence artists operating. Mr. Goodwin, it was a beautiful performance. Almost as good as the one you'll be giving tomorrow morning when Su Casa will be evacuated. The first boat to land, Mr. Goodwin, will be a Mexican police launch. And their guest of honor will be you, Mr. Con Man— I mean Mr. Goodwin. Yes, everyone, now I can tell you what I've known all along. We have had a criminal in our midst! A dangerous public enemy." Arthur's damaged voice had risen to a roar. Mystified guests of Su Casa were appearing on the terrace, on the balconies. "Look at him, my friends, Mr. Lee Goodwin, our fellow guest, and one of the most famous . . ."

Lee leapt to his feet, knocking over his chair, his glass crashing onto the tiles. He was gray with shock and terror. "No!" he shouted. And then he started to run.

"Follow him with the camera, Walter!" Arthur shouted.

Essie flew to Walt's side, clutching at his arm. "Walt! Stop! I can't stand any more of this!"

"What the fuck's goin' on out there?" E. G. shouted.

He had not long to wait. Arthur easily slipped into his new pose—sportscaster. "Yes, he's running! He's weaving and darting— now he's stopped—he's breathing heavily, nostrils flared—now he's running again! But running where? He's trapped, ladies and gentlemen. There's no place to run."

Lee ran blindly out into the garden, fell over Laddy, asleep under the avocado tree, and landed flat on the lawn.

"Hey! Ouch!" Laddy called, sitting up.

Lee scrambled up and kept on running. But where? There was the dock and there was Laddy's sailboat, bobbing and rocking on the stormy water. Lee had never sailed a boat before, but the *Sea Urchin* was a means—the only means—of escape. Stumbling and staggering along the dock, Lee leapt into the boat and fell again.

Someone was shouting to him, but he couldn't understand the words. It was Laddy. "Hey! No! It isn't seaworthy!" By the time Laddy got to his feet and ran to the dock, Lee had cast off. Tossing and pitching, the *Sea Urchin* was adrift.

Lee was free. But what do you do to a boat? There were sails—furled and lashed down. There was an auxiliary motor somewhere down in the cabin. A wave washed over the deck and knocked Lee down.

Lee was terrified. "Mommy, Mommy!" he gibbered. Another wave pitched the *Sea Urchin* on to its side. By the time she trembled aright, the boat had taken on a huge amount of water. Lee clung to the mast and sank to his knees in the rising wash as the *Sea Urchin* spun crazily.

"Oh, my God, Laddy," Liz cried, "isn't there any way we can save him? Get to him?"

"The wind's on shore. If he's blown to the beach before she sinks . . ."

Knee-deep in water, Lee clung to the swaying mast. Just as the *Sea Urchin* lost buoyancy, the hull lurched on to the rocky beach, slipped off, then caught fast as the hull split.

"Mom-meeeee!" Lee screamed.

At that moment the wind died. The sea became almost calm. It took only a few minutes for the two police officers to wade out to the hulk, but it was a good quarter hour before they managed to peel Lee's arms from the grotesquely angled mast and to lead the vacantly staring, uncontrollably twitching body onto the beach. The thread that held Lee together had snapped.

*

"Poor man," Essie moaned and buried herself in Walt's gentle arms.

"Poor man," Walter Dewlap repeated, but he was thinking of Rex Roman.

Marriage Is for Two

"Was my wrap-up strong enough, Malvido?" Arthur said into the mouthpiece of his headset. "Glad you liked it. That shipwreck—touch of Greek tragedy. Appropriate ending. And we have it all on film. Send over for it. *Ciao!*" He turned and smiled benignly on Walt and Essie.

"*Zut alors,* Essie, why on earth are you crying?"

Essie blew her nose. "Even if I could explain it, Arthur, I don't think you'd understand." Arthur hadn't been listening.

"Now, Walter, about the film . . ."

"Here," Walt said, handing him the camera. "Give them the whole damned thing. I've done my last shooting. And now, Arthur, would you mind getting the hell out of our room?" Walter went to Essie and put his arms around her.

"As you wish," Arthur said, gliding majestically out of the room. The Dewlaps were nice enough; pleasant in the way that shipboard acquaintances are pleasant. But they were really rather small town. Anyhow, Jaime Malvido would send over equipment and professional cameramen on the first boat to get really *good* pictures of the rescue.

Crossing the corridor, Arthur paused at the closed door of Claveles and stared distastefully at the nosegay of bright carnations Liz had painted on it. Poor Liz. Just another gifted amateur.

But Arthur was more concerned with what was going on behind the painted carnations. There was something odd about Carolyn and Bill. The humiliation of learning about his own Carolyn's own baby in a roomful of comparative strangers. Arthur should have been the first one to have been told. He wasn't exactly angry; he was offended, hurt, by his sister's negligence. But something told

Arthur to pretend otherwise, play it light. Arthur beat a gay little tattoo against the painted carnations, opened the door, and went in.

The room was dim, the setting sun casting a faint lavender glow. Carolyn and Bill were curled up on the chaise longue. Each held a large drink. They looked, well, rather grim.

"Zut alors," Arthur said jovially, "that was an exciting little chapter to wind up our soap opera."

"Exciting?" Carolyn said. "Oh, Arthur!"

"Well, I certainly need a drink after that work-out. So I suggest that we all go downstairs and . . ."

"Everybody needs a drink," Bill said. "That's why we're having one. Here. Alone."

The genial young dolt's tone was clearly unfriendly. What on earth for? Why? Arthur switched the conversation to brighter matters. "Well, I can't tell you how pleased I am about the baby. But, dear girl, why didn't you tell your old bachelor brother? I would never have dragged you down here in your . . ."

"Because I didn't know it myself. Not until a few days ago. I'm still not absolutely certain." Carolyn sounded so cold!

"Well, I do hope it's true." Arthur hoped no such thing. He had encountered only a very few small children. He considered them all to be noisy little nuisances. Besides, a baby would encumber them all. "It's going to be such fun to lead a new little niece or nephew by the hand. . . ."

"Don't you mean by the nose, Arthur?" Carolyn said.

"What's that, dear girl?" Could he have heard correctly?

"Arthur, this is our baby—Bill's and mine. It isn't going to be led anywhere, except to school, and summer camp, and places where perfectly normal, average kids go."

"And I suppose that if it's a boy you'll christen him George Babbitt Williams?" Nobody laughed.

"We were going to call him Arthur Craine Williams," Bill said. "But now we're not so sure."

"I'm sure," Carolyn said.

Arthur was stunned. This from his own sister, his own creation! "Would you young people mind telling me just what heinous crime I've committed, I, your brother, who . . ."

"You really don't know, do you? This whole, vulgar, shoddy

309

television thing, rigged exclusively *by* Arthur Craine *for* Arthur Craine . . . That poor Mexican woman, dying in agony. Did you care about her, about the baby? No. You cared about lights, and camera angles, and the glorification of Arthur Craine."

"Carolyn, you're talking like a silly, spoiled little girl."

"Why wouldn't I, Arthur? You've done everything in your power to make me that way. And you've tried the same with Bill. You've used us as your ornaments, your props—like your clothes, or your French furniture. It's always been *Arthur Craine*, starring Arthur Craine, with Bill and Carolyn Williams, the cute young couple, as supporting players. I thought that I didn't mind it, that Bill didn't. But we did—we did!—desperately. Oh, but Arthur, your performance this afternoon . . ."

"You mean that cheap little rat, Lee Goodwin?"

"Yes, I mean that cheap little rat, Lee Goodwin."

"Well, you've certainly undergone a radical change, Carolyn. You couldn't stand him. I remember how horrified you were when he goaded Rex Roman right into the Pacific Ocean."

"That's right, Arthur. And I was even more horrified when you, my own brother, did the same thing to him today."

"Carolyn, my dear, this pregnancy thing has unsettled you. Everyone detested Lee Goodwin, a petty crook, a boor, and a bore, a tenth-rate person . . ."

"Yes, Arthur, but still a person. Everything you say about him is true. I hated him. But he *was* another human being and you destroyed him just as effectively as though you'd shot him with a gun."

"Oh, come now! I *destroyed* Lee Goodwin?"

"Yes, Arthur. The police would have taken care of him tomorrow. You said so yourself. But for the glorification of Arthur Craine, you bullied him right into that boat and God knows what now. It was horrible, but you can't even see that. Arthur, you are a bully, a manipulator. You've bullied me since the first day you took over my life."

"So this is the scrawny, inarticulate little girl I took into my home, educated, taught poise and self-confidence, introduced to the most stimulating . . ."

"Arthur, those were the things you wanted, not what I wanted. I would have liked to have gone away to school, college, found a job, been able to stand on my own. But that wasn't what you wanted for me."

"What does a teen-age girl know about life, Carolyn?"

"Nothing. But finding out firsthand is part of growing up. You never gave me that chance. Now I'm a wife and, I hope, a mother. Marriage is for two, Arthur—for Bill and me. And we're going to try to work it out alone. We've never really been alone before."

"I see. So I am to be dismissed. Do you plan to cut me if we meet on the street?"

"Arthur, you're being ridiculous," Bill said.

"For a while, Bill and I simply want to be alone together," Carolyn said.

"Like some little clerk and his wife?"

"Exactly like some little clerk and his wife."

Arthur was desperate, although it would never do to reveal his feelings. All of his favorite old tricks—logic, wit, sarcasm—were useless now. Nothing was left but pathos. "And so now I am to be deserted by the only family I have. Left to grow old and crabbed all alone—a life without love."

"Never Arthur. You will always have Arthur Craine to love— the only person you've ever really cared about. And now if you don't mind leaving us, I'd like to have a good, old-fashioned cry."

Bill opened the door.

Dr. Craine did not join the others at dinner that evening.

Bought and Sold

As promised, the next morning was fair and warm. The "guaranteed" weather of Acapulco returned as though it had never suffered a moment's interruption. The sky was blue and cloudless, the sun hot, the breezes gentle.

Su Casa itself took on the air of the last day aboard a cruise ship.

The luggage was all set out in neat little clumps on the terrace. The costumes were decidedly hatty and suity, the clothes of people prepared to return to civilization. The ladies chirped and chattered about shampoos and sets, manicures, and rich, creamy facials. Everyone wanted an hour's soak in a deep, hot tub. Addresses were exchanged—"Now remember, if you're ever anywhere near Anthrax —that's not far from Pittsburgh—"

Liz moved among her guests with the cool, efficient cheer of a Sunday-school supervisor at the annual outing. These people had been so dear—most of them. Now Liz wanted only to get them safely back onto dry land before any other catastrophe occurred. There would be plenty of work for Liz once they were gone—legal matters, death certificates, insurance claims, the rooms and rooms of furniture. And then the widow Martínez would once again be at loose ends. Where next? But first things first, and first came breakfast.

Before the meal was even started, the island swarmed with strangers. It seemed to Liz that anyone who owned anything waterborne between water skis and the *Queen Elizabeth* had sailed across to Su Casa. First came a police launch, then the Coast Guard, and then a great flat barge chugged over the water. It was covered with people, with television cameras and odd equipment. At the helm, like Washington crossing the Delaware, stood an odious cigar-puffing man, accompanied by a sluttish girl. The man leapt nimbly ashore and hurried to April May. To Arthur's fury and Liz's amusement, he undid the top three buttons of April's blouse and April was on camera before the camera was even on land. Liz was less amused to see a brash young man bawling orders in English and Spanish through a bullhorn. She recognized the voice and hated him anew. It could only be Jaime Malvido, the perpetrator of this tawdry carnival.

A rangy girl, who looked vaguely like William Buckley wearing a Cleopatra wig, cantered across the garden on thong sandals and embraced Liz. Was she insane? Presumably not. Her name was Priscilla and she was somehow connected with the television crew. "What an experience it's been," the girl gasped as Liz deftly ducked out under her half-Nelson.

"Yes, quite an experience," Liz said. "And now, if you'll excuse me . . ."

"It was so stark, so spontaneous, so real and true and vivid," the girl said, clutching Liz's shoulders.

"Yes," Liz said. "Terribly vivid. Perhaps even more vivid right here on the spot. Now, if you'll forgive me . . ."

"As I said to Jimmy . . ."

"Jimmy?"

"Jaime Malvido. I'm starting with the network on the first, but I was his production assistant. And I said . . ."

"Jai-me Mal-vi-do?"

"Yes, Liz! May I call you Liz? Jaime's such a real person. One of the freshest, most original minds in television. And a saint to work with. He . . ."

"Then would you ask him to be saintly enough to stop standing on my husband's grave? Excuse me." Liz strode back to the house.

"Well, I'm very sorry, I'm sure. I merely intended to convey . . ."

By now the press began to arrive—hundreds of reporters and photographers scrambling up the rocky slopes of Su Casa from hired boats. Flash bulbs exploded, newsmen asked impertinent questions in a melange of languages.

At the risk of life and limb, the curious began to arrive by canoe and kayak, by dinghy and rubber raft, by motor and sailboat. They trampled the garden, uprooted flowers, yanked at blossoms, invaded lonely, empty Poincianas, pocketing ornaments and ashtrays, tearing curtains from the windows and pictures from the walls as mementos of April May and Rex Roman. Only by stationing policemen at every entrance was it possible to save the main house from the rapine of souvenir hunters.

"Laddy, I know it isn't much, but it's still private property and it's still mine," Liz said. "Can't we get these ghouls out of here?" Liz thought that she was losing her mind. She was sure of it when a helicopter descended into the center of the garden. From it stepped the *deus ex machina*, Sam Houston Noyes, an importunate Zeus, followed by Martha (Punkin) Noyes, his querulous Hera. Mr. and Mrs. Noyes felt like Wilbur and Orville Wright. Other aircraft would be landing and taking off later in the day. Acapulco

313

was back to what it called normal. But, as in all other things, Sam Houston Noyes had got there ahead of everyone else and chartered the first helicopter into the heavens.

"Who's in charge here?" Mr. Noyes asked Liz.

"No one, as you can see. But, nominally, I guess you could say that I am. I'm Elizabeth Martínez."

"I'm Sam H. Noyes and I demand to see my daughter."

"Julie? Well, you're certainly welcome to. I can assure you that she hasn't gone anywhere."

"And I can assure you that if anything has happened to my little girl . . ."

"Relax, Mr. Noyes. How could anything happen with a woman like Mrs. Bullock in charge? Laddy, would you please find Julie and tell her that her father is here."

"*And* her mother," Mrs. Noyes said. "*And* her mother. And now I have quite a lot of other things to attend to. It's been such a pleasure meeting you. But I'm sure everyone tells you that."

Julie sighed. The scene had been going on, repeated and repeated almost word for word, for the better part of an hour. It was just what she had known it would be—the bombastic father, the whimpering mother—only worse. What Mr. Noyes failed to accomplish by bluster, Mrs. Noyes tried to achieve with cajolery and, as a last resort, tears. Punkin had a wondrous facility for turning them on and off without missing a beat.

"Yes, Daddy," Julie said again. "I know exactly how old I am. Even if I didn't, you've told me four times. And I've told you that in two weeks I'll be eighteen and you can't forbid me to marry Pablo or anyone else."

"A Mixicun!" Mrs. Noyes sobbed. "They've been our blood enemies for years."

"Maybe that's why you named me Juliet." The Shakespearean reference was lost on Mrs. Noyes.

"A dirty greaser servant!" Mrs. Noyes continued.

"Don't you think you might hold off judgment until you've seen him?"

"I don't wanta see him!"

314

"I'm glad of that. I'd hate to be ashamed of my own parents in front of the man I love."

"Love? What does a girl like you know about love?"

"Only a little. I'm just beginning to learn."

Now Mr. Noyes thundered forth. "You don't know innythang about love. No girl in the state of Texas was ever given so much. You were brought up like a princess—clothes, the best schools in Dallas, parties, your own horses, your own car. . . ."

"But nothing I really wanted. I want this and I'm going to have it."

"You do, young lady, and you'll never see another cint of my money."

"Good."

"Oh, Gawd, I give up!" Mr. Noyes threw his arms upward and walked away.

Mrs. Noyes did not give up. Now she switched to a simpering sycophancy. "Why, Julie, you're one of the prettiest, most popular girls back home. Why, your party is going to be talked about for ages. . . ."

"I hope someone will tell me about it."

"Now I'm sure this Pablo is a nice boy. Some of them are very well bred. Same as you and me. But, Julie, honey, you and he just come from different worlds. Would you want to introduce him to our friends?"

"No, I certainly would not."

"Well, then, Julie," Mrs. Noyes said, with a tinge of triumph in her voice. And then Mrs. Noyes became the modern mother. "Now, honey, you bin under a terrible physical and emotional strain. No wonder you're not seeing things as—ah—sinsibly as you usually do. You've always been so level-headed. Now we got a doctor and a nurse waiting right over there and . . . "

"Why, mother? I'm not pregnant. At least I don't think so."

"*Juliet Noyes!*"

But Sam Houston Noyes hadn't really given up. Mr. Noyes never gave up on anything. Instead, he went to the main house, passed the policeman at the door with a hundred-peso bill as his card of admission. Mr. Noyes knew all about money and what it could do. In the

315

sala he found a Mexican servant stacking chairs. "Uh, hey! Amigo? Hobla in-glaze? Speak English?"

"Yes, sir. I speak a little."

"Good. I'm looking for a—for an imployee called Pablo."

"I am Pablo, señor."

"Is that a fact?" Mr. Noyes said. "And I'm Sam H. Noyes."

"The father of Julie?" Pablo beamed and stuck out his hand.

Mr. Noyes placed both hands behind his back. "Well, as long as you speak English so good, I think you and I can get along real well. I'd like to have a little talk with you, Pablo. Alone."

In less than half an hour a beaming Mr. Noyes returned to his weeping wife, his obdurate daughter. "Well, girls, about ready to shove off?"

"No, Daddy. I've told you, I'm not going. Not with you. I'm going with Pablo."

"'Fraid not, honey. Yer Mex boy friend's already gone. Flown the coop."

"You're lying!"

"Julie, baby, when you get a little older you'll realize that these people can be bought an' sold like steers."

"Pablo's no steer!"

"And, Sam," Mrs. Noyes wailed, "speakin' of that, Julie's even been . . . Julie! Come back!"

Julie dashed into the house and raced up the spiral stairs to Pablo's room. It was neat, bare, and vacant, the mattress rolled, the bedding folded, the crucifix and pictures gone from the walls. Julie ran to the window and gripped the grille. She could see Pablo at the opposite shore getting out of a boat, paying the boatman, picking up his suitcase. "Pablo!" Julie shouted. "Pablo! Wait!" He could not hear her. In anguish, Julie watched him melt into the crowd of on-lookers on the mainland.

Through her tears, she saw an envelope lying on top of Pablo's empty chest of drawers. It was addressed merely, "Julie." The mucilage on the flap was still damp when Julie tore it open and pulled out the single sheet of paper.

316

Julie querida—
You was rong and i was rait. It
never wirk for us.
    Always i love you,
        Pablo

And then, at the bottom of the page, there was a postscript written in Spanish:

El dinero ($500 dólares) es para tu papá.

Money? What money? Julie shook the envelope. Five crisp one-hundred-dollar bills glided to the floor.

"Women and children first!" Flossie called. It was too good to be true. She had poured the last drop of Su Casa's vodka supply into her glass just as the government launch arrived to evacuate the island. It had worked out perfectly.

Mrs. Bullock stiffened. "If you thank I'm goin' in any boat with that Mixicun brat . . ."

"Not with my kid, dearie. Hop aboard, honey! Age before beauty. Junior and me can wait."

Mrs. Bullock, to no one's surprise, followed by her charges, was the first passenger on the first launch. A bribe to a government official permitted Mr. and Mrs. Noyes to accompany them. There was something so odd about Julie—almost menacing. They wanted to keep an eye on her. The helicopter whirled back empty of passengers. While Lou Ann and Susan shrieked at the McIvers and the Holts, who were shrieking from the shore, Julie sat tensely, staring straight ahead.

Mr. Noyes was not a cruel man. He loved his daughter and thought of himself as kind and generous and sacrificing. "Don't take on so, Julie. Isn't it better to know now?"

"Hush up, you jackass!" Mrs. Noyes hissed. "Let *me* handle her."

The launch reached the shore and its passengers and their mountains of luggage disembarked. Flash bulbs popped, a television camera soared and dipped on its crane. Through the crowds of the curious, three ambulances inched forward. There were four ambulances in all: one hired by the television network for dramatic

317

effect, three engaged by the parents of Mrs. Bullock's girls in case their daughters were too infirm to reach Hotel Pierre Marqués by ordinary limousine.

"Well, I guess we got 'em back, safe and sound," Mr. Noyes bellowed.

A second-string bilingual announcer approached Julie. "Please, miss, just a few words for the television?"

Julie smiled sweetly. "Oh, I've been interviewed already—more than once. But why don't you ask my mother and father? They're terribly nice and they have such interesting things to say. Wait. I'll call them. Mother! Daddy! They want you for an interview."

Mrs. Noyes was already fluffing her hair, smoothing the lapels of her blouse. "Just look at that, Punkin," Mr. Noyes said. "Smiling like an angel. She's forgotten all about him already. Comin', Julie!"

"Here, Daddy," Julie said, passing Pablo's envelope to him. "Pablo wanted you to have this."

"Pablo? Me? What is it?"

"It's the last thing you'll ever buy for me. Smile, Daddy, you're on camera."

As Mr. and Mrs. Noyes leered into the television lens, Julie darted into the crowd. She hurried to the road where more than a dozen empty taxicabs waited. Julie got into the first one. "*El centro,*" she said.

Julie had no idea where Pablo might be; didn't even know where he lived. But she thought she knew enough about his family to find him. A brother was a handyman at the Gallery Victor, a sister was a seamstress for Lila Bath, a nephew was a busboy at Sanborns. Somehow Julie would find him. She'd find him if it took all the rest of her life.

On the Rocks

"All right," Liz said, as the launch returned for its second load, "next, April, you have your own luggage and all of Rex's; Bernice,

318

and careful of that sable jacket; and then you, Flossie, with Queenie and the baby. The baby's got more equipment than all the rest of you put together."

"Darn tootin', honey!" Flossie said, brandishing her glass. "An' just wait'll you see the shoppin' spree I'm goin' on with a whole fam'lya kids ta dress. Them and me, too."

While the men were loading the launch, Bernice gazed across the water. She gasped. There it was, unmistakably; Ralph's terrible blue suit. Her first reaction was, "Oh, God!" And then she felt the tears starting. How much he must love me! I'm not too good for Ralph —he's too good for me.

Flossie looked as odd as she had on the day her bungalow had been swept away—worse. Laundering had done nothing to revive the splendor of her dress; the "Mahogany" nail enamel was chipped and peeling; the mahogany "glamor" bob had gone quite white at its parting; the good, gray pantie girdle had given up the fight. And yet Flossie looked different, better, almost beautiful. In the space of a week she had become the most popular person at Su Casa. People talked to her and, better than that, they listened. Flossie had something to live for—activity, friends, the baby. And Flossie was finally alive again.

With the baby sleeping soundly in her arms, Flossie laughed and kidded with the reporters who surrounded the improvised landing place.

Liz felt tears come to her eyes. "Flossie! Darling Flossie. What would we have done without you? How can I ever thank you?"

"Honey, what would I of done without you, an' this little fellah here? It's me oughta thank you."

"This isn't good-bye, but . . ."

"Yer darn tootin' it's not g'bye. You gotta help me find the resta the family, get a house, somebody like that Pee-dro, a Spanish teacher, a lawyer. Honey, yer job's just beginnin'!"

"Ya listo, señora," the man at the launch below said.

"Huh?"

"He says he's ready, Flossie."

"Well, here goes nothin'. Liz, honey, you hold Queenie. Then pass her down after I get Junior here inta the boat."

319

"Just one more picture, *señora?*"

"Sure thing, han'some! C'mawn, kiddo, let's givum the ole Betty Grable cheesecake." Flossie, vain as ever of her legs, stepped back.

"Flossie!" Liz cried.

For the eternity of a split second, Flossie's face was a study of fear and horror. And then she went over backward, twisting her body to protect the baby.

"Oh, Flossie!" Essie wailed. Flossie lay on her back on the rocks and rubble at the water's edge, not ten feet below.

Followed by the reporters, the police, the people who were left at Su Casa, Liz scrambled down the stony slope to where Flossie lay, her neck twisted to one side. The baby began to cry.

"Flossie! Flossie, are you . . ."

"The baby?" Flossie said. "Is the kid okay?"

"Yes, Flossie. He's fine," Liz said, taking the baby from her arms. "But, you . . ."

"Me?" Flossie said. "It's like always—on the rocks." And then Flossie said no more.

V

PARADISE REGAINED

It's Not Very Likely

Liz stood on the microscopic balcony of her room in the Palacio de Guerrero holding Queenie in her arms and staring out at the blob of land that had once been her dream. In the twilight, and from this distance, Su Casa looked as though nothing had ever happened to it. She put the dog down gently, returned to the chill efficiency of her air-conditioned cell. The baby lay sleeping in the Kurtesee Krib provided by the hotel. "Poor little thing," Liz said. "Not a chance."

"Not a chance." That was what they had said at the hospital when Flossie had been removed from the ambulance that had raced along the Costera, lights rotating, sirens whooping. "Fractured neck, fractured back, fractured hip. State of acute alcoholism. Not a chance. Nothing you can do, Señora Martínez. Nothing we can do. But we'll telephone you in the event that . . ."

"I see. Thank you."

Liz knew that there was so much to be done. And she'd do it. But not tonight. She was just too tired.

"Poor little thing," she said again to the baby. "And poor Flossie. Not a chance."

The few guests of Su Casa who chose to remain in Acapulco had been billeted in a mammoth new hotel. Now that Su Casa offered no competition—not that it ever really had—the management could afford to be generous. And think of the publicity! The PR girl, standing drinks to reporters in the bar, was already calling it the Acapulco Sheltering Arms (she was a great wit), having passed out mimeographed press releases that said, in part, ". . . at the insistence of Omar D. Brackish, Chairman of the Board of Brackish International Hotels and Motor Courts, Inc., the victims of the disaster of unknown origin that isolated the tiny Su Casa guesthouse from the life and gaiety of beautiful Acapulco have been placed in the new thousand-room, air-conditioned Palacio de Guerrero, where they will receive medical care and every personal attention, free of charge . . ."

In room 1414, Bernice lay in bed beneath a gay swag that read *Duerme con los Angeles*—Sleep with the Angels—and watched Ralph getting back into his blue suit. She had given herself to him on purpose. She told herself that it was the least she could do. And it had been terrible; Bernice unmoved, Ralph blubberingly ardent and inept. He had wept on her sternum and sobbed out something about being married—right here and now.

"Well, Bern, how's about it? I mean you and me."

Oh, God, how he loved her! How could he? She hated herself more than ever, but there it was: Bernice didn't love him. "Ralph, you're so dear. So sweet. But, Ralph, I just don't know. I'm so tired and so confused. You've got to let me think it over."

In the presidential suite, thus named in the hope that the president of some place might someday visit the Palacio de Guerrero, April May was receiving star treatment. E. G. d'Enker moved right in with her. Debbie had been sent back to Los Angeles in care of Mr. d'Enker's young assistant. Debbie was a sweet kid, but, after all, April was a star and a damned good lay.

At a reproduction Philip IV desk in the living room, April puzzled over page twenty of her three-year contract. It danced with whereases and notwithstandings, with footnotes and parenthetical asides. Riders fluttered like the wings of a hummingbird from its margins. "But lissun, Mr. d'Enker, whatsis mean when it says, 'In the e-ven-chew-al-utty that the a-fore-men-chunned . . .' "

"Fer Chrissakes, jus' sign it, baby, an' let's send down for some drinks." Mr. d'Enker was throbbing to get April away from the reproduction Philip IV desk and into the reproduction Philip V bed.

Bathed, barbered, and scented, Roland felt a lot better. He had even been able to get some sun on the little balcony outside his room. It was a small single, identified by the Brackish Hotel chain as a "junior suite," whatever that meant.

Arthur, as a celebrity, had been given a very senior suite. Roland had been a bit surprised that Arthur had not invited him to share it, but Roland understood. Arthur would be inundated by reporters and television executives winding up the story of Su Casa. There would be no hope of privacy, no opportunity for the two of them to be alone—at least not until tonight.

Roland tucked his see-through shirt into his poppy-printed pants and considered knotting a scarlet scarf at his throat. Then, in a flash of inspiration, he tied the scarf around his waist. There! He was ready. Should he telephone Arthur first, or simply tap at his door?

Arthur despised his suite. What would you call all of this bogus Spanish stuff: Early Hollywood, Middle Palm Beach, Late Stern Brothers? As far as Arthur was concerned, it was Mexican Grand Rapids in the hands of a contract decorator. These rooms were so commercial, so impersonal, so empty. It had been a long time since Arthur had traveled anywhere without Carolyn and Bill. Now they were gone. With a cool kiss and a cold handshake, they had ridden to the airport to take the direct flight home with Essie and Walter Dewlap. Well, let them! If there was anything Arthur hated it was an ingrate.

First the barber, then the press, then that smart-assed little Jaime Malvido with the vulgar E. G. d'Enker had come and gone. Arthur had been terribly gracious. Malvido had discreetly given Arthur his fee. Arthur had waited with remarkable patience for Mr. d'Enker to mention a contract. He had not. No matter. He would. Or some nicer network would come round with an offer. In the meantime, there were cables from both *Life* and *Look* requesting exclusive rights to Arthur's own inside story of the siege of Su Casa. A long letter from his publisher suggested a book-length treatment of the same thing submitted in time to catch the Christmas trade. . . .

There was a tap at Arthur's door. Really, if the management had to shut him up in this string of hideous rooms, the least they could do would be to furnish some sort of servant to answer the door! Arthur tied the sash of his dressing gown, marched from the bedroom through the living room to the foyer, and opened the door just a crack. It was Roland.

"Yes?" Arthur said.

"Here I am."

"So I see. But what on earth are you got up for?" Arthur braced his foot against the door.

"I-I thought we might have dinner together."

"What a pity. I've already dined." Arthur had not.

"Or possibly a drink?"

"Afraid not. I'm really exhausted. And so . . ."

"Yes, you must be. But could we get together sometime tomorrow?"

"Well, it's not very likely. I'm anxious to get out of this hell hole and so I'll be leaving as soon as possible. Well, good-bye, Roland. Do let me hear from you once in a while."

The door closed in Roland's face. He heard the pronounced click of the safety lock. Dazed, he stood there for a moment and then stumbled toward the elevator. The doors slid open. Roland stood aside waiting for a fat couple to pass. They were in their sixties. The man wore a huge sombrero and a harlequin jumpsuit; the woman wore a bikini and orchid mink. As the doors closed, Roland heard her shrill cackle, "Honestagawd, dja ever see such an outfit!"

Back in the shiny new antiquity of his bedroom, Arthur felt lost and lonely. He wanted dinner and he wanted company.

Liz!

Now, there was really somebody. He had known Liz half of her life and almost half of his own. She was intelligent, she had style, and she was a lady. Liz had flair and Liz had taste, although not the money to support either adequately. With Arthur, that would be no problem. What a pair they might make! Liz was really the perfect hostess. She was born to be the wife of a statesman, an ambassador or—or of a famous figure. True, she sometimes had a distressing tendency to go a bit Girl Scouty, but Arthur could control that. Even boyish Laddy would be rather an attractive adjunct.

Arthur dropped his robe on the foot of his bed, sucked in his stomach, went to his dressing room and selected some new, never-

326

worn-before resort clothes. Poor Liz, how she would welcome a little dinner, à deux, at some good restaurant.

Arthur tucked his see-through shirt into his fern-printed pants and considered knotting an emerald scarf at his throat. Then, in a flash of inspiration, he tied the scarf around his waist. There! He was ready. Should he telephone Liz first, or simply tap at her door?

Liz opened the door just a crack. It was Arthur.

"Yes?" Liz said.

"Here I am."

"So I see. But what on earth are you got up for?" Liz braced her foot against the door.

"I-I thought we might have dinner together."

"What a pity. I've already dined." Liz had not.

"Or possibly a drink."

"Afraid not. I'm really exhausted. And so . . ."

"Yes, you must be. But could we get together sometime tomorrow?"

"Well, it's not very likely. I'm anxious to get out of this hell hole and so I'll be leaving as soon as possible. Well, good-bye, Arthur. Do let me hear from you once in a while."

Arthur had the eerie feeling that he had heard this conversation before. But where? When? Extrasensory perception or some nonsense like that.

The door closed in Arthur's face. He heard the pronounced click of the safety lock. Dazed, he stood there for a moment and then stumbled toward the elevator. The doors slid open. Arthur stood aside waiting for a fat couple to pass. They were in their sixties. The man wore a huge sombrero and pink terry-cloth shorts, the woman wore a bikini and blue broadtail. As the doors closed, Arthur heard her shrill cackle. "Honestagawd, dja ever see such an outfit!"

Some People

Some people change. But most people never do.

Today in Dallas, Texas, Lily Lee de Camp Bullock is known not only as a great lady, but also as something of a heroine, remarkable for her cool courage. Still gloating over the large profit of her Mexican "finishing" tour, she is now writing haggling letters to the management of English hotels demanding youth hostel rates for her Cultural English Theatre Tour—"girls from the finest families." London, Glyndebourne, Stratford-upon-Avon. *Quo vadis?* Both Lou Ann McIver and Susan Holt have said some rather unsettling things about Mrs. Bullock, but no one pays much attention. As everybody knows, Lou Ann is no better than she should be, sleeping her way through the twenty-to-forty set at the club. She always has and she always will. As for poor Susan, she's dimwitted—always has been, always will be.

Absent from Dallas is Julie Noyes. She found her Pablo and married him on her eighteenth birthday. But from their authentic copy of the Petit Trianon, Sam H. and Martha (Punkin) Noyes still rage at a firm of private detectives over long distance. The search is well-nigh hopeless as Sam never bothered to learn Pablo's last name.

Mrs. Noyes had been right about one thing: Julie and Pablo *did* come from two different worlds. The adjustment was not easy. At first Pablo's family treated Julie as though their son had married Lady Bountiful. The best chair, the best plates, the choicest morsels were lavished on Pablo's *novia*. But when ample hints concerning color television, a washing machine, a Volkswagen—even a second-hand one—went unfulfilled, their attitude changed. In the eyes of her in-laws, Julie became the dumb *gringa* who had married their most promising son for *his* money—a girl with no dowry, not even bedding; a girl who couldn't cook, couldn't sew, couldn't speak proper Spanish, *and a Protestant!* Julie found neither attitude especially endearing. As for Pablo's opinion of Julie's family, well! But as neither Julie nor Pablo especially relished the worlds they had come from, they managed to manage.

Julie, who had never in her life dreamed of haggling over anything, is now the scourge of the marketplace, shrewdly knocking ten centavos off the price of a head of lettuce, fifty off half a kilo of butter, two whole pesos off a chicken in rapid, colloquial Spanish. "Don't be so sting-gy—no, stin-jee 'oneybun," Pablo says. "These poor people have to live, too." Yet Pablo is amused and immensely proud of the frugal young woman, more Mexican than the Mexicans, who is his wife. But whatever became of the American girl-goddess he had worshiped from afar?

Pablo's rise had been meteoric—from waiter, to captain, to desk clerk at the Palacio de Guerrero. Handsome in his striped trousers and tropical-weight morning coat, he is everyone's favorite. He has had better offers from the Hilton, Sheraton, and Western International Hotel chains and refused them. Appalled at the sloth, the waste, the inefficiency that goes on about him, Pablo dreams of the day when he and Julie will have their own hotel—"Somp-ting we could swing, 'oneybun. Somp-ting 'long the lines of Su Casa. May-bee nex year. But firs' tings firs', eh, 'oneybun? The baby." Their baby is but weeks away. Julie fancies the names of long-gone Mexican leaders—Benito, Venustiano, Plutarco, Sebastian. Pablo prefers names like Franklin, Ike, Dick, Lyndon. " 'Ow about callin' 'im Lyndon, 'oneybun?"

"My Latin lover," Julie sighs. "Close your eyes and you're in Big D." And then she closes hers.

Bernice Potocki returned the sable jacket to Madam Kaye, who claimed that it was irreparably damaged. As gently as she could, Bernice took her congé of Chicago and of Ralph. It would never have worked. She is now a major force in a smart California specialty shop. Her salary is high and her commissions astounding. She is called "Our Miss Potocki." A title is tacitly implied. She makes seasonal buying trips to New York, and next year her itinerary will include Paris and Rome. She has a modest stable of beaux—young actors, junior executives, and such.

From a blue-tweed office at the network—small, but on the same floor as President d'Enker's—the Girl Friday has placed a series of embarrassing telephone calls to Our Miss Potocki. Our Miss Potocki, having no idea who any Priscilla is, simply hangs up. Last week a traveler for a line of better coats and dresses asked for Bernice's hand in marriage. He was refused. She still thinks of Ignacio de la Vega y Martínez. Perhaps, before it is too late, Bernice will find the right man. Who knows?

As for Ignacio, he is still in Acapulco. Having settled the affairs of Su Casa, his law practice is at a standstill. Out of season he keeps in condition by sending vacationing secretaries and school-teachers into orbit. But there is no real future with any of them. Possibly next winter the right woman will come along. She must. Ignacio's hairline is beginning to recede. We are none of us growing any younger.

April May is now, as everyone knows, a star with her own show. It will not last. Her moronic appeal is wearing thin. She is last year's joke. Mr. d'Enker will buy off her contract at the end of the season. In a way April is glad. It's hard to learn all those lines— especially when you don't understand them. And a Mr. Gottlieb has asked April to make him the happiest man alive. He will not be alive much longer, but he is enormously rich with no known heirs. Even now Our Miss Potocki is helping April to choose her wedding gown—white satin with a five-yard veil falling from a crown of orange blossoms.

Jaime Malvido is very much in television—both North American and Mexican. The Volkswagen convertible has been replaced by a Jaguar with two telephones. He is known for his real-life documentaries. The most recent was "Esclava Blanca," a candid study of the Mexican white-slave trade carefully staged in an obscure village with a cast of drama-school dropouts who will never embarrass Jimmy by appearing anywhere again. The famous find him to be polite, charming, and self-effacing. Underlings say that Jaime Malvido is something of a snob. That is not true. He naturally shies away from opportunists, arrivistes, and toadies. As Jimmy says, "I hate ass-kissers."

Mr. and Mrs. Walter Dewlap are, as always, Mr. and Mrs. Walter Dewlap of Anthrax, Pennsylvania—upstanding, well-to-do, and interested in everything. They will never change. Essie is in sporadic correspondence with Carolyn Williams, and after Carolyn's baby was born the Dewlaps and the Williamses spent a week together at the Plaza in New York. Essie was amazed to see that svelte Carolyn was up to a size twelve and astounded to hear that Carolyn didn't even care.

Bill and Carolyn really did change. They abandoned the penthouse in Astor Street for a place in the country. Carolyn rarely ventures into town. Bill must. And although Bill grumbles about the commuting, he is happy. Both of them are. They exchange Christmas and birthday presents with Arthur Craine although they have not met since Acapulco. Arthur is much too busy to visit them. Carolyn is relieved, Bill overjoyed. Carolyn has just dutifully written her brother to announce that a second child is on the way. Arthur will respond with a long, brilliant, witty A.A.A. (All About Arthur) letter. Even with the best intentions in the world, Carolyn will somehow find herself too busy to sit down and read all of it. The chains are severed.

Roland's heart was, naturally, broken again. It remained so for almost a day. On the flight out of Acapulco, Roland happened— just happened—to choose the seat next to the curly-haired young man who stood ahead of him in line at the airport. They were friends before the plane was off the ground. The young man has more above his melting eyes than curls. Not for nothing did he work in the Gift Department at Bonwit Teller. Today the Chic Boutique and the young man are almost self-supporting.

Roland is not without a streak of vindictiveness, and at their parties he is not too reticent to imply that he and Arthur Craine were more than friends to anyone who will listen. All the boys in Allentown listen. Half of them believe the story, the other half state flatly, once they have left the party, that Roland doesn't even know Arthur Craine!

Chip? Florentino? Who knows? Who cares?

The Princess-up-the-Hill is off the hill. The silver palace stands empty awaiting her return, like her real estate all over the world. The Princess has given up silver and gone back to white. Avid for islands, she lives in an ancient white-washed castle on Malta, where she dresses as a nun to the outrage of the Maltese. She is receiving Catholic instruction from a handsome confessor. It is nip and tuck as to which will occur first—her reception into the church or her expulsion from Malta.

Arthur Craine goes on forever, though not on television. He has never been exactly certain what all three networks meant when they used the term "overexposure." Arthur, too, has deserted Chicago and is more than willing to tell people what a smug, boring, provincial place it is. He has no fixed address, moving peripatetically from one fashionable spot to another. Arthur's mail is forwarded by the firm that handles his affairs.

His magazine piece on Su Casa and the widely acclaimed book that followed in time for Christmas won him thousands of new fans, but no friends among the people who shared his adventure. Even Laddy Parkhurst was able to read between the lines. But Arthur is big and, while he deplores their smallness of spirit, he is perfectly willing to forgive them all—even Carolyn.

By the time Laddy got to Mexico City, Mr. Ackerman and his lovely niece had vanished. Deported, some said, as undesirable aliens, leaving behind a paper chase of bad checks. Laddy still can't believe it. How could a man whose money literally grows on trees write a bad check?

Lee Goodwin? In the small room where he sits staring, he appears to be content. It might be said that, in one sense, he made good his escape—no one can reach him now.

Su Casa is no more. The house was emptied, dismantled, and sold off to demolitions dealers. The land on which it stood continued to disintegrate until the last little lump that was left was condemned by the government and blown into oblivion with one mighty charge of dynamite.

Liz knew when the explosion was scheduled, but she wasn't around to watch it. She had been too busy. On that day Liz and Queenie had flown to the capital to collect Meyers, Florence, Mrs.

Flossie lived. "Hell, honey, I'm too mean to die."

But she had come close. Liz and Laddy had hovered for three days at Flossie's bedside in a tiny clinic in Acapulco. The woman shouldn't have lived, but she did. On the morning of the fourth day, Flossie, had finally spoken. She had said three words: "Baby," "Queenie," and "Vodka," before lapsing into a coma again.

"That settles it," Liz had said. "She'll pull through. Laddy, get going."

"B-but where?"

"To the telephone. Find out the names of the best bone surgeons in the world—here, the States, Europe, Russia, anywhere. Just get them. In the meantime I'll get her out of this pesthouse and into a really good hospital in Mexico City."

At astronomical fees, the great surgeons circled. They were unanimous in their opinions. Flossie's was a hopeless case. She had no right to be alive. Her three-word vocabulary had dwindled to two—"Baby" and "Queenie." The No Visitors sign was posted. Again Liz had taken matters into her own hands. With the aid of Laddy, a large market basket, and ten dozen carnations, Liz had smuggled Queenie and the baby to Flossie's deathbed beneath a squirming, writhing bouquet. The yapping of the dog, the cooing of the baby had brought the whole staff of the surgical floor down around Liz's head. But Liz's flagrant violation of the rules and regulations had turned the tide. With the baby at hand, the great surgeons agreed that Mrs. Meyers just might possibly live. And then Flossie croaked out "Vodka!"

Encased in plaster from jowls to knees, sucking vodka through a plastic tube, calling for the dog and the baby, Flossie's recovery had been a milestone in medical history. "Hell, honey, I'm too mean to die."

There is a certain kind of person who can be spotted at a hundred paces as Quality. There is something about them—can it be the cut and quality of their clothes, the way they carry themselves, or simply the aura of discreet wealth?—that announces in carrying, but well-modulated, tones, "Class." Today Mrs. Florence Meyers quietly, but forcefully, projects that message—at least until you hear her speak. "Shit, honey, it's more staples than surgery that make me stand so good." Literally riveted together, Flossie, her hair the color of burnished pewter, stands like a dowager empress in the stark whites and severe blacks selected for her by Liz. ("Charming! Such taste!")

In her enormous house on the beach at Acapulco, Flossie is pointed out as one of the local highlights, almost as impressive as the bay itself. Described as anything from "society saint" to "lovable eccentric," Flossie is almost as much in demand as the large checks she writes to worthy causes. She is forever being urged to be on the committee for this, to sit on the board for that. Amazed and flattered, Flossie simply hasn't the time. "Hell, honey, cantcha see I'm upta my tits in kids?"

Up to her T's in K's, indeed. She has taken all of Aurelia's children under her wing, cursing, scolding, and bawling endearments to them in her odd English and execrable Spanish. There are those who suggest that Doña Florencia drinks too much to be a suitable parent. But the children are healthy and happy, and so is Flossie.

Flossie has not changed. Only her circumstances. She loves and is loved.

Before Su Casa was consigned to eternity, Liz had undergone the grim and mystifying experience of having Salvador's body disinterred and submitted to a solemn requiem mass in the hideous Acapulco cathedral. It had come as something of surprise to Liz to find that, in addition to Salvador's elegant cousin Ignacio, the cortege was joined by a gnarled Mexican woman, decidedly more Indian than Spanish, who said that she was Liz's mother-in-law. Liz was also surprised that Salvador's remains were to be buried not in a family crypt in Spain, but beside his father in a small plot in the Acapulco cemetery. Liz declared that she simply hadn't understood Salvador's Spanish. She still agrees with her newfound mother-in-law—Salvador was the dearest, the finest, the most loving husband and son any woman could have. She will mourn him as such forever. That was it! Liz just hadn't understood his Spanish—or his English.

But Liz is no longer interested in understanding Spanish. Fluent Italian is her aim.

When everything in Acapulco was signed and settled, Liz found that she still had some money—about half as much as she had invested in Su Casa. The question was: What to do with it? The answer came the very day she deposited the check. Italy!

Well, it seems that this elderly English couple had been running a little tearoom and gift shop ever since the end of World War II. Now his health was shot—or was it hers?—and they wanted to sell the place. Immediately!

Liz has seen photographs. Hideous, of course. Chintz, ivy wall-paper, skimpy little net curtains: just what you'd expect from a pair of unimaginative, middle-middle class, fuddy-duddy old Britons. And their menu! Potted prawns, Windsor brown, boiled mutton, haggis, fruit salad (tinned, you may be sure), trifle, sponge cake with custard sauce. The inventory of the gift shop is just as de-pressing: gritty postcards, bogus cameos, raffia bags, mass-produced antiquities, machine-embroidered luncheon sets. Typical!

But the building has good lines—excellent. With a coat of paint and a little imagination, anyone could turn it into a stunning, really inviting restaurant. Possibly severe black and white, with riotously bright flowers everywhere. A bar? Oh, yes! By all means a bar! That's where the profit really lies. Add a dining terrace just here at this side, near the dreadfully inefficient kitchen. (That would have to be done over completely.) And jazz up the dismal garden with bright little tables under the fig trees. It should take about two weeks—three at the longest.

As for restocking that tatty little souvenir shop, why, Italy is full of the loveliest stuff—the traditional old regional things, of course, and the starkly modern output of Milan and Rome. All it needs is a little taste, and everyone always says that Liz has taste. "Charming. Such taste!"

"But, Laddy, what really appeals to me is the location. Pompei!

I've never been there myself, but I'm about the only tourist who hasn't. I mean they cart them out there in busloads all day every day. Literally by the thousands. People who are dying for a drink and are willing to pay for a really *good* lunch, served with wine and a little style—not this station buffet fare."

"Pompei?" Laddy said. "Oh, yes."

"I could make a go of a place anywhere," Liz said, "but the location of this one is just too good to be true."

"Well, where, exactly, is it, Liz?"

Liz paused, her eyes bright with optimism. "It's right at the foot of Mount Vesuvius!"